THE CANADIANS
by
Robert E. Wall

IV
PATRIOTS

BANTAM BOOKS
TORONTO · NEW YORK · LONDON · SYDNEY

PATRIOTS: THE CANADIANS IV
A Bantam Book / October 1982

ISBN 0-553-22686-X

Published simultaneously in the United States and Canada

───

Bantam Books are published by Bantam Books, Inc. Its trademark,
consisting of the words "Bantam Books" and the portrayal of a
rooster, is Registered in U.S. Patent and Trademark Office and in
other countries. Marca Registrada. Bantam Books, Inc., 666 Fifth
Avenue, New York, New York 10103.

───

PRINTED IN THE UNITED STATES OF AMERICA

H   0 9 8 7 6 5 4 3 2 1

MEN AND WOMEN CAUGHT IN
THE TURMOIL OF WAR . . .
AND IN THE
TUMULT OF PASSION

MATTHEW NOWELL: A Yankee officer sworn to reject his Loyalist father's land, driven by a desire for war, shaken by a passion for a forbidden love.

AMY NOWELL MORIN: A Loyalist woman who paid the terrible price of love and war, now her new-found happiness was threatened by a lost child's terrible secret.

ETHAN MORIN: An intrepid Yankee soldier. He must choose between the land of the woman he loved and the country whose uniform he once wore.

GEYASADA: A treacherous Seneca chief. He vowed to keep the white-skinned girl he captured and to kill anyone who dared to claim her.

MAGGIE NOWELL: A lovely child torn from her mother's arms, raised by the Indians who stole her, now doomed by her beauty to a heartbreaking fate.

AARON BRANT: A courageous sachem scarred by betrayal. The drama begun in BLACKROBE would explode in a shocking climax as a father's love led him into the white man's world . . . and war brought a nightmare of blood and violence.

THE CANADIANS
A PEOPLE DESTINED TO ACCEPT
THE CHALLENGE TO PROTECT
A WILD AND GROWING LAND

For my mother
 Sabina Daly Wall
  on the occasion of her 80th birthday

A Genealogy

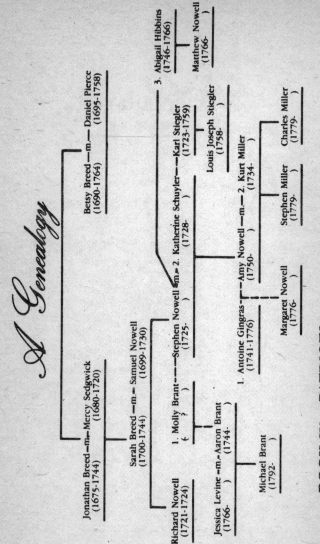

Jonathan Breed —m.— Mercy Sedgwick
(1675-1744)   (1680-1720)

Betsy Breed —m.— Daniel Pierce
(1690-1764)   (1695-1758)

Sarah Breed —m.— Samuel Nowell
(1700-1744)   (1699-1730)

3. Abigail Hibbins
(1746-1766)

Matthew Nowell
(1766-   )

Stephen Nowell —m.— 2. Katherine Schuyler —m.— Karl Stiegler
(1725-   )   (1728-   )   (1723-1759)

Louis Joseph Stiegler
(1758-   )

Richard Nowell
(1721-1724)

1. Molly Brant —m.— Aaron Brant
(?   )   (1744-   )

1. Antoine Gingras —m.— Amy Nowell —m.— 2. Kurt Miller
(1741-1776)   (1750-   )   (1734-   )

Jessica Levine —m.—
(1766-   )

Margaret Nowell
(1776-   )

Stephen Miller
(1779-   )

Charles Miller
(1779-   )

Michael Brant
(1792-   )

BOOK IV - PATRIOTS

Prologue
1792

1792

Rain soaked the streets of Albany, turning them into rivulets of muddy water. The old Dutch-style houses seemed to droop under the weight of the humidity. At the riverfront, the downspouts from the houses poured a flow of rainwater onto the banks. Once the soil had been thoroughly soaked, sections of the muddy bank crumbled into the river, turning the Hudson a darker brown.

. The richly dressed black man waded across Pearl Street. He leaped the submerged curb onto the brick sidewalk and took refuge under the eaves of the Albany Inn. He ran his hand through his steely gray hair and tried to wring some of the water out. He stamped his feet to free his expensive leather boots of the brown muck that clung to them. The boots would have to be carefully dried and polished this very night if they were to be of any use to him in the future. He smiled. Stephen Nowell had turned Josiah the ferryman into Josiah Ferryman, a partner in the firm of Breed, Nowell and Vaughan; yet he still thought like a servant. He would never get used to the idea of someone else taking care of chores like muddy boots.

He swung open the inn's front door. His senses were overwhelmed by the rank stench of stale beer and day-old spilled rum, mixed with the pungent odor of burning pine in the hearth. Josiah surveyed the room until he caught sight of Nowell sitting alone by the fire. He too was richly dressed. His greatcoat was thrown over the back of his chair. It still dripped rain onto the bare hardwood floors of the taproom. But the cloak had served him well. His dark blue coat with polished silver buttons had been untouched by the downpour. His silver gray hair was almost exactly the same color as the breeches he wore. And he still wore breeches. He would have nothing to do with the new revolutionary radical style of pants. To him they were a symbol of the French Revolution and radical Jeffersonian democracy in America, both of which he detested. He had grown heavier over the years. His

2

middle had thickened and there were unmistakable signs of a pot belly protruding over the edge of the waistband of his breeches. His face was chubbier, displaying a flabbiness about the jaw that in profile could only be described as a double chin. He looked every inch the wealthy, conservative merchant-gentleman he was.

But there were aspects of him that did not fit the mold. A thin white scar ran through his left eyebrow and lid, and his empty left sleeve was pinned against his shoulder. He had not always been a merchant. He held a silver-headed cane in his hand. The cane's tip was wedged in a broad space between the floorboards. He rested his hand on the silver head and his heavy chin on his hand, staring at the leaping flames of the hearth.

Josiah walked to his friend's table and sat down. Stephen looked up at him, startled by his sudden arrival. "Josiah, is everything taken care of?"

"We leave for Saratoga in the morning by hired coach."

"Have you any word on her condition?" Stephen asked.

"The old woman lives—although just barely. We can't waste any time getting there."

Stephen sat quietly for some minutes, lost in thought. "I'm glad we arrived in time," he said finally. "But I'm sorry Katherine could not be with us. She loves that old lady. But I couldn't take the chance."

Josiah nodded. "There is something else you ought to know," he said. "Major Nowell is living with Miss Margaret."

Stephen smiled wanly. "How many years has it been since we last saw him, Josiah? It was just before Bunker Hill. It's been seventeen years since I last saw my son. I don't know how many times I've tried to see him. When Katherine and I built the house in Saint John, we asked him to come to Canada and join us. He never even responded to my letters, and when Katherine and I visited Israel and Margaret in Saratoga, we discovered he had been posted to Fort Pitt. I don't even know what the man looks like, Josiah. As a boy he favored Abigail."

Stephen grew silent and began to stare into the fire again. A sadness seemed to descend upon him. Josiah had seen this happen whenever he mentioned the girl-wife, Major Nowell's mother, who had died so tragically almost thirty years before. But now he did not mention her often and never in the presence of his wife, Katherine.

3

"It's ironic," Stephen said suddenly. "The son I hoped would make up for the loss of the others is estranged. My daughter writes to me and her mother regularly from Upper Canada, and even Aaron—Molly Brant's wild Mohawk—acknowledges me as his father and has sought my help. But this youngest will have nothing to do with me."

Josiah said nothing. He knew from long experience that talk did little good when his friend was in this mood.

The door of the inn swung open again, and a heavyset man with a ruddy face half hidden in his dripping cloak entered the taproom. He too searched the tables with his eyes and, catching sight of Josiah and Stephen, he came to their table.

"My esteemed brother-in-law, I presume," he said with a smile.

"Phillip?" Stephen responded. "I mean Senator Schuyler, or do you still prefer General Schuyler?"

"I prefer Phillip. Your associate," he said, glancing at Josiah and not sure just what their relationship entailed, "was at my home earlier making inquiries about Aunt Margaret. I simply could not let you slip out of Albany without greeting you."

Stephen laughed. "I wouldn't do that, Phillip. The word I received was that you were in Philadelphia trying to help your son-in-law, Secretary Hamilton, keep Jefferson from turning my unfortunate native land into a vile democracy."

Schuyler ignored his barb. "My sister is not with you, I gather."

"No," responded Stephen. "She's not really well. The doctors diagnosed a slight stroke last year. She has recovered from that. But she is not yet strong enough to travel. We have moved from the city to our country home in the St. John River valley. It is quiet and very beautiful there. She loves it very much."

"We've seen each other only twice since we were children. But I know she is happy in Canada—from her letters."

"It's our home now," said Stephen. "We are at peace—with a sensible and conservative government in New Brunswick."

"I'm happy for you both. It is important to have a place you can call home. My aunt has taught me how important that is. She nearly drove me to distraction for years until I rebuilt the mansion at Saratoga Flats. And she has lived there in peace and has given me my peace ever since." He hesitated a moment and then added with sadness, "Until now."

4

"Will you come with us?" Stephen asked.

"No," responded Schuyler. "Margaret and I have taken leave of each other already. She finds good-byes difficult. She wouldn't appreciate having to see me again. Just carry my love to her."

The coach followed the course of the Hudson north to Saratoga. The rain of the night before had given way to a smoky fall sun. The trees that grew along the riverbank were a blaze of reds, oranges, and browns. The river beyond Albany was almost empty of traffic. Stephen recalled former days—days of invasion from the north or from the south, when the river was so busy it was difficult to reason how the *bateau* men avoided collisions. But with the peace of the past decade, no invasions disturbed the tranquillity of the northern Hudson.

Josiah had fallen asleep. They had risen early to begin this journey, and the black man could not sleep at all the night before a trip—not that Josiah or Stephen traveled that much any longer. Stephen looked back at the river. He remembered this bend in the river road. The old Saratoga house had stood almost on this spot until it had been destroyed by Burgoyne's soldiers in 1777. That British invasion had gone no farther, and its members had reached their goal of Albany only as prisoners of war. And earlier, from this spot, the Abenacki sachem, Socono, Stephen's Indian father, had taken him across the Hudson and taught him to be a man again, saving him from the life of an invalid filled with self-pity. The new house would come into view any second now. Stephen would face two difficult tasks once he reached it. He would have to say good-bye to a lady whom he loved but who he was not sure cared for him, and he would have to greet a son whom he loved but who he was sure despised him.

The old lady lay propped in her bed. She was so thin and frail that Matthew was afraid to move her. She had asked him to bring her into the front bedroom, to give her a view of the river. He had moved the whole bed rather than hurt her by lifting her from it. At ninety-two, Margaret Schuyler demanded everything and got precisely what she wanted. Matthew saw to it. When Kip died the year before, at the age of seventy-six, Matthew asked for leave from his regiment to be with her. He was the only family she had left, and he was not even

5

a blood relation. But this old lady had raised him since he was ten, and he loved her as much as he could have loved his own mother.

He was nervous this morning. Word had come from Albany that his father, a man he had not seen in seventeen years, was coming to Saratoga to visit the old lady. The last time his father and his father's wife visited, he had missed them by volunteering for service on the frontier. But there was no avoiding this visit, and for this meeting Aunt Margaret made him promise to be present.

Matthew sat looking out the window of her bedroom. The delicate lace curtains stirred slightly in the soft breeze. The day grew warmer as the morning wore on. They would be blessed with a few days of Indian summer before the cold came down out of the mountains to the north. He rose from his chair and walked over to the great fourposter bed. Margaret was dozing, but each breath was followed by a slight gurgling sound in her chest. He heard the noise of a carriage coming down the Albany road, and he went back to the window.

Matthew could not help but be curious about his father. His memory of him was so faint. The carriage stopped in front of the veranda, and a black man stepped out. Matthew recognized him instantly. It was the ferryman, Josiah. Then the other man climbed out. He did not immediately recognize his father. He had changed greatly, but Matthew knew him by his cane, which he carried to balance himself and compensate for his lost arm. Matthew left his aunt alone to go downstairs and greet the guests.

"Gentlemen," Matthew greeted them from the first landing.

Josiah smiled at Matthew. "Mr. Matt," he said. The black man would have preferred to go to Matthew and throw his arms about him, but he knew the father would not, and he could not embarrass his friend.

"Matthew," said Stephen, in a greeting rivaling his son's formality and coldness. "You've grown into a strong-looking and handsome man. Your mother would be proud."

"How is your wife, sir?" Matthew asked, trying to keep the conversation going.

"Not as well as I'd like. I had to leave her behind, much against her will. Gave me the devil for breaking a long-standing promise by not taking her with me. But she wasn't

6

up to a long trip down to New York, and then the packet boat ride to Albany would have done her in. How's Aunt Margaret?"

"I doubt if she'll last the week," said Matthew with some feeling. "Her birthday is coming up, and she insisted I send for you."

"She'll be disappointed that Katherine is not with me. It couldn't be helped. Take me to her; I want to see her."

Matthew turned back up the stairs, and Stephen followed. They entered the old lady's room together. Margaret was still dozing and did not hear them enter. Matthew stood beside her and touched her frail shoulder. She awoke with a start.

"Aunt Margaret," he said, "Mr. Nowell is here."

She looked around. Stephen stepped into her view and she smiled. Her teeth were now completely gone, and he was shocked to see how truly frail she was. But then next week she would be ninety-two. No one in Albany or Saratoga could truthfully remember her as young. She had outlived all of her contemporaries and many born well after her.

"Where's Katherine?" asked Margaret.

"She couldn't come, Margaret. She's not well."

"You always were a disappointment to me, boy," she said. Only Margaret could get away with calling a sixty-seven-year-old man a boy.

"But then you were no better and no worse than most men. I never liked men. That is, except for Kip. He died last year."

"I know," said Stephen sadly.

"I liked Kip," she continued. "The only man worth his weight in spit. I decided not to hate you as much as I really could and as much as you really deserved because you introduced me to Kip."

Stephen smiled.

"I called you here, Stephen, because I am dying. I'd rather have told this to my Katherine, face to face, but you'll have to do it. I'm leaving all of this," she said, waving her frail arm wearily, "my house and my lands, to Matthew. I want Katherine to know that I had not forgotten her. I always said I would leave it to her, but she's got so much from you, and your son has nothing."

"You know, Aunt Margaret, that I will provide for my own son."

"I can't be sure. The boy is almost as obnoxious as you are.

7

You probably won't be able to stand him, and you'll probably disown him."

"I never would," said Stephen indignantly.

"Good. You hear that, Matthew; your father promised me on my deathbed that he'd never disown you, no matter what you did. Remind him of it when he tries to disown you." She cackled her familiar laugh, a much weaker sound than it had been in the past.

"Get out of here, now; I want to die in peace."

Stephen looked at her with some concern. But Matthew merely chuckled.

"You say that every day, old woman, but you never do it."

"One of these days," she said, holding up her hand, "one of these days." And she began to doze again.

The two men went down the stairs.

"You realize that it can never be," said Stephen to Matthew.

"What do you mean?"

"She couldn't leave you this house; she doesn't own it. She never did. It was willed in the Schuyler estate, and Cornelia Schuyler and then General Schuyler allowed her to live here. When she dies, it reverts to the Schuylers."

"I know that," said Matthew, "and she knows that. Why do you think she went through the charade of getting you to promise not to disown me? I know that was a sham too."

"Matthew, I meant what I said. When I die, you will receive your proper portion of my estate in Canada."

"I don't want any of your Tory loot."

"Oh, Matthew, the war has been over almost a decade. Why continue to fight old, tired battles?"

"If the war is over, why do you continue to hold the forts that were ceded to us in the treaty—Detroit, Niagara? No, sir, the war won't be over until our army enters Canada and drives the damned British and you damned Tories into the sea. There is room for only one nation on this continent, and that nation is going to be the United States. So help me God, I'll lead an army across the lakes and I'll take for us all that God intended for us to have—the whole continent."

Stephen was shocked by his son's outburst. Matthew was not really angry; he spoke in a cold and calculated tone. It sent a chill through the father. Stephen was suddenly frightened for the peace he had come to cherish in his new home, and he was suddenly frightened for Canada.

I

Aaron

1783–1794

1

Aaron pulled his army blanket about his body to keep out the cold. The snow was deep—to his midcalf already—and the winds off the lake would surely carry more. He could barely see the trail that led along the Niagara River. He had to be at the fort before the worst snows came. The Buffalo Creek Seneca had treated him with the respect due a Mohawk sachem—the stepson of the Great Johnson and the son of Molly Brant. But the old ties of brotherhood were broken. Geyasada, the Seneca sachem, had been conspicuously absent, and when Aaron had raised the question of the ransom of his niece, Maggie, he was met only with hostile stares.

Earlier in the war against the Americans, Aaron had led a raid on a garrison house at Fort Vaughan. To his horror he learned that it was the home of his half sister, Amy Nowell. He had saved the lives of all of the family present in the house. Her husband, however, had been captured by Onondaga earlier and probably killed. Aaron had saved Amy and her twin sons and had later released them. But Maggie, her red-haired daughter, had been taken by the Seneca sachem; Geyasada had been persuaded to spare her life and had adopted her. His wife doted on this child. But Aaron had promised his sister that he would work for Maggie's return although he knew that it would be close to impossible. In her last letter to him, Amy wrote that she would move west to Canada to be near her child.

The trail was almost gone now, and the snow blew directly into his face. Aaron stopped. For the first time it occurred to him that he might not be able to reach the fort on this night. He had taken these trails many times and knew where his people took shelter along the way. There was a cave not far from the shore of the Niagara. He would strike out for it. It was only about a half mile from the last landmark he had noted.

He left the trail and trudged through the snow into the forest. He wished he had carried snowshoes with him. The

11

going would be difficult without them. He was sweating under his blanket but if he stood for only a few moments the cold would creep through and chill him to the bone.

The wind rose as Aaron trudged on. Its roar through the pines made him shiver. The sound, he thought, was the loneliest one in nature.

He was halfway to the river when he saw the flicker of a fire. No fire that size could have existed without some sort of shelter. Aaron made straight for the light. He lost it twice as gusts of wind drove snow into his eyes. It collected on his eyebrows. At first it melted from the warmth of his body but then it froze and encrusted the tips of the tiny hairs.

He found the light again. This time it was off to the right but definitely closer. He trudged on. He was determined not to call out but to approach the fire cautiously. Better to freeze to death in a blizzard than to roast over an enemy fire. His caution made him smile. That was the thought of the forty-year-old battle-scarred Aaron Brant. The twenty-year-old warrior, Kenonranon would have preferred the fire.

He was close enough now to see that the fire had come from the cave he had set out to find. The chances that someone other than Iroquois would be in the cave were small. He dropped behind a fallen birch tree and called out a greeting in Mohawk. The response came back in the unmistakable dialect of the Seneca. The Seneca and the Mohawk were loyal to the king and to each other, unlike the traitors—the Oneida.

He rose to his feet and struggled the last few yards. The snow was piled high at the entrance to the cave. He had been lucky. In another half hour the drift would have blocked out the light from the fire. Aaron crawled over the drift and tumbled into the mouth of the cave entrance.

He found four faces wrapped in blankets staring down at him. He recognized one; it was that of Geyasada—the very man he sought. Behind him were huddled a woman and two girls. One, about sixteen, was clearly Indian. The second he recognized instantly by her flaming red hair. It was his eleven-year-old niece, Maggie.

Aaron smiled at them. "Your fire saved me," he panted. "I owe you much."

Geyasada smiled, revealing gaps in his teeth. "You'll need something to warm you, Kenonranon," he said.

Aaron was almost overwhelmed by the stench of rum that

12

came from the man. The Seneca lifted the small keg to his mouth, gulped several mouthfuls more of the liquid, and then handed the keg to Aaron while wiping the rum that had dribbled down his chin with his forearm. Then he staggered to his feet and, grabbing his wife, pulled her over toward Aaron.

"This is my woman, Jenny. She's good. If you want to try her out she'll give you a good time."

Otsegenni or Mother Jenny, as she was known, was shocked by her drunken husband's offer. She resisted his pull and he smacked her, leaving a welt across her cheek. The young girls cried out in fear.

Jenny was embarrassed. Geyasada had struck her many times in the past, especially when he was drunk like this. But never before had he humiliated her in front of a stranger.

Aaron was disgusted by Geyasada's drunkenness, but he was cold and wanted some of the rum. He threw his head back and took a large swig of the sweet liquor. It burned all the way down his gullet. He took a second swig but then felt the keg wrenched from his hands.

"You drink too much, Mohawk. Mind your manners. You are a guest in my cave." Geyasada's words were slurred.

Aaron was enraged by the insult but he kept his temper under control. It would not do to humiliate a man before his wife and children.

"Sachem," he said coldly, "I believe this cave belongs to all travelers." He emphasized the title to remind Geyasada of the obligations of the office they both held.

Geyasada took another swig of rum. Again he lunged for his wife, who stepped aside nimbly for a large woman. Then he collapsed on the floor of the cave with a thud. This time he passed out and stayed put.

The young Indian girl took his blanket and covered him with it. Then she turned to Aaron.

"My name is Ruth," she said. "My sister is Maggie and this is Mother Jenny—the sachem's wife."

The girl spoke with dignity, and Aaron felt for the disgrace she suffered. He guessed from her words that Geyasada and Mother Jenny were not her parents. Like Maggie, she had probably been adopted by the pair.

Aaron nodded to the girl and then took his blanket to the far side of the cave and sat down. The person who really interested him was the white girl. He looked at her and

13

noted that she stared at him brazenly. He smiled. It was clear that Geyasada had his hands full with her. She would not be easily intimidated. Even if he couldn't persuade the sachem to return the girl to Amy, at least he could report that she was healthy and unbowed.

Mother Jenny waddled across the cave toward him and offered him some dried meat and water made from melted snow. When he finished eating, he motioned to Ruth.

"I need sleep," he said. "You keep watch for the next three hours and then wake me up."

The girl looked puzzled.

"We are still at war," said Aaron. "Our enemies, the Oneida and the Tuscarora, take the scalps of girls along with those of sachems."

Ruth nodded and went to the mouth of the cave, Geyasada's worn musket in hand. Aaron did not know if she knew how to use it but he was exhausted and had little choice but to rely on her. He turned his back on the fire and was soon snoring lightly.

He did not know why he awakened. He was tired enough to sleep through the whole night but something deep inside him rose and pried into his brain, causing him to awaken with a start and to look about him anxiously. Jenny and Maggie were huddled together next to the fire. Geyasada snored loudly where he had fallen. Aaron realized he should be moved. If he rolled the wrong way he would be in the fire.

Ruth still sat with the Seneca's musket across her lap at the entrance of the cave. When she saw Aaron was awake, she motioned him to join her. Aaron grabbed his musket but realized that it might still be wet with snow and reached instead for the tomahawk at his side. He rose and moved silently to the shadows near the left side of the cave entrance. His nerves were on edge. The girl was staring out into the grayness of the night snow. He stepped past the girl and crawled through the drift. He had moved no more than ten feet into the snow when he heard a war cry. A small party of about six Oneida came dashing directly toward him. When they saw him leave the cave, they knew they had been detected and gave up all pretense of stealth. Aaron stood up in the knee-deep snow and threw back a challenging cry to the Oneida.

"The traitors of the longhouse track down women and children for scalps. They are geldings."

One of the Oneidas raised his musket to his shoulder and aimed at Aaron. But he was distracted by a terrible scream that arose from inside the cave. Suddenly Geyasada came racing out of the cave, his blanket aflame. The man had awakened from his stupor to see himself on fire and had panicked. Aaron tried to trip him. If he rolled in the snow, the flames would be extinguished. Aaron's attempt to stop him failed, but Geyasada pulled up short when the musket ball originally meant for Aaron came screaming over his head. Ruth shrieked as the lead ball struck her in the hip. Aaron grabbed Geyasada's shoulder and dragged him back into the cave. The Seneca complained bitterly of burns but Aaron could see that they were superficial. Quickly he doused the fire with a gourd of water. Mother Jenny and Maggie stood huddled together at the back of the cave. Both were paralyzed with fear. Ruth moaned in agony. Jenny, seeing for the first time that she was hurt, moved across the cave on her hands and knees to assist her. She and Maggie together dragged Ruth back toward the relative safety at the rear of the shelter.

Aaron grabbed his musket and powder horn and stepped back into the darkness as well. Geyasada stood up. A musket ball came crashing into the cave and ricocheted against the stone walls. Aaron ducked instantly.

"On the ground," he called out to the Seneca and the women. "Keep low."

Suddenly it seemed darker at the mouth of the cave. Aaron raised his musket and fired. Nothing happened. Snow had soaked into the pan. He dropped the gun and raced toward the opening. The Oneida could not see him coming. Aaron crashed his knee into the other man's groin. The dark form in front of Aaron screamed.

As Aaron turned, a musket fired behind him. The ball passed his head by inches and struck the Oneida in the shoulder. Aaron's knife slipped into the muscle of the Oneida's stomach and buried itself to the hilt. The Oneida collapsed backward into the snowdrift at the cave's mouth.

The dark form of Geyasada crawled past Aaron, who heard a gurgling noise as a throat was cut. Then Geyasada crawled back to Aaron's side. He held the dead Oneida's scalp clutched in his gory hand. Even in the cave's darkness, Aaron could see the look of triumph in his eyes. Aaron ripped the scalp

15

from the sachem's hands and held his own knife against Geyasada's throat.

"What's wrong?" croaked the Seneca.

"You," said Aaron through clenched teeth. "You're so anxious to take a scalp that you nearly put a musket ball into my head. Never fire into a melee like that. You can kill friend or foe, you don't really know which. Just whoever makes the mistake of getting in the way."

Geyasada was sullen. He pulled away from Aaron's knife. He was frightened and angry at the same time. He had killed the enemy. He was a sachem. He deserved honor, not the anger of this Mohawk. He crawled to the other side of the cave to sulk.

Jenny was terrified and now started a wailing noise—a dirge for the dying. Beside her, the wounded Ruth whimpered with pain. Aaron moved to her side. He examined the wound in the girl's hip as best he could in the dark. She was not bleeding badly and she was in no immediate danger from her injury. He hushed her and told her to be brave. He kept his eyes steadily on the cave entrance, watching for a shadow that would indicate that another Oneida had worked up the courage to try to enter. Jenny's wailing grew less loud. Aaron heard a rustling and thought it might be Geyasada coming over to confer with him. He was startled when the face of Maggie came peering out of the gloom at him.

"Kenonranon," she whispered, "I'm frightened."

He put his arm around her shoulder and pulled her close to his side. She shivered and he held her even closer to him to try to warm her with his body. Tears streamed down her face. She mumbled something and he placed his ear closer to her mouth to hear her. Then he realized that she prayed to the white god, Jesus, a prayer she could only have learned from her mother, Amy Nowell, years before. He held on to her while she prayed and even after she stopped. He decided he would tell her that he was her uncle and that he had come for her to return her to those who loved her. But her head fell against his chest and she slept. He would tell her all in the morning. Still he held on to her and all the while his eyes never moved from the entrance of the cave.

Several hours before dawn, the Oneidas rushed. Geyasada fired first, blowing the top off the skull of the first Oneida to dart into the cave. Maggie awoke with a scream as Aaron's musket—its powder now dry—roared inside the cave and a second

16

Oneida was spun around before falling dead. Geyasada tried to reload but Aaron did not bother. He rushed toward the entrance and dived at the feet of a stocky buckskinned warrior. He upended the warrior and they fell into the snowdrift, grabbing at each other. Aaron worked his knife free. His opponent had fallen on top of him, knocking Aaron's wind out of him. He felt the Indian's fingers on his throat—tightening. His eyes bulged as his wind was cut off, and he lost his grasp on his knife. It fell into the deep snow. In desperation he reached up and grabbed the Oneida's face with his fingernails. His thumbs slipped into the enemy's eye sockets. Aaron pressed with all of his remaining strength. The Oneida screamed as blood shot out of his now empty sockets. The grip on Aaron's throat loosened.

Geyasada came out of the cave, his musket reloaded, but the last two Oneida, terrified by the screams of the blinded man, turned their backs on the slaughter and fled. Aaron sat up in the snow. Geyasada took his tomahawk and split the skull of the screaming one and then scalped him. Aaron wiped the gore from his hands on the icy whiteness. He felt sick. He walked back into the cave to find Ruth and Maggie staring blankly at the blood-covered ground. Jenny rose from her bed still dazed.

Aaron stepped in front of the girls. He grabbed them by the arms and pulled them away from the sight of the Oneida corpses. Ruth hobbled. Her hip clearly pained her. Geyasada busied himself by removing the scalps from the dead warriors. He offered one to Aaron. The Mohawk shook his head. Geyasada shrugged and took it for himself. He ordered the women to haul the corpses out into the snow. Aaron objected. Ruth could barely stand and Maggie was too young for so gruesome a task. Again the Seneca shrugged his shoulders and watched Jenny pull and tug the bodies of the large men out into the snow alone.

"My Mohawk brother has brought good luck to me," said the still unsteady Seneca sachem.

"Geyasada has done the same for me," responded Aaron. "In fact, he has saved me much effort trying to find him. I must discuss the one with the red hair with you. Her mother still weeps for her."

Geyasada deliberately misunderstood him and glanced over at Jenny. "Her mother sweats and smells foully because of it, but I do not see any tears."

"You know of whom I speak," Aaron responded. "My sister longs for the return of her child."

"Will Kenonranon side with his stepsister against his brothers and sisters of the longhouse? You know our laws. The red-haired one is my child—Jenny's child. We love her as our own."

"My sister has come across the lakes and will pay much for her return." Aaron hoped that Geyasada was as greedy as he appeared to be. And at the mention of ransom Aaron noted that the Seneca's interest in their conversation increased.

"What would she pay?" he asked.

"Our father is a wealthy man. He could be persuaded to reward Geyasada. Muskets, a medal from the king—anything is possible to the blackrobe. Surely he loves his granddaughter and wants her back."

Geyasada remained silent but Aaron was convinced that he had triggered the man's interest. Jenny rekindled the small fire, and Aaron and Geyasada stared at each other across it in silence. But Aaron knew that he could not continue the negotiations. He was past exhaustion. His eyelids drooped. And it was an effort to keep his mind attentive to what the Seneca said. The exhilaration of combat had given way to a lethargy not unlike that he had felt after making love. He could barely move his limbs, yet courtesy and the importance of this negotiation required that he not insult the Seneca by requesting a halt. But he feared if he did not, he would commit the grossest of insults by falling asleep while the Seneca spoke.

Geyasada noted Aaron's exhaustion. "We have a few more hours before dawn," he said. "I think it not a time for serious discussion. My friend, you need sleep and so do I. We will begin our negotiations with the first light."

Aaron was puzzled by the Seneca's gesture. It was totally out of character. Any kindness from Geyasada was suspect. But he could not let the chance to end this conversation slip by him. He accepted Geyasada's suggestion gratefully. He spread his old blanket out on the ground carefully and rolled himself up in it. Within minutes, he was asleep.

But Geyasada did not sleep. He remained seated, watching the Mohawk's breathing. Kenonranon was a fool. He thought that trinkets would buy the prize from him. He could have Ruth for trinkets. When he and Mother Jenny adopted Ruth after her parents died ten years ago, he had known that

18

eventually she would provide him with a bride price. But he had no such plans for Maggie. From the first, she had fascinated him. Now he loved her but not as a father. His passion was of a different sort. But he had to do something about Brant. Brant would never allow him to have the girl in peace. He should kill him. It would be easy. He could blame it on the Oneidas. He rejected the thought, as attractive as it was. He could never silence the tongues of the women. Eventually word of what really happened would leak out and the Brant clan would seek him out and take a bitter revenge. He stared at Aaron. Look at him, he thought. He sleeps with the carelessness of the secure. Well, the joke would be on Kenonranon. When he awoke, he was in for a surprise. He almost wished he could be here to observe the expression on the Mohawk's face.

Maggie had overheard the men talking, and she knew they spoke of her. She had a powerful grandfather who would come and buy her back from Geyasada. She hoped her grandfather was as kind as Kenonranon. She had been terrified after the first attack and he had comforted her. He had not slapped her when she tried to crawl into his lap—not like the pig. She always thought of Geyasada as the pig. It was a name that Jenny called him when he was not around. She and Ruth picked it up from Mother Jenny. Once Ruth had forgotten herself and used the name within the sound of Geyasada's ear. He had beaten her. But the Mohawk sachem was no pig. With him she could feel safe—a feeling she could never remember having in the past. She lay pretending to sleep on her blanket. In the morning the Mohawk would take her away from here. That was all she could think of.

Suddenly she felt a finger probe sharply into her back and a hand clasp over her mouth. She could smell the rum and knew instantly that it was Geyasada.

"It's time to leave here, my pretty one," he whispered in her ear.

She sat up, wiping the sleep from her eyes. She saw that Jenny had already strapped the heavy pack filled with their belongings onto her back. But Ruth and the Mohawk were still wrapped in their blankets, fast asleep. She started to say something when again the Seneca's hand went over her mouth.

"One word and I'll roast your heart over my fire," he said.

She was terrified. She did not know what Geyasada was up

19

to but she knew that the warm feeling of security that had possessed her a few moments earlier was already a dim memory from the past.

Aaron awoke slowly. Normally, when he was on the trail, he was awake as soon as his eyes opened. But this morning, wrapped in warmth in the darkness of the cave, he did not wish to move. Then he heard her call and the sleepiness left him.

"Kenonranon. I need you."

It was Ruth. He crawled to her side. He felt her forehead. She was feverish, but it was not the raging fever of the pox. Then for the first time he realized they were alone.

"Where are the others?" he asked, suddenly very wary.

"They're gone, fled," said Ruth. "Geyasada took Maggie and Jenny and he has run away with them."

Aaron's first thought was to follow Geyasada. The Seneca had only a few hours' head start and the woman and the child would slow him down. But then he realized how badly he had been outwitted. Geyasada had left Ruth behind, knowing that Aaron, the noble sachem of the Mohawks, could never abandon a wounded woman—especially a woman from his own Turtle clan. How would he explain that to the noble clan mother of the Turtles, Molly Brant? His sense of responsibility to his people would require him to remain in the cave until the girl could walk. And even then, he would have to bring her to safety—probably to the Mohawk encampment at Fort Niagara. Geyasada's head start would be weeks, not hours long, and by the time Aaron was back on the trail, it would be a very cold trail indeed.

They arrived at Fort Niagara the next week. The gray stone of the fortress with the black muzzles of the cannon gaping out of their embrasures matched the bleakness of the winter day. The clouds still hung over the lake, and the ice was piled up just offshore.

The Indian village that surrounded the walls of Niagara was little more than a slum. The neat rows of longhouses of the Iroquois castle had been replaced with shacks and shanties nailed together from whatever green scrap wood they could beg or steal from the British army inside the fort. Some families lived in open-sided lean-tos, which did nothing at all to keep out the winter. Aaron had seen it all before—the muddy streets littered with dog droppings, the cold, the poverty—but Ruth had never been here. She had come to see Niagara as refuge. As she looked about, her hopes were dashed. A toothless old man came out of his hut onto the planks that served as a path from one hut to another. He removed his loincloth and squatted. He stared up at the two strangers. He was not at all embarrassed. He merely smiled, revealing his gums.

"Things are worse now than when I left," said Aaron. "There will be disease here soon."

He led the newcomer toward the fort. Joseph Brant, his uncle, a captain in the British army, had quarters inside the fort. Molly Brant, Joseph's sister and Aaron's mother was a frequent visitor from Kingston.

He recognized his mother's slim form approaching the village from out of the fortress gates. He waved to her. She smiled and changed direction to come to him. She was older now but although her face had some wrinkles and still showed the marks of a childhood case of smallpox, Aaron thought she had changed very little over the years. Her walk still had pride in it. She was still the clan mother of the Turtles, even if the clan itself was dispersed and broken. The Oneida he had killed back at the cave might well have been his Turtle cousin. The Six Nations were in shambles. But not Molly Brant.

Aaron kissed the cheek she offered him.

"Was your mission a success or was Geyasada still the pig he always was?" she said.

Aaron shook his head. "He will not surrender my sister's child to her. Worse yet, he has fled from me rather than discuss it."

"Well, at least that is an end to it. You won't be running off to the Seneca any longer. Who is this person?" she asked, pointing to Ruth. Without giving Aaron a chance to respond, she took a closer look, her eyes squinting. She no longer saw very well. "You are a cousin, aren't you?"

Ruth nodded. "I am of the Turtle clan, clan mother, and like you, I am a Christian. My adopted mother is Otsegenni of the Seneca. She raised me in the longhouse of Geyasada, the sachem. I know nothing else of my origins."

"I know your mother. She has become the size of a cow," Molly said cruelly.

"Your son is a brave warrior. He and Geyasada killed many

21

Oneidas and he saved me from death—a lingering death from wounds alone in the forest." Ruth continued. "Kenonranon could have taken many scalps."

Molly's face twisted in disgust. She wrinkled her nose.

Aaron chuckled. There was a time when Molly Brant would not have thought the taking of an enemy scalp disgusting. He described the raid on the cave to her. Now she became even more concerned. Not because Oneida were dead or because Geyasada had fled. Her concern had been for Aaron. That death had reached out to him twice, once when a ball from Geyasada's musket passed close by him and once when the fingers of the Oneida pressed about his throat. Twice he had come close to leaving her.

"I must find a place for our cousin to stay," said Aaron, turning from his mother.

"Let her fend for herself."

"You forget, mother, I too must find lodgings."

"You stay with Joseph and me."

"I think it more appropriate for a sachem to live among the people when times are hard."

He turned from her and signaled Ruth to follow him.

Molly looked on in annoyance as he disappeared down the street of shacks. But soon annoyance gave way to pride. It was true, she thought, the sachem should live with his people.

Kenonranon heard the sound of thunder in his sleep. He remembered how frightened he had been by it as a child. Old Brant, his great-grandfather, who made him toy masks with protruding tongues and wild crossed eyes, had comforted him and told him of the two giants who had angered the great spirit and who were forced to bash their heads together whenever the spirit snapped his fingers to make lightning. Kenonranon knew that the old man had been joking and had laughed. But still, he had feared the thunder less. He awoke with a start. It was not thunder but cannon fire coming from the fort. He sat up quickly and looked about. The hut was a small one, nailed together loosely from old boards. Because the wood was green it had warped, allowing the cold air to pour through when the wind blew. The girl slept next to an old Onondaga Christian woman, who guarded her as a dog guards an old bone.

Again the cannon sounded. Aaron stood up. He knew the

girl had been awakened by the same noise because he heard her giggle at his nakedness.

The cold air blew through the cracks in the wall as it had all winter. Aaron shivered and reached for the British army blanket to cover himself. The blanket was gray and worn thin from washing. There were enough holes in the wrong places to do almost as little for his modesty as it did for his warmth.

The months of winter had dragged on and on. Disease was everywhere. The old woman became ill, followed by Ruth, and then Aaron himself had contracted the numbing stomach cramps and sweating fever.

With the coming of spring they had all recovered, but the closeness of their living quarters brought new troubles. The Onondaga woman first thought that Aaron sought her as a partner. When Aaron made no move toward her, she concluded that it was not her but her ward that he desired, and she was determined that as a Christian she would guard the girl's virtue. Aaron could have her only after the vows were exchanged before a clergyman. In reality, Aaron had not thought of the girl very much at all since that night in the cave. She was a pretty child with large brown eyes and black hair, which, when she allowed it to hang straight, came down to her waist. But he had come to live with these people because they needed him and his own family did not. The British treated Joseph Brant and his family with enormous respect but they had little use for teen-age girls and old women.

Cannon roared again, finally waking the Onondaga. She stared suspiciously at Aaron, who stood wrapped in his blanket not much more than six feet from her prize. Aaron walked to the skin door of the hut and pulled it aside. Spring rains had fallen, turning the streets of this makeshift village into quagmires. The inhabitants had laid boards along the streets to keep their moccasins dry, but now even these boards were covered with an oozing brown mud.

Several Indians stood ankle-deep on the boards and stared up at the fort above them. The British flag flew proudly from its stone ramparts, and small red-coated sentries could be seen pacing back and forth. The guns facing the riverside were covered with clouds of black smoke. They had been fired in salute. No hostile force of Americans could have come this far west without detection. That they had fired in salute was the only possible conclusion. There was no living enemy of the king within a hundred miles of Niagara. That was why his people had flocked here, to flee the hated Americans and the Americans' even more hated allies, the Oneida and the Tuscarora, traitors to the longhouse. While Aaron watched, the Redcoats poured powder into another gun and touched the slow match. The gun leapt back; smoke and fire belched out of its bore. Aaron stepped back, almost tripping over the grandmother, who had come out of the hut behind him.

Ruth was dressed already. She took some kindling and placed it in the center of the floor to start the fire. Soon the house was filled with smoke as breakfast was prepared. The older woman emptied a sack of cornmeal to make a paste in her bowl. She shook every last bit of the meal out.

"We will have to get more meal from the British now," she said in Iroquois. "And if the British insist on treating Christian Indians badly, I hope you complain to your relatives. They're good Christian folk. They will take our side."

"The British treat us all the same," said Aaron with disgust.

Aaron went to the small trunk in which he kept all his possessions, including his letters from his sister, Amy. The two women followed him with their eyes. He was a large man; his legs were heavily muscled. His waist was thin and his shoulders enormous. Those who met him for the first time were startled by his fair skin and penetrating blue eyes. His father was a white man, the Boston merchant Stephen Nowell, now a Loyalist exile like his son.

Aaron fixed his loincloth in place and then put on his oldest pair of moccasins. He walked out into the chilly morning, past the huts that the Indians had built, then the palisade and ditch of the front gate of Fort Niagara. He recognized his uncle, Joseph Brant, standing on the parade grounds talking to the white commandant. Joseph's face was flushed with anger and he screamed at the white man. Aaron rushed to his side and touched his uncle's arm. The older man started to pull away. Then seeing that it was Aaron who touched him, he relaxed.

"Kenonranon," he said, switching to Mohawk, "the British have signed a treaty with the Americans. The war is over."

Aaron smiled. "At last." Now he could return to Canajoharie, his home. Molly Brant could get her house back. Joseph could go back to his study of the Christian scriptures. This most-feared of Mohawks, the scourge of the frontier to the

Americans, was interested more in translating scripture into Mohawk than he was in raiding white settlements. He would defend his people's rights to the death but Aaron knew him to be a kind and gentle man. He was no demon.

But his face was now demonic, which puzzled Aaron greatly.

"It is good that peace has come, uncle. Why are you so angry?"

"Because the British have treated us as a subject people. We are not to make our own treaty with the Americans. They have given away our homeland to the Americans. The longhouses will never be constructed along the banks of our river, along the shores of our lake."

Joseph had feared as much when the Americans had driven them from their home and they had fled to Canada, but he had expected that the dignity of nationhood would have been left to them. He could establish a new longhouse here in Canada, but he had hoped and he had been promised that they would be allowed to preserve their dignity.

The British officer looked on as the two Indians spoke. It was clear that he was embarrassed and distressed. He liked these people and he was sorry. They lived miserably here at Niagara. Once they had been proud and now they were beggars.

Joseph could not face the commandant. He pulled away from Aaron's grasp and with long strides began to walk out of the fort and toward the village of huts. Aaron called after him to wait, but Joseph kept right on walking, down toward the village of huts. Aaron had to run to catch up with him.

The cannon fire and the warming sun had awakened the entire encampment. Men sat on empty rum kegs before their huts. Several were already in the process of creating future seats for themselves. They staggered about in the mud. Some children ran between the huts playing a game whose rules only they could comprehend. When Aaron reached Joseph's side, his uncle waved his hand as if to encompass the whole village.

"Look at us," said Joseph, his anger still showing. "We have become beggars living in filth. It is time to leave this place of death. Remember what happened after the battle of Oriskany? The Seneca went home because seventeen of them died in the battle. You recall that?"

Aaron nodded.

"Well, five Oriskanys would not have cost us as many lives

25

as have been lost to disease here at Fort Niagara. Oriskany took the lives of the men. Niagara steals the babies and the old."

Joseph Brant led his followers along the deep gorge of the Niagara River south of the old fort. The heights loomed above them. They had left their place of sickness behind them and now journeyed to their new home on the Grand River and Lake Erie.

Aaron noticed it first. It was again like the sound of distant thunder rolling toward them and never ceasing. The waters of the river raged beneath them as they hugged the path heading south. The sound grew closer and closer. Aaron's adopted family, Ruth and the Onondaga grandmother, followed closely behind him. Ruth pushed up close to Aaron as they went forward toward the noise. He could almost feel her breath on his bare back.

The waters swirled around the curve in the channel and formed a whirlpool, which crashed against the solid rock embankment. The noise grew louder as they proceeded south. The girl and her adopted guardian had been chatting but Aaron, who had been annoyed by talk on the trail, could no longer tell if they persisted. Their voices were drowned by the rush of the river.

They passed the whirlpool and rounded a bend in the river. The vista that opened before them was breathtaking. The waters of Lake Erie, forced into a narrow channel of the Niagara River, plummeted into the thunderous mists and then rushed to enter Lake Ontario.

Aaron had seen them before, but the falls of Niagara still overwhelmed him. The great Horseshoe Falls were directly ahead of them, and the second falls, smaller and less dramatic, fell into the gorge on the left.

Aaron turned to look at Ruth and Grandmother, as the girl now addressed her. He noted only then that they had stopped in their tracks from fright when they first caught sight of the cataract. Aaron's face broke into a smile. He walked back toward the girl. Grandmother caught hold of herself and started to yell, complaining that they had held up the whole line of march, but she was not quick enough to fool Aaron. She had stood openmouthed like the others; she had merely recovered more quickly.

Aaron took hold of Ruth's hand. The girl looked at him

26

through enormous brown eyes. He smiled at her and began to tug gently at her arm.

"Don't be frightened, our people have followed this path through both war and peace. The spirit of the white waters is friendly to us."

Ruth smiled back at him and began to step slowly toward the falls. They climbed even higher up the embankment of the riverside. The noise was almost deafening now, and the mist cloaked them completely. Aaron had to push his long hair off his face to keep the water out of his eyes. The path was a well-used one but dangerous to those who grew careless. A mist shrouded the river below now. The top of the mist was crowned by rainbows that broke up and then reformed as the travelers moved upward. Aaron kept hold of Ruth's arm long after her initial fright had disappeared. She voiced no complaint. They were past the top of the horseshoe now; all danger had passed. The river widened once they passed the island that split the falls. And the sounds of falling water began to recede slowly at first and then more quickly as they continued south.

Brant met them with his advance party at Chippewa. Here the Niagara split into two branches about Grand Island. He had canoes, brought from the Seneca, ready for his party. Ruth expected Aaron to paddle her, but Molly intervened and decided that Aaron should come with her. She assigned Aaron's young cousin, Isaac Brant, to Ruth. They launched their canoes into the west channel. The river currents were less strong now, but paddling against them was still hard work. Isaac's canoe went ahead while Aaron and Molly followed behind. Aaron had hunted and fought all of his life. His build was thick and solid. Ruth could not take her eyes from him, and she turned around in her canoe several times as they moved rapidly up the river toward Lake Erie. It was poor canoe etiquette, she knew, but the strength and beauty of the man behind her, his light skin and his blue eyes forced her to turn to look at him again and again and to break all the rules of behavior her mother had drilled into her. She was a Christian, and young Christian girls were not supposed to have thoughts like those that crept unbidden into her head when she looked at Aaron's body. When they had glided past Grand Island and the two channels were joined, Aaron guided his canoe toward the west bank. They rounded a point and the broad expanse of Lake Erie opened before them. The clouds hung low over the lake, and the wind moved from the southwest. To the south lightning broke through the grayness of the sky and flashed downward into the waters. The waves seemed to respond to the shock and grew more violent.

Aaron had hugged the shoreline as they left the river but other canoes in the flotilla were not as cautious. Aaron lost sight of Isaac and Ruth's canoe and drove his canoe with all the strength of his arms toward the beach. When the canoe ground to a halt on the beach gravel, given a final shove by a breaking wave, he jumped out quickly, pulling the front of the canoe up farther on the beach. Molly climbed out and Aaron began to hand her the skin-wrapped bundles she had brought with her for this visit.

A wave broke against him, forcing him to stumble. Molly ran back to the canoe. She realized Aaron intended to go back out into the lake to help those who might have capsized. Aaron steadied the canoe and then jumped over the side into the front. His mother called out in fear but she went unheeded. Aaron balanced the canoe against the next wave and then plunged his paddle into the water. The fragile craft crested the top of the wave and then shot out into the raging inland sea. He steered the canoe to the left. He saw Joseph Brant with two of his half brothers, Molly's sons, striving to make the shore. They were taking water but they were well on their way to safety. The waves seemed gigantic now. Aaron had to fight to keep the nose of the canoe headed into the wind. Ruth had not been that far behind him. He should have seen their canoe before this. Then he saw them. Their canoe had capsized. He saw Grandmother clinging to it. Isaac was hanging on to the other side, but he did not see Ruth. His heart pounded within his chest as he dug his paddle into the water and awaited the next wave. It lifted the canoe high into the air and then he saw her. She was trying to swim to shore but the waves drove her back. She would never make it. Aaron realized he could not turn to reach her. If he tried, his canoe would present its side to the wave and he too would capsize. He dived out of the canoe and swam with powerful strokes toward her. But then he had lost sight of her again. A wave lifted him and he saw her again. She was going under. He struck out in her direction. He had her in sight. He reached for her and missed. He reached again and caught hold of her deerskin tunic. He pulled her to the surface. She was gagging. She clutched at him in desperation. He grabbed her under the arms and kicked his legs, pulling her over onto her back behind him. He whispered in her ear and told her to relax, he would protect her. He could not fight against the wind-driven waves. He gave in to them and let the waves drive them both. They were tossed about like corks. He knew that, had he been alone, he could make it to the shore, but Ruth acted like a drag anchor. He had to keep moving. It was their only chance. Maybe if he yelled someone would hear him. He opened his mouth and swallowed water. He started to cough and gag. Ruth had stopped struggling and lay limply in the water.

He thought she was unconscious, maybe even dead. It would be so easy to go limp as she had and sink to the bottom. A new wave lifted him. He was tired. He couldn't swim anymore. His body plummeted into the trough between the waves. He started to sink and then his foot touched bottom. It shocked him out of his trance. He was near shore. He lost his footing with the next wave but let it carry him and Ruth along. He heard breakers crashing into the rocks. They could make it. Again his foot touched. He stood and pulled Ruth forward. A wave crashed against him and sent him rocketing into the shore. Aaron smashed his shoulder into a large boulder. He felt the pain down to his fingertips. He regained his feet and dragged Ruth up into the pines that grew on the shore's edge. He fell down next to her. He placed his ear over her breast. He could hear her heart beating. She still lived. He fell face forward on the ground. He felt his stomach churn, and he threw up over the soft rain-soaked earth in front of his face.

The storm continued through the night. They could have used a fire to warm themselves but Aaron had nothing with which to start it. The wind-driven rain had soaked any potential kindling. There was no shelter available. Aaron was too exhausted to search for any even if there had been some. He lay stretched out on the beach while the cold rain drenched him all the more. The girl lay huddled next to him, unconscious.

Toward dawn the winds let up. The rains came down straight rather than at an angle. Aaron stood up. He gasped when he moved his arm. His arm and shoulder were stiff and swollen. He remembered crashing into the rock. He moved it gingerly and determined that he was badly bruised but had no broken bones. He wiped the water from his eyes and looked down at the girl. Her teeth chattered with the cold and she shivered. He had to find them some shelter. He stood up and realized for the first time how destitute they were. He was entirely naked. Somehow or other he had lost even his loincloth in the desperate swim to shore.

The rain clouds had lifted to the south and the sun was pushing to break through. Ruth stirred and then her eyes opened. She looked about her in surprise. She had no idea where she was or how she had arrived at this beach. Aaron sat down beside her, partially to reassure her and partially to make his nakedness less obvious.

"Are you all right?" he asked her.

She nodded. "Just cold."

"As best I can make out, we're on an island about a half mile offshore. Once the waters calm down we can make a swim for the mainland."

Ruth shook her head. "No, I'm not going back into the water. I was terrified. I was sure I was dying."

The girl shivered again as the wind blew across the lake and struck the small beach, bending the pines almost in half and forcing the evening rain from their needles onto the ground.

"I don't mean to embarrass you," said Aaron, "but I believe you should take off your tunic. The doeskin is soaked through and it will take hours to dry. We could hang it up on the limb and let the wind do its work."

She blushed. "Is that what you did with your clothing?"

"No," said Aaron as he stood up. "Whether either one of us likes it or not, this is how I arrived on this island, just like a newborn baby."

"Not quite," said Ruth, blushing but nevertheless staring at him.

Aaron ignored her remark. "We need a fire or we're both going to come down with the bloody flux."

Ruth took her tunic by the hem with both hands and pulled it up over her head in one motion. Then she handed it to Aaron. The tunic had decorative cut fringes. Aaron took one in his mouth and bit it at the point where it joined the main garment. Then he tore the strip of deerskin from the tunic proper.

"I need a sharp stick and some wood, dry wood if possible, and some pine needles or dry leaves."

For the next half hour Aaron worked on his fire-starter.

After several false starts a wisp of smoke finally arose from a birch log as the deerskin string drew the pointed end of a stake deeper and deeper into the wood. Aaron fed the smoke a diet of pine needles and leaves. The smoke grew more and more intense as he blew on the heated wood. A small flame flickered, seemed to die, but then flared again. Fifteen more minutes of intense care ended with a good-sized but smoky fire.

The wind still blew, and Ruth crept closer to Aaron, huddling before the fire for warmth. She placed her tunic close to the fire. It would shrink, but she was cold and wanted something to cover her.

"If no one sees our fire, we must try to swim to shore once the wind dies down," Aaron said.

Ruth merely shuddered. "They will come looking for us," she said finally. "I think we should stay here until they find us."

He knew she was probably right but he hated the inactivity—the helplessness. He was hungry, but if any game existed on this tiny island he had no weapons to hunt it. Then he remembered the first time he had returned to the longhouse with game. His father, the white man, Nowell, whom his people still called Blackrobe, had taught him to set a snare. He had not done it in years. But it should not be that difficult if there were rabbits or chipmunks about.

He grabbed Ruth's tunic again and bit at a piece of fringe. He had fashioned and set his snare within minutes. There were signs of rabbit runs. Rabbits were plentiful on the island. Probably their only danger came from the sky. He sat down again across the fire from Ruth, placing his hand in his lap to cover his nakedness.

"I'm still cold," she complained.

Aaron sighed and rose. He walked to the pile of wet sticks and rotten logs he had collected and tossed two more crumbling logs into the flames. Their first effect was to cause a column of sparks to rise into the air, followed by a hissing sound as the water-soaked wood was heated by the flames. More and more smoke rose into the gray sky.

"I'm not sure we'll generate any more heat with logs like these." He walked back to her side and sat down, placing his heavily muscled arm about her narrow shoulders. He looked down at her serious and still-frightened face. There were tiny wrinkles at the corners of her eyes. They became more

31

pronounced when she smiled. Even if one could not see her mouth one could tell she was happy when the smile-wrinkles appeared. He bent down and kissed her on the mouth. She responded with warmth. His hand wandered to her small breasts and he stroked them, causing her nipples to harden. She touched him and he was soon erect. She did not know what to expect from him but she wanted him. Her mother would have ranted at her about Jesus and the grandmother would probably try to haul her off to the priest to confess. But to her at this moment this sachem of the Iroquois was all that counted. She lay down on her back when his large hands pushed her gently backward. He seemed so large towering over her. Her eyes widened with fright as he loomed above her. She felt him trying to enter her. It was impossible. But he pushed harder. She gasped with the pain. He was too much for her. She tried to pull away from under him. But he held her tightly. She couldn't escape. The pain was shooting up her thighs into her stomach. She started to cry out but his mouth closed over hers. She couldn't stand it any longer. She pulled her mouth away and sank her teeth into his shoulder. But then she felt the tearing in her body and stopped resisting. He entered her as she gasped for breath. Then he lay still with his weight on his arms. He leaned down and kissed her eyes, her lips, her throat. He began the rhythmic motion so very slowly. At first she still wanted to cry out in pain but gradually a warmth began to fill her. He moved faster and faster. He was breathing heavily now, and as she placed her arms about him she could feel his back covered with a film of sweat. Then he held his breath and let out a moan of delight and collapsed his weight upon her.

She felt crushed lying under him. The warm glow began to fade. This act that she had only heard in the dark recesses of the longhouse was now part of her experience. She did not think it was as mysterious and wonderful as the other girls she knew had said it would be. But still she felt it was worth the pain. The seed of the sachem was now in her belly.

That evening Aaron found a rabbit in his snare. He skinned it and roasted it over their fire. The meat was tender and both of them were ravenous. One little rabbit would hardly have calmed the hunger pains of one of them, much less satisfy both. But nothing else appeared in the snare and both went to sleep that night still very hungry.

Aaron spread Ruth's now dry and stiff tunic on the ground

32

next to the hot flames of the fire. They lay down upon it. He opened his arms and she felt herself enclosed within them. Aaron felt himself grow stiff again as soon as his body came into contact with hers. He wanted to enter her again. He kissed her nipples, taking the soft delicate rosy skin into his mouth and sucking gently. She stirred and arched her back, crushing her small breasts against his mouth. She cried out in pain when he entered her the second time. She was sore and aching from the first. But this time he entered her quickly, pushing himself deeply within her. He moved quickly and soon he found her body arching under him and moving in unison. He could feel himself building to a climax. It would be quick again. The girl cried out. He held his breath as the pressures within him built and then he felt the release. He stopped, his breathing coming in great gasps. The girl continued to move against him. As he softened he saw a look of disappointment cross her face. He smiled at her.

"I'm an old man, Ruth," he said. "Maybe someone of your age who could rest a moment and then start all over again would be better for you."

She stared into his face to see if he was serious and then she shook her head. "I feel protected with you on top of me," she said. "You're strong and powerful. No one can harm me as long as you are there." She hesitated out of shyness but then blurted out, "Tell me that you'll always be there, that it will always be like this, on this island, and not like it was in the cave."

"Are you asking me to your platform in the longhouse?"

"Oh, yes," she gasped.

He withdrew from her and she grabbed for him. He pulled away from her, laughing. "I told you, girl, I'm old. I need my rest, no more."

"In the morning?"

"Maybe."

"And the next morning?"

"I hope we get off this island by then," he said.

"You know what I mean."

"I must speak to the clan mother about you."

She smiled at his words. He turned from her and she began to stroke his powerfully muscled back. It had been better the second time, she thought, and it would get better each time they made love. Perhaps the girls had known what they spoke of after all.

33

Isaac and Joseph Brant arrived in the middle of the night. Aaron heard them approach the fire and was on his feet to greet them. Joseph looked at him, smiled when he saw the sleeping form of the naked girl, and embraced his nephew.

"Your mother is nearly hysterical. She is convinced that you lie at the bottom of Lake Erie feeding the fishes. We must get to the mainland immediately to ease her mind."

Aaron smiled but the smirk on Joseph's face when he spied Ruth sleeping naked by the fire forced his smile to disappear.

"Uncle," he said quickly, "the girl and I have agreed to speak to my mother about becoming husband and wife." Then Aaron laughed. "She is a Christian and we may have to go to Joseph Brant's favorite Anglican priest just as soon as we can find him."

Brant smiled. "I'll build a church at Grand River first thing and then we'll hunt up a priest."

Ruth awoke finally. Her hand immediately sought to cover her nakedness before the three men. She grabbed for her deerskin tunic and held it in front of her. Even in the dim light of the dying fire it was possible to see the blush of embarrassment on her cheeks.

Joseph Brant offered her his blanket, which she took gratefully, wrapping herself modestly. Aaron had already left the campfire and had reached the canoe beached on the shore. Joseph had stored an extra blanket and tomahawk, which Aaron appropriated for himself. By the time the three others arrived at the beach Aaron was dressed and seated in the front of the craft, paddle in hand and anxious to cast off. Isaac and Ruth sat in the middle of the canoe, and after shoving off, Joseph leapt into the stern. The lake waters were calm now. The winds had died completely. After a few moments Aaron halted his paddling and looked up into the cloudless night sky. There was no moon and the sparkle of the stars in the ebony sky seemed all the brighter for it. The air was warm. The chill winds of the storm had fled. The lake was a black mirror reflecting the tiny blue lights in the sky above. Aaron breathed in deeply. It felt good to be alive after so close an encounter with death. He sat back on his heels. He felt a soft hand on his back. He did not turn around, but the girl's touch reminded him of the intimacy on the island. She was only a girl—shy, insecure, frightened. Aaron knew he did not love her. But he knew that this time was not merely a jump under the robes with a girl, as all his other experiences had

34

been. She was gentle and quiet and she needed him. And besides, he didn't mind. It was time for him to have a wife and children of his own. And she was pretty and the sex had been more than satisfying. He sighed contentedly as the girl continued to stroke the small of his back. Finally Joseph complained from the stern.

"I didn't realize that I was expected to bring all four of us to the mainland alone."

Aaron laughed. He leaned forward away from Ruth's gentle strokes and dug his paddle deeply into the still waters of the lake.

The first pink light of dawn appeared in the east as they approached the clay cliffs of the north shore of Lake Erie. They turned west and sought the mouth of the Grand River. The sky ranged from deep purple to light orange. The cliffs gave way and they found the river's broad mouth.

The Grand was about a thousand feet wide at its mouth. It would be large enough to accept ships like those that the English sailed, thought Aaron. But even as he entertained the possibility he saw drawbacks to the site. Even in the poor light of dawn he could see the sandbar as the canoe glided above it. It was spring. The waters were high, and the bar was under several feet of water. Under the hot suns of August, the water level would fall, and the sand would block even a craft with a slight draft like this canoe. Joseph directed them to paddle upriver. The current was moderate but Aaron felt strong. He dug his paddle in. He put the strength of his broad shoulders into the stroke.

"The best sites are upriver," shouted Joseph just loudly enough to be heard, as if awed by this new river of the Mohawks. "Here we will plant anew."

They arrived at the first camp of the Iroquois after hours of paddling against the current of the river. Molly Brant had been informed well in advance that they approached, and she stood quietly on the riverbank as the canoe cut through the mud flat and came to a halt. Aaron climbed out. He halted and turned and gave his hand to Ruth and helped her out of the canoe. Molly's back stiffened and a blank look erased the warm smile at the first sight of the son she feared had perished. She seemed to sniff the air to find the source of some disturbing odor.

Aaron took Ruth by the arm and walked to his mother. She offered him a cheek to kiss. He complied dutifully. Aaron

35

knew his mother well enough to know that she had already guessed his plans regarding the girl. There was no sense in trying to avoid the issue.

"Mother, Ruth and I plan to marry."

"Marriage? Sounds Christian. When did you convert, Kenonranon?"

Aaron knew that Molly herself had adopted Anglicanism. Her objection, if there was to be one, would not be based on the religious issue.

"I haven't converted. Ruth is the Christian. It is her wish to have a priest."

"That might take time. Joseph is particular about his priests. He'll have only a good one. He might take a long time finding one. Meanwhile, Ruth," Molly said, giving her attention to the girl for the first time, "you and I must become acquainted. Joseph will be building me a house, Aaron. I assume you will help him. In the meantime, Ruth, I have a lean-to constructed for myself and Aaron. You must come and visit Aaron and me at my lean-to."

"I'll be staying with Ruth," Aaron stated firmly.

Again Molly's back stiffened. "Your mother, my dear," she said to Ruth, "is our cousin. It's Jenny, isn't it, dear? You must visit me. We have much to discuss."

She turned her cheek again to Aaron and he kissed her. Then she offered the same honor to Ruth. The girl shyly touched the great woman's pockmarked cheek with her lips, and Molly pulled away just as soon as she felt the girl's touch.

"Remember, I wish to speak with you."

The grandmother danced a little jig when Aaron told her of his decision to make Ruth his wife in the Christian church. When the man and the girl came before her campfire in her hastily constructed lean-to, she rushed to them, throwing her long, thin arms about Aaron's waist and kissing the girl mightily. She broke out some venison and cornmeal that generous Turtle clansmen had given her to make up for her lost provisions. And she began to cook a meal. She wept as she prepared the cornmeal cakes and skewered the meat over the fire. She brushed tears away from her cheeks with the sleeve of her red-and-white checkered blouse.

She served the meal with the tears still flowing. Ruth tried to comfort her but it was of no use. She was too happy to be comforted.

After the meal the fire grew dimmer and the cold spring air began to flow freely into the open face of the shelter. Aaron sat next to Ruth. He had placed his sleeping mat next to hers. He looked at the grandmother, waiting for some sort of outburst. The woman looked as if she was about to protest in some manner but instead she went to the next shelter and borrowed another blanket. If her ward was not to be at her side to warm her, she would need it.

Ruth cuddled next to Aaron. His large body blocked the wind from reaching her. She was under his blanket and the warmth that came from his body was more comforting than any fire. They had made love just as soon as they heard Grandmother's snores. Afterwards Aaron stroked her and she placed her head on his arm and buried her face in his warm, heavily muscled side. His odor was musky and strong but not unpleasant to her. He was to be her husband. There was nothing about him that was unpleasant.

Before the dawn came, Molly Brant entered the lean-to and poked her finger into Ruth's shoulder.

"Come to my shelter," she hissed.

Ruth shook herself awake. She was startled and frightened. The clan mother did not make social visits at dawn. She rose from her bed and wrapped her blanket about her body. She followed Molly out of the shelter and down the path toward the Brant hut.

Aaron had watched the exchange without interfering. But he knew Molly well enough to know that there was trouble.

"How dare you let this happen?" said Molly haughtily. "You and my son are of the same clan. It violates the ancient laws of our people. You pig, you were so concerned with stepping before a priest that you forgot the laws of the Iroquois."

"What?" stuttered Ruth. "The clans are in disarray. The tribes are in chaos. No one is observing the old ways."

"My brother brought us here to reestablish the old ways and the first marriage planned here in Grand River, our new home, violates our customs. The marriage is not to occur. Do you hear me?"

Ruth looked at her openmouthed—too flabbergasted to respond.

Molly slapped her in the face. Welts raised by the angry hand appeared almost instantly. Ruth began to grow hysterical.

"Yes, mistress," she screamed.

"Good, now we must plan how to undo the damage that has already been done."

"There will be no undoing of anything." Aaron's voice startled Molly, who had not noticed him standing in front of the open side of the shelter. But it was the tone of his voice that really startled her. Never before had he sounded so hostile.

She turned and fixed her dark eyes on her son. "Kenonranon will challenge the clan mother of the Turtles on this question?"

"Yes!"

"This child means more to you than all that old Brant, Nicus Brant, my father, and I have taught you concerning the history and traditions of our people?"

"There is no conflict."

"The girl is of the Turtle clan. You are of the Turtle clan. It is forbidden."

"Much that was forbidden is now allowed," responded Aaron. "It was once not permissible to reject the gods and spirits worshipped by old Brant, by Nicus Brant, your father, and by yourself. And it was not permissible to take up the worship of my father's god. You pick and choose which traditions to observe and which to reject. So do I."

"I will not have you marrying. You are my son. I am the clan mother. I shall forbid it."

Aaron took Ruth by the hand, turned from his mother, and walked back to his own shelter. Before he was halfway there he heard his mother scream out so that the entire settlement could hear.

"You will not marry that slut."

Aaron did not turn around but continued to walk to his own shelter. Once inside, he dropped to his knees beside Ruth and took her into his arms. She was terrified. He could almost feel her drawing into herself for protection against the great woman's ire.

"Don't be afraid, Ruth," he said. "She can't harm us."

The girl started to cry, and Aaron cradled the back of her head with his huge hand and then stroked her long black hair with his fingers. He held her until she stopped shivering.

The grandmother stared at the two of them. "What's happening?" she asked finally.

"It's my mother. She objects to Ruth and me becoming man and wife."

"Are you going to marry her anyway?" she asked, her eyes

narrowing to slits as she looked into the sun that poured into the shelter.

"Of course we'll marry," said Aaron angrily. "I've given my word. I've promised Ruth. She will be my wife." He pulled the girl to her feet as he spoke. "Enough of this weeping now. I'm going out to test Joseph Brant's claim that the country of the Grand River is rich in game. I shall bring home a week's meat for my woman to cook. And she had better prepare it well or I'll beat her."

Ruth's eyes opened wide with fright.

"I'm teasing, girl," said Aaron, pulling her gently to his chest. "Can't a man tease you?"

"My father, Geyasada, beat me sometimes," she said, hiding her face in his shoulder.

"Well, no matter what," interrupted Aaron, "I'll not be beating anyone. I am sorry, I did not know."

She smiled at him. It was a radiant smile, dispelling all the pent-up fears that had been released within her by the screams of the clan mother.

"I'll take my cousin Isaac Brant with me. It is time he learned what it is to try to feed a family."

Several hours after Aaron and Isaac had departed, the grandmother returned to her lean-to. She was sniffling and attempting to hold back the tears. She went to her cooking pot and hauled it, dragging it on the ground behind her, and walked to the riverbank to wash it. Ruth watched her intently. She wondered when she would speak. The older woman returned, carrying in her skinny arms the cast-iron pot half filled with water. Some of it spilled on her front, soaking her shrunken breasts with cold river water, which she seemed not to notice. She trudged ahead to her shelter.

Ruth went to her and held out her arms to help her with the pot, but the old woman passed her without even noting her existence and went straight to her embers. She put the pot over the fire.

"There will be no wedding," she muttered finally.

Ruth stared blankly at her. "Aaron said we would be married."

"Gonwatsijayenni—Molly Brant—his mother and our mother says no."

"I'll marry him anyway," said Ruth, her voice breaking.

"Challenge her and the clan mother will destroy you."

"But no one observes the clan taboos anymore. It's her, it's

39

really Molly Brant. She wants her son to herself. She is a selfish old witch."

"You're right," said the Onondaga, "but because it is her, the most powerful woman of the Six Nations, perhaps even more powerful than any man since she is the widow of 'He Who Does Great Things,' she can enforce her will on anyone. If she approved of you, you could marry her son even if King George himself forbade it, but if she disapproves, all you can do is obey, gain her sympathy, and hope to come out of it with some profit."

"But I love Aaron,"

The old woman looked at her ward. Great tears welled up in her black eyes. "I am sorry," she said, "but you are to leave here for Buffalo Creek and the Seneca village. Our cousin, the clan mother, has sent for your father, Geyasada, and he comes to fetch you."

Ruth's look of bewilderment changed to panic. "He'll be here before Aaron returns, won't he?" A low moan escaped from her lips. He was not her father. He could be no one's father. She wanted to run but she had nowhere to run. Why had Aaron left her? She was abandoned. No one would or could help her any longer.

2

Aaron hoisted the buck up by his hind feet. The antlers touched the ground and twisted the neck of the deer at a grotesque angle. He opened the belly with his knife. The messy part would now begin. They would take back only what they could carry and leave the rest to the wolves. They were a full day's journey from the Grand River camp. When they had left two days ago, they had fully intended to return that night, but once the buck was sighted, the chase began and it was only now completed. The buck had led them many miles before falling before Aaron's musket. The boy, Isaac, had cost them at least two chances to kill earlier with his inexperience. But now he could be useful. He could skin the buck and butcher it. Besides, the young had to learn sometime.

Isaac complained good-naturedly when assigned the task, but Aaron ignored him. This boy, even though, or perhaps because, he was a son of Joseph Brant, was not very promising.

But because Joseph was his uncle, he would not insult the youth as long as he knew his place and did not push him too far.

Aaron walked to a small stream about a hundred feet from where Isaac worked. He despised the work he had assigned to Isaac but as a boy he had been forced to do more of it than he liked to remember. He knelt down by a deep pool formed in the rocks and washed the gore from his hunting knife, from his hands, and from his forearms. Then he took the clear water into the cup formed by his hands and raised it to his lips. It tasted sweet and cold. In the reflection that appeared in front of him he saw the face of Isaac. It was twisted into a smug grin.

"Have you finished so soon?" asked Aaron without looking up.

The smugness was replaced by astonishment. Aaron smiled to himself. The boy would now believe that he could see behind him. That was just as well. His back would always need every ounce of protection he could scrounge together. Let Isaac Brant spread the story that Kenonranon could see without looking. He turned as the young man left the stream and went back into the woods to finish his work.

Aaron sat with his back against a large oak. He rested his head against the bark and looked up into the branches. Every once in a while the wind blew the green roof of leaves aside and he caught a glimpse of blue sky and pretty white clouds.

Molly was the one he had to watch. His mother feared no man. She would destroy his plans if he let her. But why should she? He had always been a dutiful son. He had always provided for her, protected her, been at her side when she needed him. She loved him. Why should she attempt to thwart him? When they returned tomorrow he would confront her about her objections to Ruth.

Aaron stormed into Molly's shelter just as she poured tea for her brother Joseph Brant.

"Where is she?" he demanded.

"If you mean that dear child, your Turtle cousin Ruth, she has gone to visit her Seneca kinsmen among the Americans."

"When does she return?" he asked, his face stoical and his anger checked.

"Her stay is indefinite. The child is extremely upset. As

41

you know, my son, she was a virgin. To have deprived a Christian kinswoman of her virtue was not a noble act."

Joseph looked interested in their exchange for the first time and he stared at Aaron in surprise.

"She is my betrothed," said Aaron angrily. "There is no harm in loving each other and entering her body. It brought no shame to her. It has always been so with our people. Does my mother claim to have come to Johnson's bed a virgin? If she does, she must have some difficulty explaining me. But perhaps that would explain her treatment of me now—her disowning of me."

"Ruth is of the Turtle clan, as are you. It is forbidden for you to marry her. Besides, you are not ready to marry. You must stay with Joseph and me and help us rebuild our nation."

"I'm thirty-nine, mother. I am ready for a wife. It is time I had children of my own."

"That's hard to argue with," interrupted Joseph Brant. "I have a grown son and I'm not that much older than Aaron."

Molly's eyes blazed in anger at her brother. "I am the clan mother. You need me, Thayendanegga. If you wish my support at the council, stay out of it."

Joseph looked at Molly with an anger equal to hers showing in his razor-tight lips and the nostrils that quivered as she spoke to him. He placed the half cup of tea on the ground before the fire. Then he rose and, without uttering a word, walked from the shelter.

After Joseph had left, Aaron remained silent for some minutes. Finally he spoke softly to Molly.

"Don't do this, mother."

"You don't even love the girl."

"I gave my word to her."

"It's too late. It's already done. Geyasada has come and taken her home. I gave him some money. The girl was delighted too. She really wanted someone closer to her own age."

"You brought Geyasada here?"

"Yes, and I gave him money. It will help him find another man for his simpleton daughter. I tried to persuade him to trade Maggie for Ruth, but as you know he is quite unreasonable about the little girl. Besides, the laws of our people are on his side in the matter."

"I'm going after them."

"I thought you might try that," said Molly, "and so I

42

informed our dear friend, Geyasada, sachem of the Buffalo Creek Seneca, that if you should arrive there and if you should violate our law in attempting a union with the girl, then I was on his side in your argument about your sister's child. If you take Ruth, your sister loses any chance of seeing her red-haired darling again. Without my support, Kenonranon, Maggie Nowell, dear Stephen's granddaughter, will remain as Indian as did dear Stephen's son."

This time it was Aaron who left the shelter in a rage. After he had gone, Molly sat before the fire sipping her tea. She had won. His promise to his sister to undo the damage done by the Iroquois raid in the last war and the return of her daughter to her would weigh heavy with him. He would come to see it her way in time. She poured leaves and hot water into her pot. She would have another cup.

Aaron left for Buffalo Creek the next day accompanied by Isaac. The village of the Seneca was on the New York side of Lake Erie, on a creek a little way up from its union with the lake.

Two men made rapid progress across the large lake. They did not strike boldly across the water. The lake was shallow, and as both Isaac and Aaron knew so well, winds and storms could turn it into a hellish, boiling cauldron in no time at all. Sudden storms killed many bold enough to venture out of sight of land. Aaron insisted on keeping within striking distance of the shore at all times. He paddled vigorously, driving Isaac to keep up his pace. Then he would stop and allow the canoe to glide along under its own momentum while he studied the woods along the shore. Isaac twice asked him what he was looking for but Aaron ignored him. They made camp that first night not far from the headwaters of the Niagara. Aaron had brought pemmican with him but Isaac had failed to carry any supplies. If he had asked his mother to prepare for him she would have babbled to the clan mother.

They sat on opposite sides of the small fire. Aaron was in no mood to talk. He was worried. He had been to Buffalo Creek before. Geyasada, the sachem of the Senecas, was a coward. They had campaigned together in the war and the Seneca had behaved badly. In addition, Aaron would never forgive Geyasada for refusing him his request to return his niece, Maggie Nowell, to her mother. And he could never forgive him his treachery in the cave. He did not know how much truth his mother had told or how deeply she had schemed with the Seneca. He imagined she had revealed future plans more than past plots. This would give him some chance if he acted swiftly.

The night was chilly and Aaron threw another rotting log on the fire. It was birch and its bark caught fire almost instantly, making a cracking sound followed by a hissing as the moisture in the rotting wood boiled to the surface and was engulfed by the flames. Young leaves on the trees above them rustled as the night breeze passed overhead and began to stir the dark waters of Erie. All was silent except for the occasional wind. Finally Isaac spoke.

"You must be getting old, Kenonranon. You need a fire bigger than two men traveling could possibly use."

Aaron merely smiled. "Wait until you are my age," he grunted.

They were silent for some moments. Finally Isaac spoke.

"Will you defy your mother and marry the girl?"

"If she'll have me."

Isaac looked at him in awe. He could not conceive of defying Molly Brant. She was the most powerful of women. Even his own father, the clan mother's brother and the bravest man in the whole world, did not dare to cross her.

"She has power over everyone," said Aaron, reading Isaac's thoughts. "But I will defy Molly Brant or anyone else to get Ruth back."

Aaron laid his blanket on the ground before the fire and stretched out upon it, pulling the far end up and over his body. Isaac sat and watched him doze off and then he too stretched out on his blanket and was soon fast asleep.

Isaac had a dream he had dreamed often. The rattlesnake came toward him, its forked tongue darting in and out of its gaping mouth. Its fangs were bared and dripping venom. But he lay helpless as it came closer and closer. He tried to yell but not a sound escaped his lips. He tried to get up and run away but he was paralyzed. Not a muscle would move. Terror took hold of him. His heart pounded in his chest. Again he tried screaming and this time a tiny moan escaped his lips. But it was cut off. He awakened to find a hand clasped over his mouth. His eyes were open wide now and filled with fear. The dream was over. It was supposed to be followed by relief that it had been merely a dream, but terror gripped him instead. The form leaning over him had him in a grip every bit as irresistible as the paralysis in his dream. He couldn't move. Then a voice whispered in his ear. It was Aaron. Fear began to give way to confusion until the sachem's words began to register in his mind.

"Don't jump up," said Aaron's whisper. "The fire has burned out. No one can see us. There are enemy in the woods waiting for us. I picked up their signs while we traveled today. They were careful but not careful enough."

"How do you know they are enemies?" Isaac croaked in a whisper.

"Friends would have greeted us, not spied. Roll slowly out of your blanket and fill it with my gear." Aaron released his grip on the boy. "Here, put this unburned log under the blanket, too. It will appear that you are still sleeping by the fire. Now let's slip into the bushes."

Isaac started to follow Aaron.

"Idiot," whispered Aaron, "take your musket and powder with you."

They crawled into the underbrush away from the glowing embers of the campfire.

"Is your musket loaded?" asked Aaron.

The look of chagrin on Isaac's face was all the answer Aaron needed.

"Hurry and load. We don't have much time. They'll come soon."

"Why?"

"The moon—it will rise soon. They won't risk it if it is bright."

Even as he spoke Aaron cut himself short. Dark forms could be seen moving at the far edge of the camp. There were four—no, six—creeping low to the ground and approaching the stuffed blankets that they thought were Aaron and Isaac. They raced toward the forms. One leapt over the embers and crashed into Isaac's blanket, jamming his tomahawk down with a thud into the rotten log that Isaac had covered at the last minute. The attacker pulled away the blanket in surprise and then yelled in anger when he realized he had been deceived. He was quicker than his companions, two of whom tore Aaron's blanket repeatedly with knife thrusts.

Aaron rose to his feet and raised his musket to his shoulder. His ball blew off the back of the skull of one of the knife-wielders. He dropped the musket and charged the man who had attempted to finish off "Isaac". His tomahawk rose in

45

his right hand. His opponent blocked the descent with his own tomahawk but he failed to stop Aaron's left hand, which held his hunting knife. Its razor edge sliced through the muscles of the man's belly and then tore down through the groin, spilling torn intestines and their contents onto the ground in front of him. The man screamed in shock and then fell backward into the embers of the fire, stirring up a small flame and sending sparks up into the dark night.

Now Aaron faced four opponents, but Isaac's musket blasted at last from out of the bushes and destroyed the face of one of the opponents in front of him. That was enough for the other three. They realized that the shot from the bushes would be followed by another just as soon as the reloading was accomplished. They panicked and ran toward the forest.

Isaac rose from the bushes and joined Aaron. The sachem bent down over the form of one of the dead men.

"Let's chase them," said Isaac, the excitement of the fight causing his face to flush.

"I don't think it would be wise to chase three armed enemy into the night. Not if you wish to avoid becoming the victim of the same tactics I've just perpetrated."

A moan of pain from the wounded attacker drew their attention to him. Aaron walked over to him and shoved his back out of the embers. He leaned down to the man, who gripped his belly and tried to force his guts back in with his hands.

"Why have the Seneca attacked their brothers?" Aaron asked him.

He could see a mask descend over the man's face. The wounded man had steeled himself to pain and to death. It would do little good to ask him questions. With one swift motion Aaron drew his hunting knife across the Seneca's throat, across the jugular. There was a gurgling sound and then nothing.

Aaron sat back on his haunches, puzzled. These men had been sent to meet him and to murder him. Why? What was Geyasada up to that he had dared to murder the favorite son of the clan mother and the sachem of the Mohawks?

Aaron had seen Geyasada flee from a fight with an ancient Abenacki, a fight that he himself had had to finish, but that would not be sufficient reason for him to stoop to murder. It must have something to do with the girl Maggie. Geyasada had been obsessed with Aaron's niece the moment he had captured her as a four-year-old. The thought that he might order her uncle's murder because of the girl forced Aaron to fear for her.

Isaac went from body to body. He returned to Aaron's side and removed the scalp from the dead Seneca at Aaron's feet.

"Two of these are yours."

Aaron waved his hand at Isaac.

"Keep them if they please you."

"But I didn't kill them," the boy protested. "We must follow the traditions."

"Following the traditions has led Ruth into Geyasada's clutches. So much for tradition. Help me haul these bodies into the underbrush. I intend to sit out the rest of this night and be off to Buffalo Creek with the first light. You can join me, wait up with me, sleep, return home with your scalps, whatever, it makes no difference to me."

Isaac decided to remain silent while the sachem was in so foul a mood. He dragged one of the bodies away while Aaron handled the other two. Then he picked his blanket up off the ground and wrapped it about his body to wait.

The whole Seneca castle at Buffalo Creek came to a halt as Aaron and Isaac's canoe landed on the riverbank. Women, upriver from the landing beach, were pounding cloth against rocks and scrubbing deerskins with their knuckles. They stopped their work to stare at the strangers. Boys running naked, screaming novice war crys, and dancing into the river to cool off on this hot spring morning gathered together in knee-deep water and stared at the newcomers wide-eyed and suddenly silent.

Only the men pretended not to notice them. Most sat in front of their huts preparing bows and cleaning muskets. Some, even this early in the day, sipped from jugs of trader's rum. But for all the feigned indifference, every warrior already knew who had arrived and why.

Aaron stepped from the canoe onto the riverbank.

"Follow me and do what I say," he said to Isaac softly. He walked past the young boys and ruffled the hair of the closest one with his hand. The boy stepped away as if the hand contained the sting of a bee.

"They're expecting us. Every bloody one of them is prepared for this," he whispered, really to himself since Isaac

47

following on his heels paid almost no attention to him but gaped in awe at the size of the Seneca encampment.

"So many of them," he said aloud.

"The Seneca are as numerous as the other five nations combined. Had they been as courageous as they were numerous, we would all still be living in the lands of our ancestors."

"Spoken like a Mohawk," said a man from in front of a hut they passed on the path to the village center.

The man rose. Despite the darkness of last night, Aaron was sure that this man had been one of the ambushers.

"I come with business to discuss with the sachem of the Seneca. Unless you have been elevated to that post by the clan mothers, I suggest you hold your tongue and lead me to Geyasada."

The Seneca leered at Aaron. "Unless you can run with the speed of the deer or swim as fast as a trout or fly like an eagle, you will have no talks with the swift Geyasada."

Aaron looked at the warrior quizzically.

"He has fled, Mohawk. Our brave sachem has taken his women and fled in the middle of the night just after he received certain news that the sachem of the Mohawk would visit us. He has left us without a leader."

Several other Seneca warriors joined the group. Then an ancient white-haired woman, bent in half with rheumatism and supporting herself with a thick wooden cane, approached them from the direction of the village center. The warriors stepped aside to make a path for her. She was clearly a revered personage.

"Mohawk," she called when she sighted Aaron. "You visit us now in our hour of shame. We have no sachem to greet you with honor."

"Grandmother, I assume I speak to the clan mother of the Bears. My mother, clan mother of the Turtles, has spoken of you to me."

"Your mother is a great lady—worthy to carry on the traditions of our people. But you did not come to this last castle of the Seneca to trade compliments with an old witch like me. You seek our sachem. He has fled. He made decisions and he could not face the consequences. He is a coward. Now we clan mothers must oppose him and select a new leader in his place."

"He was always a coward, grandmother. How is it that you only discover this now?"

"He spoke well."

Aaron looked away in disgust. "That has been our trouble all along. We choose our leaders for what they say and not for what they do. Among the Six Nations the only important thing is how well you say something."

"It is not that bad a system, child," she responded. "If only our men had talked of war against the Americans instead of making war, I might now still be living in my longhouse at Genesee Castle, and you, Mohawk, might still be at Canajoharie. But enough banter. You seek Geyasada. He, his wife, and his children have left. We know not where."

"The red-headed child, he took her also?"

"She is his child."

"His adopted child."

"You know well enough that among us that makes no difference."

"She is my sister's daughter. I sought to ransom her."

"Clearly Geyasada thought little of your efforts."

"And the girl Ruth?"

"She is also his child. The Christian women, Ruth and Jenny, have disappeared with Geyasada."

Aaron grabbed hold of Isaac's shoulder when he heard the woman's response. "We must follow them."

The old woman smiled and shook her head. "Where would you go? East, west, north, or south? You pick the direction. He could seek refuge with the Oneida or the Tuscarora to the east, or he could flee to the Delaware to the south or the Shawnee or the Miami to the west. They are all the adopted children of the Seneca. They would find room to hide a Seneca sachem, even a deposed one."

The ambusher of last night pushed closer to Aaron. "What is it, Mohawk?" he asked. "Has your whore run away with our sachem? Your balls mustn't exist at all if she seeks the company of the coward, Geyasada."

Aaron turned to look at the Seneca warrior. "Do you address me, night-stalker? Come visit me during the daylight sometime and I will show you where I dumped the remains of your carrion brothers."

The Seneca reached for his knife. Aaron grabbed his wrist and squeezed. The Seneca screamed in agony as Aaron's grip grew tighter and tighter.

"Drop the knife," said Aaron, his face totally impassive.

The Seneca could not, not in front of the whole nation. But

the pain grew worse. Then suddenly it was gone. Aaron released his wrist. He stepped back from his opponent.

"I don't wish to make war on the Seneca," Aaron said.

He turned his back and faced the clan mother. The look in her eyes was sufficient warning. He ducked and the knife slashed into his shoulder. He had been a fool. He thought he had cowed the man but he was wrong. Isaac moved toward the Seneca. Aaron called him off. He had to keep this a personal matter or they would both be cut down. Blood from his wound poured down his arm and dripped onto the ground. He pulled his knife from its sheath and faced his foe. The man seemed almost startled by his success. Aaron's knife flicked out and caught him on the side of the head, slashing a gaping wound on his skin's surface. Blood gushed down over his eye and onto his neck and shoulder.

Suddenly strong arms grabbed both Aaron and his foe. They struggled but the Senecas who grabbed them were strong, and Aaron, who might have broken away, had no stomach for this fight.

The clan mother spoke. "Enough, you two—Soyeghtowa— you violate our hospitality with your petty disputes. Come, you two, I'll mend your wounds. We'll treat them with healing herbs. Follow me."

"I'll go nowhere with the Mohawk," screamed the blood-covered Seneca. The high pitch of his voice betrayed how close to hysteria he had come.

"Well then, child," said the clan mother, "heal yourself. But the son of Gonwatsijayenni, I'll take care of him."

Aaron felt the clawlike hand of the ancient woman touch his bicep and pull at it. He looked about at Soyeghtowa, who had removed his shirt and was wrapping it about his head to stem the flow of blood.

"Isaac," Aaron called out. "Go back to your father. Take care until you get there." As Aaron watched, Isaac retreated nervously to their canoe at the landing beach. Once Isaac was out of sight Aaron let himself be led by the clan mother to her hut.

They entered the gloom of her one-room house.

"Sit," she ordered.

He saw no chairs, so he sat on the floor. She reached up into the exposed rafters from which hung dried plants as well as a jug of beans and dried corn. She took hot water from the cooking pot in her hearth and washed Aaron's wound. Her hands were surprisingly gentle and deft despite the fact that they were gnarled and bent with arthritis. Then she took her special dried herbs and made a tea from them. Finally she soaked a cloth in the hot herbal tea and placed it on the wound. Aaron jumped in pain as the cloth slapped against the skin.

The old lady cackled. "The brave Mohawk sachem," she said sarcastically. "How long would you last in a Huron fire?"

"Longer than the Seneca sachem, old lady."

Again she cackled. She seemed totally undisturbed by the desertion of Geyasada.

"He was a poor choice," she finally admitted. "But his departure saves us the trouble of removing him. The men would have insisted," she laughed, "and they would have made a mess of it. Just like you and Soyeghtowa. Quick to grab knives. It takes us a lifetime to train you to use something besides your knives and your cocks. And when we find one with half a brain he turns out to be a coward—someone the men won't trust."

She sighed. "Here, drink this," she continued, offering him her herbal tea.

"What is it?" he asked suspiciously.

"Poison, what do you think? Drink it. It will put you to sleep. That wound is deep. You'll need rest."

Aaron tasted the tea. It was sweet and he began to sip it. After he had finished it he felt a great lethargy come over him. The old woman placed an intricately woven blanket on the ground and gently but firmly pushed his great shoulders down onto it. He could not resist her force. By the time his head touched the blanket he was breathing the slow, rhythmic breath of sleep.

The clan mother of the Bears looked down at him. He was a handsome one—she could understand the girl's falling for him. If she had known a man with blue eyes when she was a girl she surely would have opened her arms to him. Now the clan mother of the Turtles owed her two favors. She had cared for her son's wound. He would recover. She had carried out Molly Brant's request. She had hidden Ruth from Kenonranon and she had fulfilled Molly Brant's request far beyond the Turtle mother's fondest dreams. She had guessed that Geyasada would flee after the attempt on Kenonranon's life failed. What a stupid plot it had been to begin with. So male, so unsubtle. It was she, the clan mother of the Bears, who had persuaded the disgraced sachem of the Seneca to flee and to take the woman and girls with him.

She checked Aaron's eyelids to see if he slept. He would be out for some hours now. It was a healing sleep.

"Two favors," she chuckled. "I had better hurry to collect them from Gonwatsijayenni. Before too long the sleep which does not heal will be upon me."

But not all favors must go to the Turtle clan mother. Kenonranon was a sachem. In the future her clan might need his help. A few favors in his direction could prove useful.

He awoke with a pounding in his head.

"How do you feel?" she asked him.

"Almost well," responded Aaron, his voice husky from drugged sleep.

"I'm sorry I can't report the same for your opponent. The man is gravely ill."

Aaron looked at her in shock. "How? His wound was not a fatal one."

"He rejected my potions and my herbs. Evil spirits entered his head and now he raves like a lunatic."

Aaron raised himself on his elbows. He turned onto his uninjured side and rose to his knees. He felt dizzy. The old lady steadied him as he stood. He looked about the hut for his loincloth.

The old lady chuckled. "What do you think I did with it? Took it to bed with me and stuffed it between my legs? I used it to pillow your head, boy. It's right in front of you."

Aaron smiled at her. "I bet it wasn't always my pillow. Now take me to Soyeghtowa. You must be mistaken about him."

The Bear clan mother led him out into the bright sunlight. Aaron had to shade his eyes against the glare. The old woman walked toward the river and stopped in front of the hut of the man who had first stopped Aaron and Isaac as they entered the Seneca village. She pulled back the deerskin doorway and entered. Aaron followed, stooping to avoid hitting his head on the rafters.

The one room was dark and filled with smoke. Once again Aaron's eyes were forced to adjust. He could see nothing. He felt the old woman's clawlike hand grab his. She led him to the far side. Lying on a mat, his entire body covered with a heavy blanket, lay the Seneca. His head seemed twice its normal size, and the side where Aaron's knife had slashed oozed a foul-smelling combination of blood and pus.

The man was delirious and tossed his head from side to side, except when the wounded side touched the edge of his mat and the pain forced him to groan aloud.

Aaron looked to the clan mother.

"What are you doing for him?" he asked.

"Hot compresses, a good sweat to get the evil spirits from his body. But it is all for naught. He will die before the sun sets."

"From a wound as meager as the one he suffered? I don't understand."

Aaron had found it difficult to like the man, but he was a brother Iroquois and he had never meant to harm him.

The man's feverish eyes moved. Aaron lowered his head and placed his ear near his mouth. He couldn't make out what he said at first but then he realized that Soyeghtowa could not accept the disgrace Geyasada had brought on his people.

He repeated over and over aloud, "He's not a coward. He's a Seneca warrior—a brave warrior." Then his body relaxed and he began his tossing once again.

Aaron sat staring at him as the life slipped from him. As the clan mother had predicted, his struggle ended before the sun disappeared. Aaron sat alone in the smelly, smoke-filled hut, staring at the corpse. Why had all this happened? Ruth was lost to him—driven into the hands of his enemy Geyasada. Now both she and Maggie had disappeared. His promise to help Amy find her daughter seemed a false one, and now this senseless death. Anger swelled within him as the source of all his troubles became more and more obvious to him. It was always the same answer. It was Molly Brant—the clan mother of the Turtles—his own mother who had brought about all these tragedies—all to satisfy her own selfish whim.

He rejected her and her whims. He had been a dutiful son from the day he had been returned to her from his father's arms after Stephen Nowell's vain effort to kidnap him. He had rejected his white heritage, adopted his Indian one to please her. Everything had been to please her. But no more. Nothing tied him to her or to his Indian heritage any longer. Maybe his father had been right from the beginning. He shook his head to clear it of these thoughts, thoughts that he had suppressed for years. He needed more time to think and

53

the Seneca village was not the place. He would leave Buffalo Creek. Some of the Soyeghtowa's kin would surely come looking for him. He was finished with this violence. It was all pointless. He needed new ways. But first he had to fulfill old promises. He would find and return Maggie, as he had promised, to his sister, Amy. And he would marry Ruth as he had promised himself.

He walked slowly back to the clan mother's hut. She was nowhere to be found. But lying on his bedding was a tiny rawhide message. It was a map—at the base of the great lake there was the black-and-white painted form of a skunk. He knew what it meant and he knew what it had cost the clan mother of the Bears to reveal this information to him. But he knew why she had done it. It was the Iroquois Disease— neutrality—even worse—it was their nature to be on both sides of every argument.

Lake Erie was choppy. The winds blew steadily from the southwest into Aaron's face. He had been paddling within sight of the southern shore for days. He could not be far from the mouth of the Maumee. He knew he should enter it and strike out for the St. Joseph River after he passed the Maumee rapids. From the St. Joseph, he would carry his canoe the long distance to the Grand River of Michigan, which would take him to the lake he sought. But he knew he would delay his journey. Instead he turned the canoe and boldly set out toward the northern shore of Erie.

He was lucky in the crossing. The winds stayed steady, driving the great puffy white clouds across the deep blue sky. The paddling was easier now, although the waves seemed to want to push the bow of his canoe back toward the east. But he persisted—always keeping the bow pointed north. The winds cooled him and he kept a steady but relaxed pace.

The far shore loomed up out of the waters by midafternoon and then grew closer and closer. Before the sun set, he entered the strait called the Detroit River. There were white settlers this far west. The French had been living here for years. Their orchards, the trees alive with pink blossoms, dotted the shores on both sides of the strait. Since the end of the war, American Loyalists in small numbers had moved here and the English town of Amherstburg had been established. The American Rebels were supposed to occupy the western or Michigan shore of the river, but despite the treaty of peace

54

signed in 1783, British troops still held Detroit, and the British flag was planted on both sides of the river.

Aaron pulled his canoe ashore at the English town and made inquiries. When he found the information he needed, he launched the canoe again into the river and paddled north against the current. Two miles further upriver—near the mouth of a creek—he saw the half-completed house. Again he pulled to the shore and beached his craft.

The sun was now dropping rapidly. It touched the tops of the trees of the virgin forests of Michigan across the river. Then it dropped even lower, scattering its golden light amid the branches. Glimmering rays appeared to break through gaps in the forest denseness. They touched the choppy waters of the river and broke up into jewellike patterns.

"Amy Nowell?" Aaron called out.

The door of the barn beyond the house swung open and a little towheaded boy—no more than four years old—came running out, preceded by three hens that screamed in anger at the boy for some unseen outrage.

He saw her then, carrying an identical version of the running boy on her hip. She squinted into the setting sun and did not at first recognize him.

"Who's calling?" asked a voice from out of the barn. It was a voice Aaron did not recognize. It was soft in tone despite the fact that it came shouted from the inside of the barn. And the accent was strange to Aaron's ear.

Suddenly recognition came to Amy. "Ethan," she cried. "It's my brother, Aaron. It's all right." She set the second twin down on the ground. He raised his arms up to her and began to whine when she ignored him and ran toward Aaron. "Hush, Charlie," she called back as she ran. "It's your uncle. He may have news. He must have news of your sister."

She threw her arms about Aaron and kissed him. "Where is she? Has Geyasada agreed to ransom her?" She stopped speaking when she saw his solemn face. Her joy turned to terror in an instant. "She's dead, isn't she?" Great tears formed in her eyes.

"No," said Aaron quickly. "Geyasada has run away with her and with my betrothed. It is no longer a matter of legalities and ransom. It is a matter of revenge and blood. I know where they are. I am going after them."

Ethan Morin, Amy's husband, came up behind her and

held on to her shoulders. He heard the last part of Aaron's remarks. He held out his hand.

"I'm Amy's husband," he said in his South Carolina drawl. "I'd be very pleased to go with you."

"No," Aaron responded quickly. "It is dangerous and I have caused my sister enough grief. I will go alone."

"Maggie is my wife's child. I don't much care if there is danger."

Aaron dropped the subject. He had no intention of debating with this white man. He would merely leave without informing Morin.

The twin boys now stood side by side surveying this giant of an Indian.

"Charles, Stevie," said Amy. "This is your uncle, Aaron Brant."

Aaron looked down at the boys. They were strong children. They would grow into powerful men. Charles looked shyly up at Aaron. When his uncle smiled at him, he grabbed hold of Ethan's leg and hid behind it. Stevie looked at him boldly. This one, Aaron thought, this bold one will give Amy trouble. He wished he could live close by and fulfill his duties as uncle. His sister clearly needed him.

The sun was gone now, leaving the sky above Michigan pink and gold. Amy took Aaron's arm. "We must apologize to you for our living accommodations. Ethan's just now building the house."

"Me too," said Stevie.

"Yes, you and Charles are a big help to Ethan. We are living in the barn," concluded Amy. "That may seem to you to be doing the whole thing backward but it was standing from an earlier settler and it will have to do until we get ourselves a proper house."

Aaron entered the barn with them. Amy had an outdoor fire with a pot hanging over it. In the pot an Indian stew was brewing. She smiled when she saw his look of surprise.

"The months I spent as your prisoner are now put to good use," she said.

Aaron looked embarrassed. "You were not my prisoner. I tried to protect you and the boys until your people could come for you."

"You had hoped I would stay, Aaron. You said so."

Aaron looked uncomfortable. His sister spoke the truth. "I

have no real nephews except for these two." He gestured toward Charles and Stephen.

Ethan offered Aaron a stool to sit upon. He took out his clay pipe and lit it. He then offered it to Aaron. Aaron took a puff and passed it back.

Ethan started to laugh. "Sort of like passing the peace pipe, isn't it? Where is the girl, Mr. Brant?"

Aaron grew very wary. "Geyasada has fled to the west," he said. "I will follow him down the Maumee to the Wabash and there I will receive news of where he is." He lied to Ethan because he did not wish the man to follow him.

Amy brought bowls of stew to them and to the boys. "Have you seen Margaret?" she asked.

He nodded. "Last winter—on the trail to Niagara. She traveled with Geyasada and his wife and another adopted daughter. The second daughter, Ruth, was to become my bride. But Geyasada and my mother interfered—and now he has fled with them all."

There were some moments of silence. Then Amy returned to the only topic that really interested her. "How did she look?"

"She is well," said Aaron, after waiting until he had swallowed a piece of meat he had been chewing.

She looked longingly out of the barn door toward the darkening western sky.

Aaron reached over and touched her hand. "Sister," he said. "I will return her to you."

Amy smiled at him.

"You're damned right, we will," interrupted Ethan.

Aaron slept out of doors that night. Well before dawn, he crept out of his blanket, picked up his musket, and rolled his belongings up into the blanket. He walked noiselessly to the riverfront. He found Ethan asleep in his canoe. He shook the man's shoulder. "I have to leave," he said.

"Not without me," said Ethan, rubbing his eyes. "And Amy agrees."

"You'll slow me down."

"I don't know if I've heard that theory before—that two men paddling a canoe are slower than one—it's a new one on me."

"You're not a woodsman."

"Try me," said Ethan stubbornly.

"My sister . . ."

"She knows. She packed my things for me."

Aaron could think of no other objections. He tossed his

57

blanket and musket into the middle of the canoe and shoved off from the shore. Leaping into the rear, he picked up his paddle and dipped it into the waters of the Detroit.

Ethan rose to his knees and picked up a second paddle. "I guess this means I'm going with you," he said softly, and a broad smile broke across his face.

3

The Miami spoke a funny language, the little girl thought. And the funniest word of all was the name of the village she lived in, Chicago—the place of the skunk. It was an ugly word and a terrible name for such a pretty spot. She stood on the sandy beach looking out on the vast sea that the Miami called Michigan. The waves broke on the beach and rushed up on the sand with a hissing sound. The wind came in from the north, causing a high surf. Above her a gull swerved into the breeze and its progress came to a sudden halt. It flapped its wings but made no progress. Finally in frustration it swerved again to the left and was hurled quickly away inland toward the village.

The girl was dressed in a deerskin tunic. She wore a beaded headband and her hair was worked into a single braid that hung down her back, reaching almost to her waist. She was every inch a young Indian girl of nine or ten except for the obvious fact that her hair was a bright red and her complexion was fair.

She turned from the beach reluctantly when she heard her mother call her name. She hurried to go back to the lodge. She hated the village. The other children teased her about her inability to speak the Miami language. She was a Seneca, a proud people of the Six Nations. The Miami were the children of the Seneca and she resented their teasing. It never dawned on her to think that if she looked like a true Seneca the Miami children would probably have left her alone. But to them she looked every inch the white child she really was.

Even more than the teasing of the village children, she hated to return to the family hut—to him—to Geyasada. She loathed the man who claimed himself her father. Back at Buffalo Creek when she had been younger he had fondled her and she had loved his attention. But then all had changed. She could not forget it. She had been listening to her mother snore. He had waited. Then he had come to her mat and talked to her. He told her pretty stories of the forest animals and the legends of the Seneca. Then he had stroked her back and helped her to sleep. The first time he had allowed his hand to wander, it frightened her, but then he had given her such pleasure and she had fallen asleep content. The next night he did the same thing. Every night for two weeks he had come and given her comfort. But then he had insisted that she touch him. She had not liked that. He was big and red and ugly. But he was too large and she had cried out. Her mother had awakened.

Geyasada claimed that their adopted daughter was having dreams troubled by the spirits and that he soothed her. He went back to his own mat. Maggie had lain alone, sore, terrified by what the man had tried to force her to do.

Nothing had been the same afterwards. The wife of Geyasada, Otsegenni, was suspicious. The next day they had a terrible fight. That night Geyasada dropped all pretense and came to Maggie's bed before Otsegenni had even begun to get ready for bed. He lay down next to Maggie, naked and aroused. She had screamed but he clamped his hand over her mouth. Otsegenni ran from the hut and did not return for the rest of the night. When Geyasada was finished he returned to his mat, leaving Maggie terrified, torn, and bleeding. Soon she heard him snoring. She knew where he kept his knife. It would be easy to take it and sneak up next to him and plunge it into his heart in return for all of the pain he had caused her. But she could not work up the courage to do it. Instead she lay awake sobbing and terrified that if she cried too loudly it would awaken him and he would return for more.

In the morning Otsegenni returned to the hut and Geyasada left. Maggie couldn't stand. Her adopted mother came to her with warm cloths. She took Maggie into her arms and kissed her cheek and rocked back and forth. She brought the child some warm broth.

"My little fire-hair," she wept, whispering in the girl's ear.

"I didn't like it, mama," she cried. "Please make him stay away."

Otsegenni began a low moaning wail and Maggie knew that he would come back and that Otsegenni could do nothing to protect her.

He came back and he revisited her almost every night and gradually she found her position changing from child and daughter to wife. It poisoned completely her relationship with Otsegenni, who came to be jealous yet at the same time was forced to hide this disgrace from the entire community.

They had fled Buffalo Creek, when they were rejoined by Ruth. Geyasada had been angry with Ruth and had beaten her when he learned she had slept with Aaron. But he never slept with her. He tried but she claimed to be pregnant with Aaron's child. For a while after that Geyasada lost interest and turned his attention back to Maggie. Ruth would be safe from him until her child was born. Now all the women in the lodge shared a common disgrace. This warrior was an animal who molested and raped his own child. It was a secret they guarded carefully.

Ethan lay on his stomach amid the scrub pines on the edge of the sand dunes. He had grown thinner. His face was drawn and haggard. The Indian had set a backbreaking pace. He was sure it was going to exhaust him and force him to turn around and go home. But he had fooled his brother-in-law. He had kept up with him. And he had forced Aaron to respect him. Those first few days he had never been so tired in all his life. But now he felt he had left all that behind him. He was growing tougher with each passing day.

Aaron was up ahead scouting the Miami village. He had been out there for over two hours. The Miami camp was only a few hundred yards away from the Lake Michigan shore. It was clear that it was to be their camp for the summer. Some sand had lodged in Ethan's boots. He longed to take them off and scratch the itch. He felt a hand touch his back. He jumped involuntarily with fright.

"Sorry," whispered Aaron. "But I couldn't call to you." He dropped down beside Ethan.

Ethan shook his head with relief. "What did you find out?"

"They're all there—Jenny, Ruth, and Maggie."

"What do we do now?"

"We go in and get them out."

"How?" asked Ethan.

"Tonight. I will visit Ruth. She sleeps alone. I saw her move into the lodge for women who have their flow." He spoke of her with some bitterness.

"What's wrong with her?" Ethan asked.

"Nothing, it is the custom. But she has been beaten. I saw her. I wanted to call out to her. But I could not risk it. When I see her tonight, I will tell her to go to Jenny and say she is lonely by herself and ask if Maggie can spend the night with her. Once we have them both, we can make a run for it—but not back through the Michigan rivers. That is what they would expect us to do. We must take the long route instead—up Lake Michigan to the straits of Mackinac and then down Lake Huron to Detroit."

"That will take weeks," offered Ethan.

"It will be safer."

Once dark descended on the village, Ethan and Aaron crawled in closer to the Miami encampment. Aaron pointed out the low bark hut where Ruth was staying. A giant orange moon seemed to rise up out of the depths of Lake Michigan. Its light fell on the hut, casting a shadow that hid Ethan and Aaron as they reached it. Aaron peeked through the cracks in the bark. He could see Ruth sitting before a small smoky fire. She clutched herself with her arms almost as if trying to keep warm. Aaron called to her softly. She was startled at first but then recognized his voice. She moved to the back of her hut—toward his voice.

Aaron pulled off a sheet of bark effortlessly and, bending low, he entered the hut. Ethan followed him. Aaron took hold of Ruth and pulled her against his chest. She seemed both happy to see him and terrified at the same time.

"Kenonranon, how did you find us?"

"No matter," he responded in Iroquois. "I'm taking you and the red-haired girl, my niece, away with me. This man is Maggie's stepfather—my sister's husband."

"How will you get away? Geyasada will track us down and kill us. He is a devil, Kenonranon."

"What has he done to you?" Aaron asked.

She looked away from him.

He shook her. "What has he done?"

"He beat me." She turned her back and Aaron gasped. The girl's shoulders and the top of her back as well as the backs of her arms were bruised.

"I lied. I told him I was pregnant with your child so that he would leave me alone. When he discovered that this was not true, he tied me down and whipped me."

Aaron's face, lit only by the tiny fire, seemed to harden.

"Can you bring the girl here?" he asked. "Will he grow suspicious if you do?"

"I don't know," said Ruth, "but I'll try."

"Good girl," said Aaron. "See if you can bring some blankets and food as well. Tell them you have the chills and that you're hungry."

Ruth stepped out of the entryway of the hut into the moonlight. Aaron watched her until she disappeared. Then he turned to Ethan. "So far, so good," he whispered.

"What is she doing?" Ethan asked.

"She goes for Maggie."

Ethan's heart was pounding. Soon—very soon—he would see Antoine and Amy's child. The restoration of this child was Amy's overwhelming desire.

An hour passed, and Aaron grew impatient. "What's keeping her?" he asked himself. Then he saw her walking through the village. She had a bundle in her arms but she was alone.

Ruth entered the hut.

"Where's Maggie?" Aaron asked.

Ruth looked confused. "Jenny wouldn't let her come. I argued with her and then . . ."

"What is it?" Aaron asked in distress.

"I gambled. I told her you had come for the child. She loves the fire-hair and Geyasada abuses the child. I told her you would take her to her real mother and the girl would be truly happy for once in her life."

Aaron looked about him. He could not panic. He had a line of retreat. He still could take Ruth and escape—half his task achieved. But how could he face his sister? He had to wait and he had to place his trust in Geyasada's woman.

As if to mock his decision, the voice of Geyasada came from the rear of the hut where the bark had been torn off. "The Mohawk wife-stealer is hiding in the female house."

Aaron froze and then turned slowly to face his enemy's musket.

"It is an even more appropriate place for the Seneca coward to enter. I am told he lost his testicles to an ancient Abenacki at Oriskany."

"Your last insult to me, Mohawk."

Ruth rushed at Geyasada just as he was prepared to fire. The musket went off with an impact that seemed to echo throughout the village. The girl collapsed on the floor, her chest spewing blood.

Geyasada ignored what his musket had done. He pulled his hunting knife from his side and threw it at the charging Mohawk sachem. The knife was badly thrown. It struck Aaron handle-first on the side of the head. But the force of it staggered him. He buckled at the knees and fell facedown.

As soon as Geyasada released the knife, he ran out of the hut screaming that his enemies were attacking the village. Ethan looked at Aaron and Ruth, both of whom lay on the floor of the hut. He knew he could do nothing for Ruth. He had been a soldier long enough to recognize a mortal wound when he saw one. Instead he grabbed Aaron and tossed his heavy body outside the hut. He stepped through the hole and hoisted the Mohawk's dead weight onto his shoulders. Then he began to run down toward the beach, toward the dunes where they had hidden their canoe.

He could hear the whole Miami village up in arms behind him. If he was lucky there would be enough confusion to give him a few minutes' head start. Aaron seemed to grow heavier as he ran and his shoulders ached with each step he took. The dunes were directly ahead of him now. He stumbled and fell forward. When Aaron's body hit the ground, he grunted. Ethan was truly frightened. He could imagine what these people would do to him and Aaron if they caught them. He could imagine what the Seneca would urge them on to do. He lifted Aaron's body again and continued at a trot toward the beach. He thought they had hidden the canoe behind the dune in front of him. He circled around it but there was no canoe. He began to panic. All these damn hills of sand looked exactly alike. He had to find the canoe. They were dead men without it. He dropped Aaron in the sand. He raced on to the next dune—to his right. His heart leapt when he saw the tail end of the canoe jutting out from behind the dune grass. He pulled the craft down to the water's edge, floated it, then ran back toward Aaron's body.

The village was filled with commotion. Some muskets were fired. But as yet no one had followed his obvious trail to the beach. He cursed the moon, which was now high in the sky. Earlier it had provided shade to hide in. Now it gave off light to help his pursuers.

He dragged Aaron's body to the shoreline and shoved him into the canoe. He steadied it and hopped in himself. The lake was calm. He had no waves to battle. He dug his paddle deeply into the water and the canoe shot ahead. Now he could hear voices on the beach. There was a shout. They must have discovered his trail. A few more minutes now and they would find where he had launched the canoe. He was sure they would follow him in their own craft, and he was sure they would see him out on the lake, driving toward the north, trying to get beyond musket range.

Then suddenly things became darker. He looked up into the sky. A huge black cloud was passing in front of the moon. His fears eased a bit. It would not be easy for Geyasada to tell which direction he took. As Aaron had explained it, they would expect him to strike for the mouth of the Grand River in Michigan. But as Aaron had advised, he would go the long way—through the straits. He hoped that soon his brother-in-law would regain consciousness and show him where these fabled straits lay. They had failed. They had failed miserably and now Aaron would have a grief in his heart—a grief akin to Amy's.

Amy waited daily by the shore of the river. The boys could play in the water and cool off their bodies in the summer heat. Today she had already weeded Ethan's garden and cooked a noonday meal for herself and her sons. But her mind was elsewhere. When she finished she took the boys to her spot on the riverbank and searched in both directions for signs of her brother and her husband. She could not bring herself to think that she might ever see her daughter.

And then they arrived—from the north, from Lake St. Clair—which surprised her. She strained her eyes to see. The canoe moved rapidly but there was no flash of red hair in the sunlight. Only her brother's golden skin color and her husband's sunburned torso. She stood and waited for the canoe to come to her. Ethan leapt from the craft and wrapped his arms about her, kissing her passionately on the mouth.

Aaron held back. He looked embarrassed. When Amy looked beyond Ethan's shoulder at him, he lowered his eyes. "I've failed you, sister."

"Don't listen to him," interrupted Ethan. "He came as close as humanly possible to getting her back." Then he whispered into Amy's ear, "The girl he was going to marry was killed trying to help us. He's given all to us."

Amy knew that although she had not let herself hope that Maggie would be with them, she had in her heart of hearts felt that her brother, the sachem, would have made good on his promise.

"It's hopeless for now, Amy," Aaron said. "The Seneca pig will run off now, and I have no clan mother of the Bears to tell me where. Eventually word will surface, but until then it is hopeless."

Amy nodded but inside the sadness was overwhelming her. "What will you do now?" she asked.

"I have to begin anew," he said. "So far I have lived the life my mother set out for me. It has led to all this grief. Maggie's lost—Ruth is dead. Now I reject her way. I think I will seek out our father and try the way he wanted for me so many years ago."

Amy smiled at him. She reached behind her neck and loosened the latch on the locket she wore. It had belonged to their grandmother, Sarah Nowell. She handed it to him. "You've grown since he last saw you," she said. "He may need this to identify you."

4

It had begun as a dull ache in the bone on the side of his left foot. It was sore even to touch. Then the pain had moved to the base of his big toe, and with that pain came swelling and more pain than Stephen Nowell had known since that time so many years ago when he had lost his left arm.

The doctor had diagnosed it as the gout and told him he was lucky to have contracted it in late spring. Normally, the old quack claimed, it disappeared with the onset of summer. But Stephen did not regard himself as lucky. Not only could he not walk, he couldn't even touch his foot without excruciating bolts of pain running from his toe up his leg. He could not stand even the touch of a linen bedsheet on his foot.

He sat on the porch of their country house on the shores of South Bay outside the town of Saint John. The trees were fully covered with their blanket of leaves now and the lush green of the river valley would last through the summer.

Stephen's foot was propped up on a pillow. It felt better and it did not throb as much when his foot was elevated. He picked up a glass of port from the small candlestick table that his servingman, Jonathan, had placed beside him. Katherine was upstairs napping. It was just as well. She would have yelled at him and taken the wine from him. She had left word with the servants, Jonathan and Agnes, that Stephen was to eat no rich food and drink no wine. The old quack who came up from the town at enormous expense for Stephen came out onto the porch.

"Mr. Nowell, sir, I must protest. This wine can only do harm."

"This wine, sir," responded Stephen, "if I consume enough of it this afternoon, will make it possible for me to endure the pain in my foot tonight."

Dr. Grey of Saint John had treated many cases of gout but never had he had a patient as difficult as Nowell. He picked the decanter of port up off the table and whisked it out of Stephen's reach.

"Damn it, man, how dare you take my wine."

"It will be necessary to bleed you to remove the foul elements which you have allowed to enter your body, especially from bad eating and drinking habits and which your body cannot eliminate."

"Come near me with your lancet, quack, and I'll eliminate all over you."

Stephen's yelling had not gone unnoticed. Katherine Schuyler Nowell came from her bedroom on the second story of the house. Her brown hair was now streaked with gray and tied in a bun at the back of her head. Her middle had thickened and she had a slight hint of a double chin, but her face was unwrinkled. Her complexion was still perfect.

"Stephen," she called, "what in God's name has riled you up so?"

"This butcher wants to bleed me. Nobody bleeds me."

"Mrs. Nowell, it is my customary treatment for gout. But I think your husband is more agitated about my having confiscated his port."

"Stephen, how did you get your hands on the wine?"

"Loyal servants."

"I'll tell Jonathan what-for," she scolded, placing her hands on her hips.

"Come here, Katherine," said Stephen, grabbing for his wife.

Katherine's eyes flashed toward Dr. Grey and back to Stephen. Her signal was obvious and in exasperation Stephen shifted in his chair. His foot slipped from the pillow and his bare heel smacked against the hard wood of the chair on which it rested. Stephen howled in pain. Katherine gave him a look of concern, but seeing that he had done no serious damage to himself, she grabbed hold of the patchwork quilt with which she had covered him, all but the offending foot, and adjusted it to make sure he did not take a chill.

"Mistress Nowell," said Grey, his face pinched with concern, "I believe that bleeding is the only solution and will effect quicker relief of the symptoms."

"I am sorry," responded Katherine, "my husband has an inherent dislike for men of your profession. I believe he picked it up in his years as a soldier when he was very much younger."

"You're right," interrupted Stephen. "A man whose judgment I respect—Israel Kip—always told me that the only thing more injurious to health than a disease is a doctor."

Grey seemed to puff up with indignation. "I don't know why I continue to treat you, sir."

"I don't know why either—except that maybe my wife is paying you a fortune in good money and providing you with a room in a good house and a fare at a table which is the best in the province of New Brunswick."

Grey turned in anger and walked back into the house.

"Katherine, get rid of that fellow. I can't abide having him around me."

"Not until you're entirely recovered. Do you want to come inside with me?"

"No, I enjoy it out here in the fresh air."

She saw him glance at the decanter of wine, which was within reach of his right arm. She pushed it a few feet farther away with her foot. He said nothing but she could see the crestfallen look on his face.

"I'll come out for you at dinnertime," she said, and left him alone.

Stephen sat for some minutes in silence. He loved this spot and came here from the town more and more often. Now that Josiah had become introduced into the business, he found more and more time for Katherine and more and more time away from his offices. He had built this house as their retreat away from the city but now it had really become their home. He had been able to salvage some furniture from his house in London and had shipped it to Saint John. But he had lost everything in the Breed-Nowell house in Charlestown. Katherine had hoped that some of their things from Fort Vaughan would have survived, but that entire garrison house on the Mohawk where they had spent their early years together had been destroyed in the Indian raid in the last war. Their daughter, Amy, had survived the raid along with her twin sons, Stephen and Katherine's grandchildren. But she had lost her husband, Kurt, and her daughter, Maggie. Now she also lived in Canada but in the province of Upper Canada, far to the west near the strategic post of Detroit.

But for all their losses and all the destruction Stephen was content. After years of separation and second marriages for both of them, they had come back together closer than they had been in those first years. Stephen had failed Katherine again and again in the early years but it was his love for her when they reunited on Isle d'Orleans that had restored her to good health. They had been inseparable ever since.

The late afternoon sun was reflected in gold on the calm waters of the bay. The waters were so calm that every few minutes one could hear a fish leap and return to the waters with a splash. Stephen was not the only auditor. A fish hawk appeared high in the sky circling impatiently. Stephen shaded his eyes to get a better view of the circling bird. But then suddenly it plunged downward out of the sky at great speed. It struck the flat water with a smack and then rose again with a struggling fish held tightly in its talons.

But by that time Stephen's observation of the hawk had been distracted. As his eyes had followed the bird's descent, he saw off in the distance a canoe paddled by a single occupant, its bow high in the water. It was headed toward the shore directly in front of the Nowell's porch.

Stephen did not have many visitors and none at all coming down from the north from the St. John River. Stephen tried to get a better fix on the traveler but the glare was too strong. There was no doubt, however, that the traveler was heading toward the Nowell house.

After some moments Stephen was able to determine that his visitor was an Indian. The natives from New Brunswick were, on the whole, friendly and so there was no reason for concern. Even if he were a hostile, he was alone and posed no threat to Stephen's home.

"Katherine," he called out. He waited for her to respond. "Katherine."

She came to the front door of the house.

"It appears we have a visitor. I don't think we need to be concerned but you might alert Jonathan and Agnes."

"I've been alerted already, sir," said Stephen's valet.

Stephen had hired him in London and he possessed all the pretensions of one who had spent his life in the service of the British upper classes. Stephen was not a member of that privileged group and could never quite understand why Jonathan Wills had entered his service, much less understand why the man would follow him to North America. Actually the answer was quite simple. Nowell paid his salary in full and on time—a feat that not even his last employer, a duke of one of Britain's noblest families, had been able to emulate.

"Should I alert Dr. Grey?" said Jonathan, as coolly as if he were asking if he should serve dinner.

"No, maybe the Indian will scalp him and then he can spend his life working on a cure for baldness and leave gout sufferers alone."

"Stephen," said Katherine, laughing at his comment. "You grow more and more like Willie Vaughan as you grow older. That was a Vaughan remark."

Stephen chuckled. "You're right. God, how I miss that man. All of us Nowells loved him. My mother and he—well—all the gossip about them was true. He was my closest friend and benefactor and my boy Matthew viewed him and not me as his true father."

A note of sadness entered his tone when he spoke of his son by the young girl Abigail Hibbins. He had not seen Matthew since just before the battle of Bunker Hill almost a decade ago. The boy disliked him before the war and truly hated his "Tory father" now.

He grew silent, and Katherine knew better than to pursue the topic of Matthew Nowell.

The canoe was close enough now for Stephen to make out the features of his visitor. His dress was like that of most Indians at this time—part European and part Indian. It was difficult to tell anything about him from his clothes. But Stephen became suddenly alert when he observed the canoe. It was not sleekly constructed like those of the local New Brunswick tribes. Instead it was clumsily made, like those of the Iroquois. Stephen had only enemies among the Iroquois, but Saint John was a long way from Iroquois country.

"Jonathan," he said, "would you go inside and load my set

of dueling pistols for me? You will find them in the bottom drawer of the armoire in my bedroom."

Katherine looked at Stephen anxiously while Jonathan disappeared without a word. He returned with the two pistols. Stephen checked them and placed them out of sight under the quilt that covered his legs.

The canoe slid to a halt on the sandy beach. The Indian crept to the front of the craft, hopped out, then pulled the bow up higher onto the beach. He looked up at the house and began to approach it.

Stephen squinted to get a better view and then he called out in Mohawk. "Welcome to my home. What brings the son of the Six Nations so far from the longhouse?"

The Indian stopped and looked at Stephen. He responded in English. "You are Mr. Nowell, aren't you?" Then he came closer.

Recognition came swiftly to Stephen, but it was the locket the Indian wore that finally convinced him.

"Kenonranon?—Aaron? Is that you, my son?"

Aaron nodded and stepped onto the porch.

Stephen took his pistols from beneath his quilt and handed them to Wills. "Jonathan, I won't be needing these. Aaron, you may recall my wife, Katherine."

Aaron acknowledged his father's wife with a slight bow of his head.

"My God, let me look at you," said Stephen, reaching up and touching Aaron's forearm. "You're not a boy, are you?"

"I am now older than you were when we last saw each other."

"Katherine, call Agnes. We must have a feast. My son has returned."

There was such a sparkle in his eyes, such a joy in his voice that Katherine felt swept up in it. She ran into the house calling Agnes, a local girl hired as a cook and maid. Jonathan followed her inside. There would be much for him to do. He didn't understand how this Indian could be the son of his employer but he was too well trained to inquire. Nowell would not be the first man he had served who had recognized and cherished his bastards.

Suddenly Stephen and Aaron found themselves alone on the porch.

"Have a seat, Aaron," said Stephen. "I'm sorry I can't get up. The gout has me—bloody painful complaint."

70

The moment was awkward. The father and son had been separated for years by the determination of Molly Brant to raise her son within her own culture.

"I've come to seek your pardon, father, and if that is granted to request your advice."

"Pardon? For what?"

"For neglecting your existence all these years. For being so totally wrapped up in my mother's world that I neglected my father's."

"The battle for the soul of Kenonranon," said Stephen softly, "was fought between Molly and me over thirty-five years ago. You were the stakes. You weren't a party to the contest. I lost. Molly won. It was a colossal foolishness on my part to start the fight. If anyone should apologize, it is me. I was so self-righteous I drove your mother to do what she did, barring me from your life. She was afraid I would steal you from her for good and she had good reason to be afraid. I would have done it. I beg your forgiveness."

There were tears in Stephen's eyes. He quickly rearranged the quilt on his legs to force himself to concentrate on something else. He could not cry before this man, this son he was seeing for the first time in years.

"How can I advise you?" Stephen blurted out gruffly, still trying to fight back the tears.

"I've broken with my mother," said Aaron. "It is a long story but she interfered once too often in my life for her own benefit. Her actions have caused immeasurable harm to many, including your own granddaughter, Maggie Nowell, and to someone else who was very close to me. I could not stand it any longer. I left her. It was as simple as that. Now that I have left the Indian world, I need to enter the white man's world. Although my skin is light enough to do it and my eyes are the same color as yours, I don't know how to be a white man. But I must start a new life. The old one is dead—very dead."

"Well, step number one, the whites always celebrate a happy turn of events. And," he said suddenly, his eyes piercing directly into the identical blue eyes of his son, "for me this is a happy moment. Not because Molly has lost you, but because I have found you again. See that fine crystal decanter just out of my reach? It contains a beautifully rich port wine, thirty years old. You pour yourself a glass and hand me the rest of the bottle."

71

Aaron poured a glass of the wine. He had tasted rum and some cheap French trade brandy. He hated both. He raised the glass to his lips and sniffed it. It smelled sweet. He tasted it. It was delicious. His face broke into a grin. Stephen laughed aloud.

"I knew you'd like it." Then he himself took a gulp from the decanter.

The door of the house swung open and Dr. Grey stepped out onto the porch. He took a look at Aaron and his face went the color of his name. He opened his mouth to speak but nothing came out. The muscles in the side of his face began to twitch in fear. Wild Indians had invaded Saint John.

"Aaron," called Stephen, "get hold of the man before he faints."

Aaron reached for the doctor's arm. The man yelped at Aaron's touch and pulled away and then collapsed on the floor.

Stephen started to laugh while Aaron looked on in dismay.

"Pour the rest of your wine on him."

Aaron allowed the contents of his glass to fall onto the doctor's face and mouth. He stirred, licked the wine from his mouth, and Stephen swore he made an appreciative sound. Then his eyes fluttered open.

"Dr. Grey," said Stephen, leaning over the side of his chair to get a look at his fallen tormentor. "This is my son—my prodigal—he has come home and we are about to kill the fatted calf in his honor unless he'd prefer to eat you."

Grey screamed and fell into another faint. This time Katherine came running from the house.

"Stephen, what have you done to the poor man?" She rubbed the doctor's wrists until he came to again. He looked fearfully at Aaron when his eyes opened.

"Your son, sir, an Indian?"

"Did you ever see an Indian with blue eyes, Doctor? You're a man of science. Where are your wits?"

"Oh, of course." He rose and straightened his cravat and brushed off his coat.

Katherine took him by the hand. "We are going inside for dinner, Doctor. I'll walk with you. Aaron, please help your father."

She gave Stephen a withering glance. He would hear about his mistreatment of Saint John's leading and most prominent physician later when they were alone.

Stephen produced his silver-headed cane from off the porch floor. He put his right foot onto the floor and, using his cane, tried to raise himself. He howled in agony when his left foot touched the side of the chair.

Aaron went to his side. He offered to grab his father's left hand and then shamefacedly switched to support his right hand when he remembered that his father had lost that arm in the battle of Lake George early in the war with the French.

"You forgot about it, didn't you?" said Stephen, still gasping from the pain in his foot. "You visited me right after. Such a brave young fellow—Molly Brant's son all right. Her determination, her courage, her pride, they were written all over you and you've still got all of them. You'll be a better man than I was because of them. Here, I'll reach up and pull myself up on your arm. I've just got to keep the foot from touching the ground. But even lowering it below the level it has been is agony."

He raised himself and gasped again, but with his son's support he hobbled indoors to the dining room.

Katherine had been working on the room for the past year. Originally it had been a dark room. The windows looked out on the porch, but the porch roof had cut down on the amount of light that could enter and the oakwood-paneled walls had been brownish gray and gloomy.

The wood now wore a coat of off-white paint. A new carved mantelpiece sporting miniature Corinthian columns on each end had replaced the old oak beam and it too was now the same off-white as the walls.

In each of the two far corners of the room were floor-to-ceiling closets. Katherine had each closet door covered with rows of paneled mirrors. They looked almost like floor-to-ceiling windows. But their reality was only a reflection of the front of the house. The ceiling border had been wonderfully carved by carpenter-craftsmen into fine rosettes and laurel wreaths. The rugs that covered the brown-stained oak floor were from China and depicted scenes from an aristocratic Mandarin life against a royal blue background.

Katherine's success with the mirrored doors was instantly noticeable when they entered the room. The two sets of candelabra on the mantelpiece reflected into the mirrors, whose reflection in turn was mirrored on the opposite walls. The finely carved mahogany table was covered with a daz-

73

zling white cloth of fine Irish linen. Katherine's cherished porcelain, again from the Far East, this time from the mysterious isles of Japan, was set on the linen for dinner.

Aaron helped his father to the head of the table and eased him into one of the softly upholstered but delicate-looking mahogany chairs. The sachem felt ill at ease in these surroundings. His buckskins and his moccasins were out of place. He was grateful he had decided to wear his shirt before visiting his father. His leggings were dirty and he did not wish to sit on these chairs. He looked at his father in silent despair but Stephen was busy placing his foot in the most comfortable position he could find. Katherine understood his dilemma. Without hesitating, and as if it were something she had done all of her life, she picked up the linen napkin from beside her dish and spread it out on the silken upholstery of her chair.

Jonathan, who stood by the door that led to Agnes's kitchen, raised one eyebrow only. Dr. Grey looked at Katherine as if she were mad. But Aaron did not notice the men. He quickly followed Katherine's example and sat down much relieved.

Jonathan took a soup tureen from Agnes's hands and began to serve a light consommé. He ladled it into Aaron's bowl. The Mohawk warrior was disappointed. How could the whites maintain their strength with this stew as thin as colored water and totally lacking in any meat? He started to pick up the bowl with his hands and checked himself. Katherine had picked up the metal spoon beside the bowl and began to bring the liquid to her mouth in it. His father and the doctor did the same.

Aaron picked up his spoon. He grabbed it as he would his hunting knife or his tomahawk, holding it as if he would thrust it lethally at a foe. He tasted the liquid, slurping it into his mouth. It was tasty but he knew it would never fill him. After his ordeal he would go down to his canoe and cut himself a slice of beef jerky.

"Aaron," said Stephen, who was already finished with his "stew." "We have so much to talk about. You mentioned our granddaughter, Maggie Nowell. Amy's last letter to us still sounded hopeful that the Seneca would trade her for money and goods."

"She's disappeared. My enemy Geyasada, sachem of the Seneca, never intended to share the child with my sister, much less return her. He ran off with her and Ruth, the woman I planned to make my wife. I almost got both of them back, but he killed Ruth and I only escaped because Amy's husband helped me."

"And Molly was involved in this?"

Aaron grew silent. His anger was colossal but it was still private. He had no intention of revealing the depth of it—even to his father, especially to his father.

The man who pretended not to be there came from behind him and lifted his food from his plate.

Aaron grabbed his arm. He was not finished. It was poor fare to begin with, but to have it stolen before he was finished was intolerable.

Jonathan looked at Aaron with haughty tolerance. "I presume, sir, you are not entirely finished with the consommé. I beg your pardon."

Jonathan was angry. It was asking too much to have him serve this barbarian who held his spoon like a four-year-old. He had not tasted his soup in five minutes. It was already cold. What was he supposed to do? Everybody else was ready for the next course.

Aaron let go of Jonathan's arm. "Take it away. I don't want it," he said gruffly, realizing that he had looked foolish again.

Aaron rose from his chair. He looked at the quizzical faces in front of him.

"I don't belong here. I'll go down to the beach and feed myself." He left the table and walked swiftly to the hallway.

Katherine followed him and caught up with him as he stepped out on the front porch.

"Aaron," she called.

He stopped and turned and looked at her, his anger and embarrassment showing all over his face. He had stopped only because it was Katherine who followed him. He remembered her warmth and friendliness to him as a child and he had seen the gentleness still present when she took care of his father and even in the way she looked at him.

"Aaron," she repeated. "Please come back and rejoin us."

"I can't. I can't face—I don't know what I can't face."

"You can't face not knowing the right little thing to do in the white man's everyday life, things your father and I and even Jonathan Wills were trained to do from childhood. I'm sure I would make a perfect fool of myself in a longhouse."

"Just like I did in yours?" said Aaron with some bitterness.

Katherine smiled wanly.

"I didn't mean it to come out that way, Aaron. I don't know why you have come here. I presume you have told your father. I presume you have come to some important cross-road in your life."

"I came to ask him to help me enter the white world. But I despair. There is too big a gap—too much to learn."

"Come back with me," said Katherine, tugging at his arm. He followed her reluctantly. They reentered the quiet dining room. Stephen exhaled loudly with relief when he saw Aaron in Katherine's grip.

"Thank you," he said to her quietly. "Son, you just had a brief taste of how difficult things are going to be for you. Right now you know next to nothing about living in this world. You are going to have to spend the summer here in Saint John. Katherine and I will teach you and even Jonathan will help."

He said this last with a side glance at his servant, whose eyes rolled up toward the sky.

"And by the time fall comes you'll be ready to learn even more. I'll send you to Dr. Wheelock's in New Hampshire. He trained your uncle when he was a boy—taught him to write, and your uncle taught your mother."

"Uncle Joseph is a student of scripture now. He is very learned. He told me his teacher was in Connecticut. But no matter where he is, I cannot pay for a school."

"They moved the school closer to the pupils. There were more of your former gang in the north country than down in Connecticut and your education is free. You have only to pay for your room and board. Even Dr. Grey here, a man of science, will help us."

"Mr. Nowell," interrupted the doctor. "I have my practice in town. I doubt if I'll have the time."

Stephen fixed a stern glance on the doctor. "I've contracted you for your time for as long as I have the gout, you quack, and right now your time is mine and I feel that my illness is getting worse."

"On the contrary, sir," said Grey. "Summer is at hand. Gout always improves with the coming of the warm weather."

"Not mine," said Stephen slowly and with great emphasis. Katherine recognized his tone. She had heard it before. It was a tone he used only when his mind became stubbornly fixed on a course of action.

76

The night descended slowly in the northern province. The last gasp of the setting sun still lightened the western sky across the bay. The sky in either direction was dotted by the brightest stars in the heavens.

Aaron lay on his bedding on the Nowell guest room floor. He had placed his blanket next to the open window so that he might look up into the night sky. He could not sleep. The reunion with his father had touched him. The kindness of his father's wife had moved him deeply. Their plan to educate him in the white man's way of life was a generosity he had not expected. He came to his father because his father was the only white he knew who had loved him. He came because he needed help, and he found it.

He was going to try his best to learn what they had to teach him. He would begin right away. He threw his light blanket off his naked body and got to his knees. He stood up and sat on the edge of the bed. The mattress felt soft. He did not understand how anyone could sleep on it. He would sleep in the white man's bed, damn it. He would learn to be comfortable even if it killed him. He glanced at the gleaming white nightshirt that lay at the foot of the bed reflected in the moonlight. He lifted his blanket off the floor and wrapped it around him as he lay back on the bed, his head sinking into the goose-feather pillow. He lay on top of the covers, the nightshirt unused. Some things the whites did he would have more than a little trouble adjusting to.

Before he fell asleep, he thought of Ruth. He knew he had not really loved her. Yet she had loved him—enough to give up her life for him. He was filled with regret. He thought he could have learned to love her. But now he would never know.

The Connecticut River twisted through the New Hampshire and Vermont hills on its way to southern New England. On the flat plains at the foot of one hill sat the village of Hanover, New Hampshire. The village was really little more than the college buildings. Dartmouth College had been founded by Elias Wheelock of Lebanon, Connecticut, back in 1769, as a school for Indian boys, but since the war it was populated by white boys as well.

The founder had built an eighteen-square-foot log house

with the help of his sons and students back in 1769. The school had grown since. John Wheelock, son of the founder and president, sat in his study in one of the school's new buildings. Before him on his maplewood desk were the plans for a new and even more elaborate structure. Built of sturdy local stone, it was to become the main hall of the college, three stories high, with chimneys at each end and a cupola with a weather vane and a fine clock. It would be every bit as fine a college classroom and dormitory as could be found at Cambridge or New Haven to the south.

The president sat back in his chair, touching his fingertips together. There was a knock at the door.

"Enter," he called out absentmindedly. As the door opened he looked up. "Yes, ah, Mr. Brant."

Aaron stooped as he entered the low-ceilinged room. He was wearing his good suit of clothes. His father had ordered the suit made by his own tailor. Aaron still could not get used to the knee breeches and stockings, but most of all he hated the confinement of shoes.

"Have you decided, sir?" asked Aaron, his anxiety revealed by the slight break in his voice.

"I have your father's letter here, Mr. Brant, along with his extraordinarily generous contribution to the construction of our new building. But it is all highly unusual. You are thirty-nine years old and your relationship to your father is, shall we say, unusual as well."

"I guess you would call me a bastard, sir, and I guess you must accept the fact that he has decided to acknowledge me."

"Yes," said Wheelock, coughing slightly. "And your father was a well-known Tory."

"And my uncle is a better-known Loyalist. One trained in English by your father."

Wheelock looked at him in surprise. "Joseph Brant the Mohawk is your uncle?"

"Yes, sir."

"Good God," said Wheeler, rubbing his chin with his fingers. He sat silently for some moments. "That makes you a relation of Sir William Johnson the baronet."

"My mother was his wife."

Again Wheelock coughed slightly. "I can't accept you as a regular student."

Aaron's disappointment was obvious. "But," he began to protest.

78

"Wait a minute, Brant, let me finish. You're too old to enjoy the companionship of the men of the college. I can't see you among them. To be quite frank, although your uncle is a Christian, I have no assurances from your father of your beliefs or your moral education."

"My uncle was not a Christian when he came to Dr. Wheelock."

"Your uncle was a child when he came to Lebanon. I remember him. I was a child then too. You come here to Hanover a grown man. But hear me out. I will allow you to attend classes with the boys, but you will have to find lodging on your own."

"But there's not much about."

"I am sure you can improvise. You may begin classes tomorrow. How is your Latin and your Greek?"

Aaron looked chagrined. "I studied with my father all summer but we studied primarily English. We only began the other languages."

"Did your father have an education?"

"He studied at College Louis le Grand in Paris."

"He's a Papist?"

"Even worse, he was a Jesuit. But he renounced all that."

Wheelock shook his head. The story grew more and more complicated. "I can't say much for Jesuit theology but they are competent scholars, and tolerably well educated. I'll see you in class tomorrow. Good night, Mr. Brant."

After Aaron had left, Wheelock shook his head in amazement and then looked back at the plans for Dartmouth Hall. People called him haughty and autocratic. They'd change their tune after the groundbreaking.

Aaron walked out into the cold mountain air. The leaves, struck by the late afternoon sun on the mountaintops, were ablaze with color. He was overjoyed. He didn't give a damn if he were accepted for a degree. What he wanted was the knowledge the teachers at the college could give him. The man had not thought to question him on his ability to read and write. He had learned those skills only this summer. His writing was a primitive scratching and his spelling was almost nonexistent. Katherine had spent hours with him but to this very minute he could not distinguish "though," "through," "threw," and "thought." Whites said Iroquois was difficult as a language. But he saw his native tongue as logical. His people called wine "the fermented juice of the grape." It

79

made a long word but it was exact and precise. One would never mistake it for the sound made by a hurt dog. But now he had his chance. He would learn the white man's way of life. He walked down the road away from the college. He had left his belongings in the woods after his long journey from the St. John River to the Connecticut.

But he would have to find a place to live. There were some farms outside the village. He would have to try them. Perhaps a farmer would give him bed and board in return for meat. He could always hunt. He found his canoe where he had left it. He pulled it out from under some bushes and threw the bundle of his possessions across his back. He followed the trail south along the river until he came to a small farmhouse. It was set back from the road and had an unpainted wooden fence around it, and a crushed stone path that led to the front door. When he opened the gate, it creaked loudly and a dog began barking ferociously. He knocked on the door. It opened and a great black dog burst through and knocked him off his feet.

"Kaiser," a girl called out. She grabbed at the dog's collar and pulled him back. The dog continued to growl and bark.

Aaron picked himself up off the ground. He was angry. His good suit would be stained. The dog still pulled at the girl's restraining hand. Then a man's voice rang out in a language that Aaron did not understand and the dog's deep bark turned into a whine and it sat down meekly, its huge tongue hanging out of its mouth.

The man appeared behind the girl and the dog. He was old, with a long gray beard. He was dressed shabbily in a black coat, black breeches, and a black hat.

Curious as the man looked, Aaron had little time for him. He was struck instead by the beauty of the girl. Her hair hung loosely down her back and was a raven black. Her eyes were brown and huge. They seemed to stare right into him as she searched his face, seeking to know where this huge, blue-eyed stranger had come from and what he wanted. Her complexion was fair despite her dark hair and her skin looked soft—so soft he was tempted to reach out and touch it.

"Can I help you?" said the old gentleman in heavily accented English.

Aaron brushed off his clothes. "I'm looking for a place to stay while I attend the college. I'd be willing to do some hunting for you in return for a place to stay."

"You're a college boy? How long were you left back?"

"Papa," interrupted the girl, "that's rude."

The old man was laughing at his own joke and Aaron joined him.

"I respect scholars, however, Jessica," he said in Yiddish. "Call your aunt. I want Elizabeth to see this fellow before we house him or sic the dog on him."

The girl disappeared and then returned with a heavyset lady who was removing her apron as she came to the door.

"We are visited by a scholar, sister, who claims he can keep us in meat in return for a bed while he studies at the college."

"He can't stay in the house," said the older woman.

"Why?" asked the girl.

"Because he is a man—a Christian. Your father travels from farm to farm about the countryside in New Hampshire and Vermont peddling his goods and leaving his women alone with Kaiser. You can't have a strange man living here, and a Christian besides. He is not one of us. It is too complicated. The laws must be upheld."

Jessica pouted and then turned to her father. "Papa, there's the barn. He could sleep there."

"He could," said the old man, "and I could buy a pig. I don't know what we'd do with either one. I won't eat the meat he provides or the pigs."

"He could do chores. We need wood for the fire."

Levine the peddler paused for a moment. Then, turning to Aaron, he asked, "What else can you do other than hunt game? I need someone to chop my wood, feed and groom my horse, and milk my cow. Can you do any of those things?"

Aaron swallowed hard. He needed a place to stay and this farm was the closest to the village. Yet what the old man asked of him was the most demeaning labor a warrior could undertake—women's work among the Iroquois. But, he reminded himself, he was no longer an Iroquois. Now that that issue was settled, all that was left for him was to find out how to do the chores. He had never done any of them in his life.

"I can do those things for you," he lied.

"Good, you can have a bed in the loft of the barn. Jessica, show Mr. . . ."

"Brant, Aaron Brant."

"Aaron is a good name. Show Mr. Brant his bed."

Jessica stepped out of the house. As Aaron followed her down the dirt path toward the barn, the giant dog Kaiser followed behind him, occasionally nipping at his heels and forcing Aaron to ask Jessica to make the dog behave. She laughed and chased the dog back to the house. When she rejoined him they walked together to the barn door. From inside, the warm aroma of animals rushed out at them.

"These are your wards," she said, laughing.

"So long as it doesn't include the dog I won't mind."

Jessica laughed. "The loft is up that ladder. There's hay and a bucket for water. And on the wall behind the door my father keeps his ax, shovel, pick."

She pointed to the tools and then went over and took the ax from the wall. It was too heavy for her and she let its head fall to the wooden floor of the barn.

He took it from her hand and swung it onto his shoulder. His movements lacked the fluidity of one accustomed to swinging an ax every day to split wood to heat his home. She noted it instantly.

"You're not from a farm, are you?" she asked.

Aaron bristled. "Of course I am," he asserted.

"Step outside, we have wood to split. Let's see you do some."

"I'm very tired now. I'd like to get some rest."

"The wood," she commanded.

Aaron followed her outside the barn, slowly trailing the axhead on the ground. The log pile was next to the barn. Pieces of birch, maple, and some oak lay strewn on top of each other.

Jessica kicked an oak log out of the pile and gestured to Aaron. He lifted the ax high in the air and struck the oak as it lay flat on the ground. The ax sank deep into the wood with a thud but the blow had no other effect.

Jessica giggled. "I thought so. I know more about splitting wood than you do."

"And I suppose you'll give me away?"

"Why shouldn't I? It's me that has the cooking to do and it's me who will be cold this winter."

"And I suppose I won't be."

"You have the barn—the animals keep it warm. You have blankets."

"Then you won't give me away?"

"Not if you learn to split wood." She bent down and stood

the log on its end. "You hit it this way," she said, taking the ax from Aaron and striking the head softly on the exposed butt of the log.

Aaron took it from her and swung again. This time the blade bit deeply into the dry oak with a crack. The edge cut cleanly through to the ground.

She smiled at him. "You learn quickly."

He shrugged his shoulders. "If only I could pick up grammar and spelling as quickly. The college simply assumes I am a Latin scholar with a smattering of Greek and Hebrew."

"I know Hebrew," she offered. "And I am good in English composition. I could help you with that as well."

He looked at her strangely. "Would you?"

"If I have time. My aunt keeps me busy learning to cook. My father always wanted a scholar son. He taught me to read and write in Yiddish and Hebrew. I taught myself English."

Aaron found himself more and more in awe of her.

There was a yell from the house.

"That's my aunt—protecting my virtue from a Christian. Next thing she'll be doing is sending Kaiser down here."

"Aren't you a Christian? I thought all whites were Christians."

"Of course not, we're Jews—Hebrews."

"What's a Jew?"

"That's a question I can't begin to answer. Not while Aunt Elizabeth is screaming at me. We'll talk about it later. I have to run now. I'll bring you your dinner later. Good-bye."

"Good-bye, Jessica," he said.

She started to run up the path.

"Jessica," he called after her.

She stopped and turned toward him.

"I'm not a Christian either," he said.

She looked at him strangely, "What are you, then?"

He smiled broadly. "That too would take more time to explain than Aunt Elizabeth would allow."

Moishe Levine the peddler set out early in the week, his wagon loaded with wares he had picked up as far south on the river as Springfield. He carted them along the few trails that ran along the river shore, occasionally setting inland over even rougher old Indian trails to reach some isolated farmhouses he knew about. His customers referred to him as "that dirty old Jew," but they were happy to see him arrive because

83

for many he was the sole conduit to civilization. He carried pots and pans, needles and thread, gaily colored cloth to be turned into shirts, aprons, dresses, curtains. In turn he seldom received cash; instead he traded for someone's junk, scrap iron, burned-through pots, and broken utensils. Those beyond repair he carted with him to the smith at Deerfield, south in Massachusetts, to be melted down. He was paid cash for the scrap. Anything possible he fixed. And he had a genius for that. His cabin was filled with clocks, some chiming and some silent, that he had fixed, was working on, or planned to make work again.

Winter came to Hanover in mid-November. It was a bit early, claimed the old man to Aaron, as they rode together into town. Aaron was on his way to class. Levine would travel for a week even further north on the river.

The snow was six inches deep on the road. No one had yet traveled it and it was powdery and unpacked. The mare's breath came steaming from her mouth as she pulled the wagon, runners having replaced its wheels.

Aaron was fascinated by the old man and his business. He wished he had more time to speak with him but he could see smoke from the college buildings up the road. He would be getting off soon.

"Mr. Levine," he asked, "when will you be returning?"

"In about ten days, God willing. Watch out for Elizabeth and Jessica for me."

"I shall," said Aaron absentmindedly. "Why don't you use the river instead of a horse and wagon? Water travel, I'm told, is cheaper."

"Because I am a stubborn old man," said Levine with a chuckle. "In Poland I had a horse, so in America I have a horse."

"But a canoe can carry so much and you don't have to groom it and you don't have to feed it."

"In so brief a period of time you have grown tired of grooming and feeding horses. But I don't have to feed Sophie, you do."

"Well, you must pay for it."

"Look, my young friend. The canoe is something you know about. Horses I know about. A horse is your friend. She takes you where you want to go, you can talk to her and she doesn't talk back, something my dear Elizabeth and my dear dead Esther had no knowledge of. Stick a feed bag on her nose,

84

rub her down, clean up her shit, which by the way you dump in the garden and get better vegetables and flowers— that is all this mare asks of me. Tell me who talks to a canoe. You talk to a canoe and they think you are crazy. They lock you up and take your money—the relatives, that is. But it is safe to talk to your horse. And can a canoe shit and make your flowers grow prettier? No. For me it is a horse."

Aaron laughed at Levine's logic. "But I know you struggle to make a living, sir, and the canoe could bring you more money."

As they turned a bend in the road, Hanover and Dartmouth came into view. There was a little bay formed by the riverbank and here the current was practically nonexistent. The river water stood still, stagnant. The cold and snow had had its effect and the tiny bay was covered with a thin film of ice.

Levine smiled and pointed out the frozen eddy to Aaron. All of Levine's talk about a horse was put into a new light for Aaron by the simple gesture. The mare and the wagon made the journeys into the wilderness in winter. A canoe would be finished as soon as the ice came. Levine knew that the winter trade, as risky as it was, was the difference between subsistence and prosperity, and although few would have guessed from the way he looked and dressed, Levine was a prosperous man.

They pulled up before the cabin where Aaron's classes were held. Aaron climbed down and Levine clucked to Sophie, who pulled away amid a jingle of horse bells.

Aaron returned to the Levine cabin in the evening. The snow had continued to fall all day. Then in the evening the flurries stopped and the cold descended on the New Hampshire hills. Aaron opened the barn door and found Jessica waiting for him. She had a woolen blanket wrapped about her body. At her feet sat the great black dog, Kaiser, who began to growl as soon as Aaron entered. Jessica patted him and quieted him.

"How do you stand it in here? It is too cold. Come to the house for your dinner."

"I think not," said Aaron. "Your father is away and your aunt does not enjoy having me about."

"But she's not a cruel woman. Why, if it got any colder, she'd want me to bring the cow into the house."

"As I learned this morning, a cow is more important. You

85

can survive without a scholar from the college, but you'll have no cream, butter, or cheese without a cow. But then, on the other hand, I've lived all my life until now without cream, butter, or cheese."

Yet the barn was dank and cold and the smoke rising from the cabin chimney was inviting. Aaron allowed Jessica to grab his arm. He stepped out of the barn and carefully closed the door behind him. He followed Jessica and Kaiser up the path to the house.

Aunt Elizabeth was lighting candles now that the sun had set. She had a shawl on her head and she seemed to be praying. She turned as the cabin door opened. She did not complain when she saw Aaron enter.

"I hope your father has reached his shelter for the Sabbath. It is just as well he can't travel tomorrow. The weather is dreadful."

"There is not that much snow. Certainly not enough to stop his mare. He'll be able to make progress tomorrow," offered Aaron.

The older woman merely glanced at him and walked over to the stove that was set in the hearth. It glowed red and the whole cabin was comfortably warm.

Jessica whispered in his ear. "It's against our law to travel on the Sabbath."

Aaron was embarrassed by his mistake yet annoyed at the same time. How was he to know their strange regulations? Why should he feel guilty for not knowing them? He followed Jessica's lead and sat at the family table.

Elizabeth set bowls of chicken broth in front of them and on a separate dish placed the boiled chicken meat. There was fresh warm bread with raw honey and a rich red grape wine of great sweetness.

Aunt Elizabeth ignored his presence and spoke only to Jessica. All the while Aaron grew more annoyed.

"Miss Levine," he said to Aunt Elizabeth, "I'm sorry I did not know your law. I hope I was not offensive."

Elizabeth took note of him finally. "Mr. Brant," she said in her highly accented English. "My brother took you on as a handyman against my advice. I told him that you could not come into this farm without causing great confusion and difficulty for me. He put you in the barn and that is where you should stay. My niece has seen fit, as an act of charity, to invite you into the house. It was her decision and I'll abide

86

by it. With her father absent and knowing my feelings, it was foolish of her and I do not approve. I'll not try to make you think I do."

Aaron sat back in his chair. He was surprised by her.

"Let me be blunt, madam. At school I am teased by the boys as a Jew-lover. Even the professors are surprised that I live on your farm. I was raised an Iroquois—a Mohawk—and I have felt the hand of hatred, race hatred, during my lifetime. I reject it. I reject it totally. I can live as a white man if I choose and that is my decision. But I will not hate my brethren because of that choice and so I reject the comments of my young classmates and even my instructors. But I find it difficult to deal with you because in so many ways you are as prejudiced against them as they are against you."

"On the contrary, I do not insult them, persecute them, nor have I any intention of interfering with their lives. The same cannot be said for these Christians. They persecute us whether it is in Poland or in New Hampshire. I do not persecute you, sir. I merely ask you to leave us alone. It is our ability to take care of ourselves—one Jew protecting and caring for another—that has kept us as a people and as a religion surviving these seventeen hundred years since the destruction of our temple and our homeland. We don't interfere with you. Don't interfere with us."

They ate the rest of their meal in almost total silence. On two occasions Elizabeth sat up straight in her chair and pounded her chest. Finally Jessica questioned her.

"Your indigestion again, aunt?"

"Yes, but it never used to act up when I ate proper food. Only when we were forced to eat improperly prepared Christian food."

When they had finished, Jessica rose to clear the table and Aaron sat back and drank the hot tea that was served in a glass cup in a pewter holder. While he sat drinking, the older woman searched his face and watched his eyes as they followed the girl.

"How could you be an Indian with blue eyes?" she asked finally.

Aaron did not answer.

"Hey, Indian," she called more loudly.

"What?" said Aaron startled by her question.

"Your eyes are blue, your skin is almost white. Who are you? What are you?"

"My mother is a Mohawk clan mother. My father is a New Brunswick Canadian merchant. I'm a mongrel, raised an Indian and trying to become a white."

"It won't help if you become involved with her. She's no mongrel. That will only make things more difficult for you and impossible for her."

Aaron hadn't realized how he was staring at Jessica. He was embarrassed.

"You can't fool an old woman like me. I know what goes through a man's mind when he looks at a pretty girl."

Now Aaron was blushing. He felt as if somehow his interest in Jessica was disloyal. He had asked another woman to be his wife not that many months ago. And he had seen her murdered. Yet he could not even remember clearly what Ruth's smile was like. Did her cheeks dimple when she smiled, as Jessica's did? He shook his head. He had to stop this.

"It is time for me to go back to the barn," he answered.

"No, you're not," said Jessica, turning from the washbasin where she scrubbed the dishes. "You stay in here tonight. You can have my father's bed."

Aunt Elizabeth stared at her for some moments.

"And you, my pretty one," she said finally, "you will share my bed with me. With a strange man in the house one can't take chances."

Jessica turned on her aunt with anger.

"That's awful, Aunt Elizabeth. How can you say such things? How can you embarrass Aaron? How can you embarrass me with such remarks?"

"I only do what your father would want me to do."

"My father doesn't have your evil mind," said Jessica, pouting.

The peddler returned home at the end of the week in time to celebrate the next Sabbath with his family. Aaron remained in the barn studying Latin authors, attempting to put their thoughts into English, a language in which he was not fully comfortable writing and reading.

When Sunday came Levine took off again, this time to the south. It would be his last trip of the winter. By Christmastime the snows would be too deep even for his sleigh.

Aaron saw Aunt Elizabeth and Jessica wave the old man off. He stood in front of the barn. He had helped hitch up the mare. He waved at Levine, who waved back. Then he walked back into the barn and closed the door behind him. In so doing he turned the enclosure pitch-black. He climbed up into the loft and opened the hay door to let in sunlight so that he might read. He rubbed his hands together. His fingers were so cold he could barely move them. Letting in the sunlight also let in the cold wind. He could not wear the mittens Katherine had sent him in his pack because he had to turn pages. He could not recall any time in his life when he had been as miserable as this. He heard the barn door open and saw light pouring in below.

"Aaron," he heard her call.

"Up here."

He started to climb down but she stopped him. "Let me come up. I haven't been up there since I was a little girl. It used to be my favorite spot."

Her face appeared above the rough ladder. Aaron gave her his hand and helped her climb. They sat together on the hay that was Aaron's bed.

"It's cold up here," she complained.

He took her hands and put his mittens on them. They reached halfway up her forearm.

"How can you live here, Aaron?" she said, looking at him sadly.

"Oh, it's not so bad when the mare is here. I talk to her a lot. Something your father taught me." He laughed at his own joke.

"My father's favorite pastime."

"I know. He told me." And they laughed together. Then for a moment they were silent and just stared into each other's eyes.

"I think I am falling in love with you," said Aaron with his inflection raised as if asking himself an amazing question.

He leaned over and kissed her on the lips. She kissed him back passionately. He moved closer and touched her breasts. She pulled back from him with a look of surprise on her face.

"Why do you pull away?" he asked her.

"It wouldn't be proper," she responded.

"But I think you love me too. Why shouldn't we come together?"

"Because we are not married." A look of panic came into her face. Her eyes flickered about almost as if searching for

89

something hiding in the loft. The dog began to bark back at the cabin.

"And I fear we never can be," she said. "I must go."

She rose abruptly.

"Don't go," he called out. "Jessica, stay with me tonight."

"No," she said, looking back over her shoulder. She leapt from the ladder when she was two rungs from the bottom and then she raced out of the door and up the path to the house.

Aaron watched her go from the loft. He sat back down in the hay. "Damn," he whispered.

He picked up the play he was reading, a comedy by Terence. He didn't see how it could be called a comedy. He hadn't laughed once since he began reading it. Nor had any of his classmates or Mr. Proctor the instructor. This comedy was very serious business indeed.

He had read only a few lines when he heard Jessica cry out. He glanced out the loft door and saw her running down the path to the barn. He was halfway down the ladder when the door swung open.

"Aaron, come quickly. It's Aunt Elizabeth."

Aaron ran past Jessica up to the house and flung open the door. The woman was on the floor. Aaron ran to her and scooped her into his arms and placed her on her bed. He put his ear to her chest and then he felt her pulse. There was none.

Jessica arrived at the door as Aaron stood up from the bed. He turned to her, a look of dismay dominating his face. The girl began to weep.

"You must bring my father back," she said, sobbing.

"I can't leave you alone," he said.

"Bring him back, Aaron," she said, desperation creeping into her voice. "Kaiser will stay with me." At the sound of his name, the dog, who had been sleeping by the fireplace, raised his head.

Aaron nodded. The old man had a forty-five-minute start in a horse-drawn sleigh but he would camp for the night. Aaron would find him with no difficulty. He walked over to Jessica and took her into his arms and held her while she wept.

Aaron ran along the river road heading south. He wanted to make as much time as possible while the sun still shone. The sleigh's tracks were easy to follow. They were the only tracks on the road. At this pace he would be fairly close to the old man's camp by the time night fell. Even in a failing light he had only to follow the road. If the drifts should pile up he had the river itself to guide him. He was warm now. The coat he wore was beginning to weigh him down. He stopped and took it off and tied the sleeves about his waist. Standing still for just those few moments allowed the cold wind to penetrate his shirt and his skin. He shivered and then began his loping pace once again.

The sun set behind the mountains to his right. The sky was still bright but the shadows cast by the hills covered the valley of the Connecticut in blackness. He picked up his pace. Soon he would have to begin searching the riverbank to his right and the woods to his left for a campfire. He stopped again. His chest was heaving. He must have come fifteen miles. The sweat poured off him. He had to rest to get his breath back. He had set a pace faster than he had ever tried in any long-distance run. His calves and thighs ached and his lungs burned, but at the same time he felt an exhilaration, a joy felt deep down within him that he could run seemingly without end, without barriers.

Then he saw it, off to the left in the woods—a flicker of light. He moved from the road into the forest. Levine would not camp too far off the road. Aaron called out to him.

The old man answered back. "What is it, my Indian friend? How in God's name did you get here?"

Aaron entered a small clearing where Levine had built his fire. He was seated on his bedding, which he had spread out before the fire. The mare was unhitched and hobbled not far away.

"Mr. Levine, it's Aunt Elizabeth."

A look of fear came into the old man's eyes.

"What?" he asked.

Aaron walked over to him and stretched out his arm. "She's dead, sir. Jessica asked me to come and get you."

The old man allowed a low moan to escape his lips and then without warning he tore his new coat in a straight line from the right side of his neck to his waist. Then he opened the torn coat and did the same thing to his shirt. Silently he rose from his bed and walked to the mare.

"We go back home. Help me hitch up the animal."

They rode back in silence. Aaron kept shivering on the way back. The wind had penetrated through his coat. Finally Levine asked Aaron for the details of his sister's death.

"I suspect it was her heart. While you were away on your last trip she complained of pain and blamed it on her indigestion."

Levine nodded and rode on in silence, clucking only absent-mindedly to the horse. About a mile from his house he turned to Aaron.

"She was gruff and rude at times. But she was a good sister to me and a mother to my daughter from the time my wife died. We shall all miss her. We must offer prayers to God thanking him for the memory of her."

There were candles lit in the windows of the house as they came to the fence gate. Aaron hopped down from the wagon seat and opened the gate. Levine drove the wagon down to the barn and left Aaron with the task of putting away the animal. When he had finished, Aaron walked swiftly to the house. He found Aunt Elizabeth, her body completely washed and redressed, lying on the bed. Levine was sitting on the floor staring at his sister's body. He rocked back and forth from the waist and Aaron assumed that he prayed. Jessica was standing by the door waiting for him.

"Aaron, we'll need your help. My father is now in mourning and so am I."

Aaron noted that she had torn the top of her dress but had pinned it modestly closed.

"We are all alone here in the wilderness. There are no others of our kind to help us while we mourn. We are not allowed to do things for ourselves. We will need a grave dug tomorrow. We'll bury her then, and if you would feed us for the next several days . . ."

Aaron nodded. "Where do you wish to bury her?"

"Behind the house there is a grove of evergreens. In front of the grove. But do it tomorrow. It is not appropriate to leave an unfilled grave overnight."

Aaron nodded again and then left the house. He went back to the barn and took the pick and shovel from their hooks on the wall. He shivered with a chill. Tomorrow might be the appropriate time to dig the grave but he knew he had been chilled and he was not sure what shape he would be in by tomorrow. Already he felt feverish. The grave would be dug tonight.

Aaron awoke when the sun first struck the east side of the barn. Normally he awakened earlier. He knew for certain now that he was sick. His muscles ached and his skin burned.

He pulled on his clothes and brushed the straw from his bed out of his hair. He climbed down the ladder. He was unsteady on his feet. When he pried open the door of the barn, the reflection of the sun on the new-fallen snow was blinding to him.

He walked the path to the house, stepping on the part of the path where the morning sun was turning the snow to slush. He knocked on the door of the house. Jessica opened it. She was dressed in the same gray homespun dress she had rent when her aunt died. She was dry-eyed but there were heavy black marks under her eyes. She was close to exhaustion. He saw the old man still sitting in the same spot on the floor. He still rocked back and forth in a rhythmic motion. Aunt Elizabeth's body, dressed in her best clothes, now lay atop an old door that had been set carefully on the floor.

"We have no coffin," said Jessica. "We'll place some boards on top of her." She glanced over at her father. "He's not doing well," she said.

The old man had slipped into a trance, not moving at all now.

"Help me," whispered Jessica. "We must bring her outside. Normally she would have been buried before sunset but propriety demanded that my father be here to mourn."

Aaron cringed. He wanted to tell her that he had not the strength to help her, but that would leave her alone. It was clear that her father would be of no help. He had to find the strength. He had to steel himself for one more effort. He picked up the front of the board. Jessica struggled with the rear.

"If you get tired," Aaron said almost hopefully, "let me know and we'll set her down together and rest."

"Wait," yelled Levine, surprising both of them. "I must get something."

He rose and went to his bed. He pulled out a trunk from under it and removed a leather bag.

"Now," he said, "we can proceed."

He seemed to have come suddenly to life. They carried the body of Aunt Elizabeth in procession down the path and out toward the grove of trees beyond the house.

The old man brought up the rear, weeping silently. He ordered them to stop. He prayed. Then he told them to move on again. Several times he stopped them. Aaron was growing weaker and weaker and the pauses did nothing to aid him since they did not set their burden down. He slipped once and caught his footing only at the last moment. Jessica held on to her end with all of her might and kept the door steady. He realized that for all his strength, it was she who was better able to bear the burden at this moment. Finally they came to the gravesite.

Levine told them to place the board on the ground. He took the leather sack and went to the edge of the three-foot hole that Aaron had dug in the frozen soil. He wanted to dig it deeper but he knew it was hopeless. He hadn't the strength. But the old man seemed not to notice. He took some soil from the bag and threw a handful into the empty hole.

Aaron looked at Jessica in puzzlement.

"It's soil from the Holy Land—Palestine. My father's father gave it to him when he left Poland when he and my aunt were young."

Levine nodded to them and Jessica and Aaron lifted Aunt Elizabeth's body off the old door and lowered it as gently as they could into the grave. Again Levine threw handfuls of dirt on top of his sister's body. Then he turned and, again weeping, left the gravesite.

Jessica followed him, leaving Aaron behind. He picked up the shovel from behind the mound of dirt and began to fill in the grave after he had placed boards over the lonely body of Jessica's aunt. When he had finished he followed them back to the house and opened the door to find Levine sitting again on the floor.

"Jessica," he called out. Then the room began to reel and he collapsed on the board floor of the cabin.

The fires of the enemy burned low like a coal fire but the heat was intense. It coursed up his legs into his groin and then spread to his belly and chest. His whole body was heated to furnace level. His mouth was dry. He could feel a film cover the roof of his mouth and his lips were dry and cracked. If he ran his tongue over them he could loosen dead skin, which peeled away from his lips but left them sore and bleeding. There was a pounding in his head that consumed his ability to think or even to identify where he was. The pain in his chest made every motion an agony.

Someone was torturing him, piling weights upon him and placing burning stones at his feet to blister the skin of his soles. A nonconsuming fire possessed him but it could not kill him. It just heated him beyond endurance and then heated him some more.

But not everyone about him was merciless. Someone, taking pity, wet his lips with cold water from melted snow. It was the pity of this friend that kept him going through the heat—the torture of burning. The light, cool hand on his face and the cold water touching his mouth—they were what kept him going.

Then the heat started to diminish. From all the pores of his body he felt beads of sweat emerge. Little rivulets formed on his bare chest and trickled down toward his navel. His whole face was covered with sweat. His groin was so wet he feared he had pissed himself. Again the cool hands, this time with a cold wet cloth, washing his face, his chest, his stomach and groin. His legs and even his toes were bathed in the soothing cool. And then the process began again: the heat, the pain, the sweat, and the cool.

Finally he could see only blacks and grays. Shadows moving before his film-covered eyes. Then suddenly he was awake. It was nighttime and he was in Aunt Elizabeth's bed in the Levine cabin. Pain gripped his chest when he moved his arm. He coughed and the pain grew so excruciating that he cried out.

Jessica's face appeared from the dark in front of him. She had a cloth in her hand. She noted his fevered eyes focusing on her and she smiled.

"You're awake."

He tried to speak but his lips were cracked and his tongue coated.

"Don't try," she said. "You've been down for four days. The best we can tell is that your lung is inflamed and you've been running a high fever. I thought I'd lost you at least twice but now I think you'll be all right."

Aaron had thrown his blankets off his chest in his delirium. Jessica pulled them back up to his chin.

"You must keep warm. You can't catch another chill. It will be the end of you if you do."

Aaron's eyes followed her as she washed his face with her cloth. He couldn't speak and moving his lips pained him. But he still moved them as if to say thank you.

She understood him.

Aaron slept the next few days, with only occasional lucid moments. Jessica fed him chicken broth and potato and beet

95

soups. Slowly his fever subsided and the pain in his chest became less and less intense. The sores on his lips developed scales and then began to heal.

Old Levine had finished his mourning and helped Jessica care for her patient. Finally, when he was sure Aaron was recovering, he began to complain to him, asserting that as hired help he was a failure.

"You're more of a hired burden," he said straight-faced as he finished feeding Aaron some hot borscht.

"And you stink!" he added. "How can someone stink as bad as you do?"

Aaron sniffed at his armpits. "Not bad," he joked weakly. "I've smelled some bears who were worse."

"I've smelled skunks who were better," said Levine in much disgust.

"I've not bathed in some time."

"Not true," interrupted Jessica. "I bathed you just two days ago."

Aaron didn't know how to respond.

"Don't worry," said the old man. "I did that part of the job not appropriate for an unmarried woman."

"I owe my life to both of you," he said.

"Nonsense," said Levine. "It is we who owe you. It was you who came to our aid in our hour of sorrow and it nearly cost you your life. It is Jessica and myself and even my poor sister who are in your debt." As he said this last a tear came to his eye.

Aaron lay back on his pillow and was quiet. Finally it registered in his mind just how many days of classes he had missed.

"Oh, no, I'll be so behind. I must get dressed and get to the college."

"No, lie back," ordered Jessica. "I've taken too good care of you to let you ruin it all. Why are you going to that silly college anyway? You're a man and not a boy like the others. Why do you humiliate yourself by sitting in a room with little boys and allow men, some even younger than you are, to humiliate you before these children?"

"I must have an education of the white man if I am to be one. My father advised it and his wife helped me with reading and writing English."

"I read and write English. My father speaks Yiddish, Polish, German, and English, and he can read Hebrew fluently.

The spoken language is sensible. His customers in Europe spoke them. The Hebrew serves his needs as a religious man so that he may read Torah. Why do you need this Latin and this Greek? I have seen you struggle with English. It is the reading and writing of the language of this land that you must master. You stay here with us and I will teach you English."

Aaron swung his feet over the side of the bed. The floorboards were cold. He tried to get to his feet. He did not realize that he was naked until he stood up. Then his knees buckled.

Jessica grabbed the feather comforter from the bed and threw it over him. Moishe came to her aid. They picked Aaron up and put him back down on the bed.

"I'm sorry," said Aaron. He wasn't quite sure for what, whether it was for standing up without clothes or for being sick.

"Silliness," said Jessica. She wrapped the comforter about his body. "You're to stay in bed. We'll work together."

Aaron sighed. "I don't think I have much choice. I can barely move."

"You'll get your strength back," said Moishe Levine. "Just keep swallowing my daughter's cooking; not only will you get well but you'll get fat," he said, patting his own stomach.

The days moved along swiftly for Aaron. The harsh January snows came. He sat in a chair finally, huddled next to the glowing stove. Jessica sat at his feet and they read together. Aaron had a copy of the King James Bible in English and they began with a reading of Genesis. Aaron said that he felt that the Bible story of the Creation was far more unbelievable than any Indian myth, and Jessica became upset with him and called him a heathen.

He laughed at her but then realized that she was serious and scandalized by his lack of belief. He teased her about hers no longer. Instead he concentrated on the words—the reading and the speaking of the language.

He found his command of written English expanding every day. Inquiries came from the village from Mr. Wheelock about his return to classes. But Aaron was no longer sure he wanted to return. Jessica's criticisms had affected him.

The reading had been proceeding for forty-five minutes. The girl had cooked their meal and placed herself at his feet. For thirty of those minutes she had tried to remain alert but finally her exhaustion overcame her and her head fell against

Aaron's knee. Her father was across the room reading the Hebrew text of the same book.

Aaron stopped reading and pushed a lock of Jessica's hair from off of her face. She slept quietly while Aaron stared at her. She was so beautiful. In repose her beauty was intensified by the lack of worry and concern that had appeared so constantly on her face during the course of his illness. But the longer he looked at her, the more concerned he became. A feeling was building up inside him. Dartmouth meant nothing to him any longer. More and more his waking hours were filled with Jessica—her face, her voice, her kindness to him. When he fell asleep his dreams were filled with her as well. He reached down again and began to stroke her head.

"Aaron, my friend," said Moishe from across the room, "don't make a serious mistake. She was your nurse and your teacher. She can never be any more than that."

"I know," said Aaron with sorrow, "but I wish she could be more."

Moishe looked troubled. But he went back to his Hebrew text. He noted that Aaron continued to stroke Jessica's hair and his expression turned to one of worry.

5

February came and went. The snows deepened in the New Hampshire hills. The roads were lost in wind-piled drifts several feet deep. At night as the temperature fell and the winds rose, the frozen branches would snap like the sound of a rifle cracking.

Aaron could move about now. He tried to help Jessica with household chores but was too weak for most duties other than helping her prepare the vegetables for dinner.

Levine was housebound now until the spring thaws came. Even then the muddy roads would limit his wanderings. He had always chafed against the inactivity of winter but this time he knew it was the blessing of God. Jessica and this man, the barbarian, were becoming close, frighteningly close. He watched them now practically head to head before the fire, peeling potatoes for tonight's dinner. He should never have taken this uncircumcised heathen into his care. Elizabeth, poor Elizabeth, had been right. It was too dangerous with a young girl like Jessica.

The dog, Kaiser, growled and his legs began to twitch as he chased some mysterious varmint in his sleep. Aaron reached down and scratched the dog's head. Kaiser's eyes opened. Then he rose, stretched his enormous body, crossed the room to where Levine sat, and stretched out to sleep again, perhaps this time without interruption.

The old man made himself a promise to watch these two. He had lost his sister; he couldn't lose his daughter as well. But not many minutes after this resolve formed in his mind, his eyes, like the dog's, closed and he dozed off to sleep.

Jessica placed the potatoes in the cast-iron pot. She poured water to cover them, fixed the lid in place, and set it on the stove.

"We're all a bit tired of potatoes, Mr. Brant. Was it not you who promised to provide us with meat for the winter?"

Aaron looked embarrassed.

Jessica had become more and more familiar with the serious nature of the man. He did not understand teasing, and his sense of humor was quickened only occasionally and probably most successfully by her father.

"Aaron," she called his name softly. "I'm teasing you, my love."

"Am I?" he asked.

"What?"

"Your love?"

Her dark eyes looked directly at him. "God help me, yes," she said.

Aaron smiled. "Why God help you?"

"Because I want you and I want to be your wife, and if I become your wife, it will kill my father."

Aaron broke eye contact with her. His face hardened as he attempted to control his own emotions.

"I love you, Jessica."

She started to weep.

"And I will not be deterred from making you my wife—not by your father. It happened to me once already. This time it will not. This time I am in love and no one can stop us." He looked up at her. "That is, if you love me."

"I don't want to hurt my father."

"Neither do I, but I'll be damned if we can allow his feelings to suppress our own. That happened to me once before."

99

Jessica looked puzzled.

"It wasn't quite the same. I didn't love the girl. But I gave her my word and she trusted me. My mother is a very powerful woman and very domineering. She interfered and drove the girl away. It caused my break with her. It is because of that that I am trying to live in the white man's world. But, Jessica, I'll not lose you to your father."

"He will regard me as dead. It is our religion."

"My mother invoked clan taboos on me. I did not then honor them and I will not honor Jewish taboos. Will you?"

Jessica did not answer. The tears welling in her eyes finally flowed down her cheeks.

"You don't know what a hard thing you ask of me."

She went to where her father slept. His white hair was standing almost straight out from the sides of his head. She pressed his locks down with her hand. The old man's head jerked and nodded. In his sleep his hand went to his mouth and he stroked his moustache. She leaned down and kissed the top of his head.

Aaron walked to her side. He placed his own arm about her waist. He leaned down and reached for her chin with his hand. He raised her head to meet his kiss. His tongue pressed against her lips. It startled her but she opened her mouth and his tongue entered her. Their bodies came together. She could feel his groin pressed against her.

She pulled away from him. His face registered disappointment.

"Mr. Brant," she said, "not until I am Mrs. Brant." But no sooner had she said it than again the tears began to flow. Aaron pulled her to him again. But this time not in passion but to comfort her.

"We won't think about it," he said to her, whispering in her ear as she sobbed. "We'll not think about it until spring."

Aaron never returned to Dartmouth College, and the college officials seemed not to notice his absence. In March when he felt recovered and the weather turned mild, he announced his intention to return to his sleeping quarters in the barn. He had little excuse to remain with the Levines in Hanover—especially now that the peddler was making preparations for his spring journeys—except for his overwhelming love for Jessica Levine.

He continuously returned to the cabin during the day to

assist her. He could not keep his eyes off her as she worked. She was sweeping the floor vigorously, raising a pile of dust. All the curtains had been removed and were soaking in a tub of lukewarm water and soap. The chill March air blew through the open windows and forced the fire in the open stove to burn hotter. The metal stovepipe that ran up to the old chimney actually glowed red.

Despite the open window, Jessica was sweating. Aaron walked over to her and for the third time offered to take over the sweeping. But she would have none of him.

"I'm a mess, Aaron Brant. Stay away from me." The dog, huddled next to the stove, raised his head at the tone of apprehension in Jessica's voice. But seeing that it was Aaron, he put his head back down and returned to sleep.

Aaron put his arms around Jessica from the rear and held her close to him.

"Aaron, don't. I'm sweaty."

He knew she really meant that her father could return from the barn at any moment. He cupped her breasts with his hands and she pulled away from him.

"No liberties, sir," she said as if shocked.

But Aaron knew from the mocking tone of her faint anger that she teased him.

"You're a grown, mature man, Mr. Brant, yet you behave like a boy."

Again Kaiser raised his head. He sniffed the air and then pulled his huge body to his feet and paddled over to the door.

Moishe Levine knocked the snow from his shoes by stamping them on the ground before the doorway. He pushed open the door.

"Jessica," he yelled, "it's as cold in here as it is in the barn. What are you doing?"

"Cleaning."

"Can't you wait until winter's over?"

"Father, you know very well that every year since we've been here by this time you had already left on your first swing to the farms. What's holding you up?"

Levine went to the stove and spread his hands in front of him. "Your aunt's gone. I'm not so sure I can simply take off like in the past."

Both Aaron and Jessica knew he meant not with Aaron Brant hanging around.

101

"Mr. Levine," Aaron said. "I think it is time you and I spoke."

"No, Aaron," Jessica interrupted.

But Aaron ignored her. "You should know that I love your daughter and I want to marry her."

"You can't," said Levine. "You're not one of us."

"Then I'll become one of you."

"You don't know what you're talking about," said the older man. "You're going to have to leave us."

Jessica's face, flushed with the heat of her work, grew redder now with anger. "And what do you expect, father? How was I supposed to meet 'one of us' here in the middle of this American wilderness? Where would I find 'one of us'? Was I supposed to grow into a middle-aged hag—childless, manless, taking care of you? Where was I supposed to find 'one of us' to love?"

"There are places. Newport, Rhode Island, where we first landed. There is a community there. I could have sent for someone."

"No, thank you, father. I found someone I love and who loves me."

"You can't marry a Christian. I won't have it."

"I intend to marry Aaron Brant and I seek your blessing to do it."

"You've gone mad," shouted Levine, his eyes wide, bulging with anger. He turned to Aaron. "Brant, you will leave my home immediately. You have connived behind my back. You have stolen my daughter's love for me. You've made her turn her back on her people, on her God. If I see you here again I'll sic Kaiser on you."

"Father, you can't throw him out. I love him and he has no place to stay."

Aaron was filled with a deep pain. He did not wish to anger Levine, who had befriended him when he needed friends. But he had no intention of losing Jessica because of her parent's objection. That was not going to happen to him again. Not with Jessica.

"I can take care of myself," he said softly.

"Oh, no, you won't. I brought you back from the brink with care and love. You're mine, Aaron Brant. My father will not chase you away."

Levine's heart sank. He saw in her the defiance that was his—the courage that took him across the ocean and into the

102

wilderness. The courage of his race that had seen their ancestors survive pogroms and persecution.

She knelt at his feet. "Father, I seek your blessing," she said. "I beg you to give it to me. But, give it or not, I intend to marry this man."

Levine sat silently. The time seemed to stand still; the loudest sounds in the room were the cracking of burning wood in the stove and the breathing of the sleeping dog.

Then Levine began a low wail and, with a sudden jerking and tearing motion, tore his coat and shirt, ripping them just as he had done on hearing the news of his sister's death.

Jessica began to cry, sobbing deeply. Aaron came to her side, helping her to her feet.

"Father," she called out, near hysteria, "I'm your daughter, your only child."

The old man turned away from her. "I have no children," he said, spitting the words out through clenched teeth. "My daughter has just died. I must sit shiva."

Jessica backed away from her father as if he had struck her. Her hand covered her mouth in horror. Aaron grabbed hold of her just as she started to fall. He caught her before she hit the floor.

"You stupid old bigot," he said to Levine. "She loves you."

"Take that slut from my house. She is no daughter of mine."

"Are you crazy?" Aaron said, now enraged. "It's still winter out there."

"Get out of my house—you uncircumcised pig, you destroyer of a father's soul. May God curse your union. May she be barren. Believe me, my curse is a blessing because never will you be forced to feel the pain you and my daughter have brought to my heart. All I wish you is emptiness. The numbness I now seek."

Aaron could see the pain of loss in Levine's face and so he said no more. He laid Jessica down on her bed. He went to her dresser and pulled her clothes out of the drawers. He tied them all in a large bundle. He picked up her small body in his huge arms and grabbed hold of the bundle with his hand.

"If you come to your senses," he said to Levine, "we shall be in the barn."

"Be off my land tomorrow" was all the old man said.

The next day Aaron found his canoe by the river. He loaded his meager possessions in the middle of the craft, he

103

sat Jessica in the bow, and then he shoved off from the shore. There were still ice floes in the river and he would have to navigate carefully, but the water was high with some of the spring melt-off.

They had spent the night in the barn loft. Jessica had not slept but instead had wept and grown angry and then wept and grown angry again. Aaron could do or say little. He held her to him, attempting to cover her exposed soul with his massive body. But his brawn and his muscle could do little to protect her from the soul-numbing grief she felt. His love for her was strong enough to allow the suggestion to arise in his mind that he should lead her back to the house and beg her father's forgiveness, losing her, which would destroy him. But if it saved her, it was preferable to watching her suffer. She had told him once that all Jewish male children were circumcised and that men who wished to join them underwent the same painful surgery. He would submit to that if it made a difference. He mentioned it to her and she simply wept the harder. She did not take him seriously. She shook her head from side to side, crying uncontrollably but conveying to him that she did not want that for him.

Aaron made her lie back in the straw. He covered her body with his, holding her tightly. He would keep her warm in the chill of the March night and he would tell her soul that she was not alone even if her mind could not communicate with him.

The town magistrate in Hanover married them. He was not sure he had the authority to do so but Aaron gave him a piece of his father's gold and his objection was forgotten. He led her to a lean-to he had built on the Vermont side of the river. A large fire in front of the hut would keep them warm. He still had the Indian blankets his mother had made, which had kept him warm in the Levine barn in the long winter. He spread dried pine needles over the floor of the hut and then spread out his blankets.

She sat on a blanket. She shivered but smiled at him. It was the first smile he had seen in the days since her father had thrown them out. It lifted his spirits. He had purchased a small bottle of rum in Hanover. He lifted it from his sack, which he had hauled from their canoe. He pulled the cork with his teeth and offered her the bottle.

She shook her head no.

"Go on," he urged. "It will warm your insides."

Just as he said this, she shivered a second time and then

104

took the bottle from his hand. She took a gulp and coughed, spitting the rum out of her mouth.

Aaron laughed. "Take another swig," he said.

"Never."

"You'll need it if you are to stay warm."

She took the bottle a second time from his hand and this time she sipped some of the liquor. She kept this down.

"It's really very sweet, isn't it?" she offered.

"But it is like a fire in your belly once it goes down. And speaking of fire . . ." He turned to the pile of logs and kindling he had constructed before the hut. He struck the flint and soon wisps of flame and smoke rose from the pile.

Aaron blew on them gently until he heard the first crack of burning wood. He removed another package wrapped in paper from his sack. He took generous slabs of deer meat from the paper, skewered them on stakes, and placed them before the fire. Finally he placed two oldish potatoes directly in the flame. He saw Jessica's eyes fill when she saw the potatoes. She knew he had taken them along from the Levine cold cellar.

He offered her the bottle again. Again she sipped it. He took a large gulp and reveled in the feeling of warmth that filled him. He could tell the rum and the fire had had their effect on Jessica. She sat on the blanket and her arms, instead of hugging her body, were now free. She brushed her dark hair off her face. Aaron sat next to her, his eyes watching the meat as it cooked. He did not wish it to become tough from overcooking.

Jessica reached out for his hand and took it in hers. She smiled softly.

"Thank you," she said.

"For what?" he asked.

"Just for being there," she responded.

He took hold of her and brought her closer to him and kissed her eyelids and the tip of her nose. Her tears had started to flow again. He licked them from her salty cheeks with his tongue. Then he kissed her mouth. Remembering the last time, she opened hers for him to enter, and felt his tongue explore the tip of hers gently. And then it began to roam and finally his passion built within him and she felt him drive his tongue forcefully toward her throat again and again.

His hands were touching her breasts and moved to her back, undoing her buttons. He slipped her blouse off her shoulders and then turned his attention to her skirt and petticoat.

When she was totally naked, he removed his jacket, shirt, and breeches. He had been fully aroused well before he appeared naked before her. She took him into her warm hands and began to massage him gently.

Suddenly he pulled away from her and started to chuckle. "When you have a lover my age," he whispered into her ear, "you don't run the risk of doing that and then waiting for him to get into condition again."

She didn't know what he was talking about. She felt perhaps her boldness had led her into doing something wrong.

But then he gently pushed her down on her back. He lay on top of her. She felt his hardness and then his fingers finding the right spot and then the hardness again. She gasped in pain as he pushed it against her. Then she felt even greater pain as he continued to push.

This is not what she had expected. But it did not deter her. She loved him, this giant of a man, and she wanted his body within hers—pain or no pain. She bore down and felt the ripping as he entered her fully.

He waited a few minutes. He whispered into her ear that he would love her until the day he died. She smiled and wrapped her arms around his neck. He began to move slowly in and out and with each movement the pain gave way before pleasure.

He burned the meat. The potatoes were small and black when he reached into the fire with his fingers and gingerly pulled them out.

"You are a terrible cook," said Jessica as she lay back looking into the warmth of the fire and eating a tough piece of venison that he had cut for her with his knife.

"But I'm a good lover."

"I've no one to compare you with," she jested, but when she saw the hurt look on his face she sat up and kissed his bare shoulder.

"You're a wonderful lover," she whispered in his ear, "and I too shall love you until the day I die."

"Jessica, do you want to stay here in case your father changes his mind?"

She shook her head. "He won't."

"Then I want us to leave here and return to Canada."

She looked at him quizzically. "Why?"

"Because it is my home. I want to bring you home with me. I severed my ties with this land during the war. I have a new home now, a place where I can be free to be myself."

"But you can be that here. That's why my father and my aunt came to America."

"These lovers of freedom, as you call them, drove my father, my mother, and me out because we disagreed with them. In my new home no one will be persecuted for disagreeing."

"I don't share your view of this land, Aaron. You did more than disagree. You took up weapons and fought them."

"Only after they fought us."

"That sounds like a little child's 'he hit me first.' But I love you and I respect your love for your Canada. And I will go there with you."

He smiled at her and kissed her again. "Until the day I die," he repeated.

The canoe veered to the New Hampshire shore to avoid a chunk of ice that the swift-flowing spring flood sent hurtling to the south. Aaron's muscles tensed as he steered the canoe toward clear water. On his right the village of Hanover appeared.

Jessica sat upright when she saw the old wagon and the mare on the road ahead of them making for the village. The old man was huddled down in his seat as if to avoid a wind—his coat pulled up high about his neck. Jessica's lips moved and Aaron heard her call out faintly, "Father," as the wagon disappeared around the bend in the road. All that was left was the distant jingling of the mare's bells announcing the coming and going of the peddler.

Aaron and Jessica left Hanover behind them. They paddled with their few possessions against the strong current of the Connecticut to its farthest reaches. Then they carried the craft overland, launching it on streams and small lakes until they reached the southern tip of Lake Memphremagog. As they paddled the great long lake with its looming mountain peaks on all sides, they crossed the line that the diplomats in Paris had drawn across this lake, separating the new United States from Canada.

At night Aaron beached the canoe at a likely campsite. He built a fire and snared small game. They cooked and ate their

107

food. Then Aaron spread the blanket and they lay in each other's arms all night. They made love, a hard, sweaty love-making that left both of them exhausted but satisfied.

From the northern reaches of the lake, they followed small streams and portages until they arrived at the St. Francis River. Aaron could not have known, but he was inadvertently tracing the path that his father and grandfather had traveled in a journey of pain over 50 years earlier—a journey that had altered his father's life and had ended in the death of his grandfather.

They passed the Abenacki town of Saint Francois at night and in silence. Aaron saw little reason to give old enemies the chance to greet a Mohawk from the south.

The St. Francis River entered the St. Lawrence at a wide part of the river called Lake St. Peter.

The easy paddling down the St. Francis gave way to a journey up the St. Lawrence that turned south past the French village of Sorel and then on to the port of Montreal. Here the ocean vessels had to stop. They could not proceed beyond the rapids of Lachine. But beyond Montreal were the Great Lakes and the Mississippi, the vast prairies and the mountains.

Aaron and Jessica had used up their supplies by the time they reached Montreal, although Aaron still had some of his father's gold. They found lodging at the auberge on Rue St. Gabriel and dumped their few possessions there before touring the town.

The city of Montreal was growing rapidly. Its docks were filled with ships from Britain and enormous *voyageur* canoes, laden with furs from the whole winter's trappings out on the western lakes and beyond. Gangs of men loaded furs from the canoes into the shore warehouses of the great Scottish merchants who had come to dominate this soon-to-be-English city in an overwhelmingly French province.

There were shops on Rue St. Paul that Jessica wanted to visit. She had seen no city larger than Springfield, Massachusetts, and that when she was a child. And Aaron had almost never been out of the forest in his forty years. The two walked about, looking up in awe at the three-story warehouses, and were nearly run down by carriages and wagons whose wheels on the cobblestones drowned out the other noises.

They entered a tailor's shop. Aaron's good suit, the one he

had worn so proudly to classes at the college, was now threadbare. He had to be measured for a new one. He had worn his buckskins while they journeyed, but here in the city they were out of place except along the waterfront. The tailor had eyed him suspiciously as he ran his measure along the inside of Aaron's leg. Although Aaron's eyes were blue, the tailor was not at all sure that he wasn't measuring a wild Indian whose tomahawk would split his skull while he worked. Aaron was aware of the tailor's discomfort but did not know its source. He was sure, however, that he would not buy this suit unless Jessica too was measured for a dress at a seamstress's shop. Jessica placated him but she had seen a mercer's shop where bolts of cloth were on display. She would go there on her own later. She would make her own dresses as she always had done.

They walked back on the Rue de la Commune along the waterfront. The workmen all spoke French, which neither Jessica nor Aaron understood, much less spoke. Yet, because of his buckskins, workmen greeted Aaron warmly, assuming he was one of the *voyageurs* and knew their language.

They returned to their inn on Rue St. Gabriel. Aaron ordered a roast hen and a bottle of rum sent to their room. The innkeeper asked for payment in advance and was surprised by the sight of gold coming from the leather pouch Aaron carried about his neck. His attitude of suspicion immediately gave way to one of submissiveness, and the bird, roasted a golden brown, was accompanied not only by the rum but by a bottle of fine Quebec fermented cider. Jessica found she liked the cider far better than the rum.

The two sat before the small table, picking apart the chicken with their fingers, which they frequently burned and stuck into their mouths to soothe and cleanse. They laughed and occasionally fought in jest over one piece or another that they both coveted.

The room was turning darker, although the sun would not set until very late. The buildings opposite the inn cast shadows in the early evening, darkening the guests' rooms.

They had finished eating and Aaron had consumed all the rum and most of the cider. He was more than slightly tipsy. He reached over and took his wife's hand in his.

"Mrs. Brant," he said, slurring his words, "I want you to know that I am very happy and that you are the source of all my happiness."

She smiled at him. He rose to come to her but knocked over the table and nearly fell to the floor.

"I believe I am drunk," he announced.

"I know you are," she responded. She took him by the hand and led him to the large double bed. The bed had been turned down for the evening and the red rays of the sun coming through the window struck the white linens, turning them a pale gold.

Aaron sat on the edge and started to remove his moccasins, but he lost his balance pulling off the second one.

Jessica knew he would achieve no more on his own. She removed his second moccasin and then reached up to undo his leggings. As she touched his waist he began to laugh and twist his entire body. He was violently ticklish.

"Jessica, hold off," he cried out, breathless with laughter but still too drunk to protect himself.

She finally got his buckskin pants off and was working on his shirt. Every second motion was interrupted by the thrust of her fingers toward his armpits and new howls of laughter.

Finally he lay naked and sleepy on the bed. She took the sheet and the comforter and pulled them down to his feet. Then she covered his entire body with them. He was snoring within a few minutes.

Jessica went to the window and looked out across the Rue St. Gabriel. Across the street there was a second inn with its own courtyard for horse-and-carriage traffic closed to the street by a brick wall. The sun would set soon, she thought, and she knew what she must do. She stepped out into the hallway with a paper and took a light from an oil lamp that stood on a small table at the top of the stairs. Then she went back to the room. She covered her head with a shawl and lit the candle and prayed. It was little enough, for the next day by her own reckoning was the Sabbath.

They awoke late the next morning. Aaron stretched out in the bed enjoying the luxury of soft clean sheets. His eyes hurt slightly and his mouth tasted foul but he still felt enormously relaxed. All but one part of him, which stood rigidly at attention.

Jessica was awakened by his stretching and yawning. When she saw his condition she reached over and boldly began stroking him, but suddenly she stopped. He looked over at her about to protest when Jessica suddenly jumped from the bed and crossed the room. He saw the blood spots on the bed linen and on the floor. She had taken a small hand towel and dabbed it against herself.

Aaron rose from the bed. He was naked and still aroused. It embarrassed him but he still walked to her side. He was surprised to find her weeping. He put his arm about her and kissed the top of her head.

"Why are you crying?" he asked finally.

"I want to bear your child."

"We've time for that," he said, "a lifetime together. Don't weep over that—rather weep over what the landlord is going to say about his linen. I'll get some water and wash up."

When he left her side, Jessica again felt the cold gripping her as it had when she first came to the window. It was not the air but rather the coldness of fear. She had abandoned her father's faith and she had sinned against her father. She knew his curse would prevail and she would have no children.

But she was wrong. She became pregnant the second month of their stay in Montreal. They had left the expensive Auberge and had taken rooms in back of a small warehouse off the docks. Aaron's money was gone and he was searching for some sort of employment in an accountant's office. But his arithmetic was rudimentary and no one would hire him. Finally in desperation he went to the docks. He knew no French but he was strong and willing to work. Many men were needed to carry the bales of furs from the canoes into the warehouse. It was temporary—spring work. In summer the men would have nothing, then in fall they would be employed again, loading supplies and trade goods into the canoes for the long journeys west.

The work boss was a huge French Canadian, Jean Luc Lambert. He spoke a few words of English, most of them blasphemous. He hired Aaron without question as soon as Aaron approached him. Then he set him to work in the unloading. Aaron carried bale after bale from out in the hot sun into the cool of the warehouse building. He was sweating almost as soon as he began to work. He stripped down to his waist, removing his buckskin shirt. Each bale weighed about as much as he was able to carry and he staggered as the morning burned on. He knew that others took advantage of him. He carried three bales for every one that the others toted.

At noon the other workers sat down, broke out their long

111

bread with cheese and wine. Some carried pieces of maple sugar, which from past experience they knew would restore their energies.

Aaron was exhausted. His arms ached so badly that he was afraid that if he stopped carrying he would not be able to lift them to his mouth to eat, much less to carry anything more. He collapsed in the shade of the warehouse.

Jean Luc looked over at him and jested to his comrades in French about the skin color of the Anglais, casting doubt upon the complete purity of his mother's behavior.

After ten minutes Jean Luc rose and stood towering above Aaron.

"Anglais," he said, "*tu* work."

Aaron did not know what the man wanted but he got the point when the Frenchman shoved him with his foot.

Aaron rose to his feet.

"*Tu va*—work now—"

Aaron stood waiting for the rest to join him. But nobody else moved. They continued eating the bread and cheese.

"What about the rest of you?" Aaron asked.

Jean Luc laughed in his face and turned to join the others.

Aaron sat down again. The Frenchmen stopped chatting and looked directly at their leader. Jean Luc turned slowly and let loose with a bull-like yell when he saw himself disobeyed. He came charging at Aaron. Aaron leapt to his feet and deftly sidestepped the work boss's onslaught.

Jean Luc tripped and fell when he missed Aaron. The workers bellowed with laughter, which only enraged their leader all the more. He approached Aaron more carefully the second time. He was a frontier fighter, which meant no holds were barred. He lunged at Aaron's waist to get him in a bear hug but instead found himself bent in half clutching his throbbing testicles, which had received a paralyzing kick.

But Aaron did not make use of his advantage. He backed off when he saw Jean Luc throw up his lunch. He didn't want this fight. He wanted the job. He had to have money for food for Jessica and himself.

Jean Luc wiped the vomit from his mouth on his sleeve and again he stalked Aaron. This time he circled three or four times. Jean Luc feinted with his right hand and then caught Aaron's powerful forearm with his left. Earlier in the day Aaron would have broken his grip, but his arms were tired from the morning work. He felt himself pulled toward the

112

giant, whose other arm was now about his back. His breath was knocked out of him. He could not regain it. Jean Luc squeezed tighter and tighter. Aaron's legs were off the ground and his arms were pinned to his side. He had no leverage and nothing to help him to pull away and breathe again. Finally in desperation Aaron used the one weapon left to him. He sank his teeth into the fatty tissue under Jean Luc's cheek right under the eye. Blood squirted into his mouth and then poured down the Frenchman's face.

Jean Luc screamed in rage and pain. His grip loosened and Aaron dropped to the floor. Jean Luc, blood streaming through his fingers, stumbled about the room. Several of his companions made a move toward Aaron but were called back by their leader. They were, in fact, relieved to be recalled—the Anglais fought like the savage he looked to be.

Aaron realized that his career on the docks was over. He picked himself up off the floor and walked out of the warehouse into the hot sun. He found his shirt and then continued down the Rue de la Commune toward the marketplace and the Bonsecours Church, to where he and Jessica lived in their tiny back room.

Jessica sat sewing the cloth for her new dress and was surprised to see him home. They had celebrated a bit last evening because his search for employment was over. She had hoped to tell him her news but she had postponed it for tonight when he had finished his first day on the job. Aaron came into the room and slammed the door behind him. He was angry with himself for fighting but he did not understand how he could have avoided it.

"What's wrong?" asked Jessica.

"Nothing!" He went to the pine cabinet that served as their clothes dresser and food cupboard. He found the old half-filled bottle of rum and pulled the cork. He took a long swig. He turned to her.

"I've had a fight. I won't be going back to that job."

She said nothing but went back to her sewing. He took another swig of rum.

"I'm told Indians can't handle that stuff," she said finally.

He started to laugh bitterly. "Well, I guess I can half handle it, then."

She rose and went to him and he opened his arms to her.

"I'm sorry. It was cruel of me to say that," she cried. "But

113

I'm worried about us. We have no money left and the job seemed like a godsend."

"I am sorry too, Jessica, but I had no choice. I tried to mind my own business but they dumped all the work on me. At the rate it was going I would have collapsed completely before three days were up, and if I had backed down it would have only gotten worse."

Jessica sighed. "So be it," she said.

He looked about the room. He saw that she had bread rising on the shelf above the stove and she was cooking a half chicken in the pot.

"For poor folks we eat well," he said in surprise.

"I'd planned a celebration. I was not going to tell you until I was absolutely sure, but the job looked like the perfect time."

"Tell me what?"

"I'm expecting."

He reacted almost instantly. He kissed her on the mouth and hugged her tightly.

"Good news?" she asked.

"Good news," he said softly, and then he started to chuckle.

"What's funny?"

"At the Auberge you were convinced your father had cursed you and that you were barren. Well, you were barren for exactly two months." Then he grew quiet. "I see now," he said finally, "why you were upset about the job. It all becomes more and more difficult. Well, tomorrow I'll go out looking for work again."

He searched that week and the next and grew more and more desperate. There was nothing for him in Montreal. He returned home empty-handed and more desperate every evening. The rent on their room came due. It was Jessica who paid it. At the end of the first week she decided she had to do something. She had seen advertisements in the seamstress's shop window for someone to aid in the sewing. She applied and was hired. Every day after Aaron left, she stepped out of the room and made her way from the market area up to the Rue St. Paul and the shop. In the back room she sewed until her fingers ached. Then before sunset she returned home to make supper of bread and cold meat. Aaron was so desperate he never noticed. Nor did he remember rent day and so took

114

no notice that the landlord did not show up at the front door demanding payment.

Aaron sorely wanted another bottle of rum but without funds there was little he could do. Maybe he could find someone with cash who would buy him a drink. He walked to the Rue de la Commune. He failed to see the huge man approach him from the rear until the man's meaty hand clamped down on his shoulder and spun him around. Aaron was instantly alert and ready to strike out. Instead of anger, he saw a great smile break across the stitched face of Jean Luc Lambert.

"The Englishman with the teeth," he said in French. "*Mon Dieu*, that was a short fight. Let's have another. I have been looking for you."

He took a roundhouse swing at Aaron, which Aaron blocked with his arm, although the force of it numbed him. He smashed Jean Luc in the face and started it bleeding again. The Frenchman shouted almost in joy and kicked Aaron in the shins with all his might. Aaron collapsed on the ground and the Frenchman fell on top of him, punching and kneeing him.

Aaron felt himself sinking and reached up and grabbed Jean Luc's ears and smashed the Frenchman's head against his own. He blacked out from the force of his own blow.

He woke up looking into the smiling, bloody face of his antagonist.

"*Bon*," Jean Luc said. He grabbed Aaron by the shirt and pulled him to his feet. Aaron was still gasping and offered no resistance when the Frenchman shoved him along the docks back toward the warehouses. He led him into a merchant's office and demanded something Aaron did not understand from the clerk. A full day's pay was placed in his hand. The clerk explained that Jean Luc had vouched for his character and despite several weeks' absence he would have his job back. They returned outside. Aaron tried to thank the Frenchman but Jean Luc touched his head.

"Damn' *bon* fight," he said in atrocious English.

When Aaron arrived home with his news, he was deeply disappointed. Jessica was not there. He waited for her, sure that she had gone to the market. As the hour grew later he became concerned and then frightened and finally desperate. He went to the market and searched for her. The vendors were yelling in French, selling their vegetables and meats. It

115

was not difficult for an English-speaker to understand their cries, since each would hold aloft a sample of his goods.

Finally at sunset Aaron went back to his room. He was close to hysteria. He opened the door to see her calmly setting bread and a heated chicken soup on the table. From the look on his face she knew that she was in trouble. He ran to her and hugged her and then, like a parent reacting to a child who has been lost and then found, he just as suddenly grew angry.

"Where the hell were you?" he shouted. "I've been looking everywhere. "What's that?" he asked, looking at the coins she had left on the table.

"Money. It buys food and pays rents," she responded.

"Where did you get it?"

"The same place I got last week's. I've been working." She walked away from him and went to the stove and toyed with the teapot as if preparing some tea. They had run out of tea some time ago. She wanted to turn around and see the look of surprise or perhaps anger on his face but it was she who was surprised. He started to laugh. She swung around in time to see him place his smaller pile of coins on the table.

"I've got my old job back," he said. "So where before we had nothing, now we have a little fortune."

"Those are coppers, my love," said Jessica, "not your father's gold pieces."

"If only they were," Aaron laughed, "we could go back to the Auberge and live in luxury again."

"Not likely," said Jessica, "those days are over. I'm in charge of the finances now." She scooped up the pennies in her fist and walked to the shelf above the stove. She placed the coins in the empty tea tin.

"From now on we work and we save."

"From now on I work and you save," interrupted Aaron.

"I want to keep working," said Jessica, her eyes flashing in challenge.

"You don't understand, Jessica. I was raised a Mohawk warrior. I'm accustomed to seeing women perform manual labor on my behalf. As a Mohawk I was raised to expect it. A woman with child was given the lighter tasks. But now I am a white man. I can't allow my wife—my pregnant wife—to take on the duties that her husband must perform."

Jessica said nothing. She served him his soup and they ate in silence. At night, after he had fallen asleep, she made up

116

her mind. As soon as he left for work in the morning she would be off to the Rue St. Paul and her needlework.

For the next two weeks Aaron worked steadily on the docks. He was treated as one of the regular workers. Jean Luc greeted him every morning with a thunderous smack on the back. The first morning Aaron had not expected it and he tensed, his fist held high, ready to fight back against the giant Frenchman who seemed determined to turn every one of their meetings into a struggle for survival. But Jean Luc stepped back from Aaron's stance of defiance.

"*Non, mon ami,* no more." He laughed, holding up his hands as if to ward off Aaron's blow. And Aaron from that day recognized his thundering back-pounding as a gesture of friendship.

The third day on the job the crew found another English-speaker. He was a skinny man, at least ten to fifteen years older than Aaron, with a long hatchet face and a razor-sharp nose. His hair was stringy and he had lost most of it. His arms and legs seemed only loosely tied to his body and he walked with a flat-footed jerking motion. He announced his name to Aaron in a nasal twang.

"Elisha Stoddard," he said, "call me Eli. I'm a Yale man. We Stoddards are all Yale men, although my original domicile was Northampton in the Bay Province until those hoodlums Hancock, Adams, Warren, and Washington came along and deprived me of my sustenance. I'm a doctor of medicine, although I did not study the healing arts in academe. Rather I learned them from cogitating on the ills and failures of my fellows of the genus homo."

Aaron understood only every other word Eli spoke. He had far more success understanding Jean Luc. But Stoddard kept right on speaking.

"I've encountered a temporary embarrassment here in this city of this regal mountain and am forced into manual servitude. I believe the gargantuan Gallic gentleman over there has assigned you to me as my assistant. We are to haul those bundles from those rivercraft into these premises."

Aaron looked at Eli Stoddard in amazement. Without speaking he left the warehouse where he stood. He grabbed a huge bundle of furs in his arms and carried it back and dumped it at Eli's feet.

"Your turn" was all he said.

"Bravo," clapped Stoddard. "I'll wager you can't do that a second time."

Aaron smiled. "I'll wager you can't do it the first time."

A frown crossed Stoddard's face. "I am far stronger than I look." He walked to the next canoe and reached into it with his ridiculously long, skinny arms. Then to Aaron's shock the bale of furs came swiftly out of the canoe and into Stoddard's arms. He stumbled once coming back, tripping over his feet, but he did not drop his load. Instead he dropped it at Aaron's feet.

"Doubting Thomas," he said, smiling.

"That's quite a feat, Eli," said Aaron.

"You may call me Dr. Stoddard," said the other man. "Or Doc, if you like. I shall call you Tom."

"I think you're crazy," offered Aaron.

"So did my father and my redoubtable uncle, Mr. Jonathan Edwards, before his self-inflicted demise at the College of New Jersey. He wanted me to transfer from Yale, sir, from Mother Yale to his miserable Presbyterian hovel in Princeton, New Jersey. Sir, I would rather die than leave Mother Yale and live in New Jersey."

"So now you live in Quebec."

"Only temporarily, my good Tom, only temporarily. Anyone who gives thought to the matter will leave this province for the west, for the lakes. The country is better, the land is freehold, and the divisions of this society are better left behind. The wealth is in the west, Tom."

"My name is Aaron."

Stoddard ignored him. "This city, Tom, is controlled by a pack of pestilential Scotch-Presbyterians. They petition the Crown for assemblies, trying to speak in the name of all loyal subjects of the Crown. But this province is French and Papist. These Scots can't speak for the people here. Their priests will do that for them. I'd head west for freehold and free Englishmen. All true Loyalists—those who sacrificed for King George, not like these pecuniary Presbyterians who sat here throughout the war getting fat on victualing and robbing the troops—all true Loyalists will head west."

"I've been to the lakes," offered Aaron.

"Well, by God then, Tom, what are you doing back here?"

"Like you, I find myself temporarily embarrassed and in need of sustenance." Aaron started to laugh. A few moments around this man and he began to speak like him.

They worked together the rest of the day. Aaron said little

118

but Eli never stopped speaking of the Upper St. Lawrence and the land along the shores of Lakes Ontario and Erie.

When the day was over, Eli had no hesitation about inviting himself home with Aaron for dinner. He had no funds and he would not be paid until the end of the week.

They arrived at Aaron's room to find it empty. Aaron asked Eli to sit down.

"Oops, not there," he said as Stoddard was about to plop his skinny rump on a stool that rested by the table. "The leg on that is weak and I've got to repair it."

Then Aaron poured Eli some tea, which they could now afford. Through the window he saw Jessica running down the street from the Rue St. Paul. He was angry with her. He knew where she had been. But with Stoddard present he would say nothing.

"Mr. Stoddard, this is my wife, Jessica Brant. This is Mr. Eli Stoddard."

"Dr. Stoddard, sir, Dr. Stoddard."

"You're a doctor?" she asked, saying the words almost reverently.

"I am indeed, madam. And you are a lady in need of a doctor—not so many months down the way."

Jessica turned red. "Am I showing so soon?"

"Hardly. But I could see the look of relief on your face. Never will a healthy individual show any desire to meet a man of my profession, and sick people fear my coming because I bring the news of pain and death. Only young ladies who will be delivered of a child look upon me with the look you gave me—the look of one who has faced an ordeal alone and sees succor in my countenance. But alas, fair lady, by the time you come to term I shall have left this rotten burg and made my way to the free country of Upper Canada."

Eli left after eating an enormous quantity of meat pie. He went off in search of a bed and Aaron was enormously relieved. He was convinced that his new friend might seek to sleep in their room, that, in fact, they might never get rid of him.

As soon as Stoddard departed, Aaron turned to Jessica.

"He's a lonely man," said Jessica, looking away from her husband.

"Don't avoid me."

"What do you mean?"

"You were working in the seamstress's shop, weren't you?"

"What if I was?" Jessica answered arrogantly. "I'm healthy

and strong. Why shouldn't I work? It's not that hard for me. I enjoy it and I get paid."

"You're pregnant. You should be resting."

She ignored him and went to the washtub to soak the dishes from the evening meal.

"From now on, you are not to leave here during the day when I am gone," ordered Aaron.

Jessica turned with fire in her eyes. "You didn't seem to worry when my money was paying the rent and buying the food. You just moped about feeling sorry for yourself—the unappreciated, educated, but disadvantaged Mohawk sachem who took solace in his rum bottle."

Aaron became equally angry. He turned away from her. He had to rise early for work. He stepped out of his clothes and climbed into bed. Jessica was always after him to wear a nightshirt for warmth rather than modesty and sometimes he did to please her, but tonight he had no desire to please her. He turned his back on her and faced the wall as she undressed to join him. She climbed into bed next to him. She reached over and touched his bare back but he was in no mood to wake up. He feigned sleep and ignored her until, after the passage of a few minutes, his pretended sleep gave way to the real thing.

In the morning Aaron rose early. He grabbed a heel of Jessica's day-old bread and shoved it into his pocket. It would have to suffice for breakfast.

Jessica was only beginning to stir in the bed when he left. He closed the door to the room and stepped out into the street. And then he took his key to their home and locked the door from the outside. That would teach her to defy him. She would spend the whole day in their room. There would be no sneaking off to any seamstress's shop.

When Jessica realized that Aaron had left without kissing her good-bye, she in turn grew angry. He had no right to treat her in that manner. All she wanted was to help them. She was determined that she should have her way and her job. She too dressed quickly. She splashed some water from a pitcher on the nightstand on her face and dried it with a small hand towel. She was troubled still. Perhaps it was wrong to go against his wishes, but with a baby coming they would need everything they could get. She placed a bonnet on her head and went to the door. She pulled on it and jerked back suddenly when the door did not respond in the anticipated manner. She tried it again. Only then did she realize that it had been locked. She looked for the key that normally hung from the hook by the left side of the door. It was gone.

"He's locked me in!" she said half aloud in amazement. "Damn him! How dare he!"

She twisted the knob once again in disbelief that he would do such a thing. Well, he wasn't going to get away with it. She walked over to the window and calculated her chances. The windowsill was four feet above the floor. She pulled a stool from under the small eating table over to the window and climbed onto it. She shoved at the window. It refused to budge. She pushed harder. The window opened but the pressure on the stool was too great. The weak leg collapsed and the entire stool, along with Jessica, came crashing to the ground.

She started to cry, more out of frustration than hurt. She picked herself up off the floor and turned for the second stool. Before she could reach it she was stricken by pain that felt like a dagger sticking in her gut. She sat down on the stool and caught her breath. The pain left her. She started to breathe normally. She rose to place her stool next to the window when it hit her again. She clutched her abdomen in terror. She knew instinctively what was happening. She staggered over to the bed and collapsed upon it. She should go to the waterfront to get Aaron. But then she realized she couldn't get out of the room. She was locked in.

At noon Aaron left the docks and walked home. He told himself that he came because the heel of bread was insufficient breakfast, but his real reason was a sense of guilt for what he had done to Jessica. When he came to the front door he felt a certain smugness as he realized it was still locked. He opened it with the key and stepped in. He stared at the bed frozen in terror. His wife lay on her back, her skirt drawn up above her knees. The bed was covered with blood. He ran to her side, calling out her name.

She was feverish. Her lips were dry and cracked.

"Oh, my God," he wept aloud. "What's happening?"

Then it dawned on him that she had been alone all this time, unable to summon help. He froze with horror. He turned from Jessica and ran out the front door. He turned frantically to the left and raced toward the docks. When he was within shouting distance he screamed at the top of his lungs,

"Doc, Doc Stoddard, come quick."

* * *

Eli cleaned Jessica up and examined her carefully. She wept silently but continuously. Aaron sat at the table across the room as Stoddard worked.

"She's slightly feverish now," Stoddard said softly to him, "but I can see no real complications. Perhaps it was just as well. Nature has a way of forcing things when all is not well."

"No," Jessica said. "It was an act of God, not a correction of nature."

"I'm sorry" was all that he could say.

"So am I," she responded sadly.

Eli looked over at Aaron. Brant rose and walked to his side. Jessica turned away when she saw him.

"I'm sorry for failing you," he said to her.

She made no answer. Aaron knew she would not forgive him. Nothing would be the same. He dropped to his knees and placed his head on her breast.

"Please forgive me, Jess. My damned stubborn pride forced you to go through this all alone. How can you ever forgive me?" Tears welled up in his eyes.

"I so wanted to give you this child," she replied. "You and my father work hand in hand to punish me."

Aaron raised his head and looked into her eyes.

"I love you, Jessica," he said. "There will be other children."

Jessica turned her head to face the wall. The words of her father's curse came flooding back into her mind and she was gripped by fear.

The dead lay everywhere. Geyasada had crept into the field of battle when the moon went down. He had been there for Little Turtle's battle. It should have been his battle. He was a Seneca chieftain while Little Turtle was a Miami, and the Miami were the wards of the Seneca. He should have outranked the Miami but this collection of Hurons and Shawnee and Delawares and Miamis had no respect for him.

He knelt down to feel in the dirt. He found a corpse already stiff with rigor mortis. He felt the head with his hands. He cursed. This one was already scalped.

This general of the Yankees, this one they called St. Clair, he had been a fool. He crept through the Ohio country building forts and telling all that he would crush the red men once and for all. He had not been challenged until he reached the bend of the Wabash with his two thousand drunken ruffians and their women. That is when Blue Jacket and Girty, the white man, and Little Turtle had decided to strike. Geyasada had argued against it but they had ignored him. The insult was too much for him to bear, and so without telling his comrades, he sat alone watching the battle. He saw the whites across the river panic when the Indians struck. He saw his comrades chase the militia and saw them pursue the fleeing Americans as they poured into the main camp. Some, under General Butler, the whites' second in command, attempted to rally and charge, but the general was soon riddled with bullets and his men fell back into the road that took them back to their forts. St. Clair escaped but Butler lay dead and scalped in the field.

No one had seen Geyasada on the battlefield. But, he reasoned, no one could say he had not been there either. And tonight he had already taken one scalp that the others had missed. It was a woman's scalp but he did not care.

He heard a moan from the bushes to his left. He moved quietly in that direction. He stopped and listened. He could hear someone breathing heavily. He pushed aside the bush and looked into the pain-filled eyes of a militiaman—a boy really—about eighteen years old. The boy was wrapped in his blanket, his back propped against a rock. He had removed his trousers to use the cloth as a bandage to stem the flow of blood from a gaping wound in his thigh. Not even the cold of the ground where he was seated seemed to touch him any longer.

Geyasada smiled. It would be good to take a prisoner back for torture. Then no one would deny his part in the victory. The white boy's hand came from behind his back. He held a dueling pistol in it. Geyasada let out a yelp of fear and made a dive to get out of the boy's range of fire. But the boy did not aim at him. Instead he placed the barrel of the pistol in his mouth and fired. The ball exploded through the roof of his mouth and into his brain and out his skull. The boy's eyes went blank and blood gushed from his mouth. He slumped over onto the ground.

Geyasada waited a second and then he rose from the ground, brushing leaves from his leggings and shirt. He took out his knife and walked to the white boy's body. The pistol ball had damaged his scalp. Geyasada wanted it anyway. He would need it to proclaim himself one of the victors.

When he arrived back at the lodge with his grisly trophy, he insisted that his wives sing his praises. He broke out a bottle of his rum and he drained most of it and then began to look over his women to complete his triumph. Mother Jenny stepped into his path but he slashed her across the face viciously with the back of his fist and sent her flying across the hut. Maggie cowered in her bed. Geyasada pulled back his loincloth, revealing his aroused self to her. He leered at her and approached her bed.

"I'm beginning my flow," she cried out in desperation.

Geyasada continued to leer. It would not matter. He would not touch her—there.

When Mother Jenny awoke she went to her daughter, who lay weeping and humiliated. She would tell her mother nothing of what had happened.

Aaron knew that nothing had been right since Jessica lost the child. He told Eli the whole story and told him of his despair. She had lost all interest in their quarters, in herself, and in him. Eli had listened—a rare compliment from him. But even that consolation was gone before long. Just as suddenly as he had appeared, Eli Stoddard was one day no longer in Montreal.

When Aaron went home every evening, he faced a Jessica who barely spoke to him. She would place his dinner in front of him and return to her sewing. The seamstress's shop where she had worked allowed her to bring home her work and do it there. Aaron no longer cared but Jessica refused to return to the shop—in fact, she hardly left their rooms any longer.

At night, when he would reach over to touch her, she lay there perfectly still. Aaron could not make love to someone who showed no feelings, no emotions. She did not seem to be angry with him any longer. He would almost have preferred that. Anything was better than her indifference. When he tried to speak with her about it, she became even more uncommunicative.

Aaron's distress increased with the passing weeks. He was angry. Not with Jessica. After the pain he had caused her he would never be angry with her again. Strangely enough, he was angry with Eli. Eli was his friend. Eli was his doctor. Where was he in this time of need? Gone off to his fabled Upper Canada, most likely. But Eli had had influence with

Jessica. She respected him, honored him. If he had remained in Montreal, Aaron was sure that Jessica would not be in the state she was in.

She sat across the room from him sewing. He had nothing to do. He was bored.

"Jess," he said finally, "I'm going to bed."

"Fine," she responded. "I have this hem to finish. I'll be along later."

He rose from his chair and began to strip off his clothes. When he was entirely naked, he went to the washstand and began to clean himself. He reached under the stand into their clothes cabinet and found his nightshirt. He pulled it over his head and let it fall about his ankles. He hated these night garments. But it pleased her when he wore them and he desperately wanted to do something, anything, to please her. He knew it would do very little good. She would continue sewing until she heard him snoring. Then she would creep quietly into the bed.

He climbed into bed. He remembered the softness of the bed in his father's house. He wished Katherine, his father's wife, were here now. She could talk to Jessica and bring her around. He had written his father and told him of his marriage but there had been no response as yet from Saint John.

Aaron had just about drifted off when there was a pounding at the front door. Jessica was startled.

"Who could be calling at this hour?" she asked. She picked up her candle and walked to the window. "My God, I think it's Eli."

Aaron sat up in bed as Jessica swung open the door.

"Ah, the rose of Hebron," Eli shouted. "Don't stand there gaping, madam. Invite me and my companion into your domicile."

The door was pushed open all the way by the wind, which also extinguished Jessica's candle. A second figure entered the room with Eli.

"My partner in my travels wishes to address the beautiful Jessica Brant."

Jessica nearly collapsed when the voice that came out of the darkness spoke the lilting Yiddish tone of Moishe Levine. Aaron leapt from the bed and stood at her side. Levine switched to English.

"My handyman. So this is how you take care of my daughter. She works while you sleep."

125

"Father," said Jessica. She went to him and he enfolded her in his arms.

"I got a little angry," he said, shrugging. "But anger you get over—a daughter, you don't. And this crazy man—this Stoddard fellow—the most learned Christian I have ever known. Although I have not known too many Christians—usually I'm too busy running away from them to get to know them—this Stoddard, he comes to Hanover out of nowhere. He tells me you need me, that this dope you married has made a mess of things. So I came."

Jessica stiffened. "I'm not going back with you, if that is why you came here."

Eli relit the candle and Jessica got a first good look at her father. He had aged.

"No, I'm not here to make you unhappy."

Jessica stared at him for some moments. "I must get you some food. You have come a long way." She went to their stove. "Aaron, I need some wood for a fire. I have some soup I can reheat."

Aaron smiled. He had not seen her so agitated in a long time. He put on his old shoes and stepped out the front door. He loaded his arms with split logs and reentered his home. Stoddard and Levine had already launched into a heated debate on some fine point of scripture. Aaron walked to Jessica's side. He threw some wood into the oven and stirred the embers. The hot coals sent off sparks and a lick of flame. The wood would catch.

Jessica stood watching the two old men. Unthinkingly she put her arm around Aaron. He realized that it was the first time she had voluntarily touched him since the accident.

"I think he has forgiven me," she whispered to her husband. "He is going to bless our union."

Aaron smiled at her. "Now maybe, wife," he said, "you can forgive *me*."

6

Aaron Brant was terrified. The man who had calmly walked through the slaughter at Mackinac and who had fought bravely at Oriskany and led Mohawk raids into New York could barely move his lips. His throat was dry and his stomach was in an upheaval. He opened his mouth to speak but only a peculiar croak came out. Sweat poured off his forehead. He opened his mouth, this time with more success.

"Good morning, children."

From the young throats came back a response in unison.

"Good morning, teacher."

This was the first day of classes in a new school in the town of York built on the site of the Toronto carrying place. The school was also Aaron and Jessica's home on Front Street opposite York Harbor. The town was new, built just the year before, and contained few children who could afford education. But it would grow and more children would come. Already this village had been made the capital of the new province of Upper Canada—itself only three years old.

It went easier for Aaron after these first moments. He assigned the children some written work to test their abilities to write. He sat at the desk in front of the rough log hut. Two boys started to fool but Aaron stared them down. This dark man with the penetrating blue eyes was not to be fooled with. They calmed down and grew quiet and went back to work.

Aaron silently sighed with relief. He did not know what he would have done had they kept up their misbehavior.

Aaron and Jessica had finally followed Eli Stoddard's advice and had moved to the new province of Upper Canada. Eli had established a practice in the capital rather than in the more established Kingston. His medical practices were unorthodox, and he knew they would never withstand the scrutiny of medical colleagues. In York he was the first physician on the scene and there was no one about to question him. But if Eli's medicine was unorthodox, his politics were not. He was a Loyalist through and through, a fervent subject of the king who had sacrificed life and limb to protect the prerogatives of the Crown in the late war. And he had no use for "late Loyalists" who had either remained neutral or who had sided with the Rebels but who had come to Canada attracted by cheap or free land. To Eli Stoddard even these latecomers were ever tainted with republicanism. Upper Canada, he asserted, could be saved from the octopuslike embrace of the United States only by attracting to it true Loyalists, men like Aaron who had fought on the right side. Stoddard's success in treating the first settlers made ill with fevers produced by York's swampy surroundings made him instantly popular and therefore instantly wealthy. He found money to outfit a school and he had succeeded in persuading the conservative town fathers to hire the nephew of Joseph Brant to teach the children of their own class.

Aaron and Jessica had packed their meager belongings, left their one-room lodging, and Aaron had left manual labor on the docks of Montreal behind him once and for all. Moishe decided to migrate with them. They traveled south to Albany and then made their way to Upper Canada via the Mohawk. In back of the one large schoolroom, the Brants had been given living quarters, a small parlor, a bedroom, and a kitchen. They had no furnishings, but after years of being cramped in one room they both actually enjoyed the feeling of spaciousness that their near-empty lodging provided.

While the boys worked, Aaron's mind wandered over the past few years. It was incredible to think that a few years before he had roamed the forests as an Indian, while today, dressed in a schoolmaster's somber colors, he taught the children of the aristocracy of this new frontier province. He rose and walked from desk to desk for the rest of the morning, evaluating each child's level of work and making assignments for the coming week. Finally Aaron glanced at his pocket watch, a gift from his father.

"That will be enough for this morning," he called out. It was a bit early but he had an appointment with Eli in his living quarters.

The children scampered out of the schoolroom before the words were out of his mouth.

Aaron smiled. He concluded that there was much about teaching that evaded him but the post had a stipend that tripled what he and Jessica had earned in Montreal and he was grateful to Eli Stoddard for getting it for him.

Aaron went through the door that led to the living rooms. Michael Brant, his two-year-old son, waddled to greet him. Jessica was making a pot of tea and Eli Stoddard was already pontificating from Aaron's easy chair next to the stove. As usual he was unpredictable. Only yesterday morning he had announced to Jessica his impending fatherhood. When she asked the name of the mother, he said that he did not know and did not care, and that besides she was dead. He sat calmly waiting for his words to sink in. Jessica did not rise to the bait. Finally he announced that the child was the daughter of a patient of his—an unwed mother, cast from her employer's house, who had died in childbirth. He had decided to adopt the child. He assumed, he said, that the child in her early years would have to live with a mother and that Jessica would be a mother to her. He knew Jessica well. She had already convinced Aaron of the idea.

Today he had a different surprise. He had brought with him one of the most powerful men in the province, who sat in a straight-backed wooden chair dressed in beige breeches and a dark rich brown coat.

"Tom, good fellow," shouted Eli as Aaron entered, "I want you to meet Judge Richard Cartwright—one of your benefactors. It was he who insisted that this pestilential swamp, which we have misnamed York, be the seat of government for his most blessed of provinces under His Majesty of Great Britain and that it should have a schoolmaster."

"Judge Cartwright, I am in your debt," said Aaron.

Cartwright nodded to Aaron. "It was as much Stoddard's idea as it was mine, sir. I am always willing to help a fellow veteran of the war, Mr. Brant, but I am somewhat confused. I thought your first name was Aaron."

"It is."

Cartwright looked strangely at Stoddard, who was unaffected by the glance.

"The campaigns you waged with your uncle," said Cartwright, "are known to me, as is your uncle. Those of us who came to these settlements out of loyalty must work together and support each other. A man of your background—a fighter in the frontier war—you must know that I speak the truth when I say we must be vigilant."

"Against whom, sir?" interrupted Eli. "Point out the poltroons. We'll hang them."

Cartwright looked at Eli with a clear annoyance showing on his face.

"Mr. Brant, I've come to see you today because I wish to discover your attitudes toward the future of our settlement. Very little is left of the British North American empire. Nova Scotia remained loyal because of the presence of British power in Halifax. The new province of New Brunswick cut out of Nova Scotia is promising. Whole regiments of loyal troops are settled in Saint John and in the river valley. It will remain firm. But it is Canada where most of the people of British North America now dwell. And until recently Canada meant the French of Quebec, recently conquered, hostile to Britain, and placated into neutrality by a guarantee for a foreign church and a foreign law and a foreign form of land tenure."

"Mr. Cartwright," interrupted Jessica as she brought tea to the table in front of the judge, "we spent several years in Montreal. There are English-speaking people there."

"Indeed, Mrs. Brant," returned an annoyed Cartwright. In his house the women did not enter political discussions. "But those Englishmen are found in numbers only in Montreal and in Quebec City and almost all of them are Americans."

"Aren't we all?" said Jessica.

"No, madam," interrupted Cartwright, "that is precisely the point I am trying to make. Those Americans were merchants who moved to Canada before the pestilence of republicanism struck. We don't know whose side they were on. When American troops invaded Canada, they supported them. When the British troops returned, the merchants waved the old colors and cheered as loudly as anyone."

"You're right," said Eli. "Don't trust the Quebec English. They are all secret republicans. There isn't a loyal one in the bunch."

"Doc, shut up," said Aaron. "I believe Sir John Johnson has settled with many of his troops in Quebec. I served with those men and I feel I could trust them."

"You're right," said Cartwright. "My suspicions are more aimed at latecomers. The Montreal merchants joined with us in asking for an assembly, with the power to vote granted to those who had a stake in society. The king gave us our wish but saw fit to divide Canada in two. In Quebec he gave further guarantees to their priests and seigneurs."

"Small comfort to the Montreal merchant," said Aaron. He had walked to the mantelpiece above the fireplace and leaned against it, his teacup balanced in his left hand. Jessica took her cue from Cartwright's tone and disappeared angrily into the kitchen.

Stoddard slurped his tea and Cartwright again looked at him in annoyance.

"I believe the government feels that Lower Canada— Quebec—will remain French only for a time and that eventually it will succumb to the pressures of British culture. But Upper Canada, our home, along the shores of these great lakes, had to be dealt with differently. We are peopled by those who came after the war. A people driven from their homes by intolerance and treason. The American republicans call themselves 'the patiots' but it was, sir, those who fought for the king and country, it was we, sir, who were the true patriots."

"Hear, hear," said Stoddard.

"By the grace of His Majesty, we now have our own assembly, elected by true subjects of the Crown with modest property. And we have a council where those with the greatest investment in society, men of the greatest property, sit for life. It is like our own Canadian House of Lords. There was even some talk in Parliament of creating a Canadian peerage."

"We've come far, sir, I agree," said Aaron.

"Not far enough," said Cartwright. "Everything we've obtained is threatened and again it is republicans, both in America and in France, that threaten us. The king wars with the French radicals in Europe and at the same time American radicals cross the lake in ever-increasing numbers, not only here in the York area but at Kingston, and even worse at Niagara and in the far west at Detroit. Thank God the king's ministers had the wisdom to hold on to the forts that were negotiated away in seventeen eighty-three, because if war comes now, sir, we won't have to face a military threat from right across the border."

"But what are you saying?" asked Aaron. "Is it that you fear subversion by Americans who are in our midst?"

"Precisely. The governor, Lord Dorchester, feels war is imminent."

Jessica had returned to the room and she had overheard these remarks.

"Perhaps it is imminent because you kept those forts contrary to your word and have been provoking the Indians who still live on the American side of the border to attack the Americans."

"Fie on you, Jessica," Eli blurted out. "We kept the forts because the Americans went back on their word to alleviate the plight of those of us who fought for the king. My home in Northampton is now occupied by a fat merchant from New London. A lot of alleviating the bloody Congress did for me. The Americans broke the treaty first. The king heard the groans of his people and had the good sense to realize that surrendering the forts would put us in even worse danger than we are now in."

"My wife, Mr. Cartwright, is one of those late Loyalists I think you refer to. She left the United States only after marrying me. Her heart may still be rebel."

131

Cartwright smiled at Aaron. "As a good husband, sir, I am sure you are showing the lady the error of her ways."

Aaron smiled. The thought of teaching his teacher amused him. But he said nothing.

Finally Cartwright came to the point. "I want you with us, Brant. We're the men who will run this province—loyal men, men who fought for the king, men who abhor republican chaos. Men who believe in stability and giving of power to those who exercise it with restraint, men of property."

"I'm not a wealthy man, sir," said Aaron.

"But whether you like it or not, you are a man of position," said the judge. "The name of Brant is a significant one to people who have lived in central New York and who now live on this side of Lake Ontario. Most believe you to be the son of Sir William, and if there is a more significant name than Brant, it is Johnson."

"I'm not the son of Sir William Johnson."

"I know that now."

Aaron gave Eli a wicked look.

"Yes, Tom, I revealed the truth to him."

"You are the son of the richest merchant in New Brunswick—the acknowledged son. Therefore, sir, whether you like it or not, you will be a man of property as well in due course. We want you with us. We must prevent the riffraff from controlling our province as they control the American states. We must prevent Canada from going the way of republican violence. And you must be willing to serve your king either in the Assembly or in local office. Can I count on you?"

"You may," said Aaron. "I lost one home from the American disease and I'll not lose a second."

Jessica's face turned from his. He could see she disapproved and that they would argue tonight after their guests left. But he knew he had entered a new phase in his life. Cartwright's coming to his home was his entry into the white man's world in Upper Canada. Now everything was up to him. Kenonranon was gone and from now on only Aaron Brant would survive.

II

Matthew
1794–1800

7

The August sun was hot, and the general was insane. Everyone said so. The stories went back to the war with England. Matthew Nowell, a major of the regular Federal Army of the United States, had come with his general as part of his legion all the way from Cincinnati on the Ohio River. He had helped build the winter quarters at Greenville and he had helped build their last outpost, Fort Defiance, at the junction of the Auglaize and the Maumee—fifty miles from the British-held fort at the falls of that same river.

In the last ten days they had advanced from Fort Defiance and were only five miles from the British fort and its Indian encampment. It was a nest of vipers, thought Matthew. Miami, Shawnee, Wyandote, Iroquois, Delawares, and Chippewas. There would be a battle. That was inevitable. The winner would own the west. No one could try to make the Ohio River the boundary of the United States. The Indian tribes would be pushed across the lakes along with their British and Canadian mentors. And that would be the first step to pushing the British off the continent of North America.

His face was flushed red and sweat poured from his temples down his cheeks and into his collar, turning his linen stock limp and wet. His uniform coat, too light in the wilderness winter, roasted him in the heat of the summer.

The ranks of infantry marched in two columns. On his right the Maumee River flowed swiftly toward the falls on its way to Lake Erie. Out in front and spread out on the left flank of the American army rode cavalry and Kentucky dragoon volunteers. This army would not be ambushed as St. Clair's force had been in 1791.

General Wayne rode slightly ahead of Matthew. Matthew had dined with "Old Tony" every evening but as a junior officer he had said nothing at the mess. Wayne insisted that all of his officers dine together. It was one way to prevent cabals from plotting against him. Wayne shouted a lot but he had been ill recently. His leg was filled with gout. It was swollen

135

and agonizing to touch. Riding his horse, he was forced to close his eyes to keep the tears from flowing. But still, even with the pain of gout, the general seemed quieter the closer they came to battle. All of which convinced Matthew that his leader was as unbalanced as everyone said. But Matthew did not care about that. What mattered was fighting and winning.

One of Matthew's men stumbled over a root in the trail and went flying onto his face, his musket clattering on the ground.

"Shit," yelled the soldier in front of him as the muzzle of the fallen musket struck him in the thigh. The wound was superficial but the frightened, bruised man set up a wailing of pain.

Matthew took his sword and jabbed its point into the soldier's other thigh. The private looked up at him in surprise.

"What the hell did you do that for?"

"For symmetry," answered Matthew sarcastically.

Private Conrad looked at him with the blankest expression.

"Get your ass off the ground, you malingering son of a bitch," shouted Nowell. "And you," he shouted at the soldier who had originally caused the incident by tripping, "if you fall on your face again, you are to lie there until all three thousand men in this unit walk over your rump."

Jennings, the erring soldier, picked up his canteen and his musket, which clattered together, and ran forward to regain his place in the line of march. Conrad got to his feet and also took his place in the line, this time behind Jennings.

"You clubfooted ox," he whispered so that only Jennings could hear. "I'm behind you now. When we get into battle and the snot-nosed major is too busy to look, I'm going to ram my bayonet right up your asshole. You'll die of brain damage."

Jennings continued to march without looking around.

"You Kentucky bag of wind," he said finally out of the side of his mouth. "You're all perverts. There's not one of you who hasn't done it with his sheep more often than with his wife, and they tell me you have an officer called Miss Campbell." He started to laugh. "You're led by a Miss Campbell." He broke into a guffaw that caught Matthew's attention.

"Quiet in the ranks," said Nowell.

"That's *Miscampbell*, one word, you bastard," Conrad said, not being able to allow the honor of his home to be besmirched without correction—no matter what the major ordered.

The trail cut by Wayne's cavalry now gave way to waist-

136

high grass, which grew on both sides of the river. Up front the sound of musketry broke the rhythm of marching feet on swampy meadowland. Matthew raised his head and stood on his tiptoes to see what was going on.

General Wayne seemed to sit taller in the saddle. His aides had all dropped to the rear. He saw Matthew and signaled to him.

The major raced to the side of the general's docile old mare.

"Go up ahead, Major, and find out what goes on and then get back as soon as you can to report."

Matthew ran up front, slipping through the column, avoiding the soldiers. He grabbed Conrad and Jennings by the arms.

"Come with me," he shouted.

The two men looked at each other. Following this major was the last thing they wanted to do. But given their last run-in with him, neither saw any alternative but to follow.

They ran through the tall grass. Matthew stayed in front of the two privates. The musket firing seemed to have stopped. Then he heard the sound of horses galloping. He broke through the meadow grass and into a clearing. He was nearly knocked over by the cavalry falling back from their first bloody confrontation with the Indians.

Matthew tried to restrain one of the fleeing horsemen but they all raced past him.

Conrad and Jennings finally came out into the clearing. The obvious terror of the cavalry was sufficient to persuade both men to flee back into the safety of the tall grass. After the last of the horsemen had passed, Matthew called to his two companions to follow him. The two soldiers had no choice but to obey.

They went across the clearing into the woods. If they were to be ambushed it would be now, Matthew thought, and then he could count on making a stand alone since he was convinced his comrades would not be around to share his fate. But he had to know what lay up ahead. If the Indians were following up their rout of the calvary, or if they had planned to move about the Americans' flank, the fate of the army depended on his being able to report these facts. He moved through the woods silently. He remembered what the great Abenacki sachem Socono had taught him. But his companions made enough noise for a small regiment. The Kentuckian was not too bad but the Virginian, Jennings, was hopeless in the woods. They would not save themselves by stealthy approach and withdrawal.

Matthew saw a second clearing coming up in front. That would be dangerous to cross. Instead he looked up into a giant oak in front of him. He motioned to Jennings to bend before him. He climbed onto Jennings's back and hoisted himself onto the first limb. He could see nothing. The other trees blocked his view. He found a forked limb higher up and hauled himself into it. Now he had a better view. It was not a clearing at all but rather a continuation of the forest. The trees had been knocked over as if by the hand of some angry god. Their trunks lay across each other, limbs intertwined to create a natural abatis against an assaulting army. A windstorm of extraordinary strength had created this place that the Indians called Fallen Timbers.

Matthew caught sight of movement among the torn-up roots immediately in front. The Indians were using the place as a natural fort. Their line ran from the high grass by the river to deep into the woods beyond the tree stumps on their right. Thus far they had not taken advantage of their initial success. They were waiting for Mad Anthony Wayne to come to them.

Matthew slithered down from the tree to join his anxious companions.

"Let's get back," he ordered.

Jennings took off like a cow through the underbrush.

"You, come back," Matthew called. But to no effect. Jennings had disappeared before their eyes. And he was heading off toward the Indians' flank and not back toward the advancing American column.

Conrad had looked after Jennings's disappearing form with disgust.

"Asshole," he whispered.

Matthew nodded in agreement.

"Well, at least we won't be mistaken for the whole British Fort Miami garrison when we approach our own force. We've got to get this information back to General Wayne."

Geyasada was nervous about Blue Jacket's decision to face this American army. He disliked the Shawnee. They were a wandering people with no set lands of their own. He might not be living within the longhouse, but there was some comfort in knowing the Seneca still clung to the western door at Buffalo Creek. And the young Shawnee brave Tecumseh actually frightened Geyasada. He had none of the Iroquois sense of diplomacy. True, he was an orator, but he spoke only of extreme action against the whites. He did not understand the necessity of playing off white against white. His people had been masters of this game for centuries but Tecumseh was willing to risk all.

Geyasada never took risks. His family was at the fort, actually at McKees Trading Post slightly downriver from the fort. The British had made all the Indians leave Fort Miami. It made Geyasada nervous. The British were afraid of this American army and wanted no Indians within the walls to give the Americans an excuse for attacking them. If the Redcoats were afraid of these Americans, Blue Jacket and Tecumseh better be even more afraid. Little Turtle was afraid but the tribes did not heed the leader of the Miami any longer. And without doubt Geyasada was afraid. As soon as the fighting became hectic, he would disguise his actions and slip away and rejoin Mother Jenny and his red-haired wife. He had placed himself on the flanks because he saw the Fallen Timbers fort as a trap. The crazy American general would come after them there with the long knives.

He lay hidden in the underbrush. The first skirmishes were over and the Americans with their horses had fled. If he had been in command he would have been satisfied with that victory and withdrawn beneath the guns of the British fort. It did not matter that the British would not fight to protect them. The Americans did not know this.

There was a crashing in the bushes in front of him. It sounded almost like the desperate thrashing of a buck pursued by a pack of wolves. But it was not a deer. A terrified American soldier came tumbling through the blackberry bushes behind which Geyasada had concealed himself. If the Seneca did not rise and reveal himself the American would crash into him.

Geyasada reached out and grabbed Jennings by his long hair. Jennings felt the tug and then caught sight of the vermilion-painted Seneca. He screamed as the Seneca grabbed him about the throat and brandished his hunting knife. Then, with a sudden flash, Geyasada drew the blade across the white man's throat. Jennings's eyes seemed to bulge as he saw his own blood surge from his throat and spurt onto his chest and the ground. He would have collapsed but Geyasada kept him on his feet. He thrust his knife into the scalp of the semiconscious Virginian and ripped the hair from his skull. Then he let Jennings fall. He had his trophy. He would leave this place and fall back toward the fort. He had an American scalp. He could not believe his good fortune. No one would now dare to question his bravery.

"Well, Major, your scouting report coincides with what the leaders of my cavalry tell me," said Wayne to Matthew Nowell. "Brigadier Wilkinson," he said to the rather chubby, pleasant-looking officer who rode beside him, "we march forward."

The brigadier started to move.

"Wilkinson," ordered Wayne, "not through the marsh grass but through the woods. Our men have to see where they are going. And, General, use the bayonet. Don't let them fire, they'll merely waste ammunition. They are to march right into those timbers and give those savages a taste of steel."

Wilkinson rode off.

"I suspect he'll do as I ordered," said Wayne. "He's a scoundrel but there were enough witnesses to my orders. If he disobeys it is a court martial for him."

Matthew ignored Wayne's remark. It dealt with the politics of the army—far beyond him.

"May I join my men, sir?" Matthew asked finally.

"Go to it, boy."

Matthew raced ahead. He found Conrad and the rest of his troop fixing bayonets on the ends of their muskets. When their orders were given they marched toward their own left flank and advanced through the woods toward Fallen Timbers.

The troops moved rapidly. Matthew found Conrad, the Kentuckian, by his side as they passed the great oak from which Matthew had sighted the Indian fortress. Now they were among the first upturned stumps. They could no longer move as a military unit. It was each man for himself.

The Indians opened fire from their hidden positions. Soldiers fell screaming but still the Americans came on. Matthew climbed over a fallen tree that had balanced delicately against another. Both gave way under his weight and he fell headlong onto a Shawnee warrior. Matthew's sword had gone flying from his hand as he fell. The Indian grabbed his coat and swung his arm up, tomahawk held high, ready to descend on Matthew's exposed head. Then a look of surprise filled the

Shawnee's face. Private Conrad's bayonet pierced his stomach. Conrad's foot came up and struck the mortally wounded Indian's crotch as he yanked the bayonet out. The Indian collapsed in a heap.

Matthew regained his feet. Conrad picked up the major's sword from the ground and handed it to him. Matthew nodded. He would remember Conrad's deed. But he had no time now for thanks. The major climbed up onto the next log. He could see off to his right that the cavalry had regrouped and had driven through the tall grass by the riverbank and were falling upon the Indians' flank.

The warriors were now aware from the firing that the Americans could possibly cut off their line of retreat. They panicked and in large numbers began to flee the site of the Fallen Timbers and race for the falls of the Maumee and the British fort.

Matthew gave a cheer. Many of his men, struggling along with their clumsy muskets made more clumsy by the knives affixed to them, joined him. An Indian rose from his hiding place in front of Matthew and started to flee. But he was not quick enough. Matthew's sword, thrust with all his strength, pierced the Indian's back and became stuck in the Indian's breastbone. His forward motion yanked the sword from Matthew's hand but not until he heard the sickening sound of bone snapping and he felt a shooting pain rise up to his elbow. His wrist had been broken. It hung limply and awkwardly to the right.

"Conrad," he called, "keep the men moving forward. We've got them on the run. The red bastards are fleeing. We can't let them escape."

But they did escape. The Americans slowly plodded their way through the overgrown tornado site while the Indians fled downriver.

Geyasada was already at the fort when Matthew led his men into the timbers. The Redcoats sat nervously awaiting news of the battle. Geyasada waved his trophy in front of him and asked to be let into the fort. Others were coming with more scalps, he yelled up to the ramparts. The American Wayne had been beaten like the American St. Clair. Some of the Redcoats cheered at the word. But they were under strict orders to admit no one.

The Seneca realized that not only were the British un-

141

willing to fight the American but they would not even take the fleeing braves into the stockade for protection. Suddenly fear gripped him. If the Americans were willing to face even British fire they would march right up to Fort Miami, maybe even attack it. There was no sanctuary here or anywhere else. He had to flee. Mother Jenny and Maggie were at McKees Trading Post with all the other women. But if the Americans bypassed the fort they would surely head for McKees. The firing from upriver seemed to be getting closer, and the thunder of large numbers of horses could be heard along the riverbank. He could see some of Blue Jacket's Shawnees rising from the woods, making for the fort. That was enough for Geyasada. He slipped into the grass along the river. He walked the river's edge. He took off his cloth shirt and, holding it high over his head, he forded the Maumee. Once on the other side, he crawled through the grass to the safety of the woods on the far side of the river. He would return for his women later.

Matthew's wrist was hurting him. Fierce pains shot up to his elbow in a rhythmic fashion. If he moved his arm the pain reached up to his shoulder. Conrad fixed a splint with some rags and two flat sticks and tied the limp wrist in place. And then he placed a sling about Matthew's neck.

"There you go, sir," he said, patting his commander on the shoulder. He was a good five years older than the twenty-eight-year-old major and there was a certain condescending attitude in his behavior. But he had saved Matthew's life and now he had given first aid to his wound. Matthew couldn't help but feel grateful.

Conrad was bigger than Matthew, much broader in the chest and shoulders. They had the same brown hair but Conrad had less of it. His hairline had been receding on the sides, giving him a skimpy forelock, which itself would be gone in a few years.

The older man, when first assigned to Matthew's troop in the legion, was tempted to ask for a transfer. The major was an easterner from Massachusetts, somehow related to Federalist snobs, Schuyler and his bastard son-in-law, Alexander Hamilton. No good Kentuckian would be caught dead serving under a man who wouldn't vote to bring Mr. Jefferson and Mr. Madison to the executive mansion. That is, once the general stepped aside. No one could say an evil word about

General George Washington, President of the United States. Conrad, as a youngster, had served under the general in the Yorktown campaign. But as he got to know Matthew Nowell and to understand how violently anti-British he was, Conrad began to forgive him his vague Federalist connection and he had come to respect his courage. He had led his men into battle and he seemed never to be afraid to expose himself to any dangers. If he asked his men to do something you could expect to find him with the men. He had earned Conrad's respect.

The two men sat beside the riverbank about a mile upriver from the falls and the British-held Fort Miami. General Wayne, followed by General Wilkinson, came riding along the shore.

"You there," yelled Wilkinson in his slightly effeminate fashion, "what are you doing sitting still? You should be falling back to join your unit."

"Nonsense," Wayne corrected him gruffly, "get on with the fight. The enemy runs, go after him."

Wilkinson opened his mouth and then shut it. He began to sulk.

"The brigadier fears an ambush," said Wayne.

"They could regroup—falling back and making us overextend ourselves—and then they will fall on our flanks and rear."

"That could be," admitted Wayne, "but they're not. They are routed. We must follow at least up to Fort Miami. I pray to God that whoever commands that little spot of British aggression is foolish enough to harbor the savages. If he does, I'll storm the place and I'll blot the stain of it from my nation's flag. British forts on American soil! Blast it, man, it is intolerable. Detroit, Niagara, Miami, they're ours, and by God it would be sweet to take them from King George."

Wilkinson blanched at Wayne's words. He was beginning to understand why they referred to the legion's commander as "mad." Matthew stood as the two generals approached. He almost started to cheer at Wayne's words. He caught himself. His arm hurt as if someone were applying a torch to it. But he was inspired by the thought of winning Fort Miami. He grabbed Conrad for support and the two went into the high grass again, heading toward the plain by the river where the British fort stood.

They did not attack Fort Miami. The British closed their gates to the fleeing Indians. American soldiers went right up to the Palisade and bayoneted fleeing braves. Some of the Indians tried to climb the walls but the British soldiers threatened them from the ramparts. They had no choice but to drop down and to face the long knives.

Those who escaped would blame the British as much as the Americans for the death of those who did not escape. But the British commander, by keeping the Indians out and not firing on the approaching American troops, avoided a war.

Matthew stood staring up at the Union flag that flapped in the brisk wind on this hot August day. Wayne was not as mad as others thought. Unless the British fired first, now that they had refused to aid the Indians, there would be no orders to attack emanating from Wayne.

The general sent different words. They were to bypass the fort and proceed downriver to the trading post of the Loyalist McKees. They followed the river and came to the log building of the post. Some of the buildings were already on fire. Indian women and children ran in several different directions looking for shelter. The Kentuckians whom Matthew and Conrad found themselves among began to open fire on them. Nowell was aghast.

"Cease fire," he yelled, and those closest to him put down their rifles. But most merely glanced his way and, not recognizing him, despite his officer's uniform, began to reload and fire. Others began to chase after the women with tomahawks and knives.

"Christ, Conrad," Matthew yelled, "they're no better than the savages themselves."

"Don't tell a Kentuckian not to kill a Shawnee squaw. Squaws make papooses and papooses grow up and take your wife's scalp. They'll show no mercy."

But most of the women had taken their children and fled before the legionnaires arrived at the post. Those who had remained were the families of warriors who had not returned for them. Their wives mourned them for dead.

Matthew and the officer corps of the Federal Army restored discipline and most of the Indian women were spared although they were now captives. Matthew's arm had numbed during the chase to the fort and then on to McKees. But now the pain was excruciating. He needed the bone set. If the job were botched his career could be affected, unless he learned to use a sword with his left hand.

The surgeon's tent had been set up near the burned-out

buildings. Matthew walked past a pile of bodies—mostly women, but including some small children—waiting for burial. He shivered despite the heat and despite the fact that he was running a slight fever. One woman holding the hand of a young boy of eight or nine sat wailing by the body of a woman younger than Matthew. The fact that they had been murdered by American troops was shocking to Matthew. The Kentuckians were not much better than the savages in this manner. Conrad was a good man and a good soldier, but the hatred he and his fellows held for the Indians was worse than anything he had experienced in the east even during the height of the Mohawk raids during the last war.

There was a commotion in the surgeon's tent. A woman with flaming red hair, yet dressed like a squaw, came running out of the tent and slammed into Matthew. He screamed with pain and a look of consternation crossed the girl's face. She hesitated long enough in front of the agonized major to lose her opportunity to escape. The surgeon's assistant grabbed her by her great red braid with both hands and held on while she tried to pull away. Tears came pouring out of Matthew's eyes and he couldn't focus clearly on the girl's face.

"What's wrong here?" he asked finally.

"White captive girl, Major," answered the aide. "Sometimes they are worse than ten savage women combined. They sure as hell hate to go back to corsets and proper behavior."

Matthew's interest was now alerted. His niece, Margaret, Amy's daughter, was a captive but he had not heard that she would be found this far west—in the Ohio country. She had been taken in the last war on the Mohawk. His one and only letter from Amy had said the girl was with the Seneca and that their savage half brother Brant was trying to release her.

Matthew had broken with Amy over the child. His sister had gone to Canada after the war to live among the "Tories"—a people, including his own father, whom he could never forgive. She had married his friend Ethan Morin and had taken her two sons and gone west into what they now called Upper Canada, and she could be damned as far as he was concerned.

He followed the kicking, struggling girl and the surgeon's aide into the tent. The doctor was just completing an operation. His table of torture, a square one about four feet high, was covered with blood. His patient had fainted and was being carried to a cot on the far side of the tent.

"Ah, the vixen has returned," said the surgeon, leering at her. "Now, my sweet," he said, "all I wanted was a swift examination to make sure I am not returning damaged goods to the white world. Now, up on the table with you and we'll just spread your legs and take a look."

"To what point?" said Matthew coldly from the tent's entrance.

The surgeon looked up in surprise. "To no point, Major. There ain't no white bitch among the savages that ain't been knocked up plenty. No need to even look. Just tell her family that unless they watch her she'll drop her drawers at the first sight of a cock."

Maggie had stopped struggling as Matthew interfered. She looked him over. He was handsome. His brown hair was not as pretty as her red hair but much prettier than the black-haired Geyasada. She wondered if he was brown below as she was red. She didn't like the freckles that showed only faintly on his tanned face. It made him look as if the Great Spirit could not make up his mind what to color him. She wondered what had become of Geyasada. He had never returned from the battle. She was officially his daughter. If he had fallen she should be wailing with the other women. But should she mourn her father or her husband? At least she had no children to mourn.

Maggie had never conceived. But neither had Jenny. It was Geyasada who could have no children. Maggie did not blame herself. Besides, she did not care if she ever had children. They made your belly swell and your breasts sag with milk. Maggie liked her flat belly and she loved the way her breasts uplifted from her body. But now everything had changed. Geyasada, the coward, was either dead or fleeing. Jenny had rushed into the tall grass by the falls and had not returned.

Maggie was now in the hands of her own kind for the first time. She had only vague memories of the earlier times, flashes that went through her mind, flashes of a kind man dressed in black and of a fair-skinned woman lying propped in a bed, with an infant at each swollen breast. After that her memories were filled with Geyasada, with burning, and with torture.

The white man had to be important. His uniform was different from the others. And when he gave orders, the others obeyed. He must be a war chief. He sat on the shaman's table exchanging words with the magician. His wrist was broken. He grimaced when the magician touched it. The shaman's assistants came up behind him and grabbed his arms. The others took his legs. The shaman grabbed his wrist and seemed to snap it back in place. The war chief's face went white with pain but he did not yell. He was brave, not like Geyasada. They bound his wrist and then the medicine chief gave the war chief a swig of rum. The white soldier took a sip of it and then put it down. In that he was not like Geyasada either. She could like this man. She did like this man.

Matthew was feeling weak. The wrist did feel better after it was set and bound. However, he now had to find out something about the girl.

"Doctor, this captive white girl, I must make inquiries about her family. Does anyone here speak her language?"

The surgeon's aides shrugged their shoulders.

"I'll get nothing from them," he mumbled. "You," he said, pointing to Maggie, "come with me."

Maggie understood his gestures and followed him away from the surgeon's tent back along the riverbank. He walked to where the legion had established its camp within sight of the British fort. Matthew found his troop eating some salt pork and potatoes. There was Indian corn growing everywhere and the men roasted it over the fire as well.

"Private Conrad," called Matthew.

"Sir."

"This woman was a captive among the savages. Obviously she is a white woman. I have reason to suspect she could be my sister's daughter. She is the right age, the right coloring, but until I can find out for sure, she stays with us."

Without saying a word while Nowell addressed Conrad, Maggie took the mess pot and went to the river with it. She rinsed out the remains of the heated pork and brought it back filled with water. She dropped some ears of corn into the pot to boil.

The members of Conrad's mess group smiled at each other. Maggie began to gather up their tin plates for washing.

"Hey, girl, how about scrubbing me drawers," said a Pennsylvania regular army man. "I've got me a few visitors down there I could do without."

Conrad hissed at the Pennsylvanian to shut up. But Matthew paid no attention. If it was not Maggie Nowell, so much

147

the better. She would have to get used to such treatment alone in the white man's world where a woman alone was soon victim. If she was Maggie, then she could make herself useful until he could send her off to his sister. In any case, she was a "squaw" and she had been used by red filth.

Wayne withdrew from the Maumee slowly and reluctantly. The army marched back toward Fort Defiance. The general would eventually return to Greenville, where he would spend the harsh Ohio winter. Matthew received a winter's leave to recuperate and permission to travel from Fort Defiance to Cincinnati and then by route of the Ohio to Pittsburgh. There he could pick up the road east to Philadelphia and then travel to Boston.

At Fort Defiance he said good-bye to all of his troop but Private Conrad, who was assigned as an orderly to accompany him. He had no further word or even a hint of Maggie's origins, so she was to travel with them. Perhaps in Boston he would write to his sister. He did not know where she lived precisely and he had not heard from her in ten years. It might be necessary to write to his father—a man whom he despised but whom he had seen last spring just before Aunt Margaret had passed on. He knew where the man lived. Stephen Nowell would put him in touch with Amy.

The September days were still warm, even if the nights grew chilly. Their ride south was made easy by the existence of a road cut through the wilderness by Wayne's legion throughout the summer. Matthew, Maggie, and Daniel Conrad rode by day at a leisurely pace. They had plenty of time to reach the Ohio and hire a canoe for the trip to Pittsburgh. At dusk they camped and lit a fire, using the timber that Matthew and Daniel's comrades in arms had cut down so laboriously in the trek to the Maumee. Conrad would leave them and in an hour they would hear the report of his Kentucky rifle. They would prepare the fire for the game he would bring them. Maggie cooked and then doused the fire. They would lay out their bedrolls and sleep with full bellies until dawn.

They had eaten wild turkey this night. Maggie never liked the taste of the bird. It had been Geyasada's favorite food and anything she associated with the Seneca she despised. She had trouble falling asleep, but not the two white men—both snored loudly. They were at home in the woods. It surprised her. She had thought that only Indians could travel noiselessly, leaving few signs that they had passed this way. But of course the horses made them easy to track. She would have her monthly flow soon. Her cramps had already begun on the left side. It was a sure sign. By tomorrow the blood would come. It would be the first time that the flow had not meant her release. When it came among the Indians she was free to leave the hut of the pig and dwell with other women with the same flow. Those nights, even when the cramps were bad, were the only happy ones of her life. She would not awaken to find him pushing at her groin, at her mouth, or worse.

She rolled over and saw his face next to her. She opened her mouth to scream but his hand clamped heavily onto it.

"You stupid bitch," he whispered. "You'll give me away."

He looked her over, noticing for the first time that she was unbound. "Why didn't you sneak away?" he hissed. "These whites are careless. They think any white would prefer to return to their lodges." He chuckled softly.

Maggie had gotten control of herself. She had to. Her first reaction was to scream a warning to the two sleeping white men, but Geyasada would kill her before they could stop him and she intended to stay alive. But she would not go back with him. She would never again be subject to his demands, his invasions of her body. Never.

"I thought you were dead—everyone was dead," she whispered. "I had nowhere else to turn."

Geyasada grunted softly. What the girl said made sense. "We must get rid of these two," he said, turning from Maggie and reaching for his tomahawk, which was stuck in his belt at his side.

Maggie felt around the ground for something. Panic was growing inside her. Geyasada crept toward the black form that was Matthew Nowell. Maggie saw the stone—part of the ring of stones surrounding the burned-out campfire. She grabbed the heaviest one and followed behind Geyasada. He ignored her, intent on getting closer to Matthew without awakening him.

Maggie lifted the stone over her head and brought it down with all her strength. The blackened stone cracked into Geyasada's skull, sending splinters of bone deep into his brain. He collapsed almost noiselessly to the ground. Maggie's heart was pounding. She smashed the stone into his head again and then into his face, mashing his nose and knocking the teeth from his lifeless face. She withdrew his scalping

149

knife. It was razor-sharp despite the few times that it had been used as it was intended to be used. She had to rid herself of the offending face. She plunged the blade into his body again and again.

Matthew was awakened by the sound of her sobs. He saw Conrad rising to his knees. The girl sat across the burned-out campfire from them. Her knees were pulled up and her head rested on them. She was crying. But it was not the sob of a woman with sorrows; these were body-racking, heaving moans and wails. Matthew had never in his life heard anything like them. He rose to go to her aid and then saw the body about five feet from her. It was the body of an Indian. Matthew reached for his pistol and slowly approached the motionless form. He reached down and touched it. It was still warm but the Indian was clearly dead. His face had been smashed to pieces and blood oozed from dozens of knife wounds all over his body. Matthew stared down at the Indian in horror. He could feel last night's dinner rising up into his throat. It spewed from his mouth onto the lifeless body of the Seneca. Conrad grabbed him by the shoulders and led him away over to the bushes at the edge of the clearing. Matthew heaved again and again until nothing more would come up.

Daniel walked back to the form of Geyasada.

"Jesus," he said as he stared down at what had been the Seneca. Then he walked to Maggie, who was rocking back and forth and moaning softly.

"He's the one who has been screwing you," he said, making an unmistakable gesture with his fingers as he spoke.

She nodded.

"Well, he ain't going to screw anyone else ever again. Not in this world. The son of a bitch must have deserved it. What are you wailing for?" he said to the uncomprehending girl.

Matthew joined them. "Obviously, Private, this Indian was her captor and she returned a terrible revenge on him. She is distraught. She saved our lives. We grew careless this far south. If it had not been for this girl we'd both be lying here food for scavengers."

Conrad did not respond. He knew that the major was correct about their fates but he knew the girl had acted for reasons of her own more than to help them. The girl must have had a powerful hate for this Indian. It would be difficult enough for a woman to kill, but the mutilation spoke of such deep-seated horror that he was afraid to pursue it.

They arrived in Boston just as the fall rains came off the sea and turned the town gray. Matthew's carriage arrived at the foot of Copp's Hill. He leaned his head out the window to get a glimpse of the town across the river. In the old days there was a ferry here—one owned, in fact, by his father—but since 1786 a bridge connected Charlestown and Boston. Their carriage climbed up the ramp and out over the water.

It had been years since he had been in Charlestown. With Israel Kip and Margaret Schuyler both dead he had given up on Saratoga and turned his attention again to the town of his birth. He had allowed the old Saratoga Flats house to revert to the Schuylers. They had always owned it anyway. The general had allowed his aunt to live there but Matthew Nowell was no kin to the Schuylers. With the money Aunt Margaret had left him, he had purchased the old Breed estate, up for sale as confiscated Tory property. As an heir to Stephen Nowell, the Tory in question, he had obtained it cheaply and he had hired carpenters in Charlestown and ordered them to rebuild the old house. He had not seen it but they had been building all the long campaign of the summer and the house should be ready for his return.

He stretched his neck out even further as the horse clunked on the wooden planks of the bridge. It stood high above the town on Breed's Hill. It was like stepping backward in time— the house, the path leading to it.

They were across the bridge. He turned his attention to his companion. The girl was dressed in a simple frock. Her hair was combed out, scrubbed to remove lice, and then piled back on top of her head off her neck and shoulders. Her neck was long and elegant-looking. The dress had a high collar, revealing almost nothing of her, but her breasts were large and her figure in the narrow-waisted dresses of the white women was provocative to Matthew. This girl was very beautiful and she was probably very experienced. She said nothing. What she had done to the Indian was more than enough evidence that she had done things and had had things done to her that Matthew had only thought about when he was by himself. He was twenty-eight but he had never had sex except with prostitutes or army camp followers, and even with them he was ashamed to tell them about the things he would really like to do. He shook his head. He could not let this girl affect him this way. She was probably his niece.

They were off the bridge now and driving through the cobblestone streets of Charlestown. They left the paved road as the carriage turned up the path toward Breed's Hill. They drove for a few minutes around the bend and then the left side of the carriage sank in the mire. The horses halted. Conrad leaned down over the side to look in on the passengers.

"We'll not be able to take the path up, sir—too steep, too muddy. I'll have to leave you off here and drive the carriage back down to the livery stable in the village."

"All right, Private," said Nowell. "The lady and I will walk up."

He stepped out of the carriage and gave Maggie his hand. His boots would be mud-covered but that would be Conrad's problem, not his. The girl's shoes were another story. He would have to think of something for her. He didn't have to. Before coming out of the carriage, she slipped her shoes off her feet. She hated the feel of them, although they were pretty. She liked the way they looked on her feet. She dropped barefoot into the mud. Matthew started to laugh. Maggie liked the man's smile when he let himself smile. Normally he was always frowning. She laughed along with him.

They walked up the rest of the hill. Matthew held Maggie's elbow, although the girl probably was more surefooted than he was. They came within sight of the oak door. Matthew was disappointed. They had forgotten a detail that he could remember vividly. The door had been nail-studded. He would have to take care of that himself. He turned around and looked down toward the village and out across the river to the hills of Boston. It was the same—except for the narrow bridge that now crossed the gray green straits to Boston. It was the same as it had been on that day so many years before when he had watched the Redcoats form across the straits to attack this very hill. The day he had become an orphan. The day William Vaughan died.

He opened the door and stepped inside. Maggie followed him. The house had only some basic pieces of furniture. He would have to go to Boston and get whatever they needed. The parlor room had the window seat he had ordered and a good-sized fireplace. He remembered his evenings before it, listening to Vaughan tell him stories of his beautiful girl-mother and of his grandmother, whom Vaughan had loved. And the giant old man, Jonathan Breed, his great-grandfather. His father, Stephen Nowell, had been born in this house but this was not his house. He had rejected it when he had rejected America, when he rejected Matthew. This was Breed's house and Sarah Nowell's house and William Vaughan's house but most of all it was his house. His mother gave birth to him here and she had died here bearing him, loving him. He had restored it to bring back their ghosts—Jonathan Breed, Sarah Nowell, William Vaughan, Abigail, his mother.

Maggie followed the major into the house. She had heard Jenny speak of a longhouse and she imagined it must have been the size of a white man's house but it could not have been as beautiful as this. This journey to the land of the white man had left her in awe. The town of Cincinnati on the Ohio was the largest concentration of people she had ever seen until she arrived in Pittsburgh, at the forks of the Ohio, which was even larger. When they arrived at elegant Philadelphia, the capital village of the white man, Maggie could only stare wide-eyed. Boston was smaller than Philadelphia but was the source of even more amazement. That there could be enough whites to populate a second city almost as large as Philadelphia told her that there were more of her people than her imagination could handle.

And then there were the giant ships in the harbor. She had never seen their likes before. She had viewed Lake Erie and Lake Michigan, with waters extending beyond where the eye could see, and so the ocean was of no surprise to her. But that men could build such craft and use the winds to power them convinced her that men like the Shawnee, Tecumseh, who preached war with the white man, a war of extermination, simply did not understand the power of the white man. The culture of the Indians was doomed. Then and there, Maggie Nowell made up her mind. She was white and she would learn to live like these whites. Never again would men like that one—she could not say his name even mentally—men like that would never control her. She would learn the secrets of the whites and she would control her own life among them.

Matthew started a fire in the hearth and then went to the lean-to kitchen. There was a giant hearth in the kitchen with cast-iron pots and also a great black stove. He lit the stove and set a kettle of water on top of it. He opened the pantry

153

and found a giant smoked ham hanging there—a gift from neighbors in the village. He sliced pieces of the ham and placed them in a pan to fry.

Daniel returned to the house before the meal was fully cooked and the three of them ate ham and drank tea in the kitchen.

"I've arranged for a cook to come up every day from town, sir," said the private. "And the greengrocer and butchers will be making deliveries also. There is a milk cow in the barn, and if the rain stops and the ground dries out or even freezes, I'll get the carriage and the horses up to join the cow."

Matthew played absentmindedly with his wrist. It hurt him in weather like this. The physician he saw in Philadelphia told him it always would. The bone had healed well, however, and he would be holding a sword again before long.

He had to do something about the girl. He looked at her now. Her hair was lightened by exposure to the sun on the journey home and had a reddish gold hue. Her skin, where exposed to the sun, was reddish, but when she wore a low-cut gown one could see the creamy white complexion reaching down—down . . .

He pulled his mind away from such thoughts. She was probably his niece, a girl who had suffered terribly, torn from her mother as a baby, subjected to God knows what horrors, forced to live among savages whose moral standards were practically nonexistent, and forced to do things, unspeakable things, filthy things. He felt himself becoming aroused and again he pulled his mind back. He could not allow these thoughts to go on. He twisted his sore wrist and actually yelped in pain.

Conrad looked at him in puzzlement.

"I'm sorry," said Matthew. "I wasn't listening. You said something about a cow?"

In the weeks that followed Matthew Nowell's return to Charlestown, winter set in. The house was battered by sea winds from the North Atlantic. But the fires in the parlor and dining room and the warm stove in the hearth of the lean-to kitchen kept them cozy. Matthew established himself in his parents' bedroom. It was the room in which he had been born and in which his mother had died. It was furnished in a very masculine way—a large dark-stained oak four-poster bed dominated the room. The floors were also wide-board, dark-

154

stained oak. The windows were small and lead-paned, in the style of the seventeenth century, and they did not let in much light. Beneath the window was a small writing desk and chair. The only other piece of furniture was an armoire in which Matthew kept his uniforms and his few suits of civilian clothes.

The girl he had placed in what had been his room in the old house. It was the room next to his with a connecting door. At night as he lay in the bed he would listen for her; if she rose to use the chamber pot he was awake, and sometimes when she sat by the window watching the village below he could tell from the sound of the desk chair scraping on the floor. But most often she fell off to sleep, leaving Matthew alone and dissatisfied in his own room. When he did drift off his dreams were restless, filthy dreams that he did not wish to remember.

He did not quite know what to do with the girl. Perhaps her mother could identify her. If she'd learn English better she could tell her own story, and he had made it his responsibility to teach her English.

Some two weeks after they returned, he received word from the army department in Philadelphia that his leave had been extended into the spring. He would ask to be assigned to Castle Island or some other Boston Harbor defense. He felt the need to remain in his own home—his old home.

He picked up the quill at his desk and began a letter to his sister about the girl. He did not know where Amy Nowell lived but he would address an inquiry to her in care of his father at Saint John. Stephen Nowell would know where to reach her.

Then he laid the quill back down. What if the girl was not Maggie Nowell? Why raise false hopes? Perhaps it would be better to wait until she learned English and could tell him her story. Yes, he would wait until then.

Daniel Conrad was pleased with himself as he lay naked on his cot in the small bedroom off the kitchen. The cook would be arriving next week and she would occupy this bed. They had decided they needed a live-in cook. The major had promised him the small bedroom that the girl occupied. He would move her down the hall to a larger room.

Not bad for a Kentucky brawler who hadn't worn a pair of shoes until he joined the army. Orderly to a major would

155

give him the corporal's chevrons that he desired. The pay increase would be accepted without question. But the best part of his assignment was living in a fine house—living next door to the vixen wasn't a bad thought either. At the thought of her there was a stiffening in his groin. He smiled—nothing really changed. The thought of a girl had gotten him hard at sixteen and he was still the same at twenty-six. He started to stroke himself as he had done so often during the last campaign when there were no women about.

He heard a noise in the kitchen. He tried to ignore it but was startled into an upright position when the door to his room flew open. The red-haired girl looked into the dark room. The light from the kitchen window poured onto Conrad's legs and stomach. Maggie said something in Indian which the soldier did not understand. Then he saw her eyes fix on his middle. She was not embarrassed and did not look away. Daniel began to stroke himself in full view of her. Still she did not look away. He smiled. He was sure about her and what she liked. Maggie entered the room and closed the door behind her.

They made love hungrily and with little consideration for the other's needs. When they had finished, Daniel started to fall asleep. But Maggie grew angry and spit harsh Indian sounds at him. He pretended to ignore her but, remembering the fate of her Seneca captor, he determined to keep alert. He watched her face with half-closed eyelids. In the semidarkness of the room she would not be able to tell if he slept or not. Her face glistened. At first he thought it was with sweat but then he realized from the heaving of her breasts that she was weeping. He reached out with his hand and touched her face. She was startled and pulled back from him, raising her hand as if to protect herself from a blow.

"Whoa, there, little filly. I ain't that type. I enjoy pleasure. The other stuff is well out of my sights."

Maggie had little understanding of his words but the tone of his voice was soothing. This was a man who intended no harm to her. That had been her first impression and the reason she had come to him to begin with. And she had used the only device she had ever used with any success to get what she wanted from a man. In her loneliness and fear of living with these strangers, she had reached out to one of them. At first she had been disappointed. This Daniel had been no different from Geyasada—gratifying his own body by

156

using hers. But now as he spoke those strange sounds to her and stroked her cheek softly with his rough and calloused hands, she had to acknowledge to herself that she had not behaved very differently herself.

Conrad's hand moved from her face to her breasts. He stroked her softly and lovingly. For the first time in her life she felt the touch of a man that had neither anger nor lust behind it. Conrad touched her to calm her and ultimately to give her pleasure.

8

Maggie Nowell placed the last gold coin in its leather pouch and then placed the pouch in a wooden box with the others. She pressed the panel on the bottom drawer of her dressing table and a secret compartment door sprang open. Daniel had arranged to have the dressing table delivered from Boston as a gift for her. In the six years since they had returned to Charlestown so much had changed. Her first achievement had been to learn English. Formal lessons with Uncle Matthew, secret intimate lessons with Daniel in his room at the end of the upstairs hall. When they lay on his cot he taught her the words for all the secret things they did together, and then she gently rubbed his back from his thighs to his shoulders. He talked to her and she to him until he fell off to sleep. She learned far more from these lessons than she learned from her proper and formal uncle.

In those years Matthew had questioned her about her story. She told him what she could remember—the fire, the painted faces, and the fleeing across lakes in canoes. He avoided asking her about life among the Indians, and she felt that he must have completely forgotten the killing of Geyasada. But Daniel would not avoid those questions. She told him how the Seneca had seduced her. She told him how many times she had taken him into her from the time when she was too small to accommodate him and how he compensated for that. She saw the nervous look come over his face and she smiled mischievously at him. "What you do to me I ask you to do." Then she turned solemn. "I despised Geyasada. I never asked him to my mat. And he never asked if he could come. I would do it to any man who tried what he did."

157

"Jesus" was again all that Daniel could say in the face of her anger.

But he understood the girl. As time passed, he understood more and more about her. He knew that his own early years of poverty and deprivation on the frontier of Kentucky had been pure joy compared to her childhood. Maggie Nowell knew little about her beginnings but she would never forget the years with Geyasada; they would blemish her soul forever. All he could do to help her was to be gentle with her. It was a new experience for him. He had never been gentle with a woman in his life. But he found to his own surprise that her response to his love was more intense than any he had received from anyone else among his numerous loves in a busy past. Nor could he help his own feelings. His concern for her and his desire to be with her grew daily. Their lovemaking now was as far removed as possible from the lust of that first encounter. It pleased her and, he felt, it helped her. It absolutely amazed him.

In these early years her relationship with her uncle changed drastically as well. At first Matthew confined himself to giving Maggie formal lessons in English. Each evening he would sit next to her and attempt to assist her to read and write. He entered the work diligently but it became harder and harder as the days and weeks passed. He could not keep his mind on the subject matter and off her. She was so beautiful. She was so provocative. He could not say exactly what it was that attracted him to her. If he sat too close, so that their thighs touched, she would modestly withdraw an inch or so. If he touched her hand she would place it in her lap so as to be out of his way.

Each night's lesson became an agony for Matthew. He wanted to touch her but to do so was to commit a dishonorable act. She was his sister's child—his half sister's child—perhaps.

When they finished the lesson, Maggie would go upstairs to her room, leaving Matthew alone in the dining room. He would replace the books in the lower drawer of the lowboy. After Conrad retired he would reach into the opposite cabinet and take out a bottle of good port.

This evening had been particularly difficult. The wine tasted good. He actually was relieved that the girl had gone to bed. Her presence nearly overwhelmed him. He did not know how many more of these sessions he could face. He would have to call them off. Yet the girl needed to know how to read and write. As her uncle he owed her that much. He would have to hire a tutor. He could not face any more of this himself. He took a second glass of the wine and then a third. Normally he stopped after three but this evening was different. She had been so close to him. He could remember the smell of her perfume. He took a fourth glass and then suddenly she was in front of him again.

"Excuse me, uncle," said Maggie from the doorway, "I thought I might take the books to my room and practice before going to sleep."

She was dressed in a pale blue lace nightgown that set off the brilliant color of her hair. Matthew did not remember buying it and he wondered where it had come from. She walked to the table.

"Are the books in the lowboy?"

Matthew nodded without responding. She bent down and took them from the drawer. The entire front of her bodice was in full display before him. Matthew looked away in embarrassment. But gradually, as she felt around under the tablecloth for the books, his eyes were drawn back to the beauty of her breasts. His hand could have reached out and touched her. His hand moved slightly and he pulled it back as if it had reached out to touch fire.

"Ah, here they are," she said, straightening up with the books in her hands. "Good night, uncle," she said. "Don't stay up too late."

Matthew sat back down at the table. He was sweating. He had almost done an unspeakable thing. Yet he felt no comfort in a danger avoided. He felt frustrated and angry. He poured another glass of wine. He was well over his limit now. There was no reason now not to finish the bottle.

When Matthew went to his room he had difficulty standing. He threw open the door. It was the largest room on the second floor of the house, and the emptiest. He pulled off his clothes and dropped them where he removed them. By the time he stood naked at the side of his bed he was angry with frustration. He wanted the woman in the room down the hall. It wasn't as if she was some young virgin. She had been screwed by a dozen red savages at least. Why should she be off limits to him—an officer in the United States Army? A damned fine officer. He had to be as good as any flea-bitten Indian. But not tonight, he smirked, as he looked down at his limp self. Why was she playing the virginal game with him, pretending to be innocent? He was tempted to confront her but he was too drunk. He sat on the edge of the bed. Damn it, he would do something. He rose from the bed; his dressing gown hung behind the bedroom door, but for what he was going to do he wouldn't need it. He walked barefoot down the corridor and tried her door. It was locked. He put his shoulder against it with all of his might and broke the lock. The force of his pressure pushed open the door. He found himself standing in front of her. She was not studying as she had suggested she would. She sat by her dressing table combing her long red hair. He merely looked at her.

"I want you," he said drunkenly.

She rose from the table. The face that flashed in front of her was not that of her silly tormented uncle but the face of one whose image she had smashed with a rock.

In the morning Matthew awoke with a start. He was in his own room. He was frightened by what had happened the night before. His drunkenness, his lust. He concluded that he would have to leave the house. He would have to bring in a proper chaperone for her. He did not know how the girl would react to what had happened. He knew he was ashamed. He assumed she felt the same way. Although it was clear he had forced himself upon her, she had participated in their lovemaking with enthusiasm. That very day he hired the first of their lady's maids, a large homely woman whom he installed in what his father had always referred to as Aunt Betsy's room.

He brought in dancing teachers and instructors in the etiquette of the day to educate his niece. Despite what had passed between them, the lessons in English continued. Maggie's spoken English was almost perfect. The reading was coming nicely but she had trouble making her letters. Matthew spent almost every evening leaning over her shoulder, holding her hand and laboriously forming the cursive letters. She made errors, the ink smeared continuously, but she had to be taught. He guided her hand. Her red hair smelled of perfume, as did her body. Thank God he stood behind her. The nearness had startling erotic effects upon him. He could not allow what had happened earlier to repeat itself.

After two hours of work after dinner, Matthew again reluctantly called the lesson to an end. Maggie thanked him and

160

went to her room. She never looked down at him but he was sure she must have noticed how her presence affected him.

Matthew sat with another bottle. This time it was rum and he was not used to drinking hard liquor. Two glasses made him tipsy. He went up the stairs to his own room. He tripped at the top of the stairs and cursed. He went into his empty room. Perhaps the rum would let him sleep without the dreams that plagued him and without a memory of what he had done. He was just drifting off when he heard the girl cry out. He sat up in bed. He was sure he had heard her and he was sure she had called out his name. Someone had called.

"Matt."

But then she never called him that. He was always uncle or Uncle Matthew. But then he remembered this phenomenon before, just as he fell off to sleep, his name called. Maybe it was his mind playing tricks on him. On the other hand, what if the girl needed him? He threw off the covers and dropped from the high bed onto the floor. He picked up his dressing gown this time to cover his nakedness and walked down the hallway. There was no light coming from beneath the repaired door. He opened it softly and stepped in. The moonlight came pouring through the window to strike her full in the face. Her red hair lay loosely and spilled brilliantly all over the white pillow and framed the beauty of her face. Matthew stood in awe of the sight. She was so extraordinarily beautiful. He spent some moments staring at her. Then she moved slightly in the bed and seemed to mumble something. He thought he heard her speak his name. Perhaps she had called out to him after all. He walked to the bed. She wore the same blue gown she had worn that night. Somehow one of her breasts had slipped from the top and was fully exposed, bathed in the moonlight. Again Matthew reached out and this time he did not pull back. He touched the incredibly soft skin. Never in his life had he felt anything so soft. The girl stirred under his stroking. He could feel himself grow hard beneath his dressing gown. Matthew was breathing heavily. He could feel his palms grow sweaty; he wanted her. He drew back the bedclothes that covered her body. Her gown had crept up to her waist. She was naked from the waist down. Matthew's throat went completely dry. He swallowed hard but he had no saliva in his mouth to soothe the parched dryness. He bent down to the girl's milk-white moon-drenched stomach and kissed her. At the feel of him her legs spread

161

apart and she lifted her buttocks slightly from the mattress. Matthew looked down her body even further. He was completely overcome. He could not resist it any longer.

Matthew felt the joy of being inside her. He could feel the buildup. It would not be long. It was rising and ready to pour from him. He held his breath and then he screamed as he felt his seed shoot from him in rhythmic spurts.

He lay quietly for some moments. And then he felt Maggie's chest move and he realized that she wept.

"Uncle Matthew," she said after some moments of silence, "I'm so ashamed by it all."

With those words she shattered him. He withdrew from her quickly. He looked at her and took the end of the bed sheet and wiped her tears from her cheeks.

"It was not your fault, girl. It never was. I forced myself on you both times. It is I who am at fault."

Now she was sobbing deeply and Matthew felt a terrible sinking within him. What had he done to her? How could he let his lust get so far out of hand? How could he make it up to her? To comfort her. No one must know what he had done to her—for her sake. He had to protect her.

"O God, help me," he cried out, "I love you. What else could I have done but love you? Don't tell anyone, Maggie, for your sake and mine."

She had stopped crying now.

"I won't," she whispered. "But please, Uncle Matthew, I am frightened. Don't leave me. Stay with me."

"Of course I'll stay with you. I'm all you have."

"Tell me honestly, Matthew. It would be all right if I was just some child you found in the wilderness and if you were really not my uncle. Are you my uncle?"

"If it calms you, I'll tell you I'm no relation," said Matthew.

"But you'd be lying."

Matthew looked at her and did not respond.

"Where is my family?" Maggie asked.

"Dead." Matthew lied to her without hesitation. To him they were all dead—his father, his savage brother, and the sister who had gone to live with the enemy. "They are all dead," he repeated. "I am the only one you have." He reached over and began to pat her hand. He stayed the night, and before morning came, they made love a second time.

* * *

Daniel knew that things had changed between Maggie and himself. She had stopped coming to him as frequently. When she did come their lovemaking seemed strangely passionless and disturbed. He questioned her about it and she avoided giving him a meaningful answer. This evening she had gone off early to her bedroom. He thought she would come to him but she had not.

He was sure nothing had changed with him. He needed her and he was concerned for her and yes, damn it, she had grown on him. This new feeling, this aching sense of loss when she was not with him, this constant obsession with what she wanted or what would please her—these were in fact new to him. He knew it all meant that he loved her.

And if he was living in the same house with her, why was he alone all night lying in his cold bed, thinking about her? Why did he not just go to her for a change? He sat up in his cot and swung his feet down onto the cold hardwood floor. He got up. His uniform breeches were hung neatly in his wardrobe. He slipped his feet into them and pulled them up over his hips. The material felt coarse against his skin. "Shit," he whispered. Life in the east was softening him. He had taken to wearing those effete underdrawers. He threw his shirt about his shoulders and opened the door to the hallway.

His bare feet made no sound and he walked down the hall to her room. He turned the doorknob gently and opened the door a crack. The room was dark. She must have fallen asleep already. He walked into the room and silently approached her bed. He stopped before it, his eyes bulging in surprise.

"It can't be," he said aloud.

Matthew awoke with a start and sat bolt upright in bed.

"What the hell are you doing here?" he shouted at Conrad.

"I might ask the same question of you."

"Don't be impertinent, Corporal. What are you doing in this room?"

Maggie was awake now. Her eyes widened in fear as she realized what was happening.

"Daniel," she called out. Both men ignored her.

Conrad turned to leave the room.

"Stand at attention when I speak to you, soldier."

"Fuck you, Major," Daniel said. He swung his heavy fist with all his might and smashed it into Matthew's chin, snapping his head back and sending him sprawling unconscious backward onto the bed. Daniel went to the door without

163

looking behind him. He slammed it after him and stormed down the hallway to his own room and he flopped back onto his cot.

In the morning he would leave before he was arrested. His anger prevented him from reasoning to the conclusion that leaving was in effect deserting the army. He could not think clearly about it at all.

He could not fall back to sleep. He could not clear his mind of the thought of her in the major's arms. He had to get her away from Nowell. Certainly her family could not know what was going on. It was that knowledge that calmed him finally. He would inform her family of Matthew Nowell's treachery. He knew the major's father lived in Saint John in Canada and he knew that the major hated his father. Certainly the girl's grandfather would respond to the knowledge that the girl was in Boston. He finally understood at last why the major had never written to the family. He was angry with Maggie but he could not blame her for what was happening. He would not tell her family what had developed between her and the major, but he would let them know where she was. He was sure they would seek her out and release her from this bondage. He was sure the major had forced this disgrace on her. It had to be him—only him.

Matthew brought charges against Conrad and arrested him before he could escape. He was imprisoned at Castle Island and from there sent his letter to Stephen.

The response from Saint John came the next spring in the form of a visit from the seventy-four-year-old gentleman. He stayed at a run-down inn, the Cromwell's Head, at the foot of the Charles River bridge on the Boston side with his companion, a black man by the name of Ferryman, and his servant, Jonathan.

The old man sent word through Ferryman to Maggie that he wished to visit her but the rigors of his journey south had exhausted him. He asked if she might visit him.

Maggie was astonished to learn that Matthew's father lived. She had believed that he too was an orphan. Something told her to keep her visit to Stephen Nowell a secret from his son.

Her maid arranged for her to be driven across the bridge and accompanied her into the smelly taproom of the inn.

"Miss Nowell, calling upon Mr. Stephen Nowell, her grandfather," she said to the innkeeper.

"He's expecting her," said the white-faced, unkempt man who operated the Cromwell's Head. "She's to go right up."

Maggie walked up the creaking stairs to the second floor. She knocked on the door.

"Enter," said a deep, booming voice.

She pushed open the door and confronted a large, gray-haired, and finely dressed black man.

"I'm Mr. Nowell's associate, miss," he said. "Stephen, Mr. Nowell, is resting." He pointed over to the high platform bed.

Maggie looked at the pale face of the old man in the bed. He seemed to be sleeping. His eyes were closed. She went over to the bed. She could get a better look at him now. There was a faint scar running through the lid of his left eye. His right arm lay atop the blankets that covered his body but the empty left sleeve of the nightshirt had been tied in a knot at the base of the stump.

As she stared at him, the lids of his eyes flew open. Instantly those steel-blue eyes took her in.

"You're the one claiming to be my grandaughter, Margaret Nowell."

"I am Margaret Nowell," she said.

Stephen started to chuckle. He remembered when he confronted his grandfather so many years ago in almost these same circumstances, and he remembered how gentle old Jonathan Breed had been to him.

"Where is that son of mine?" he asked finally.

Ferryman stepped to Maggie's side. "Major Nowell was called to duty at the Castle," he said.

"Yes, Matthew would take his duties seriously," laughed Stephen. "Well, girl, you sure as hell look like what I've been told my granddaughter looked like, hair and all. If you're not Maggie, you'll have to do until the real thing comes along. Now, why the hell haven't you written to me? Why nothing to your poor mother?"

Maggie gasped and looked away from him. She was afraid of her own answer.

"It's a good question, girl. It deserves a good answer."

"Because until I received your summons this morning, I had no idea that you even existed and I was told that my mother had died among the Indians."

Nowell's face flushed red. "I'll be damned. The man and his hatred have gone too far this time. I'll break him. I'll turn

165

him over to my Indian son for roasting," he yelled, ignoring the fact that his "Indian" son was practicing law in York in Upper Canada.

Maggie raised her hand to silence him. It was effective—to his own amazement. Only Katherine, his wife, had ever told him to shut up in that manner.

"I want to go to my mother," she said. The thought of a mother almost overwhelmed her.

"Then it's done," said Stephen. "You can leave with me."

Maggie hesitated. The offer was enticing, but she knew her uncle's power. Their ship would never leave Boston if he knew that she was aboard. Her heart was hardening against Matthew. He had rescued her from Geyasada and he had cared for her—and loved her. But he had also deceived her. She no longer cared about what happened to him. All she cared about was meeting her mother.

"Thank you for the offer," she replied, "but I could not run off without settling matters here. In the meantime, will you let my mother know that we have met, and tell me how I can find her?"

"Certainly, my dear. Can I tell your mother that you will visit her? Will you be able to find your way to her?"

"I'll find my way. Don't worry."

There was a knock at the door. The cook, a new one, entered Maggie's bedroom.

"The major wonders if you will be joining him for dinner."

"Of course," said Maggie. She ran the silver-handled brush through her hair. First she let it hang down her back, but that was not fashionable in Boston. She lifted it and piled it up on her head and fastened it with pins.

"There'll be a guest for dinner, ma'am. Mr. Adams, the president's son."

She looked at herself in the mirror. The Adamses were such prigs, she thought. Perhaps she should wear her shawl. This dress was too low-cut.

Maggie looked into the dining room. It was a room that had been totally restored to the way Matthew remembered it as a boy, with a giant oak table and a lowboy that served in place of a buffet. The candles were lit and the pewter tableware was in place. Then she left the room and crossed the entryway into the parlor. Matthew stood by the mantelpiece next to a thin, balding man.

166

"Mr. Adams," she called out from the doorway, "I don't believe we have met but it is a distinct honor to welcome you to my uncle's house."

"We have not, Miss Nowell, and it has been years since I have had the pleasure of your uncle's acquaintance. As you know, I've been abroad in the foreign service since before Mr. Washington's election."

"You must know how distressed the major and I were at the news of Mr. Jefferson and Mr. Burr's victory over your father. Although there seems to be some doubt about who it was that defeated him."

"But no doubt that he was defeated."

Matthew looked at Maggie with approval.

"Service in Europe must have been exciting for you," said Maggie.

"The times are dangerous," said Adams. "Bonaparte has created continuous world war in a death struggle with Great Britain and I am afraid we can't help but be dragged in."

"I'll bless that day," said Matthew. "I thought our chance had come back in seventeen ninety-four at Fallen Timbers. If only Wayne had given the word or the British had given the slightest provocation, we would have struck and all of Canada would have been ours. There was nothing to stop us—north of the damned border your father helped Mr. Franklin draw across America in seventeen eighty-three."

"I do recall as a boy, as you must, Matthew, men of our fathers' generation saying precisely the same thing. But if I remember my history, Montgomery and Arnold were stopped then by General Carleton. What guarantees do you offer that the Canadians wouldn't stop us now?"

"We outnumber them ten to one and we have a professional army. They are the ragtag militia now that their imperial masters are tied up in Europe with Bonaparte. Give me an army, Adams, and set me loose at Detroit and I'll not stop until I sit atop Cape Diamond in Quebec City."

Adams laughed. "Wait until you make general, Matt. Then you'll be more cautious. I've seen it happen again and again. The first time you have to worry about how you're going to feed that army, not just fight it, you won't be so anxious to rush off to war. That's the time you'll begin to worry about engineers to build roads for wagons to carry your food. Then you'll be rushing off complaints to the secretary of war about control of the lakes and how you can't move forward until the

167

flanks are secure and demand that the secretary of the navy establish naval supremacy on the waters."

"It wouldn't take that long. Upper Canada is filled with Americans. Give the word and we'll have uprisings all over the colony. It will be a free state and part of this union in a matter of weeks after war is undertaken."

"I hope you're right. Because I'm afraid Britain will not bend to pressure by our government to stop enforcing their Orders in Council and refrain from impressing our seamen."

"I supported General Washington and your father, sir, because they supported the treaty back in seventeen ninety-four."

"That surprises me, Matthew. I would have thought you were in favor of war with Britain. In fact, I thought I just heard you say you wished we'd begun it back in that very same year."

"True, but with no war the treaty was the next best thing. Mr. Jay got the British out of Detroit, Niagara, and Fort Miami. When the war comes we'll have our own boundaries secure and we'll begin it by an invasion of Canada, not by trying to seize a post occupied by British troops that are still sitting on our own soil."

"Well, at least you're consistent. It's war—if not now, at least war later."

Maggie laughed with Adams while Matthew looked away in annoyance.

"Tell me, Mr. Adams, your last post was Berlin, wasn't it? Tell me, are the Prussians as much influenced by French fashion as we are?"

"Everyone in Europe is influenced by French fashion, even the British, although very reluctantly."

"I've been asking my uncle to take me abroad."

"It's no time for that," interrupted Matthew. "There's a war raging there. Haven't you been paying attention to what Mr. Adams and I have been talking about? There will be a war here too."

She placed her arm through his. He tried to back away but she held him tightly.

"Uncle Matthew is so protective."

"I'm afraid your uncle is right," said Adams. "It is no time for the grand tour."

The cook stepped nervously into the parlor and signaled to Maggie.

"Gentlemen, I believe we are ready for the dining room."
Maggie left her uncle's side and took hold of Adams's arm.

"Will you escort me to dinner, Mr. Adams?"

"My pleasure, Miss Nowell," he said with a bow.

Matthew watched them leave the room together. The look of pain on his face was seen by no one. He could not bear to see her pay attention to any other man. She was more withdrawn now. When they first made love she was innocent yet willing. He was the seducer, the perverter of innocence. He could not help himself. Now she was older, less vulnerable, and, he feared, less attracted to him. He gave her everything—lessons in painting, dancing, money for the finest wardrobe in Boston. He spent his savings, his inheritance from Aunt Margaret and his salary as a major in the United States Army, all to keep her happy and to keep her quiet about them and to keep her with him. Yet it seemed the more he gave to her, the more distant she became. Matthew watched Adams and his niece discourse about Europe throughout the evening. He was silent and morose. When they had finished he excused himself and went to the parlor to get some port.

"Major Nowell is very quiet this evening," said Adams as soon as Matthew was beyond hearing range.

"I'm afraid he is always that way," answered Maggie. "It's this service in the tame harbor defenses. My uncle is a man of action, Mr. Adams. This appointment is killing him. I was hoping you could do something for him."

"What have you in mind, Miss Nowell?"

"You have influence in government. Your father is still president. Could you not get someone to reassign him to the west, to Detroit or Niagara?"

Her voice trailed off as Matthew returned to the room with his favorite glass-and-silver decanter of wine carried on a silver tray along with three delicately etched wineglasses.

The cook seems to have gone off to bed. Damn it, Maggie, can't you keep these women on the job?" he said gruffly.

"No bad temper in front of guests, uncle," she chided him lightly.

Nowell growled as he flopped down in his chair. He poured wine for Adams and then looked at his niece. She shook her head.

"The hell with England," Matthew toasted. "And on to Canada."

Adams smiled and lifted the glass to his lips. They sat in an awkward silence for some moments.

"The hour grows very late and my driver must grow very weary," Adams finally said.

He rose from his seat. Maggie rose with him.

"I'll see you to the door, Mr. Adams."

She opened the nail-studded door for him.

"Major Nowell is a fine soldier. His reputation is very high. I believe your request of me for a more active service for him will be considered favorably in the District, although I suspect the new capital is not the place to find government officials. Most still drag their feet in an effort to stay on in Philadelphia. I'll send on your request. It will be in his own best interest. You are a brave and generous young woman."

Maggie blushed.

Adams took his cane from the stand at the door. His driver signaled the horses and drove to the door.

"Take care going down Breed's Hill," Adams said to his driver. "I don't wish to look like Howe at the bottom."

Maggie closed the door and smiled to herself before turning around. The opportunity had arisen and she had grabbed it. She turned to see her uncle, who stood at the foot of the stairs. He had that pleading look in his eye again. Of late she had begun to refuse him, and fairly consistently.

"Maggie," he said softly.

"Uncle, please don't ask me. What we do is so wrong, I can't bear to face myself in the morning."

"Please, Maggie, I need you."

She could hardly bear the pleading. The only thing worse would be the tirade of self-denunciation that would follow. She took pity on him.

9

Stephen awoke in the middle of the night—at least it seemed like the middle of the night; it was still dark. He reached over in the bed to find Katherine. His hand touched only cold sheets and he remembered he was living in the Saint John town house. Katherine had remained behind in the country. He had to use the chamber pot. He had to do that much more often in the middle of the night these days.

"Seventy-six years old," he thought aloud, "and almost back to wetting my breeches."

He found the pot and lifted the front of his nightshirt.

"Damn it," he cursed. He had a strange feeling in the stop of his stomach and a wave of nausea struck him and he threw up right into the chamber pot.

"Wait till I get my hands on that Jonathan in the morning." Jonathan had cooked last night's meal, the first one he had been forced to cook since he joined Stephen's household years before. He had bragged about his cooking abilities. Like a typical Englishman he had overcooked the lamb; worse than that he had made Stephen's stomach sick. Stephen stuck the chamber pot outside the bedroom door and climbed back into his bed.

He missed Katherine. When he couldn't sleep or didn't feel well he would normally lean over and look into her face. His "Are you awake?" was always greeted with a moan and then a sleepy "Yes."

From now on when he had business in town he would insist she come with him.

He turned onto his stomach to see if the pain would go away. These years with his wife had made him frightfully dependent on her. He rarely thought of the years they were apart when she had been in love with another man.

She was still in touch with the son of that relationship, Louis Joseph. He had made her a grandmother five times and was one of the largest landholders on Isle d'Orleans. He never heard from his youngest son, Matthew, but his trip to Boston and his recognition of his granddaughter, who lived with Matthew Nowell, had amused him. She was a shrewd one, this Maggie Nowell. Matthew, poor serious Matthew, had taken on more than he realized. He wished Matthew could love him. He wished he could love Matthew. But all the love intended for his son had been consumed by the boy's mother's death. Abigail Hibbins, his second wife, had died giving birth to their son. He had never forgiven Matthew, and Matthew had never forgiven him for not loving him. It was one of the great sorrows of his life.

Aaron Brant, his oldest child, was now a member of the Assembly in Upper Canada, representing the town of York. He was a lawyer. He had written his father with the news of Molly's death and an account of her burial in Kingston, an occasion for the gathering of Iroquois from Canada and the

United States. He felt her passing deeply. She had been the first woman to whom he had made love. They were children at the time. Her death killed a bit of him. But he was so proud of their son, a good, decent man with a good wife, a son, Michael Brant, and an adopted daughter, Elizabeth.

He and Katherine had but one child together. Their daughter, Amy Nowell Morin, who lived in Amherstburg in Upper Canada across the river from the American fort.

She too had written telling of the growth of her twin sons, distressed that she still had not met with her daughter—or even heard from her.

The pain grew worse and he was struck by another wave of nausea. He rose again and went out into the hall. He threw up a second time into the foul-smelling pot. He had nothing left in his stomach now but was afraid to go back to bed. He sat on the floor in the hall next to the pot. He heaved again and only a foul-tasting bile came up.

"This is ridiculous," he mumbled. He felt very sick. Normally when he felt sick and his belly ached, if he relieved his stomach of its contents he felt better. But not tonight. He rose from the floor and went back to bed. He rubbed the top of his stomach. It seemed to help the pain. He felt feverish. The night seems to drag on forever when you're sick, he thought.

The first rays of sunlight found him sitting back out in the hall. Jonathan nearly tripped over him there, dozing against the wall.

"Mr. Nowell, what is it?"

Stephen awoke with a start. "It's your damned poisoned lamb."

Jonathan lifted him under his arms. "You've a fever, sir. I'm sending for Dr. Grey."

"Oh, God, not that quack again. Why does Katherine put any trust in that man? He's a fool."

"Back into bed with you."

Jonathan helped him walk back toward the large bed. He had difficulty walking. The pain had descended lower into his belly and it had moved to the right side. It throbbed. The walking had not helped at all. The pain was worse. Jonathan eased him onto the bed. He lay back against the pillows feeling exhausted. The pain in his gut was becoming excruciating. He pulled up his knees and his whole right side seemed to burst into flame. He called out in pain and then he

172

felt embarrassed—a man his age moaning like a child over a bellyache.

Jonathan had disappeared. He licked his lips; they were dry and his tongue felt coated. But God, old man or not, his belly hurt like hell. There was a commotion downstairs and he heard the voice of Dr. Grey as he came up the stairs. The door opened and his tormentor walked in.

"Good evening, Mr. Nowell," the doctor said.

"What's good about it?" said Stephen crankily and in great pain.

Grey pulled down the covers and pushed up Stephen's nightshirt.

"Now, what have we here?" said Grey to himself.

"An old man's shrunken dick," said Stephen. "I would have thought they'd have told you what one of those was in medical school. I assume since you don't recognize it you don't have one of your own."

Grey started to press on Stephen's abdomen and ignored Stephen's quips. When he touched the lower right side Stephen yelled in agony.

Grey's face registered instant concern.

"Have you any pain on urinating?"

"Only when I piss," said Stephen. "Jonathan, get this idiot out of here and send word to my wife to come home."

Grey followed Jonathan out of the door.

"Get word to Mrs. Nowell. I believe he may be very ill. It may be a stone, and I pray that is what it is, painful as that ailment is. It is far preferable to what I fear he may have. He may be suffering from an inflammation of the abdomen, a gangrenous condition. If that is what it is, it is fatal. In either case, Mistress Nowell calms him. He is going to suffer and will need her."

Through the whole of the day Stephen lay in his bed in agony. The pains seemed to consume him. He could not stand. He could not turn on his side and he could not move his legs. The terrible white-hot pain was the only thing he was conscious of. He cried out with each throb. It hurt beyond anything in his life he could remember.

Katherine arrived in the afternoon. She rushed to his side. He felt her cool hand holding his hot one. He smiled at her through gritted teeth.

"One meal away from you and your little cook and I get a bellyache."

173

She smiled at him and threw back the hood of her cloak, allowing her gray hair to fall free to her shoulders.

He stared at her. She had not worn her hair like that in years except at nighttime.

"I didn't have any time to fix it," she said when she saw him staring.

"You remind me of a young girl."

"Which one," she jested, "the Indian, the Pole, or the Yankee child?"

"The sad mistreated Dutch girl from Albany with the beautiful gold-tinted chestnut hair and the large hazel eyes—who grew old with me."

He gasped as the pain grabbed him. She held his hand tighter.

"I think this is serious, Katherine. The pain is killing me and it weakens me."

"The doctor wishes you to drink some medicine and he wants to bleed you, Stephen."

"Katherine, do me one last favor. Throw the fool out on his ass."

Grey joined them at the bedside. He held out a cup filled with a vile-smelling thick brown liquid.

Stephen had little strength left to fight him but he turned his head away.

"I'd rather be bled," he said with resignation.

Grey smiled and put the cup down on the nightstand. He went to his leather bag and pulled out his lancet and his basin. He found a prominent vein on the old man's arm and with a flick of the blade he opened it. Blood flowed down into the tray. When he had drawn a sufficient amount, he daubed the vein with a piece of raw cotton and pressed it firmly against the skin.

Stephen looked pale and weary. The pain was growing worse. His whole belly had again become paralyzed with agony. He felt the bile building in his throat again. He gestured to Katherine to get him something. She held the basin in front of him and he vomited, a gray, ugly vomit. He lay back again and smiled at his wife. The pain was totally gone. He let his feet stretch out and his muscles relax.

"Oh, my God," he said finally, "it's gone. What a relief."

Katherine looked on in amazement. She could tell by his eyes that he was no longer hurting.

She called to Grey, who came to her side.

Stephen smiled. "To think all these years I've resisted your damned knives, Grey. There may well be something to all this bleeding. I'm feeling better. I should have let you bleed me this morning and save me the agony of this day. I'm tired," he said to Katherine.

"You sleep. I'll sit with you."

Stephen closed his eyes. Soon the rhythm of sleep took over his breathing.

The sun was setting and its golden rays flooded through the closed shutters. Katherine continued to sit with him long after Dr. Grey had left. She was tired. The journey from South Bay had left her exhausted. She dozed off, her hand entwined with his.

She awoke with a start. She could feel the heat of his hand. The room was dark but Stephen still slept. She rose and went to the bureau across the room and picked up a small hurricane lamp. She left the room and lit the lamp from a candle in the hallway. She raised the lamp next to Stephen's face. He was red and flushed with fever. She ran into the hallway and called to Jonathan to summon Dr. Grey again. Then she went back into the sickroom once more.

Stephen opened his eyes and smiled at Katherine.

"I'm sorry," he whispered.

"For what?" she asked.

"For the times I was not there."

Katherine started to cry. She was losing him. She could feel him slipping away. The time seemed to drag on and Stephen's breathing became labored. His fever was out of control. She took some water from the nightstand pitcher and soaked her handkerchief and placed it on his forehead. Some moments later Dr. Grey entered the room still wearing his coat. He felt Stephen's face and reached for his left hand for a pulse, forgetting that Stephen had no left hand. He walked around the bed to reach Stephen's right side. He waited patiently to count the pulse. He raised Stephen's eyelid. He looked at Katherine in consternation.

"Maybe I should bleed him again," said Grey. "It seemed to work last time."

Katherine merely nodded. She held on to her husband's hand while the physician took another tray of blood from his arm.

The fever continued to rage. During the night Jonathan and Dr. Grey tried to force Katherine to leave and get some sleep but she would not budge. The night dragged on and the fever continued to rise. Stephen moaned softly and occasionally called out. He spoke in French and Katherine started to cry when she realized he thought he was speaking to Karl Stiegler, his blood brother and Katherine's lover so many years ago. Then he lay quietly again. His lips moved. She bent her head to his mouth. He was praying in Latin. She placed her head on his chest and began to cry. His breathing was irregular. He raised his hand and touched her head, stroking her hair, and then his hand fell to his side. His chest did not move any longer. Katherine looked into his face. Tears streamed down her cheeks. She reached up and closed his eyes.

"Good night, husband," she said softly.

Matthew received the letter written in the careful script of Katherine Schuyler Nowell announcing his father's death. It contained a lawyer's statement and a bank letter of credit. Matthew felt indifferent at the news of his father's death, nor did he wish any of his father's money. But Maggie had expensive tastes and she was Stephen Nowell's granddaughter. He would take the inheritance. The sum was enormous. He had no idea his father had been worth so much. One-third of the estate had been left to Katherine for her lifetime. The remaining two-thirds had been divided four ways. One part to Aaron Brant, one part to Matthew Nowell, one part to Amy Nowell Morin, and one part to Louis Joseph Stiegler, Katherine Nowell's son. Even with this division, Matthew now had more money than he knew it was possible to have. As he sat in the parlor of the Breed house looking at the bank draft, Maggie entered the room.

"My father's dead," he said without looking up at her. Maggie felt a pang of sorrow. She had liked the old man. If only Matthew had half of his father's common sense he might be bearable. But there were merchants in Boston who had told her Matthew was a duplicate of his father at the same age. Perhaps there was hope for him yet.

"He left me some money." He handed her the bank draft. Her eyes bulged.

"I'm signing some of this over to your name in trust, right now," Matthew said. "You are his granddaughter and my dependent. If anything should happen to me, and mine is a dangerous profession, there is no guarantee that anything

176

would go to you. My red Indian half brother, for instance, could attempt to take it all."

"You treat me well, uncle, I am content with my lot."

"Nonsense," said Matthew, "I'm putting some in your name."

Maggie smiled and thanked him. Later in the week she discovered that he had placed one-tenth of the total in her trust fund.

One month after the visit of John Quincy Adams, Matthew Nowell received orders to proceed to Detroit and take the post of executive officer to the commandant. He was shocked. Normally such a posting would come only if he himself had requested a transfer, and he had done nothing of the sort. He was happy with his position in Boston. He had had enough of frontier soldiering. The comforts of home could not be given up easily—nor could Maggie, he admitted to himself. He knew she would never leave Boston now; she too loved the social life and the fineries Boston offered. Even if she would go, he could not continue their relationship under the close scrutiny of the fort society.

When he returned to the Charlestown house from the fortress, he found Maggie in the kitchen. She was in a dark green velvet gown that contrasted strikingly with her hair. Matthew had never seen her look more beautiful and more provocative.

He led her into the dining room. "I have been ordered to Detroit," he said with some agitation. "It is a good posting. I'm second in command, with a good chance for actual command and promotion."

Maggie smiled at him. "I'm happy for you, Uncle Matthew," she said softly.

"I suppose I should be happy too, but I can't bear the thought of leaving you."

She looked startled and distressed. "Must I stay here?" She was suddenly frightened that all her planning had got her no closer to her mother.

"Maggie," he said close to tears, "I can't live without you. But I can't live with myself with you. You must stay here."

"I can't," Maggie pleaded. "What would I do on my own?"

Matthew couldn't bear to hear her pleading. He loved her yet he debased her. She looked up into his face. Her pale complexion highlighted her coloring and the light from the candles reflected in her eyes.

"Please, Uncle Matthew, by all that's sacred, take me with you."

Matthew wanted her. He wanted her right on this spot. But he knew he could not do that to her. She thought of herself as the seducer, the temptation to sin, while he knew all along that it had been his lust. He was right. He must insist, for her sake, that she stay behind and in Boston.

She started to weep. "Maybe you better not take me after all," she said. "I'm better off alone again. I was alone and so poor for so many years when that Indian, he did things to me."

"No one will abandon you," said Matthew, relenting. "You'll be with me."

Maggie sank into a chair. "I'm so frightened, Uncle Matthew. I don't know if I can face the future."

He could see the fear in her eyes and he knew that he was doing the right thing. He vowed to make the most of his new position. It would allow him to further his dream of regaining America's rightful lands. Meanwhile, he would keep Maggie secluded. She would be his and his alone.

They traveled west along the Mohawk until near its head-waters and then they switched to wagon along the bumpy wilderness road to the small community at Buffalo. Maggie recognized no one among the many Indians who still lived in the town and clearly none of them could have recognized her. She had changed so much. She dressed in the finest gowns and the best travel cloak that money could buy. What had surprised Matthew was that she had taken only one trunk of clothes with her. Finery would be hard to obtain in the middle of the wilderness. Perhaps she had resigned herself to a simpler life in Detroit.

They boarded the small sailing vessel at Buffalo. With favorable winds they sailed the two-hundred-mile length of Erie quickly. They saluted the new British fort at Amherstburg but worked their way past its guns cautiously. They had to fight the current of the Detroit River until they reached the American fort. Above the British-built garrison houses and redoubts, on a site first occupied by the forces of Louis XIV a century earlier, the American flag now flew. The fort had been turned over to the United States legally in 1783. But not until 1796, two years after signing another treaty, did British forces abandon it and cross the river into Canada.

Matthew stood at the ship's railing as the crew brought it to the dock. He looked across the river at Canada—his goal. Someday he would raise that same flag on the other side of the river and beyond. He heard his name called from the dock. He recognized the voice first. Then he saw Ethan Morin waving. Next to him stood Amy. He had not seen them over a decade and he had not written to them either. How did they know to expect him? What could he say to them? Did they know about Maggie? Before he had time to think of answers to these questions the plank connecting the wharf with the ship was in place. Amy came rushing up it just as Maggie, dressed in a simple blue dress, far simpler than anything she would have worn in Boston, climbed the stairs from the cabin below to the open deck.

Amy stopped short when she saw the grown woman in front of her. Her last view of Maggie had been that of a terrified four-year-old. But Amy did not remain in a trance for very long. Tears welled in her eyes and she rushed to her daughter and closed her into her protective arms. Both women were crying now. Ethan climbed aboard and walked over to Matthew.

"How are you, Matt? It's been a long time since I last saw you. They've been pretty excited at our place ever since Maggie wrote to us and told us you were coming west. Just got the letter last week. It's kind of like the end of a long nightmare for Amy. But, Matt, we have some hard questions to ask you. She has been in your care for a long time—and not a word from you."

Matthew was stunned to learn that it was Maggie herself who had written to Amy. Then it dawned on him that she had contrived the whole trip. He tried desperately to find an answer to Ethan's questions. The truth was too painful—even to him. "Ethan," he answered finally, "until the girl spoke English, I didn't know the full story. I had only suspicions. I could not arouse false hopes on the basis of vague suspicions."

"Hardly vague, Matt. A red-haired girl living with western Indians. There can't be too many of them. You had grounds to be strongly suspicious and we had a right to know."

Matthew looked away from Ethan and stared at the ramparts of the fort as if searching them for defects. "I was lonely, Ethan. I don't know if you know what that means. You've got a wife and sons. I have no one. Even my father abandoned me."

179

"That's not how Amy tells it," Ethan interrupted.

"What does she know? She had her family growing up. She left it of her own free will."

"Seems to me that your father abandoned her too."

"All this is beside the point. I needed a child of my own."

"You could have gone about doing that the normal way."

Matthew ignored him. "By the time I realized the girl was Maggie, I was deeply attached—too attached," he added cryptically, "to give her up to you."

"You had no right! You kept her from her own mother."

Matthew was ashamed—but he was more ashamed of what he did not tell Ethan. "You're right," he said angrily. "I was wrong. I know it now. I'm always wrong. I was selfish. I'm always selfish."

"I can understand your needs, Matt. I just find it hard to forgive your indulging them at your sister's expense."

Matthew grew quiet.

"We'll work it out, Matt. What's important now is that Maggie's here."

While the men were talking, Amy pushed forward her teen-age sons to greet their sister. Both boys were embarrassed when Amy insisted they kiss Maggie. She in turn hugged them both. Then Maggie took Amy by the arm and led her down the gangplank. Matthew watched the two women talking. He dreaded to think what they spoke of. He never wanted this meeting. He wanted Maggie all for himself. He should have insisted she stay in Boston. Yet then he would not have had her at all.

Amy had arranged a homecoming party at their farmhouse. But Matthew insisted that, since he was the acting commander at Detroit, he could not leave the country without permission and without invitation from his counterpart at Amherstburg. He was shocked when Maggie shrugged her shoulders and announced that Amy's invitation was good enough for her and that of course she would visit her mother's home.

Maggie had not been in a canoe since her return to the world of the whites. She was impressed by the way her two young brothers handled the craft—especially the one in the rear. She thought he was Stephen. They looked so much alike, it was hard to tell them apart. The canoe seemed to fly over the surface of the Detroit River. Maggie turned around and looked at her mother, Amy Nowell Morin. Amy's husband sat behind her and was holding on to her shoulders. She caressed one of his hands with her own. She smiled at Maggie but said nothing.

The boys steered the canoe toward the Canadian shore. Up ahead a small river entered the Detroit. The canoe aimed straight for its mouth. They beached the craft only a few yards upriver. Ethan hopped out and steadied the craft with one hand. He offered the other to Amy and then to Maggie as they stepped ashore. Charles followed them shyly up the path toward the Morin farmhouse. Stephen remained behind. After they disappeared from his sight, he pushed the craft back out into the river. He was determined to bag a few ducks for their evening meal.

"Stevie, the ducks were just perfect," said Amy as she cleared the dishes from the table. Maggie rose to help her.

"Sit still," said Amy. "You're company and company doesn't clear the table."

She saw the hurt look on Maggie's face and rushed to her and threw her arms about her. "I'm sorry, Margaret," she cried. "You help with the chores all you want. You're one of us now."

The two women hugged for some time, grabbing tightly and holding each other in an embrace.

"Come into the kitchen with me," Amy said finally.

Amy dumped the dishes—her good dishes that she had received from her great-aunt Margaret Schuyler—into a giant wooden tub filled with hot water and soap.

"Duck has so much fat in it," Amy said. "I prefer chicken to duck any day. But I can't send Stevie out shooting chickens. We'd have the neighbors down on us." She sat down on a stool. "Let me look at you, girl," she said, taking Maggie's two hands in her own. "I had given up on ever seeing you again. The day your uncle Aaron and my Ethan returned without you—that may have been the worst day of my life. When I heard Matt had you with him, I didn't believe it at first. I couldn't believe that he would have kept you all to himself for so long."

Maggie swallowed hard. "I have to talk to you about him, mother."

"Who? Matthew? He's a sad man. He was a sad boy before

that. My father was a terrible mother. Poor soul, he wasn't much of a father to any of us either. What about Matthew?"

"I don't quite know what to say except that I came here to get away from him."

Amy looked at her quizzically.

"I don't know how to say this." She began to weep.

Amy pulled the girl closer to her. "What is it, Margaret? You can tell me."

Maggie hitched up all her courage. "We've been intimate, mother. Lovers."

Amy pushed Maggie to arms' length. "My brother and you," she repeated in shock, "lovers? I'll kill him for this, the scum."

"Don't blame him, mother," Maggie begged. "It's not his fault. I needed him as much as he needed me. I suppose in a way I loved him. I still do. Except that now I'm ashamed. I want to end it. But he won't. He begs me. He cries like a little boy. And I give in. I haven't the strength. I had to come to you, mother. Once I knew that you existed, I knew I needed you. I need your help, your strength."

Amy hugged her newfound child again. Maggie's grief seemed to take possession of her body. She seemed consumed by her weeping. Her whole body shook. Amy merely held on to her, rubbing her back softly with her free hand.

"You can't return to Detroit," Amy said finally.

"I have to. I have nowhere else, no one else."

Now it was Amy's turn to look hurt. "You have me, and your family here. You can stay with us."

"Oh, mother. I had hoped you'd say that, but I'm still not sure I can face starting over again. I'm not sure I have the strength."

"Of course you have, child, but perhaps it would be better if you were not so near to Matthew. Perhaps you should get away from him entirely." Tears now streamed down Amy's cheeks. "I'll arrange it, Margaret. Do you still think of Boston as your home?"

Maggie nodded.

"Then that is where you must go. You are to receive your share of your grandfather's inheritance immediately. You're to take it back to Boston with you. You are no longer Matthew Nowell's dependent—and no longer the plaything for his lusts."

"Mother, understand me, please. I'm no innocent girl. I've

182

had men since before my body was ready for them and I have loved Matthew of my own free will."

"He never forced himself on you?" Amy asked.

Maggie was silent. Finally she said, "The first time."

Amy shook her head. "He's your own blood, Margaret," she said.

"I know it's wrong."

"Then end it. Go back to Boston. Go there your own person—wealthy, beholden to no man—especially your uncle. Leave him here in this wilderness to brood over his sins."

"But then I'll lose you, mother, just when I've found you."

Amy wiped the tears from her cheek with her hand. She felt the joy of the past week and especially of this day come crashing down about her. She hated her brother now with all the passion that had built up inside her.

"There is no alternative," she said finally. "And I'll be happy just knowing you're free." She grabbed her daughter as if the tightness of the grip would make it impossible for her to follow the advice she had given her. "You've no alternative."

"How can I face the family?" Maggie asked.

"They'll question me. But they'll get no answers," said Amy. "You must start all over again, as I have done already twice in my life. You must have the strength. Now let's dry our eyes and get to work."

They washed and dried Amy's dishes in silence. Finally Maggie reentered the party room. After she left, Amy's body sagged. Her hands went to her face. "Oh, my God," she sobbed. "It's not fair. I've just found her. I can't lose her again. Please, dear God," she prayed, "at least let me have her with me for a little while. So help me God, Matthew Nowell, I'll never forgive you for this."

Maggie was very quiet as Matthew escorted her from the dock to their quarters. Once in the commandant's house, he took her cloak from her as she removed her gloves. Finally she turned to him.

"Matthew, I'm going back to Boston."

He looked at her in disbelief. "But we've just arrived."

She was silent. Then finally she said, "It's over, Matthew. I've spoken to my mother about us, all of it."

"You told her all of it?"

Amy nodded. "She is a fine person. She did not condemn me. She understood."

"What does she think of me?"

"I tried to dissuade her from it, but I believe she truly hates you, Matthew. She told me she would tell no one else—not even Ethan—but only if you stay away from me. If you come after me again, she will be forced to tell both Ethan and Aaron. And as she put it, they will come and kill you."

Matthew swallowed hard. He deserved this. Amy had every right to feel as she did about him.

"It pained my mother greatly—pained her beyond my ability to comprehend—but she was the one who told me I must return to Boston. She said that even Amherstburg is not far enough. If you were close by, in Detroit, I could never be free. She's right. I am going home to Charlestown. I really only came because I wanted to see my family—my mother and my brothers. I don't think I can forgive you either, Matthew, for keeping them from me."

"I love you, Maggie, I wanted you. I was afraid you would go away."

"As I shall, uncle. As I shall."

Three days later, she set sail back to Buffalo aboard the same vessel that had brought her. On the long trip back she thought over what her mother had said. She could begin again. A plan began to take shape in her mind.

As soon as she arrived back in Boston she wrote her grandfather's old associate, Josiah Ferryman, asking him to call on her the next time he was in the vicinity. Maggie had met Ferryman before, when she first met her grandfather. But now she approached him not as a frightened girl but as a wealthy woman of the world.

"Mr. Ferryman," said Maggie.

"Call me Josiah," he interrupted.

"Josiah, what I offer you is the return of your firm to the United States using me as a front."

"You don't know the first thing about trade. What makes you think you can do anything for me and your grandmother?"

"I learned a great deal listening to my uncle. He often explained to me the ways unscrupulous merchants got the products in and out of the harbor. I offer you entry into the American market. You give me a ship and I will meet the sister ship on a spot designated by you. My ship will wait and we'll make the switch. After an appropriate length of time my ship will return to Boston after a successful voyage. I get twenty percent of the profit."

"I know the scheme. You know you'll be violating the law."

"So will you."

"American law. I'll be safely in New Brunswick if you're caught. Nothing will happen to me."

"Does that mean your answer is no?"

"Nonsense," said Josiah, "it's good business. We'll all get rich. If the good fathers of this stinking commonwealth who robbed Mr. Nowell of what was his lose a few shekels, so be it. It reminds me of some of the things his mother did in her day. I think you've got the makings of a true Nowell, my girl. I wish your grandfather had lived to see this day."

Maggie smiled. She would celebrate this night.

Her grandfather's old partner left Boston without seeing her again.

A few months later Maggie's first ship set sail for the West Indies and returned in record time loaded with West Indian sugar. She undersold every merchant in Boston. She was selling West Indian sugar cut off to Americans by the treaties of 1787 and 1794 but very much available to a New Brunswick merchant. But as far as the Boston officials knew, this was an American ship returning with high-priced sugar from the French West Indies that was sold by its owner at incredible losses. The crew kept quiet. They were the best-paid crew in New England, and to a man they signed on for a second voyage. The only danger the crew ran was from impressment, and Maggie was quick to insist that all of her crew be American-born, with birth certificates. She would hide no deserters from the Royal Navy. She did not need prize courts or customs scrutiny of her papers in Halifax or in Boston.

The first successful venture led to the second, and the profits of the second, after sending the backer his eighty percent, were invested in a second ship. This one, a swift brig, was outfitted legally. It sailed to southern Europe, escaped French privateers off the coast of Spain, and made it to the port of Lisbon loaded with port and madeira, in desperate short supply in New England because of the war in Europe. The brig dodged the patrols of the Royal Navy that were attempting to enforce Orders of Council against trade with France. It ran the gauntlet back to Boston and made a killing. Within two years Maggie Nowell was a wealthy woman and one of Boston's elite.

III

The Patriot Sons

1812

10

The orchard was in bloom. White and pink petals were everywhere. The short, heavy-trunked apple trees planted by French settlers generations before were thick with them. And the ground at their base reminded Amy almost of the first early fall snows.

The wet winds would come down from Lake Huron and swirl among the trees in a few short days and the petals that hadn't already fallen would be blown off, to be replaced by the hearty green-and-silver leaves.

Amy sat on the front porch of her farmhouse—a house that had been her home for over twenty-five years. Ethan had built it. She remembered him, strong-muscled, stripped to the waist, sweating in the hot sun, nailing boards from the mill to the wood frame. She remembered her two towhead sons, not more than toddlers, getting in his way but convinced that they were helping, feeling so grown-up as they handed him handfuls of nails whether he needed them or not.

She put down the potato she was peeling and looked at her red hands. "Old woman's hands," she said aloud. "Well, out here at sixty a woman could be regarded as ancient."

When she came here, those many years ago, right after the war, she was still young, recently widowed, and looking to find her daughter, Margaret, stolen from her by the Indians. Ethan was an officer in the American army. As soon as they crossed the British line he had been interred for the duration of the war and then he had been paroled. They had traveled west, relying on Aaron Brant, her half brother, to find the Senecas who had stolen Margaret. The British still controlled Detroit and the whole area of the lakes, and they would continue to control it for another thirteen years.

They settled the land abandoned by the French *habitants* and began to farm. The chaplain at Detroit, up the river from Amherstburg, married them. Several years had passed with no word of the fate of her former husband and Amy felt free to marry again. She loved Ethan and he had always loved her.

Aaron tracked down Margaret's whereabouts and then she too disappeared—not to resurface for almost ten years. It was a terrible sorrow to Amy that her brother, Matthew, had seen fit to keep Margaret from her. It had estranged her from her brother forever. When she finally recovered her daughter, she had learned of her relationship with Matthew and she had lost her again. Now she was a great lady in Boston. Matthew himself for the past decade had been at Fort Detroit just across the river, but Amy had never seen fit to see him or he, her. Ethan had spent evenings with Matthew sitting up late into the night drinking, but her brother, her half brother, was not welcome in her home. She had never told Ethan or anyone what Margaret had revealed to her.

As much as her separation from Margaret was painful to her, watching her sons grow was her greatest joy. Her twin sons were in many ways a mystery to her. They looked so much alike and yet they were, in so many ways, very different. Charles was quiet, soft-spoken, and serious. He had fallen in love with boats and ships as a boy. Amy could recall having to fetch him from the river's edge. He would sit for hours watching the canoes and *bateaux* come up the Detroit from Lake Erie. When schooners first appeared on the lake, the boy's fancy was totally captured. On that day she lost him to the inland seas.

As soon as he was old enough to leave home he signed aboard a British merchant vessel as a cabin boy. He had come back to port many times since but he had left just as often. He was master of his own schooner, *Sophia*. He purchased it with money his mother had lent him after his grandfather's death. He sailed the lakes from Fort Erie at the headwaters of Niagara to Amherstburg. Sometimes he sailed past the American guns at Detroit and went up into Lake Huron and beyond into Lake Superior to pick up furs for his brother.

Stephen Miller, Charles's twin, was a vivacious, loud, hard-drinking, hard-fighting fur trader in the old Detroit tradition. He too had profited from his grandfather and namesake's death. He had his own trading post at the island of Michilimackinac. There was an American fort on that island, and American troops, and it was technically American soil, but Stephen did not care. While Charles was an out-and-out anti-American, Stephen paid little attention to politics. Amy's sympathies from childhood had been with the American cause, and her husband, the boys' stepfather, had been an American officer in the revolution. While both of her sons thought of themselves as Canadians, only Charles prided himself on being a true British subject and was as hostile to Americans as her brother Matthew was to the British.

The traffic on the river heading from the upper lakes to Detroit and to Amherstburg on the Canadian side was heavy. The winter catch was being hauled to market in exchange for trade goods and provisions for a new season. Amy expected Stephen to return at any moment. She had not seen him since fall, and without him her life was not filled with the happiness that it seemed only he could engender in her.

Charles too should be returning from Niagara in the *Sophia* before many more days.

Amy sighed when she heard Ethan call from the barn. He would want help with the cows and Amy was tired of helping with the cows. She wished her sons would come home and regale her with some of the stories of their exciting adventures—not too exciting. She suspected that neither of them in their private lives could meet the standards set by the curé of her girlhood or for that matter meet the standards set by their father, her dead husband. That part of their lives could remain secret, but meeting with government officials at Fort Erie with the latest gossip from York or even Kingston or Montreal—that news Charles gave to her. That was exciting and she could not wait to hear it. Stephen's news was just as exciting, but after her captivity in the last war it was just a bit frightening to her. He spoke of this Wyandot chief or the Sioux battles with the Ojibwa.

Ethan called again. She rose and walked off the porch, following the path in back of the house through the kitchen garden. The onions were already up and the melon hills showed tiny sprouts. Before long she would have to weed the weak ones and make room for the vines that would soon cover the ground. Beyond the low rickety fence that protected her vegetables from wild rabbits there were several acres of newly plowed fields. Ethan would have them in corn before the month was out.

She found her husband in the barn seated beside Dolly, their best cow. Stevie had named her last year when they purchased her. He said she reminded him of the newspaper accounts of the American president's lively wife.

191

Ethan had aged far more than she. The harshness of Canadian winters seemed to take their toll on this South Carolinian. She still thought of him as from Carolina, and he still retained the soft drawl of the American South in his speech. His hair had gone white and his shoulders stooped a bit.

"Amy, can you take care of Ilsa? I've got to get back to the plowing while we still have a few hours of daylight."

Amy grabbed the second milking stool and pail and sat down and reached under their other cow. They had too much milk now the boys were grown up. They could take it to the village at Amherstburg or to the fort for sale. But more often than not Amy made cheese. It was easier to keep than butter or yogurt. But they certainly had a bountiful supply of fresh milk.

On other occasions Ethan took the road to Sandwich with his milk pails. If he didn't sell it all there, he hired a boat to cross the river to Fort Detroit. He could always rely on Colonel Nowell to buy it from him.

Amy didn't understand Matthew's generosity. He hated Canadians, and his hatred, she assumed, extended to Canadian milk and Canadian cows as well. But he always purchased the Morin milk when it was offered. It became part of their fixed revenue. Surplus milk would go to Detroit for the American army.

When Amy had finished on Ilsa, she poured her pail into Ethan's larger one. Ethan would be off to the village four miles south of them or he would take the longer trek ten miles to the north to Sandwich or Detroit. As he left the barn he held the door for her.

"Come on, old girl," he said softly, "we got room for only Dolly and Ilsa in here."

"Ethan Morin," she said in mock outrage, "who are you calling a cow?"

"Well, you have put on a little in the rump," he said, patting her behind. She skipped away from his hand.

"But you're too frisky for a cow, more like a filly," he joked. Then he put his arm about her shoulder and they walked up the path through the garden to the house.

They had been lovers for almost thirty years and Ethan's arm about her felt almost as if it were part of her being. He was the third man in her life. The love of her girlhood, Antoine Gingras, her childhood sweetheart, had drowned in the American attack on Quebec. She had left Canada and fled

192

to her father's old home on the Mohawk. Here, Antoine's child, Margaret, was born and here she met Kurt Miller, the Quaker and the father of her twin sons. He had disappeared in the Iroquois attack on their home and she had been abducted by the Iroquois. Her half brother, Aaron Brant, had saved her and the boys and allowed them to return behind the American lines. Ethan, who had served with Antoine in one American army and with her brother Matthew in another, had come to her side in her hour of need. He had taken on the care of her sons and she thought of him as their father. She came to love him, not with the passion of a girl—that had been for Antoine—and not with the passion of dependency, the almost daughterlike affection she had given to Kurt; their love was more like the love of equals, calm and steady but deep.

Ethan placed a pail of milk by the door of Amy's root cellar. It was dark and cool and the milk would keep there.

"I've got but a few more rows to plant and then all the corn will be in. Then I'll be heading up toward Sandwich."

"You mean Detroit, don't you? I know you'll be staying the night with my brother."

"I've asked you often enough to come with me. Matt's a good enough fellow."

"He doesn't want to see me," she said.

"He asks about you. Why do you blame him still? What them Indians did to Margaret unnerved her. She's a grown woman now and she makes her own decisions. She could be here if she wanted to be."

"I'll never see my daughter again," she responded bitterly.

"But it isn't Matt's fault."

She did not answer him.

"We should be more of a family, but Matt can't cross the border."

"He won't, you mean. He's afraid to soil his feet on Canadian dirt."

"Times are tense, Amy. You know damned well that both sides of the river are on pins and needles. General Harrison's defeat of Tecumseh's savages at the Wabash and the Shawnee's war on the frontier have all of us nervous. War could break out at any time."

"As it could have in seventeen ninety-four after Fallen Timbers and in eighteen ought seven when the British fired on the Chesapeake. It didn't come then and I don't think it will come now."

"It's different now, Amy. It's westerners, Indian-hating, Canadian-hating westerners—Ohio men, Kentucky men, Tennessee men. They control the American Congress now. I don't think Mr. Madison will be able to resist their force."

"Mr. Jefferson did."

"As I said, Jefferson didn't have to deal with that war-mongering, brag-playing Henry Clay. And look at our boys, especially Charles. They're typical of the men on this side of the border. I'm not so sure our youngsters would mind taking a few shots across the river."

Amy was silent for a moment. "It doesn't change anything," she said. "Matthew owed me." She raised her voice in anger. "He took my Margaret and he never gave her back. All my life I've been plagued by brothers and their selfishness. Louis Joseph cost me Antoine by his stupid attempt to join the American army. If Antoine had not promised my mother to bring Louis Joseph back he might still be alive."

Ethan looked a bit uncomfortable.

She looked at him and the anger died with her. "It doesn't mean I don't love you, Ethan, when I speak of Antoine and Kurt."

She had told him this often and she knew it had real effect. But he did not like to hear her speak of her lover and her husband.

"Well," she said with resignation in her voice, "if you must be off, then be off."

She would sleep alone this night but she would sleep with the door locked and a pistol under her pillow. She did that any night when left alone—ever since that night of blood, fire, and death on the Mohawk so many years before.

Charles Miller hated riding horses. He had never been comfortable aboard any conveyance other than a ship on the water. The journey down the Niagara River from Fort Erie was one he had not expected to make. But as soon as *Sophia* docked at the wharf at Fort Erie a soldier of the Forty-ninth delivered a note to him. It was from his uncle, Aaron Brant, member of the House of Assembly. He was to come to Newark on the Lake Ontario end of the river and he was to come as soon as possible.

Charles had met his uncle on only one occasion when the

dark-skinned, strangely blue-eyed man had visited his mother. He was a little boy at that time, hardly interested in relatives. But his uncle, despite the paucity of meetings, had always taken a strange interest in his brother and in him. They could always count on him to use his considerable influence among the York elite who governed the province of Upper Canada should licenses be needed or exceptions made. His mother told him it stemmed from his Iroquois background. Uncles played an important part in the life of boys among the Iroquois.

When Uncle Aaron summoned, Charles Miller obeyed. He took a boat to Chippem downriver, but below Chippewa were the falls of the Niagara River and boats could go no further. He hired a horse and would suffer the indignity of a sore rump in the days that followed.

The road from Chippewa to Queenston ran along the bluffs overlooking the falls and gorge of the Niagara. Charles had heard and seen the falls before but they always awed him. The road rose from Queenston Heights and ran down into the village. It was a tiny spot with a handful of quaint clapboard houses, each with its own garden along four or five cross streets that divided the main road—the way north to Fort George. Charles wasted no time in the village. A reminder of the tenseness of the times they lived in could be seen from the American side of the gorge. Here was located the American town of Lewiston, dominated by Fort Grey, its guns pointed across the gorge at Queenston. He rode the six miles from Queenston to Newark rapidly. At Fort George, about a mile south of Newark, he could see old Fort Niagara on the American side of the river. Many a time he had heard his countrymen curse the day when the old fort on the American side of the border was turned back to the Americans by the king. The threat to their peace would come from those places, Detroit, Niagara, and Fort Miami.

At Fort George Charles was stopped. His uncle, he was told, had ridden south to meet him and could be found in the commander's quarters.

Charles stabled his horse and walked awkwardly across the parade ground to Lieutenant Colonel Meyers's quarters. The sentry on duty opened the door for him just as if he were expected. His uncle greeted him in the front office. He looked older, his black hair was cut short but he had streaks of silver in it, and he had thickened in the middle; in fact, he had a decided portliness to him.

He greeted Charles warmly and threw his arm about his shoulders.

"How is your mother?"

"Well."

"And your scoundrel brother? From what I hear of you, I find it difficult to believe that you two bounced into life at the same time from the same womb."

"I haven't seen or heard from Stevie since before the winter."

"And you won't hear from him as long as the whiskey and women are plentiful where he is holed up. But enough. There is someone I want you to meet."

He walked to the door on the far side of the room. He knocked on it. A brisk voice called out, "Enter."

Aaron pushed open the door and allowed Charles to step in ahead of him.

"Sir," he said, "this is my nephew Charles, the ship's master. This is Major General Isaac Brook, administrator of the province and commander of His Majesty's forces in Upper Canada."

The man confronting Charles was enormous. He towered over his uncle, who was at least five-foot-ten. Brock, Charles estimated, must be at least six-foot-three. He was dressed in a scarlet uniform covered with gold braid. He fixed his blue eyes on Charles and extended his hand. Charles shook hands but it did not feel to him that it was a greeting of equals. The general extended his hand as a prelate extended his for the veneration of the faithful. There was a haughtiness and a sense of superiority about the man that made Charles feel suddenly smaller.

"You are the young man with the ship I want."

In an instant Charles knew he no longer controlled his destiny or the fate of his beloved *Sophia*.

"Yes, sir" was all he could manage.

"That's a good fellow," Brock said in his strange British accent. "You are to take some troops. How many can you carry?"

"Where, sir?"

"To Amherstburg."

"If they don't mind sleeping on deck, perhaps a hundred."

"Take one hundred and fifty."

"Yes, sir."

196

"And you'll carry as cargo military supplies to the garrisons there."

"Yes, sir. When do I leave?"

"At any moment. In fact, if anyone dares to stop you going or on your return, you are to assume war has broken out and you are to fire on them."

"I have no guns, sir."

"Brant, you are to fix that. Get Meyers to set up a gun for the boy. Take it from the *Chippewa*. She has enough for Lake Ontario where she sails."

"Yes, General."

"Here, this is your commission. Your appointment by me commissions your ship in His Majesty's Provincial Marine. You leave within the hour—a forced ride back to Lake Erie and you sail as soon as your troops, supplies, and guns arrive."

"Yes, sir," said Charles, still stunned.

"I must be off now. Back to York. Are you coming, Brant?"

Aaron smiled. This man was enormously restless and filled with energy. It boded well for the future of Canada in the coming war.

"By the way, Brant," said Brock. "He's a good man, just as you said."

Brock left the room and entered the outer office. "Meyers," he called out, "we haven't all night. We should be sailing within the hour."

Then he went out the front door. The sentry snapped to attention but the general was already several steps past him onto the parade ground before the guard had completed the salute.

Charles stared openmouthed. Aaron patted him on the shoulder.

"High praise for a Canadian from Isaac Brock," laughed Aaron. " 'A good man.' The general doesn't much care for us. He wishes every one of us could be replaced by a hard-bitten soldier of the Forty-ninth—his own regiment, but he's stuck with us and with my former comrades, the red men. Without the militia and without Tecumseh's warriors the Americans will attack from Detroit, march up the Thames, and attack our Niagara frontier from the front and the rear."

"I've heard that before, uncle, but isn't that a bit foolish? Shouldn't they concentrate on Montreal or Kingston? If they fall, the whole province is cut off from the St. Lawrence lifeline to Great Britain and we will wither and die here on the lakes. They need not attack us at all."

"You're right. But they will attack us from Detroit and Niagara. Those fire-eating young Turks from the west in the American Congress will demand it. They want easy victories in the northwest and they outnumber us. They want no tough nuts to crack like the defenses of Kingston harbor. What's more, they want victory with lots of Indian corpses. They'll be hard to find in Montreal. Brock will have to face a push from Niagara here and from Detroit. He'll have to wait and see where. Waiting doesn't come easy to him. I'm convinced that the reports of a large American army under William Hull, coming up from the Ohio and Kentucky frontier to the Maumee, indicate that that thrust will come from Detroit. Brock will leap to that conclusion also. He'll put his Canadians on the Niagara line and rush west to Amherstburg. You'll spend the summer doing ferry duty along with every other British boat on Lake Erie."

"Mother and Ethan should be persuaded to come east," thought Charles aloud.

"You won't succeed in that," said Aaron. "But if you try, tell them my home in York is open to them. Jessica and I will be delighted to put them up. Michael is in the militia—the York Volunteers. I doubt if he'll be home this summer."

The door to Colonel Meyers's quarters opened again and Charles found himself staring at the young girl who entered. At least he thought she was a young girl. She had no figure to speak of and she was dressed in pants.

"Father," she said, "General Brock won't wait for us if we don't get a move on."

"Yes, my dear. Charles, I believe you do not know my daughter. I like to describe her as the most intelligent thing Elisha Stoddard ever did in his life. This is Elizabeth Stoddard, also the daughter of my closest friend, Eli Stoddard. Actually, Jessica and I raised her—despite Eli, who put many obstacles in our path. But she will one day be a proper young lady, even if right now . . . ?"

Charles looked at her. His horror at her pants was very evident on his face.

Elizabeth turned her back on him.

"Thomas, General Brock calls."

"You run, Liz. Tell him I'm coming."

She gave Charles a withering look and ran out the door.

"I don't think she likes you, my boy," said Aaron.

"I found her baffling," responded Charles. "Why this 'Thomas' business? Why the pants?"

"You'd have to know Eli to understand. He was in his late sixties when he took this girl in. Her mother died in childbirth. Her father . . ." He shrugged his shoulders. "Who knows? The woman came to his office too far gone for Eli to save. But he saved the baby and he never gave her up. He told Jessica that she'd have to serve as substitute mother and I would be substitute father. He said he himself was personally unfit to be her father. For himself, he took the role of benevolent spoiler. He is a bit odd, old Eli. She said once in his presence that she wished she was a boy. He said, 'Be one,' and treated her as a boy as long as she wanted. It lasted a long time. I thought my wife would go out of her mind. Liz cropped her hair, she wore breeches, climbed trees with the old man smiling and looking on benevolently. Then one day it was over. She decided to be a girl again. And he accepted that too. But we've never been quite able to get her out of the pants. She says they are more practical and more comfortable. Finally, if you want to know what I think," he leaned over and whispered to Charles, "the loincloth is best of all."

"What about Thomas?"

"That's Eli again. It's what he calls me. I don't even remember why, but once he decides something he rarely changes. But Eli is my dearest friend. Because of him, Jessica and I found our most precious possessions—Moishe, Jessica's father, until he died five years ago, and Michael, our son. All of them we owe to Eli. But I must be off, Charles. Brock will set sail as he said. In fact, when it comes to doing what he says he plans to do, there is much of Eli in Isaac."

Matthew was informed that his brother-in-law was crossing the river. Darkness had set in and the sentries during these tense times were especially alert. If war should be declared, Matthew was acting commander of the garrison and acting military governor of the village surrounding the log fort. He had every intention of crossing the river in force and seizing the town of Sandwich and silencing the British gun battery there. That would give the Army of the Northwest under General Hull, currently struggling through the wilderness swamps on the way to Detroit, a foothold for an invasion.

They had left Urbana in the Indiana territory (sixteen hundred men, twelve hundred Ohio and Kentucky volunteers, and four hundred regulars of the Fourth Infantry). Everything depended on their arriving on time. A strong American army controlling the water routes to the north and to the west and sitting astride the straits of Detroit would discourage any Indians from taking up the British cause. The madman, Tecumseh, could preach all he wanted to; no one would listen. And without Indians the British simply didn't have the manpower to break an American invasion. Hull could capture Amherstburg and then push on to strike the Niagara frontier from the rear.

Lake Erie, controlled by the British gunboats, would be a problem. An American line of supply would stretch terribly far. He laughed aloud. He recalled the conversation he had with Quincy Adams. His friend had predicted that with advance rank he would become more cautious. But he liked to think he was not too cautious. If only Hull would arrive and if only war would be declared, he would not be forced to sit inside this giant square of logs waiting to do something—waiting for word, waiting for the Army of the Northwest.

Matthew greeted Ethan at the waterfront. They shook hands and walked together back into the fort, to the commandant's quarters—but not until he gave orders to the sutlers to purchase Ethan's milk.

"You're moving out?" Ethan asked as he stepped into Matthew's sitting room. Most of his personal possessions had been packed in trunks. Matthew walked over to the trunks and patted one of them with his hand.

"You do collect an amazing number of things in a decade living in one place. Yes, I am moving into different quarters. I expect to be relieved by someone of higher rank any day now."

"It's coming, isn't it?" asked Ethan. "It's finally coming after all these years of waiting."

Matthew smiled. "I think so, Ethan. We're going to drive the damned British off this continent and bring democracy to Upper Canada."

"There's no democracy across the river, Matthew. You know as well as I do that Brock is an absolute dictator. He's governor and in command of the army. Our representative government is a joke. The council members are selected for life—Strachan and his crowd—they perpetuate their power

200

among themselves. Your brother, Aaron Brant, is right in the thick with them."

"He's no brother of mine. We have the same father of unhappy memory, but that is the only thing we've shared."

"Well, no matter. He is one of them—elected member of the House of Assembly. They get a four-year term but they can be removed sooner if Brock wants them out. He's all but declared martial law in the province. There's no democracy, no freedom in Upper Canada, and there won't ever be as long as the British aristocrats, in union with their Loyalist toadies, continue to have a say. There is only one answer. The one you and I have talked over for the past ten years, statehood for Upper Canada. You did it in Louisiana, now you have to free us."

"It's at hand, Ethan, but we'll need help."

"How much help will you need? You've got an army headed for Detroit. It's bigger than the whole British establishment in Upper and Lower Canada combined."

"Don't forget Tecumseh's people—General Harrison may have defeated them at Tippecanoe last year but there are hundreds of them ready to fight and they are effective in the woods and in ambush and in scouting. We need to completely overwhelm the British and the Indians at the outset. I want you—once war is declared and General Hull is sitting in this room—I want you to proclaim your loyalty to the United States, to renounce your allegiance to Great Britain and call on all true Americans in the province of Upper Canada, but particularly in Amherstburg, to do the same thing."

"You call us true Americans. They call us Late Loyalists."

"I don't care what you're called," continued Matthew, "I want you to rally to the flag. You are the majority of the people in Upper Canada and if the civilian population refuses to join the militia and even comes over to our side, all the troops and Indian allies won't mean a damn."

"I'm not sure they'd follow me, Matt."

"Nonsense," said Nowell. "You're one of the best-known farmers in the area. Certainly you've got the best farm, I'm told. You have money."

"Amy has money," Ethan corrected.

"Never mind. You're an American. You speak French. I suspect that some of the lazy good-for-nothing French Canadians would get off their duffs and follow you."

"Matthew, for a preacher of democracy you have some

201

strange prejudices. Being American isn't sufficient to get the folks on the other side of the river to rise in rebellion. You risk hanging if you try it. You'll only get them marching for the stars and stripes if that flag is flying over Amherstburg and your army is on the march up the Thames or on its way to Niagara. There'll be plenty of volunteers then."

"Including you?"

"Including me!"

"When can I count on you? You're an officer and you've been on our pay bringing milk and a bit of news for the past ten years."

"You describe my activities euphemistically, brother. I am an ex-officer and a spy. I'm a loyal citizen of the United States. You can count on my public support the minute war is declared."

"I'd rather have you wait until our troops cross the river. You won't be much use to us in the stockade or hanging from a tree in your own orchard."

"Whatever you say, Matt. I'll wait until you and I shake hands on the Canadian side of the river and then I'll issue a call. But I warn you, my neighbors won't heed it unless you are winners."

"Will your boys be with you?"

"They're not my boys, Matthew."

"You raised them."

"I can't really say I did. Their mother raised them and she didn't brook any interference. Amy is still a Quaker woman in many ways. She didn't take on all of her first husband's ideas, at least not enough to pass them on to her sons. There is nothing pacifist about Stevie and Charles, especially Stevie. But she didn't preach any politics to them. The boys have grown up Canadian. They'll be on the other side, as will many of their generation."

"That's why we have to move. The generation that came to Canada after the war is growing older and the children don't remember the old ways. They've become accepting of tyranny."

Ethan shrugged his shoulders. "Just come quick," he said, "and win."

He rose from the trunk he had been sitting on and stretched.

"If you have a bed for me, I'll stay over and go back before dawn. I don't like to be seen coming and going to Detroit too often."

Matthew pointed toward the guest room door.

"Oh, before you go. Amy will want to know, although she would rather die than admit it, have you had any word from her daughter?"

Matthew became silent for some moments. It was a topic he preferred to avoid.

"Maggie lives well. She is still in Boston."

Ethan looked puzzled. He said no more and went to the bedroom.

Matthew went to his desk and pulled out the bottle of claret he kept there. The mere mention of Maggie had unnerved him. In the last ten years they had seen each other twice—on his two leaves in Boston. Neither time had anything happened between them. Not because he hadn't tried. He was weak and she grew more beautiful with each passing year. She had put him off with tears. She had made a new life for herself, she pleaded. Please don't drag her down into the muck again.

He acquiesced. He couldn't do that to her again. He was reduced, as he had been in Detroit, to his own fantasies in the privacy of his own bedroom.

Stephen Miller felt exuberant. Last night's camp was back a hundred feet from the woods of the shore of the St. Clair River—a few miles south the river would turn into a broad lake. At the south end of that lake was the Detroit River and the last few miles to home. He removed his buckskin leggings and then pulled off his shirt. He would have himself a proper bath with soap and hot water as soon as he got home. His mother would insist he shave his beard as well. Although he was sure that the long blond hairs on his face and elsewhere were what made him especially attractive to the young brown-skinned girls he loved so much. Like the one last night. She wanted to see what he looked like as much as she wanted to make love. She had twisted her hands in his beard and played with the blond hairs on his chest. Then he had taken her roughly, so roughly that she complained when he had finished, and went to sleep by herself away from his bedding. She wanted no part of a second coming together. Stephen was undisturbed. If you made love with him, you took what he gave you.

He walked into the cold waters of the river. "Christ," he said aloud, "cold enough to make your balls seek shelter in your belly."

But he was not the type to enter cold water slowly. He took a deep breath and dove in headfirst. The water was numbing and took his breath away. He burst to the surface and let out a yell of joy, which was also a release of shock. It startled his companions awake.

Marc Stiegler walked down from the camp to the edge of the river to see what wounded buffalo had found its way this far from the prairies. He and Stephen were cousins who had met last winter near Lake Nipigon. He was the twenty-five-year-old first born son of Louis Joseph Stiegler, half brother to Stephen's mother, Amy. Marc Stiegler had trapped in the fur country north of Quebec but he was a raw newcomer to this life among the Indians of the west and Stephen had a sense of family responsibility. He allowed him to come along with him if only to allow him to keep his hair until he was twenty-six.

The winter had gone well. The boy knew how to keep his mouth shut. Stephen hated talkers, and not only was Marc silent but he learned the tricks of the northwestern fur trade quickly. Together they had trekked across the wilderness snows, occasionally stopping at a Cree village and finding solace in the arms of the maidens. A bottle of rum to a father or brother was more than sufficient price.

"Do you want to alert every American in the northwest that we're coming home and that we've won a victory?" yelled Marc in his French-accented English.

Stephen came splashing out of the water toward his cousin.

"We'll lick them at Detroit just as we did at Mackinac," he laughed, without even a whimper.

He came onto the shoreline and plopped himself onto the grass and let the early morning sun dry him.

"I wonder if they know about the war yet at Detroit."

"They must," said Marc. "How could we get word at St. Joseph's—the most remote place in Upper Canada—and Detroit and Amherstburg not hear of it."

"Well, our friends on the other side of the river will want to give us a warm welcome."

Marc thought a moment. "We're carrying our share of the capture of the stores of the American fort. I don't think we ought to risk it."

"Shit, Marc, you're beginning to sound like my brother—cautious Charlie Miller."

"It just makes sense, Stephen. We should land opposite Peach Island and strike overland to Sandwich."

Stephen just laughed. "Get the boats ready, my little frog. We're not sneaking home. We're going right to Amherstburg in style."

Matthew paced the wall and ramparts within the fort. He was in a rage at being forced to stay behind. This was not the invasion of Canada he had contemplated. Certainly not with him sitting still in the Michigan Territory.

The Army of the Northwest had made it finally to Detroit on the fifth of July. William Hull learned that war had actually been declared on the fifteenth of June. Hull delayed for some days awaiting official word. Once he received it, he gave orders to attack Sandwich across the river. Matthew had been selected to lead a detachment of regulars across but the bulk of the army was militia volunteers.

On the morning of July tenth, Matthew's men were in *bateaux* and canoes ready to make the crossing when there was a commotion near the Ohio men's camp. Lieutenant Colonel Nowell stepped from his canoe and walked several hundred yards to where the Ohio men camped. He saw soldiers standing about relaxing and talking to each other in little groups.

"What goes on here?" he demanded, confronting a group of enlisted men. He could not help but note that not one of them snapped to attention when addressed by an officer.

"Who's in command here?"

"Colonel Cass" was the response.

"Where's he?"

"In his tent."

Matthew followed the direction of the enlisted man's arm and located the regimental headquarters of the Third Ohio Volunteers. He walked across the littered encampment.

"No discipline," he muttered to himself. He was disillusioned with this Army of the Northwest after only ten days. He stepped into Cass's tent.

"Colonel," he interrupted Cass and his aide, "my troops are ready to cross. According to General Hull's order, you were to lead. I can't keep my men waiting. What's holding you up?"

"It's very simple," responded Cass. "My men won't go."

Matthew looked as if he had been struck in the face.

"What do you mean?"

"It means," said Cass in his slow country manner, "the boys signed up to fight Indians, kill as many as they could, and chase old Tecumseh out of the Indiana Territory once and for all. But quite a few of them say they didn't sign up to do no fighting in any foreign country. Across that river ain't the good old U.S.A."

"If they'd go across, it soon would be," responded Nowell. "You've got your orders, Colonel Cass. I'm expecting to see your men loaded in boats and ready to push off."

"Now, wait a minute," said Cass, his face flushing red. "It seems to me I heard you addressed as Lieutenant Colonel Nowell. Right?"

"Yes."

"Well, maybe you ain't got my name full straight. It's Colonel Louis Cass."

"You're a colonel of militia, Mr. Cass. I'm regular army."

"It's Colonel Cass, boy, and I don't give a shit what army you claim to be from. This is the U.S. Army and I'm a colonel and you're a lieutenant colonel. So you do what I tell you or you find yourself under arrest."

Matthew's temper was about to explode but he caught himself.

"This is an issue we must take to General Hull."

"Let's do that," said Cass.

Two days later the American forces crossed the river and seized Sandwich. Louis Cass had convinced his men and he led them ashore followed by most of the rest of Hull's army. Lieutenant Colonel Nowell was left behind in command of the depleted garrison.

The sentry interrupted Matthew's pacing. "Some boats coming downriver, sir. They're moving fast, very fast."

Matthew stepped up onto the gun platforms to get a better look. There were three giant canoes skimming along the surface of the river with incredible speed.

"They have no intention of stopping here, Corporal. We can only assume they are the enemy. Get a gun crew up here and open fire."

The corporal shouted an order and several of the regulars began working on the gun.

"Damn it!" yelled Matthew. "You're too slow. They'll be by us before we can get off a shot."

He shoved a private out of the way and began to sight the gun himself.

"Clear for recoil," he shouted. He touched the slow match to the gun. It belched forth flame and leapt backward.

Matthew went to the wall to get a better view. The heavy ball smacked onto the waves of the river, skipped twice, and then plunged downward, only to emerge on the opposite shore, where it struck a rock and came to a halt.

Stephen heard the report of the gun. He shouted, laughing to Marc, who steered the Indian canoe from the rear.

"The bastards can't fire a gun for shit." He raised his fist toward the log walls of Detroit and went back to his paddling. Musket fire erupted from the Sandwich shore and the lead balls began to send up tiny waterspouts all around the canoes. Stephen ducked instinctively lower and dug his paddle all the harder into the river. The canoes were making breakneck speed aided by the current. A musket ball smashed into the side of the canoe and tore into a bundle of trade goods with a thud. Water came gushing through the tear in the fragile bark skin of the craft.

Marc yelled from the rear. Stephen turned and looked where he pointed. Another musket ball whizzed over Stephen's head so close he could almost feel the heat of it. The cannon roared from the fort. This time whoever fired it had made corrections. The water rose in an enormous spout over five feet high just in front of the canoe.

Marc leaned heavily on his paddle and the craft shot off to the right, closer to the American shore. The second cannon opened fire but this one had not ascertained the range—the shot fired high over their heads toward Sandwich.

Stephen felt the water inside the craft lap about his knees. The more water they took on, the more slowly they would move. The water smelled peculiar and strangely familiar but he couldn't think about that now. He had to keep up the rhythm of the canoe cutting through the waters even if the craft sank lower and lower as it progressed.

The first cannon must be just about ready to fire again, he thought. And his thoughts were identical to those of his cousin, who again twisted his paddle and shoved their canoe out toward the center of the river. The roar came again from behind and this time the shot landed off to the right. Stephen whistled with relief. The shot had landed just about where they would have been had Marc not taken the evasive move.

Marc gave a shout of joy and Stephen joined him with an Indian war whoop victory cry. In just a few more moments they would pull into the overgrown estuary of the River Rouge and move out of sight. The canoe was filling more and more rapidly.

The reeds were a few hundred feet ahead. The second cannon fired but the shot fell short. Stephen counted the seconds as they paddled. The commander of the first gun, devilishly active fellow, must have figured out by now where they would seek shelter. He probably had drawn a bead on them already. But they were becoming an almost impossible target, moving away rapidly, although not as rapidly as before. But the cannon never fired. They were well out of range and the soldier who attacked them had been trained not to waste a shot when he had no chance of hitting his target.

Stephen was wet, completely soaked. His shirt had absorbed the perspiration that poured off him and his pants were covered with river water mixed with rum and whiskey. Only after they allowed the canoe to glide through the reeds did he recognize the smell. The musket balls that had pierced the canoe had also put gaping holes in the wooden kegs they had commandeered as part of their booty in the looting of Fort Michilimackinac.

"Shit," he yelled, partially in elation of having made it safely through and partially in anger for having lost his whiskey.

Marc steered the canoe to the riverbank. The other two canoes followed them into the reeds, unscathed except for an occasional musket hole from the Sandwich side. For some reason the cannon had fired only at the lead canoe.

They pulled the canoe up onto the riverbank and turned it over. Stephen pulled his drenched furs from the pile and spread them out to dry. The broken and empty whiskey kegs he tossed back into the water.

"We'll wait here," he said to the men in the second and third canoes. They beached them as well and stepped onto the soggy shore of the River Rouge.

"No fires," warned Stephen. "The Indians are supposed to be on our side but one white man's scalp looks very much like another's and Sandwich was supposed to be ours too."

He turned to his cousin. "See how smart your big cousin is?" he said, tapping his temple with his finger. "You wanted to walk right into a trap. You would have lost everything. As it is we lost our whiskey and we have some very wet furs."

Marc smiled and began to work on the canoe. "It's hopeless," he judged. "We'll have to leave it here."

Stephen pulled out his pipe. His tobacco was wet. One of his rum-runner friends tossed him a pouch of dry tobacco. Stephen lit up. They had now only to let the furs dry a bit in the sun and let themselves dry as well. Stephen lay down and stretched himself out, looking up at the white puffy clouds in the sky. He started to laugh.

"Christ, that was exciting. I'm almost sorry it is over. I was sure, Marc, that that son of a bitch had us just before you veered to the center of the river. And he did have us. The bastard had us dead cold."

"Now who's the smart one?" said Stiegler.

"I guess they know the war is on down here," said Stephen, smirking. "I think we had better wait until dark just in case they've taken Amherstburg. We'll land just below my mother's farm in any case."

He dozed while the men smoked. But suddenly he was alert. He thought he had heard the sound of metal clicking against metal. He rose to his knees and signaled his men to be silent. Suddenly there was a crashing sound of men running through the reeds.

"Run for it," Stephen yelled. He tore through the reeds, making for the Detroit River with Marc at his side. One of his friends tried to launch a canoe but was gunned down. Another raised his hands in surrender and stared down in amazement and anger at the bayonet that pierced his stomach.

Without any hesitation Stephen jumped headfirst into the river. He heard Marc splash right behind him. He dived underwater and struck out for the middle of the river, staying down as long as he could. He rose, finally, gasping for breath, and turned and looked back at the American shore. Marc's head popped up several feet to the left of him. There was an angry-looking American officer standing on the shore searching for them. Stephen recognized him from several years back when Ethan had taken him and Charles on a trip to Detroit. It was his mother's half brother, Matthew Nowell.

He looked over toward the Canadian shore and dived underwater again. He wanted to give his uncle no new target to shoot at.

Stephen and Marc arrived at Amy's kitchen door empty-handed and dripping wet. As soon as Amy saw Stephen she threw her arms around him and hugged him until he thought she might injure his neck.

"Thank God you're here. At least one of you is home."

"Charles is still out on the lake?"

"Always, ferrying men and supplies from Niagara to Amherstburg."

"Where's Ethan?"

Tears sprang into her eyes. "He's at Sandwich," she said.

"The Yankees are at Sandwich," said Stephen.

Amy sat down in the kitchen chair with resignation.

"He's joined them," she said softly. "He has issued a proclamation calling on all the Americans on this side of the river to join with the American army."

"Son of a . . . When did he decide to do that?"

"I think he had always planned it. I think it was my brother who talked him into it. For all of these years Matthew Nowell has waited for this time, ever since my uncle Philip ordered Ethan to take me west to find Margaret. I believe that hateful brother of mine has plotted this for thirty years."

Her eyes were red from crying earlier but she shed no tears now. She looked over to Stephen's companion.

"Who's he?" she asked finally, pointing to Marc.

"The son of another hateful brother. He is your nephew Marc Stiegler."

He was dark and small with black eyes, not at all like Louis Joseph. "You must favor your mother, boy," she said, giving him a kiss of greeting on the cheek as he bent down.

"I do," he said in French.

Amy, hesitatingly at first, but then with fluency, began to ask after her brother and his wife and Marc's four sisters.

Stephen watched in awe as his mother spoke French. He had heard her do it with Ethan before when he was a boy and they didn't want the children to know what they said.

"Mother," Stephen interrupted, "what do we do about Ethan?"

"Nothing," said Amy. "Come get dry by the stove. The two of you take off those buckskins. I'll get some blankets."

She opened the door to her linen closet and turned toward Stephen.

"If he's right and the Americans win this war, maybe we'll thank him for picking the right side. If Britain wins we will have to face that problem when it comes. But . . ." A look of hesitation crossed her face. "After all these years, if he was

210

planning it all along, you would have thought he would have told me what he planned. How could he keep a secret like that from me for all of this time?"

Young males who knew how to handle muskets did not remain free from the militia for very long. Stephen and Marc soon found themselves placed as advance sentries guarding the Turkey Creek Bridge. Three British regulars were assigned with them. They sat in the dark in the marsh grass on the south bank of the creek underneath the bridge. It was drizzling. One of the Englishmen had a runny nose and a hacking cough.

"Blow that stuff the other way," ordered Corporal Case, in a heavy cockney accent. "And for God's sake, if you're going to empty your snout, lean over and do it. Don't dribble on your uniform."

"God, he's disgusting," said Evans, one of the other regulars.

The man they spoke of, Private Robinson, was too miserable to protest. His nose was sore and his head ached and he could barely lift his arms and legs.

"Hey, Yank," said the corporal, "at least we get paid to sit here in the rain and die of the flux, if we don't catch a bayonet in the ass. Why in the hell are you here?"

"I ain't a Yank," said Marc.

"That's right," said Stephen. "We are Canadians and we don't plan on becoming Yanks. If they have their way, we'll have no choice."

Marc sat quietly looking over at Stephen. "You didn't give my people much of a choice. We are a conquered people. We are British subjects whether we like it or not."

"You're damned right," said Case. "You're one of them Quebec frogs. Old General Wolfe—now there was a general, not like this old lady, Proctor—now Wolfe chopped the legs right off of you frogs."

He laughed at his own joke. "Why are you helping out these Canadians?"

"It's simple. I believe Stephen's Canadians will let my Canadians alone and allow us to be French. The Yanks are so certain they are right on everything. They will have no patience with our differences and insist that we become Yanks like them—no French anymore, just Yanks."

Evans sneezed. "Damn it," he said. "Look at what you've done now, Robinson. Now I've got your bloody cold."

"It ain't my fault," said Robinson. "It's the bloody dampness. Almost reminds me of home. I always had a cold at home."

Stephen rose from the muddy ground and brushed the seat of his pants. His buckskins were wet, and even if the rain was a warm summer drizzle, his rump felt wet and cold.

"Christ, this is miserable. There's no keeping dry on a night like this."

"Not even your powder," said Evans.

"Corporal, why are we stuck out here?"

"Because the Yanks will move across the creek when they move against Amherstburg, which they should be doing at any time now."

"They'll never come on a night like this," said the miserable Robinson. "Only poor sick blokes like myself are made to go outside on nights like this and catch our death."

Stephen walked under the small bridge that crossed the slow-moving creek. The night was black. He could see no more than two feet ahead of him. His bladder was ready to burst and he looked for a private spot. Two minutes later he was starting back toward the other sentries when across the creek he heard a sudden clamor as horses came out of the blackness onto the bridge, while other horses plunged over the side of the embankment into the water. Stephen ducked back under the bridge footings and out of sight.

Someone yelled and guns fired. He heared the gurgling sound of someone strangling in blood.

"I surrender," he heard the cockney yell.

Stephen tried to catch sight of Marc, but in the confusion of horses and men in the darkness it was impossible to tell friend from foe. But there were foe out in front of him—by far the larger force. There were at least twenty-five dragoons holding three captives.

Stephen heard the soft drawling voice give an order. He recognized it instantly. It was Ethan.

"How many are there?"

"There were four. One's dead."

Stephen hoped that it was not Marc that they referred to. He recognized the second voice as well—that of Jared Ingersol—a neighbor whose farm was south of his mother's, closer to Amherstburg. They were all neighbors, men like Ethan—Americans who had gone to Canada and were now fighting for their native land. They were men whom his mother had taught him to address respectfully as Mr. Ingersol or Mr. Nichols and now they were trying to kill him and may already have killed his cousin. It was now his duty to kill them. But the greatest shock was in finding his own stepfather. How could he fire his musket at the man who had given him haircuts or spanked him for smoking cornsilk and only then because his mother had insisted? In the past they had argued about Canada and the United States. Why couldn't it have just remained a shouting match? He turned cold when he heard Ethan's softly chilling voice say the words:

"Kill the rest of them. No prisoners."

"Ethan, don't!" he called out into the darkness.

The horseman closest to the bridge jumped in fright at Stephen's call and his horse reared high into the air. He cursed and tried to get the mare under control but she reared to the right and started to try to climb the creek embankment.

Stephen stepped from his hiding place, his hands out high in the air. He repeated,

"Ethan, don't. You can't."

He saw Marc out of the corner of his eye and he breathed a sigh of relief that it was not his cousin who had been killed. He stepped to one side.

"This is Marc Stiegler—mother's nephew. You can't kill him."

He saw the look of dismay on Ethan's face.

"Where the hell did you come from, Stevie? Why the hell are you here?"

"The militia, Ethan."

"You're on the wrong side, son."

Stephen was silent.

"Ethan," said Mr. Ingersol, "this is a war. These boys will go back and inform the enemy that we scouted this far south. It will tip off the enemy about General Hull's intentions."

"Who the hell knows General Hull's intentions," replied Ethan. "I'm not about to murder my own kin. You two boys get the hell out of here. Go home and stay home until I get there. Take care of your mother, Stevie, and leave the warring to me."

Stephen shoved Marc up the side of the embankment out of the water. He whispered to him, "Let's get the hell out of here."

"You," he heard the cockney shout, "you're not leaving me behind. They'll kill me. He's your kin. Tell him to spare me."

213

Then the other regular, Evans, pulled out his musket from under his coat. He aimed it at Ethan. Ingersol's saber came slashing down and sliced into the soldier's neck. Blood spurted out and Evans collapsed with a splash into the creek water.

With Robinson and Evans both dead, Corporal Case saw little chance for himself. But he did know when to seize an opportunity. The horses, frightened by the smell of blood, reared and crashed into each other. He ducked between two of Ethan's legionnaires and was up the bank into the darkness before he could be stopped. Ingersol turned his horse to give chase but Ethan's shout halted him.

"Let him be, Jared." Then he looked at Stephen and winked. He turned his horse away, kicked its side, and rode up the embankment onto the dry land, disappearing into the blackness of the night. The other dragoons followed him and soon only the sound of their retreating horses' hooves could be heard.

Marc flopped down again into the rain-drenched marsh grass. He was breathing hard.

"I thought that was it," he said, still shaking with fright.

"Let's try to find the corporal," said Stephen.

"No use. He'll run all the way back to Amherstburg if he feels anything like the way I feel," said Marc.

Stephen knew his cousin was right and he knew everyone at Amherstburg, including General Proctor, would soon know that Ethan Morin, Canadian, commanded a unit in Hull's American Army of the Northwest.

Jessica packed Michael's cloth bag. She put in as much warm clothing as she could. True, it was August, but it could be a long campaign and winters in the west were said to be cold. As she packed his clothes, he was downstairs in their Bay Street house sitting with his father. They had given up the old schoolhouse on Front Street years ago for the elegant two-story wood-framed house more befitting a member of the House of Assembly.

Yesterday, General Brock had dissolved the Assembly, declared martial law, and called for volunteers. Almost five hundred of York's sons had responded. Half would be sent to the Niagara frontier and the other half, Aaron said, would go to Detroit.

The gambler in Brock had taken over. He would strip the Niagara frontier of his regulars, leaving mostly raw militia in their place, and he would rush with his reinforcements to relieve Amherstburg and confront the Americans.

Jessica had not raised the boy to manhood for this—to fight against a nation she regarded as her own. Michael was her pride. He was tall like his father, with jet-black hair and black eyes. His eyelashes were long and dark; most women would have given anything to have eyelashes like his. He had developed from a skinny boy to a lanky, muscular-framed man. He was quiet, handsome, and devoted to his mother. In contrast, her Elizabeth was trouble from the time she could crawl. She opened cabinets and stole food, she stole Aaron's razor and tried to shave the family dog. Discipline was impossible with her. She lived with Aaron and Jessica and regarded herself as their daughter but should they thwart her in any way, she would run off to Doc's office down the street. He would then assert his role as guardian and let her do what she willed. Jessica once called Eli's bluff and told him that he could keep the girl if he intended to interfere. And so he did. Jessica caved in within three days. She loved the girl to distraction and could not bear the thought of losing her. She got her daughter back but she knew that she did not control the child.

Aaron opened the door to Michael's room.

"Are you ready?" he asked.

Jessica sniffed and Aaron walked to her side.

"You've got to let go of him, Jess," he said, holding her to his chest. "I fought many times before I was his age."

"And you were a bloody savage," she said gruffly. "What else did you have to do? He's reading law and he should be joining you in your practice."

"Our country's at war—invaded. All of us have to make sacrifices."

They went downstairs together. The dining room was an elegant room, as elegant a dining room as would be found in this tiny capital of a pioneer province. Jessica had waited for years for the mahogany table with matching chairs. The seats of the chairs were upholstered with gold-colored damask. The same material curtained the windows looking out onto the mud of Bay Street.

Aaron sat at the head of the table. Next to him sat his son, and on the other side sat the ancient Eli Stoddard, already in his eighth decade. The top of his head was bald but the back

215

rim of hair he allowed to grow long and snowy white, falling to his shoulders.

"Benjamin Franklin style," Jessica called it. The remark outraged him but he did not change his hairstyle. Next to him sat Elizabeth. She was dressed in her best party dress and sat quietly with her head down, her attention drawn off somewhere else.

Jessica took her place at the end of the table opposite Aaron. He bowed his head, as did the others. Jessica recited the prayer of thanks in Hebrew, as she always did at the family dinner. She had dismissed the cook for this meal. She had prepared it herself. She went to the kitchen and returned with a large tureen filled with leek soup.

Michael was too excited to eat. He realized it was an emotion more appropriate to a child than to a man about to be twenty. But this was his first time away from home and from his family.

His father would always be the stern, almost forbidding Mohawk sachem who stood back and observed and judged. He was terrified that he would be found wanting in his father's judgment and he had struggled always to succeed. In most instances he had. He knew his father was proud of his accomplishments at school. He was proud that he now read law with him and would probably receive a government post before long. But this test that he faced now, this was the sternest test of all, one his father had met and conquered many times. He had now to test his courage, his manliness in the face of a lead ball or a Yankee bayonet. He was excited by the challenge and he was frightened.

He looked over at his sister. As she had promised him last night when she had come to his room to say good-bye, she was dressed in a manner that would please their mother. They were close, he and Liz, and he frequently secretly intervened in her arguments with Jessica. He chuckled to himself when he recalled her demand that he take her with him. She could shoot straighter than he could, she argued. And it pained him to admit that there was some truth in that. She was a superb horsewoman, while he rode horses at everyone's peril. He knew her moroseness today was the result of his rejection of her offer to go along with him. She was so headstrong, and she was so seldom controlled.

His father could have controlled her. He would not. There was something in his background that prevented him. He was

216

indulgent with children anyway. Michael had never received a harsh word from him. He lived in terror that someday, after failing, he would feel the lash of his father's tongue. But that day had never come.

Elizabeth had never been chastised by him either. "Father Thomas" was someone who loved and cherished her.

And Aaron also had to consider the feelings of his ancient friend, Eli. They shared the child and Eli would have to agree for "Thomas" to act and Eli could deny Liz nothing.

Jessica removed the soup bowls and returned from the kitchen with a platter on which was displayed a duck, roasted brown and lying in a bed of wild Indian rice from Lake Superior.

When they had finished their duck, Aaron poured some port wine for all. He hesitated at Liz's glass and passed it by. Michael thought she would make a fuss at this treatment but still she remained silent.

"A toast is in order," said Eli. He stood up. "Ladies and gentlemen—the king."

They rose and repeated his words, sipping some of the wine. All but Liz.

"I believe my ward has turned rebel," said Eli.

"I have nothing to toast with."

"Will you switch your allegiance back to George the Third, mad though he be, if I give you a bit of the libation?"

She nodded.

"A small price to pay to win back a rebel to the Crown."

He poured a bit of his port into her empty glass.

"A second toast," said Eli, "to the Prince Regent. May his enemies be confounded." He remained standing. "To Major General Isaac Brock," may he drive the enemy into the sea."

"Which sea do you have in mind, Uncle Doc?" said Michael innocently. "The Pacific Ocean is several thousand miles west of Detroit."

"I mean the sea of hell's fire, you little snot," Eli quipped back, "and I wish this fine young fellow, whom I have just addressed as waste matter from the nasal passages, I wish him honor, bravery, and triumph over his enemies."

"I wish him a safe return," toasted Jessica.

"I wish I were going with him," interjected Liz.

They all laughed. Then they all looked at Aaron, who had not yet made a wish to Michael.

"I wish that my son becomes a wise man and that he

217

becomes a peacemaker early in his life. And that he not wait until he is old and cannot control the rashness of the young before he learns this wisdom."

Michael was moved by his father's words because he knew they came from his heart. He knew his father favored his volunteering, knowing that Michael would have no future in York or in Upper Canada if he didn't. His father wanted the Americans repulsed but he was not overjoyed that the opportunity had arisen. Not like Uncle Eli.

Eli ignored Aaron's comments. Instead he took up Liz's toast.

"I think the girl has a splendid idea. Why should I, a man of medicine, remain behind? I could offer my services to General Brock. I should go to the front."

"Doc," said Jessica, "did we not celebrate your eighty-second birthday in this very room not that long ago?"

"Indeed you did, and it was a splendid repast. But not nearly so fine a banquet as you have rewarded us with today, my dear. And I hope to celebrate my eighty-third next year after I help beat the Yankees."

Aaron, who knew Eli well, realized he was serious.

"Doc, you're too old!"

"Nonsense, Thomas, I'm as strong as I ever was. Liz, we must say good-bye to Michael, then you must come to my office and help me pack."

Jessica hated to see the old man hurt when Brock rejected his offer but she knew him well enough to know that nothing could stop him from making the offer. Nothing could stop him from being hurt. She made eye contact with Aaron at the end of the table. His look was one she had seen often on his face when he had to deal with a difficult Eli or a difficult Elizabeth—don't interfere, there is nothing to be done. If he wishes to make a fool of himself it is his own head. She could play the game.

"Doc," she said with much irritation, "enough of your planning. This is Michael's farewell dinner. We'll have one for you later."

The old man blushed. "You're right," he said. "It's rude of me. Young man, bring me a Yankee liver for my bottled organ collection. I've never seen one and I've been told the Yankees suffer from jaundice. They are all yellow-livered."

Liz, Michael, and Aaron laughed at his joke. But Jessica puffed up in annoyance at his arrogance.

11

Lieutenant Charles Miller was pacing *Sophia*'s decks in impatience. When he sailed from Fort Erie he had orders to put in at Port Dover—sixty miles to the west. He was told to wait there and he had been waiting and waiting. He had his two longboats on board and on deck there were three large *bateaux*. The hundred-ton schooner *Nancy*, also from Fort Erie, arrived six hours after the *Sophia* did. She had the same numbers of small craft.

Charles spent the whole morning of the eighth of August unloading his boats. There were ten other leaky *bateaux* in the port, deposited there at an earlier time and waiting for a rendezvous with the commander—General Brock. In the afternoon Brock arrived with his troop of regulars and two hundred and fifty young Canadian volunteers. He climbed aboard *Sophia* and greeted Charles.

"We've met before, Lieutenant?" he said as Charles saluted him.

"My uncle, Aaron Brant, introduced us at Fort George."

"Oh, yes, Brant. Wish we could get the rest of the family to move—John Brant, the Mohawk chief at Grand River, has remained neutral. And in this struggle neutral is equal to disloyal."

"John Brant is my uncle's cousin, sir. You can be sure the Mohawks will take part in due course."

"You're sure, are you? I am glad one so young has such assurance. I hope you are sure about getting me and my men to Amherstburg."

"I'm not sure if the *Nancy* and I could carry the whole army, sir. Our holds are filled with badly needed supplies."

"I don't expect you to carry us, sir. I expect you to lead us and to protect us. My men will row and sail themselves to Amherstburg in the boats. When can we sail?"

"Not now. The boats that we brought are sound enough but the older ones brought earlier still need repairing."

"No repairs, we'll bail as we go. Damn it, man, all you colonials give me is excuses. I must get to Amherstburg and I must get there now—not next week, but now. Everything depends on speed. I've taken just about every capable regu-

219

lar from the Niagara line and substituted militia. If the Americans attack at Niagara it will collapse. I have to go west. I have to win and I have to get back and get my army back here before the clods across the Niagara figure out what is going on and jump to destroy me. Now, damn it, man, don't tell me we can't sail."

"General, I am not trying to be difficult, but I know of no sailor, not Lord Nelson himself, who could figure out how to sail a ship directly into the wind. The winds, sir, are southeasterly and we have to go to the southeast to get around Long Point or we tack back to the east toward Fort Erie and then come around the point."

Brock's confidence seemed to desert him for the first time.

"Let me see the charts," he said finally.

Charles turned and moved toward his cabin. "This way, sir," he gestured to Brock.

Charles opened the small door and bent low. "Watch your head," he called back to the general. Once down the flight of steps they entered Charles's cabin. Charles straightened up. Ducking had become natural to him. This cabin was home. Brock had to remain hunched over. His six-foot frame simply would not fit into the cabin of *Sophia*.

"You had better take the deck chair, sir," said Charles.

Brock sat down as Charles spread out the charts before him.

"This is Port Dover and here is Long Point." Charles showed him a narrow projection of land stretching out fifteen miles into Lake Erie and cutting off the direct line of sail to the west.

"Any chance of a wind change?" asked Brock as he studied the chart and pulled his chin with his long elegant fingers.

"There is always a chance," said Charles, "but you said up on deck that speed was of the essence."

"Good enough," said Brock, his mind made up. "We'll attack it directly. Mr. Miller, make sail for the narrowest point of Long Point—this part here," he said, pointing to a place close to the mainland. "It's mostly sandbar?"

Charles nodded.

"We'll portage across it, Lieutenant."

Charles looked at him in puzzlement. "But *Nancy* and the *Sophia* cannot offer you the protection you need for the rest of the journey and you'll need the supplies we carry when we arrive. It might take us days to catch up with you."

"Catch up? Who mentioned catch up? You'll not be leaving us, Lieutenant. You'll portage with us."

Now Charles's look changed from puzzlement to incredulity.

"Don't look at me as if I'm crazy, Lieutenant. I have no time. I have manpower but no time. When faced with that kind of problem you can't be subtle. We'll beach these craft. We'll unload them to lighten them and then we'll drag them, using rollers and manpower. The map indicates less than a mile across. Then we'll refloat them and reload them and be on our way."

The task seemed monumental.

"Might I suggest a variation, sir? Why not send *Sophia* around Long Point and take *Nancy* over. That way, whichever is the right way, at least half our supplies will be available to you. And you don't risk all on a gamble."

"I already have, Lieutenant. I already have. But your point is well taken. But I want you with me. You are to switch commands with the lieutenant in charge of *Nancy*. He is to take *Sophia* to sea. You are to take your new ship across the sandbar."

Long Point loomed ahead of them after a brief sail from Port Dover. Charles resented having to leave *Sophia* behind. *Nancy* was a clumsy sailer. He did not know the crew.

He had offered the cabin to Brock but the general had insisted on sailing on the open boats with his men, a fact noted by the common soldiers of the Forty-first Regiment. The general asked nothing of them that he did not ask of himself.

Charles paced the deck. The helmsman, a white-haired, foul-smelling deckhand from the Royal Navy, transferred to the lakes from a man o' war stalled at Montreal, gently held the wheel and studied the wind direction. The first officer, Mr. Morse, a young man Charles's age from Kingston, came on deck and stood deferentially several paces away from the commander.

"We'll make Long Point in a quarter of an hour, sir."

Charles sighed. "That's when our troubles begin, Morse."

"What is the general's rush? Why couldn't we wait for a wind change so that we might do this more easily?"

"I think the general is right. I think the mistake was to embark from Port Dover and place Long Point in front of us.

If we had left from Fort Erie it would have been clear sailing all the way to Amherstburg."

"True," said Morse. "Once these winds start from this direction they can blow for days until a storm comes up and the westerly blows start again."

"We have a few days to make quick time to Amherstburg and no time to wait."

"So over the sandbar we go," said Morse, shaking his head.

"See that the crew is prepared to beach her, Morse, and make sure every man is prepared to help with the unloading of the cargo."

Morse went below and Charles continued to scan the wooded north shore of Lake Erie.

"Captain Miller, sir," Morse interrupted.

Charles turned around to see Morse pushing two strange-looking creatures from below deck. "Stowaways."

Charles recognized the girl immediately. She had tried to disguise her sex with her clothing, but the effect was lost on him because the only other time he had seen her the girl had been wearing the same brown baggy pants.

"Two chaps hiding below," said Morse. "I'll place them under arrest and then turn them over to General Brock."

"Never mind, Morse. At least one of them is not a spy. You're Uncle Aaron's girl, aren't you?" he asked.

"Girl?" said Morse in surprise. "This one is a girl?" he asked, pointing to Elizabeth.

"Spy?" shouted Eli. "For whom, sir? Spy? I am Dr. Eli Stoddard of York, come to serve the troops of His Majesty George the Third. Who are you, sir? It is more likely you are a spy. And you," he said, pointing to Charles, "how am I to know you're not some Yankee pirate?"

"My name, Dr. Stoddard, is Lieutenant Charles Miller and I am master of the sloop of the Provincial Marine *Nancy*. I am also the Honorable Aaron Brant's nephew."

Stoddard smiled. "I thought so. I could tell by the way you handled your ship. I know you are a good boy. But don't you think that sandbar directly ahead should be avoided?" He turned to the helmsman. "Turn this thing around. Do you want to get us all killed?"

"Come about, helmsman, then we'll drop anchor and wait for the boats to catch up."

Elizabeth had said nothing thus far. Charles could tell from the expression on her face and her faintly green com-

plexion that she was probably in no condition to say anything.
He took her by the hand.

"Miss . . . ?"

"Miss Stoddard, I think I know how you feel. If I can be so
indelicate, I would suggest that if you're going to be sick, you
go below."

She nodded.

"Nonsense, girl," said Eli. "It's best to stay out in the fresh
air. It will lick the *mal de mer* every time."

But Elizabeth allowed Charles to lead her to his cabin. He
gave her his shaving basin and closed the door behind her.

Stoddard came down the stairway to the cabin and struck
his head on a beam.

"Good loving Jesus, this ship was built for midgets. I'm in
Lilliput," he yelled. "Where did she go? I'm her doctor. I
delivered her and I've cared for her ever since then. I've
taken care of everything she's ever had."

He burst open the cabin door. Elizabeth sat on Charles's
bed looking wretched, her soft hazel eyes staring at the
empty basin.

"Open the windows," Stoddard yelled at Charles. He seemed
never to say anything below a roar. Charles did as Stoddard
commanded.

The white-haired old man took the girl by the arm and led
her to the stern of the ship.

"Now breathe in deeply," he ordered. "There are boats
coming up quickly behind us. Those are Brock's men, aren't
they?"

"Mr. Stoddard, would you mind terribly if I asked the
questions?"

"Yes, I would," said Eli. "I want mine answered first."

"No," said Charles, his annoyance clear from the tone of
his voice. "First, you tell me why you, an old man, saw fit to
bring this child with you as a stowaway on my ship?"

"I didn't know it was yours," said Stoddard. "If I had
known that the master of this ship I had selected as our conveyance to the belligerent zones was an impertinent young prig,
I would have selected another."

"You're saying I should be grateful?"

"Of course. I am a fine physician. My ward is a trained
nurse. I trained her myself."

"Proper women do not follow men to war. And nurses are
regarded in armies as no better than camp followers."

223

"Most of them are. But if you imply that my ward, sir, is a woman of ill repute, I'll have no choice but to have my seconds call upon you."

Charles had gone beyond exasperation with the old man. He was sorely tempted to ask him who his seconds would be here in the middle of Lake Erie, but he refrained.

"I meant nothing of the kind. She's kin."

"That's not true," said Elizabeth. The stability of the anchored vessel was restoring some of her sense of control over her stomach. She looked him over from head to boots.

"You and I are no blood kin. In fact, I have no blood kin. Not even Doc."

"I stand corrected," said Charles, not wishing to continue his interrogation much further. "I can only assume you boarded my vessel with good intentions. You may remain until we reach Amherstburg. Since we are kin of sorts, if not blood kin, I'll ask my mother to take you in until we can find out what to do with you."

When Brock's small boats were beached, lines were extended from *Nancy* to the men on shore. The ship was lightened by removing the cargo until she seemed to bounce on top of the waves like a cork. A hundred men on each side pulled and hauled and the large ship found herself beached like a stranded whale.

Charles commanded one crew of workers. Morse took command of the second. The day was hot as only August days can be hot. General Brock stood watching as his York volunteers and his regulars, stripped of their red coats and their shirts, hauled on the lines and inched *Nancy* along greased rollers across the sandbar.

Charles relieved one of the men who tripped and fell after a strange popping noise came from his shoulder. Stoddard came to his side almost immediately. Charles was hauling on the rope but from the corner of his eye he could see the old man poking at his crewman's shoulder. Then the doctor yanked. The crewman yelled, but his shoulder fell back into place and the agony ceased. Stoddard said nothing. He merely glanced at Charles and stepped back to watch the work.

The girl was still dressed in boy's clothes and Charles concluded it was just as well. She went from crewman to crewman, from soldier to soldier, giving them water.

The sun beat down on them. Charles, like every other man

on the line, had removed his shirt; sweat poured off him and the hair on his chest had turned dark with dampness. His muscles ached, but *Nancy* continued to inch forward across the sandbar. His hands were raw from the hemp line. The blisters that had formed first burst and the white skin wore off, leaving behind red, raw, and bleeding sores. The seamen were more accustomed to handling rope and their palms were tougher. But the soldiers and volunteers were in agony before *Nancy* was halfway across.

At midpoint the land rose slightly and the work grew even harder. General Brock walked among the soldiers, urging them on.

As *Nancy* reached the peak of the rise there were groans from the workers. Some of them were starting to shout that ships were supposed to float on water. "Next he'll be asking us to float cannon," came another shout. Charles could feel the tension of the men around him. They were ready to quit. The task was beyond ordinary people.

Brock felt the moment as well. He removed his scarlet-and-gold coat and handed it to an aide. He spit on his elegant hands and went to join the line of haulers. A cheer went up from the men. Damn it, the general himself was going to put his back into it. They pulled a little harder, proud to be part of this group of men achieving the impossible. The midpoint of the ship came over the rise and the ship's bow, lying on its side, now had a decided incline downward. She still had to be hauled but the work was easier and soon the haulers were waist-deep in Lake Erie and on the far side of Long Point.

Hauling the small boats across the Point, which yesterday would have been greeted as an exhausting task, was now treated as incidental. The small boats, once launched, were soon hauling and tugging lines from *Nancy*, pulling the schooner into deeper water until suddenly she groaned, righted herself, and was afloat.

Soldiers, sailors, volunteers, officers, and men let loose with a thunderous cheer. It was an omen, many suggested. The campaign ahead would be a successful one. The Yankees would never stand before the courage of Brock's men.

Charles supervised the reloading of the cargo. He had to take care that these land-dwelling fellows just didn't toss things any which way into the holds. He did not like the way *Nancy* sailed, to begin with, and he was determined that he would place the cargo according to his wishes.

At one point Brock boarded *Nancy* in impatience. He came up the ladder from his boat, ordering Charles to make haste.

"Mr. Miller, I must be away," he called.

"General, if you want these provisions to get where you're going, you must allow me to load cargo properly. Your soldiers will capsize me with the first good wind if I let them have their way."

The general paced the rest of the early afternoon aboard *Nancy's* deck. Finally he returned to his small boat. The winds were still excellent and in the late afternoon the flotilla was again under way.

Toward sunset Charles came up on deck. He found Elizabeth standing at the railing.

"Are you ill?" he asked solicitously.

She shook her head vigorously. "I think I am getting used to it."

"That's very quick."

"I learn everything quickly," she responded.

"You made a lot of friends as the water boy today."

She laughed. "Not one of them guessed."

"There are some girls who would be insulted by that."

She remained silent.

"Why did you come on this crazy adventure with the old man?"

"I was jealous of Michael, my brother. It's all kind of funny. He got left behind at Niagara and I'm on my way to the real war. But he was going to be free of all restrictions. I wanted that. I hate being tied down, made to wear confining clothes, made to conform. 'Liz, nice girls don't do that.' 'Liz, why can't you be like other girls?' I'm not like the others. The others are dull people in an interesting world. I'm not going to waste my life."

"Wasn't there something interesting that wasn't quite so dangerous?"

"Captain, I find that most interesting things are dangerous."

"And the old man?"

"Well," she said, shrugging her shoulders, "he was determined to come and he is old. He needed me."

"Does Uncle Aaron know where you are?"

She nodded. "Eli left him a note. Jessica will never forgive the old buzzard for this one. She'll roast him for Friday night dinner when we get back."

Charles laughed. "I have heard that the Brants still continue some of Jessica's Jewish religious practices but I don't believe that cannibalism is one of them."

"She'll be so hopping mad that she'll serve him in a milk sauce," she said. Then they both laughed.

They reached halfway to Port Talbot that afternoon. With night they anchored just off the shore. Charles gave his cabin to Stoddard and Elizabeth. He slept on deck. He was restless most of the night. In the early morning, well before dawn, he sat bolt upright. He did not like the roll of the ship at anchor. There had been a change in the wind. The winds were from the southwest now. It would make sailing far more difficult. But worse, these changes frequently precursed violent storms coming out of the vast open prairies in the center of the continent.

Charles rowed himself ashore and went looking for Brock's tent. The camp was totally quiet. The troops were exhausted from yesterday's ordeal. There was a tired sentry standing a last watch before dawn in front of the general's small company tent.

"I must see General Brock," said Charles.

"He likes his sleep. You'd better see Major Glegg or Colonel MacDonell—his aides."

Brock pulled back the tent flap. The sentry came to attention.

"Come in, Miller," Brock said. "I like my sleep, do I?" he said, glaring at the petrified sentry. "Why don't you get some yourself, soldier? You look like you could use sleep more than I could."

"I could not do that, General. The sergeant major would take my hide off," he said.

Brock chuckled. "Well, we must not offend the sergeant major, must we?"

Brock offered Charles a chair across from his bunk. He himself sat down on his bed.

"What's the bad news, Lieutenant Miller?"

"The wind had shifted, sir."

"Which means?"

"Slow going today and perhaps a storm."

"Can we make progress through a storm?"

"No, sir. I've seen a few of these Erie storms in my career. They're violent in the extreme. The lake is shallow compared to the others. And the winds can whip it into a frenzy in no time. It would swamp your small boats. *Nancy*, if she were in

227

the middle of the lake, could ride it out but we're on a lee shore. We'll run aground and break up if the storm strikes us now."

"Your recommendation?" asked Brock, all sleep now gone from him.

"My recommendation is that we set out at dawn and make the thirty miles to Port Talbot. If we're in a storm we pull in there for shelter. It's the only shelter on this shore until we reach Amherstburg."

Brock rose and went to the front of the tent.

"Call Major Glegg and Colonel MacDonell. And then tell your sergeant major to get his ass out of bed. We must get ready to push on now."

The flotilla was under way as the rose color entered the sky behind them. The winds were weak and by short tacks *Nancy* made some progress. The small boats powered by oars soon pulled ahead. Charles stood by the helmsman watching the sky lighten. He saw Eli and Elizabeth Stoddard come on deck. They took a brief walk and then disappeared below deck again.

They inched along the coast, falling further behind the small boats. The cloud formations to the south frightened them. They were heavy and black and were moving across the lake rapidly. The clouds were even blacker further to the west in the direction of Amherstburg and Detroit. Lightning flashed through the blackened sky. Across Lake Erie he could see sheets of rain slicing through the sky into the waves. The swells increased quickly.

"Damn," he said aloud, "it's a beauty."

He ordered the helmsman to hold course until they were opposite Port Talbot and then make a run with the wind for shore.

The rain struck, drenching the sails, which helped them hold a little more wind. Charles ordered some of the sails taken in. The wind struck the schooner from the south with gale force, forcing the ship to veer dangerously toward the rocky shore. Charles ran to the helmsman's side and helped the old man hold the wheel steady. The waves slammed into the port side and sent a spray reaching up into the rigging.

"Now, sailor," said Charles.

The old man spun the wheel. The schooner responded and suddenly started to run toward the shore. If he had timed it right he should be within the modest protection of the small harbor within a few minutes. But it was guesswork combined with years of experience on the lake. A lookout, holding on to his life by a line, called out that he could see campfires ahead. That would be the army safely in port.

The winds bent the mast forward at a dangerous angle. This would not be a wild and quick storm and the shallow anchorage would not be sufficient protection for *Nancy*. Now Charles himself could see the distant shore fires. The waves were already diminished. They were inside Port Talbot. He ordered the helmsman to bring her about and drop anchor. Within a few minutes it was clear that the anchor would not hold in these seas.

"Morse," Charles yelled over the howling wind. "Take a boat to shore and get to Brock. Tell him I can't hold her here. If I am to save this ship I'll have to beach her. I'll need his boats and lines to pull us ashore."

"Aye, aye, sir," responded Morse, who then lowered the captain's dinghy and with another seaman rode the high waves toward the shore.

Within ten minutes the boats and *bateaux* were filled with men pulling toward *Nancy*. Charles recognized Brock's scarlet coat in the lead boat. He saluted. The general returned it. Then Charles heaved a line, which a soldier in Brock's boat caught. Then more lines were thrown and the boats bent their oars for shore. *Nancy* moved toward her natural foe— shallow water.

Brock's boat suddenly lifted its front end and wedged on an unseen rock. The oarsman tried to back off. One stood up and, using the oar, attempted to pull them off the rock. A wave struck the boat and knocked the oarsman overboard. He stood up in waist-deep water coughing and sputtering.

Brock stood in the boat and announced to all that the oarsmen had the right idea. He jumped over the side, up to his thighs. The others followed his lead and soon had the boat off the rock. The general climbed over the side again and fell headfirst into the boat; his feet were raised in the air and water ran down from his black leather boots. The men cheered when the line to *Nancy* grew taut again and the general's crew were once more hauling the schooner toward safety.

Nancy lay beached on her side again. The waves lopped around her and crashed against her timbers, but she had been saved. The rain continued to beat down on the beach.

Most of the men had overturned their boats and lay beneath them for protection. Charles decided to stay aboard *Nancy*. He sent Morse and his crew, along with Stoddard and Elizabeth, ashore to seek shelter. But for himself he rigged a hammock between the deck and the bulkhead of his cabin and climbed into it. He had only a few moments before sleep overtook him. But in those moments he convinced himself that this was destiny's army. No one could stop them, not the Americans, not the gods of thunder, nor the gods of the sea.

The next morning dawned bright and clear. The wind picked up and swirled back again from the west. At the crack of dawn Isaac Brock's boats were in the lake again hauling *Nancy* off her sandy blanket for the second time. The ship's timbers groaned and she righted herself once again. Brock came aboard. He had changed uniforms down to his boots and he was resplendent again in scarlet and gold.

"Lieutenant Miller," he called as he came over the side. "I am not a slow learner. The wind is contrary and this tub of yours will crawl along. I can't be forced to wait. I go ahead with the boats. If you catch up, fine. If not, take this wretched excuse for a sailing vessel alongside the wharf at Amherstburg with my supplies or sail her to hell. Those are your options."

"Yes, sir," smiled Charles.

Stoddard came from the cabin at this moment.

"General," he called out. "Do I hear correctly that you will go ahead of us?"

Brock looked at the white-haired old man. "I do believe you've kidnapped King Neptune, Miller. Who is this man?"

"Dr. Elisha Stoddard of York. By his own word, the best doctor in Canada."

Eli bowed.

"I'll be damned," said Brock.

"I must go with you, General. Men on the line may need my services."

"If you're a doctor and you can stand on your two feet, my men can use you. You're welcome."

Stoddard followed Brock over the side.

"What about your assistant?" Charles called after him.

"Oh, him," called Eli from Brock's boat, "you take care of him. After all he is kinfolk to you."

Stephen lay in the wet mud on his belly. Marc was a few feet behind him. Beyond him were two English regulars—

strange fellows, these Redcoats. He could barely understand what they were saying. He was also sure they were thieves. He had only one bottle of rum left and one of the bastards had taken it.

When he first returned to his home and found his father gone, he had not realized how precarious their situation was. There were over eight hundred members of the Amherstburg militia force. With Ethan's call to dissent and General Hull's proclamation calling for a rebellion against tyranny, at least four hundred of the eight hundred had melted away from Amherstburg. He didn't understand that and he didn't understand Ethan. Hull had addressed those who had fought for independence not to take up arms against their brethren. Ethan preached the same line. He promised peace, liberty, and security to Canadians. But Stephen had always felt liberty and security. The Americans were the only ones who threatened his peace.

So far the Americans had stayed in Sandwich and had not moved on Amherstburg. He didn't know why. The Canadian militia was untrustworthy and Tecumseh's Indians ran about the village of Amherstburg frightening the Canadians more than endangering any Americans.

The Americans had pushed as far as Rivière aux Canards—just a mile from Stephen's home.

The river was well named. He and Charles had hunted ducks here. Rather, *he* had hunted them. Charles couldn't fire anything smaller than a cannon with any hope of accuracy. He and Marc had been assigned the task of scouting across the river and reporting what the Americans were up to—why they hadn't moved south to attack.

Once the sun set they would go forward. Marc crept to his side.

"Let's go now," he said softly, "I don't see any Americans around for miles."

Stephen liked the challenge of a daylight reconnoiter, and although it was against specific orders, he nodded yes to Marc. They rose and, crawling low, ran across the bridge and into the marshes on the other side.

"Hey, you blokes," called out one of the Redcoats, "where the hell do you think you're going?"

"To a cat house to fuck your sister," Marc called out in his ridiculous English.

The British sentry, if he had a sister, might have taken offense provided that he understood what Marc had said.

They followed the river north through the marshes and then crossed through the woods to Turkey Creek. They forded the creek at the bridge. Marc gave Stephen a look that indicated he remembered how close they had come to death at this very spot just a few short days before. They were now only a few miles from Sandwich and still no sign of the Americans.

The sun was beginning to turn the western sky a silvery yellow. They would have to push on further if they were to bring back any news at all to General Proctor—the commandant of Amherstburg. Stephen began to feel a strong need to get a look at Sandwich before daylight faded. He began to throw caution to the winds and to trot toward the village. Now the sky was pink and orange. Up ahead was Sandwich and beyond it the Detroit River and the American side.

There were boats in the river heading north to the American shore. They were filled with troops.

"I'll be damned," said Stephen. "The Yanks are retreating. They are heading back to Detroit."

Ethan had led his troop of dragoons north along the Thames Valley recruiting for the American cause. He now commanded a force of fifty horsemen, well armed, well motivated—and they had been blooded. A small force of Wyandot and Delaware had attempted to ambush them on the return ride. They routed the Indians, killing three and losing only one of their number to wounds.

The Rivière aux Canards, which ran behind his farm, lay just in front of him. He had swept far south of the Canadian lines in order to avoid any more ambushes, or so he told himself. But if he were more honest, he would have admitted that he was fording this river so that he might ride directly to the west toward the Detroit River and his home.

The farmhouse was only a mile from here. Ingersol, too, was close to his home and Ethan could see the strain of it on his face.

"Jared, why don't you stop a few minutes and see Susan and the children? We'll wait for you at my house. I can't go by without seeing my Amy."

Ingersol said not a word. He kicked his mare in the ribs

and splashed through the river water and disappeared over the rise on the far side. His son followed him.

Ethan led his force across the river also. A few moments of silent riding through the woods west of the river brought them to the cleared land of his own farm. He signaled the troops to halt and wait in the woods. He rode on alone through the high corn that he himself had planted earlier in the summer. As he approached the barn he grew more cautious. There were more people in the vicinity of the house and porch than he had expected. But he did not dismount. He rode past the barn and up to the front porch. A young girl, dressed in homespun skirt and a man's shirt, sat fanning herself on the front porch. She toyed with the broom on the porch floor with her foot but Ethan could tell from the film of sweat on her face and the dark stains under the arms of the shirt that she had not been sitting long.

"Good day to you," he said. He startled her. She had been daydreaming and had neither seen nor heard him come. "Is the mistress of the house at home?"

She looked at him. "You don't come from here, do you? You talk kind of funny."

Ethan smiled. "I come from here more than you would suspect."

"Aunt Amy!" Liz called after watching Ethan in silence for a brief moment.

Ethan's wife came from her sitting room and stepped out through the porch door. She wore her work dress and she was sweating profusely.

"What now!" she called in annoyance. Housecleaning always made her irritable. But when she saw Ethan her irritation fled. He jumped off his horse in time to catch her as she flung herself into his arms. She was crying, burying her head in his shoulder.

"Thank God, you've come home."

"Only for a minute, to kiss you and then ride off again."

She pulled back from him and looked up into his tired face. "Why? Your dumb invasion is over."

He looked at her, the confusion obvious in his face.

"You don't know, do you? Hull has retreated back across the river. The Americans have gone home."

"I don't believe you," he said, almost stuttering. "Why? What could have made them do that?"

"Stevie brought the news that Mackinac has fallen. The

233

whole upper west is in British hands and the Indians are heading this way."

"So what? Hull has a regular army troop and good militia, not eastern farmers and merchants but frontiersmen, men used to fighting Indians."

Liz had stepped into the house to give Amy and Ethan some privacy. But soon the other occupants began to file out onto the porch. Stephen came over to Ethan and threw his arm about him. Charles hung back.

"He doesn't know about Hull. Stevie and Charlie, tell him. Make him stay home."

"I'm not sure that it's a good idea, mother," said Stephen. "Ethan is a marked man. If they made an example of anyone it would be him. He would be safer if he made it across the river until things cooled down."

Eli Stoddard stood next to Elizabeth on the porch.

"Are you the scoundrel, sir," he called out, "who has gone over to the enemy?"

Ethan stiffened. "I am the master of this house. Who, sir, are you?"

Stoddard stormed back into the house yelling about Yankee traitors, and Elizabeth went after him.

"The old man is an eccentric," said Stephen, "but I'm afraid his attitude will be that of many about these parts. They'll want a victim to teach the American 'late Loyalists' a lesson once and for all. Ethan, it's not safe."

Amy placed her hand on Ethan's face and stroked it softly. "You need a shave," she said gently.

Stephen knew his mother. Seeing Ethan leave again would break her heart.

Ethan looked at Charles finally. "Will a war drive a wedge between us, Charlie?"

The lieutenant looked down at his feet and did not respond.

Stephen looked over at his twin brother in dismay.

"He's our father, Charlie."

"No, he's not—not mine at least."

Amy started to say something but Ethan silenced her.

"The splits we have are bad enough," he said softly. "Let's create no new ones."

He placed his foot in the stirrup and threw his right leg across the horse's back. He bent down and kissed her on top of the head and yanked the horse's reins to the right. He kicked with his heels and he was gone, racing by the barn and across his own fields.

Amy stood watching after he disappeared. Stephen stepped to her side and placed his arm about her shoulder. She was dry-eyed but he could feel the quiver in her body and he knew how she felt.

Amy stiffened her back and placed her own hand on Stephen's, patting it softly, and then turned and went back into the house. After she had left, Stephen turned to his brother.

"That was quite a show. I hope Stoddard repeats it all to your friend the general. That really ought to impress him. His brilliant young lieutenant turns on his own father and mother for the cause. What a patriot!"

"He's not our father."

"Is she not our mother and is he not the man she loves, the man she chose to replace our dead father? Have you forgotten what he was like to us up until a few weeks ago? How can you do this?"

"As you yourself told me, he heads a band of men who don't take prisoners, who kill British soldiers without mercy. He's a traitor and beneath my contempt."

"May you never do anything you've reason to be ashamed of, Charlie—Holy Charlie. I know I have done plenty that I'm ashamed of and I'll do plenty more. Maybe that is why it is easier for me to understand Ethan right now. Maybe that is why I can't understand you and never have been able to understand you. We look alike, brother, but we're strangers."

Stephen stepped to the top step of the porch and walked past his brother and into the house.

Dinner that evening was quiet. Even Eli had little to say. He admired Amy Nowell as he admired her brother, his friend 'Thomas.' He did not understand how a woman of her strength of character could be married to a traitor. But he did not wish to embarrass her about it. Instead he remained silent. Charles and Stephen merely grunted at each other. After dinner Stephen took his bedding from the room he had shared with Charles since the day Ethan had completed building it and went into the kitchen. He made a bed for himself near the stove.

Elizabeth was impatient with the argument in the household. She and Eli should be with the advance forces of the army. Eli could help with his skills and she could help him. But if she left the house she would have to leave Charles and she didn't wish to leave him. She realized, somewhat to her dismay, that she had fallen in love with Charles.

The sun had set behind the woods across the river. Liz sat on the porch, still smacking all the mosquitoes who came to feast on her. The house behind her was quiet. She thought everyone had gone to bed. She was startled when the door swung open and Charles came outside to smoke his pipe. Amy disliked tobacco smoke. As a girl in Canada she said the house, all the houses, seemed to be filled with smoke, but after she married a Quaker, no smoking was allowed and she preferred it the Quaker way.

Charles did not see Liz in the darkness. He walked to the porch railing and stared across the river toward the American side.

"Sorry, aren't you?" she said from out of the shadows.

Charles was startled by the sound of her voice and jumped back from the railing.

"What are you doing here? I thought everyone had gone to bed," he said angrily.

She remained silent.

"No," he said after some moments of quiet, interrupted only by the summer night sounds. "I'm not sorry. I find it difficult to feel anything for him. He had no right to do what he did. He betrayed the family. He betrayed the country."

Charles began to feel a twitching in his nose. He was going to sneeze. Damn it, he thought, he always did this. He sneezed when he was about to cry. He did it as a boy and he was still doing it. He had to regain control. He couldn't cry in front of this girl. Now she stood by his side touching his arm. He looked down at her and he saw tenderness in her eyes. He bent down and kissed her soft lips gently. She put her arms around him. He brought her body next to his and held her close to him. It felt good after driving away from him the father who had provided the security of his youth. It felt good, almost necessary, to hold on to another human being for comfort and for security.

And then Liz destroyed this illusion.

"Come to bed with me, Charles."

The lieutenant pulled away from her in shock.

"What are you saying?"

"I want you to sleep with me."

"What kind of a girl are you?" he said, removing his arms from her waist. "What kind of a man do you think I am?"

She stepped back from him looking hurt.

"I thought you were a man. I want to sleep with you. Doc has told me all about how it is done and now I want to try. I'm eighteen years old. It's time."

Charles's angry reaction began to diminish. The girl had lessened it by reminding him of her age. It was true, she was eighteen—a child.

"Liz, when you marry a man, you may sleep with him, not before. Didn't Doc Stoddard tell you about that?"

"No," she said.

"Well, perhaps I should wake him and have him complete your education."

"No need," she said. "My offer is withdrawn."

"It is not an offer that a proper woman makes to begin with."

"All right, stop preaching," she said angrily.

Charles was silent for some moments. "Elizabeth," he said finally, "I think maybe I am something of a prig. I think you were trying to tell me something by your offer and I allowed my overblown sense of propriety to block your intent. Thank you for your offer," he said, "even if it has been withdrawn."

She smiled at him. Now she truly loved him.

Charles watched her go into the house and then he followed her. He climbed the stairs to the second floor and entered his room. He looked at Stephen's stripped and empty bed. He was sorry about Ethan at last. He should have been understanding of his stepfather's feelings as he had been of this strange girl's.

Liz was still hungry and she wanted another piece of Mrs. Morin's pecan pie. She opened the kitchen door. The moonlight flooded into the kitchen now from the open window that looked out toward the river next to the south end of the covered porch. There was a bundle of something under the window. Liz reached down to touch it and a hand grabbed her. She yelped.

"Shut up," said Stephen. "Do you want to wake up the whole house? It's bad enough you and my brother have been keeping me awake."

He raised his voice to a falsetto. "I want you to sleep with me, priggish sir." Then he lowered his voice. "How dare you threaten my virtue, slut." Again falsetto, "Well, screw you, big boy, you can't have me anyway."

She kicked him with her foot.

"Damn," he groaned and pulled her off her feet and down on top of him. "How about sleeping with me?" he said, looking into her face. "I won't turn you down."

"I'd rather sleep with a pig."

"Then that can be arranged too, though I think it is a bit advanced for you."

She pulled away from him and stood up.

"I came in here for a piece of pie," she said, straightening her dress.

"And all this while I thought you had come in here to see me."

She was on the verge of crying, not with fear but from anger at this man who looked so much like the gentle man outside on the porch, but who was so crude and frightened her as she had never been frightened by anyone or anything before in her life. She turned and ran out the door and up the stairs to her bedroom. She heard him laugh as she ran. Upstairs, even with the door locked and her head under the covers on a sweltering August night, she swore she could still hear his mocking voice.

The humiliation was too much for Matthew to take. He had been allowed to cross finally but his invasion of Canada had lasted only five days. William Hull was an old lady. He was terrified of his own shadow. But most of all he was terrified of Tecumseh's Indians. He saw them everywhere. If only they had a leader like Wayne or even John Sullivan, the first general he had served under. They knew how to deal with Indians. You crushed them with steel.

Matthew rose from his bed in his reduced quarters within the walls of Detroit. He felt caged within this fortress.

"Hull should be shot for treason," he said aloud, and he was not alone in his attitude. Lewis Cass, his nemesis of last month, had said the same thing publicly. The general seemed paralyzed. When word came finally of the fall of Fort Michilimackinac it was his undoing. Stories were related of hundreds of Chippewa and Sioux, traveling south to join Tecumseh, falling on Hull's exposed rear. He panicked and ordered all of his troops to return to the American side and withdrew within the safety of the fort.

Matthew opened the door and walked out on the parade ground. His room was stifling in the August heat. He needed to walk. He moved briskly across the large open field. He climbed the stairs leading to the parapet on which Detroit's guns were placed. He could look down on the village below and across the river to Sandwich with a British flag flying over it once again. He recognized the stooped form of the gray-haired man walking along the same parapet toward him.

"Matthew," Ethan called when he saw him.

Matthew stopped and greeted his brother-in-law.

"What in God's name has happened? I left an invading, confident army and returned days later, after a raid, to chaos," said the southerner softly to Matthew. "What has happened to all of us, and in particular, what in the world has happened to the general?"

"We failed," responded Matthew, "not from a lack of ability or a lack of courage from our troops. It was a failure of will on the part of our leaders."

Ethan turned and looked over toward Sandwich—toward Canada—and looked wistfully on in the direction of Amherstburg.

"My troop is dispersed. As soon as they learned of the retreat, they melted like snow in a hot sun. Even Jared Ingersol, my neighbor and lifelong friend, has returned to his home."

"No regrets now, brother?" said Matthew.

"It's too late for regrets." Ethan remained quiet, staring across the river. Finally he broke the silence. "I'll ask Amy to join me here. It will be a long time before I can go back, and I've never been without her for almost the whole of the last thirty years. I can't start being alone now."

Matthew looked away from Ethan. He knew all about being alone. He could not work up much sympathy for Ethan's plight.

"What do we do next?" Ethan asked.

"We wait."

"For what?"

"We wait until General Hull gets his balls back or until reinforcements come up the Ohio or . . ." His voice trailed off.

"Or what?"

"Or until the British launch their own invasion. Which I hope they do. Get them in an open field of battle and we'll destroy them as we did Blue Jacket in seventeen ninety-four and as we did the Shawnee last year. I just hope they try it."

"You sure we'll win?" asked Ethan.

239

"Now you begin to sound like Hull."

Ethan just shook his head and began again to look across the river—toward home.

General Brock arrived at Amherstburg after the American retreat to their own side of the river. He was overjoyed at the news of the American withdrawal and he called in immediate council of war. The room for this late-night meeting was in General Proctor's headquarters inside the walls of Amherstburg. There were general officers, gold braid embellishing their red coats, intermingled with the more drab uniforms of provincial officers. But the most resplendent of all the allies were Tecumseh and his chiefs. They were dressed in a strange mixture of colorful shirts and pants, deerskin and feathers, silver medallions. Some had painted their faces and their bodies. The Shawnee chief was simply dressed. He was, nevertheless, the dominant presence among the allies. When the British asked questions all eyes turned to this fair-skinned giant, Tecumseh.

He was in a cautious mood. The Americans had withdrawn from Canada. Fine for the Canadians. But they still controlled the Indians' homeland with their string of forts from the Ohio River to the Great Lakes. What would this new general—General Brock—do about this?

As if anticipating this question, Brock began the conference by soliciting from each of his commanders their view of the next step. To a man they advised caution. Wait out the Americans. Their supplies would run out. The Indians would wreak havoc with their long overland supply lines. Britain had control of the lake and the water routes. They could outwait the Americans.

Then Brock turned to the Indian. Tecumseh answered slowly and carefully. The American forts in the lands of the Indians would have to be taken if the Indian nation was to be created. The first of these forts was Detroit. A British army sat opposite Detroit. If the British would not help their allies to destroy that fort, what trust could be placed in their other promises?

Brock sat for some seconds weighing Tecumseh's word. He slammed his fist down on his knee.

"The man is right," he said. "I've made up my mind." The fact was that he had made up his mind before he had entered the room. He could not afford caution. He needed a total victory so that he might transfer his regulars back to the dangerous Niagara line. The British would attack.

The British opened a battery at Sandwich that began to pound away at Detroit. Matthew wanted to move a gun to respond to it but he had received no answer from his superior, General Hull. No one was getting any answer from Hull. He climbed down from the gun and made his way to Hull's headquarters, once his own, before the Army of the Northwest arrived in Detroit.

He opened the door. The sentries ignored him. The troops were dispirited since their return to the fort.

"I must speak with General Hull," Matthew said to the general's son, who acted as his aide.

"The general is indisposed," said Captain Hull.

At that moment, as if to make a liar of his son, William Hull stepped out into the outer office. He looked at Matthew with unseeing eyes.

"General, I've asked permission to respond to the British fire. I've had no word."

"Oh, it's you, Nowell," said Hull. "Have you any reports? Will the Canadians rally to us?"

Matthew looked at him in disbelief. "Not here in Detroit," he responded. "If we had stayed in Canada, maybe."

"I need more men. The enemy outnumbers us," he rambled. "The Indians, hundreds of them, are due from the north and already that devil, Tecumseh, has almost two thousand men."

"I think that estimate is a bit high," said Matthew.

"If anything, a bit low," said Captain Hull.

Matthew saw a momentary panic in the eyes of the general. And he became frightened.

"My daughter is here, you know," said Hull, "and my grandchildren as well. There are so many civilians, so many women and children."

"He's received a letter from Brock," said the general's son. "The scoundrel warns us that he may not be able to control Tecumseh's devils and that the responsibility for any massacre will lie with the general."

"All British generals have said that," said Matthew. "And the French before them."

"And sometimes that's precisely what happens," interrupted

241

General Hull. "You remember Montcalm at Fort William Henry?"

Matthew had enough for the day. The sound of cannonballs crashing against wooden palisades forced all three of them to duck involuntarily.

"No," said General Hull, after staring absentmindedly for some moments. "Don't fire back. Maybe they'll leave us alone."

Matthew stormed out of Hull's office and nearly tripped over Colonel Cass on his way in.

"Nowell, what the hell is the regular army up to?"

"Don't confuse that man with the regular army," said Matthew bitterly.

"He's a coward," said Cass. "We should relieve him."

Matthew shook his head. "He's a disaster, Cass, but he is the commander. Lieutenant colonels do not remove generals. Not unless they want a court martial and a rope as their reward."

"Well, he wants to send me and McArthur out with the volunteers to reach a supply train stuck in the swamps. Maybe it is just as well. I don't think I can stay cooped up here while the British force me to eat their lead."

He walked past Matthew and entered Hull's quarters.

Nowell returned to his own room. It was no use standing by the cold guns waiting for the word to fire that would never come.

Stephen was sweating and the sun had not yet risen. He had watched Tecumseh's braves cross the river so silently last night. Now it was the turn of the regulars and the militia. He was wearing a red coat, as was Marc. Brock had dressed up his Canadians in uniforms.

"Stevie," whispered Marc. "These jackets stink. I think they are infested. I itch." He tore at his armpits with his nails.

"Damn generals, they think Americans will be impressed with the number of regulars he has. It's an insult to our Amherstburg troops. We can fight every bit as tough as the regulars," said Stephen.

The boats had arrived empty except for their oarsmen at the Canadian shore. Stephen and Marc climbed in together and the rowers pushed off.

The militiamen took turns at the oars and pulled across the

narrow straits quickly. Stephen recognized the landing place as Spring Wells, just north of the mouth of the River Rouge and south of Detroit.

He saw Brock astride his horse. He wore his best uniform; his frame looked almost too large for the gray horse he rode. Beside him on an Indian pony sat Tecumseh, dressed only in buckskin. The Indian galloped off to join his men in the woods beyond the shore road and farms. Brock, once all of his men had landed safely, rode to the head of the column and signaled for the march to begin. The general himself was in the van.

The sun had come up and it was hot. Stephen hated this kind of war. Marching in lockstep wearing a red coat marking out his vitals to even the poorest marksman of the Yanks was madness. There were some very good men with a rifle in the American army. The sun grew hotter as the morning wore on. They could see Detroit now and Detroit could see them. All the Americans had to do now was open fire and Isaac Brock and his fine red-coated army would be no different from the ducks he took on the river back home across the straits.

Marc cursed. But Stephen did not look around to see his problem. He could see Tecumseh's men parading through the woods to his left, also in full view of the enemy in the fort.

Stephen felt as though every gun in Detroit was aimed at him. Even at this distance he could make out the gaping holes bored into iron that were the muzzles of the guns of the fortress. Yet they continued to march along the river road toward the town. There was an orchard on their left. Brock rose in his saddle and signaled the column to turn through the orchard, whose trees were filled with ripening apples and pears. Some of the Amherstburg volunteers picked the still-green apples and offered them impishly to the British regulars. Marc laughed when he saw that several accepted and began to munch on them, sour as they were.

"Let's hope we get into battle soon or else this army will be fit for nothing but latrine duty," he jested to Stephen.

The soldier in front of Stephen, without breaking stride, turned and spat on Marc's boots.

"Canadian scum," he said in a heavy London accent. "You're not fit to clean up the latrines of the men of the Forty-first, and the cast-off jackets of the foot soldiers of the Forty-first are the best you'll ever wear in your life. It's hard to forgive Brock for letting a shit-face like you wear it."

Marc moved to attack the cockney but Stephen stepped in the way.

"We have another enemy to fight," said Stephen. "Or have you both forgotten?"

"I've not forgotten," said the Englishman, "and the only thing viler than a Canadian is a Kentuckian or an Ohio man. We'll fight and lick the Yanks first and then we'll take on you bumpkins."

"Shut up in the ranks," yelled a British accent that Stephen recognized immediately as belonging to Corporal Case, who had been with them at Turkey Creek.

They were through the orchard now and marching through a gully parallel to Detroit and out of range and view of its guns. Brock called a halt and ordered the column to rest. He himself, still seemingly untouched by the heat of the August day, rode back through the column to get a proper view of the town. He ordered his Indian scouts to reconnoiter. He did not have to await their return for long. They came back bearing a blindfolded American officer who carried a white flag of truce. General Hull wanted to talk.

Brock ordered his two aides, Major Glegg and Lieutenant Colonel MacDonell, to accompany the American officer back into Detroit. As the two aides passed through the ranks, they selected regulars and volunteers to go with them as a small guard. MacDonell grabbed both Stephen and Marc while Glegg selected Marc's cockney nemesis, a West Country Englishman, and Corporal Case.

They climbed out of the ravine and out onto the plains before the fort. A giant white flag of truce flew from the ramparts and American troops could be seen falling back quickly in an orderly fashion from the plains into the fort.

"Damn," cursed Marc under his breath. "What makes these snobs, these officers, think the Yanks won't take our guns and lock us up and use the general's aides as hostages?"

"You mean that is what you'd do," said Stephen.

"Why not?" responded Marc.

"Gentlemen don't fight wars that way," said the cockney, whose name was John Dash.

Marc started to laugh when he heard the name and thought of the green apples.

"What do you know about gentlemen?" asked Stiegler.

244

"About as much as you do—nothing, but Glegg and MacDonell are gentlemen and so's Hull. They'll honor this flag-of-truce shit. It's like a little kid playing tag. We used to be able to call out 'rest' and no one could tag us when we were resting. The white flag means nobody shoots. It's rest time."

The gate was swung open for the officers and their guard. Stephen had never before seen such chaos. Blue-coated American troops seemed to be running in every direction. Hundreds of terrified women were herding little children into protective buildings to avoid the cannons of Sandwich and the two British gunboats in the Detroit River. Cattle, sheep, and goats ran wild in panic on the dirt parade ground. General Hull sat under a brightly striped tented pavilion. The British officers approached him. Stephen and Marc lagged behind, holding their muskets at their sides.

Hull seemed ill or distraught. His eyes darted from Glegg to MacDonell and back again.

"I'm asking General Brock for a three-day truce," said the American.

"You have three hours," said Glegg.

"Gentlemen," said Hull, suddenly very agitated, "I have responsibilities. Look about you. Innocent lives are at stake here. Your savages will wreak death and mutilation on the fair women and babes. I must have guarantees. I just can't surrender. There is the honor of my nation."

"You have the word of my general, who is an officer and a man of honor, that the innocent will not be harmed. That guarantee you will have to weigh against the requirements of your nation's flag. If you do not surrender in three hours, we will attack and destroy the fort and everything and every combatant in it."

Stephen recognized his uncle standing behind and to the left of Hull. He had not seen Matthew Nowell since that day on the River Rouge. It was not that long ago, but he seemed to have aged. His brown hair hung down over his forehead. His face looked thinner. He looked like a man in pain. Matthew leaned down and whispered in Hull's ear. The American general nodded.

"If I do surrender, Colonel," he said, "I must at least have some guarantee of protection for the former Americans who have rallied to the service of their country's flag."

"Impossible," said MacDonell, the Canadian, not waiting for Glegg to respond. "If they are persons who have sworn

245

allegiance to the king and gone back on that sacred oath, they'll pay the price for their treason."

Fear gripped Stephen for the first time in this entire campaign when he heard MacDonell's words. He was sure he knew now where his stepfather, Ethan, was. He had not fled into the woods like any sensible traitor would. Instead he had behaved like an "honorable traitor." He would probably surrender when Hull gave up, as Stephen was now sure he would. He had seen beaten men before and Hull had that same confused look about him. Stephen felt he should be overjoyed at a bloodless victory but now he was afraid for his stepfather's life.

The American army, regulars and militia, marched out of the great wooden gate of Detroit and stacked their arms and battle flags on the esplanade in front of the fort. Some were openly weeping, but most, like Matthew Nowell, were grim-faced and silent. Inwardly they cursed the weak man who had been placed over them by an inept and unprepared government. When Hull fixed his signature on the articles of surrender, Matthew turned his back, took his sword, the same sword he had held in his broken wrist at Fallen Timbers, and broke it in two over his knee. Then he stormed from the pavilion back toward his quarters. If he was to be a prisoner of war, he would need to pack his essentials.

He had recognized Stephen Miller with the British negotiators. Ethan was his stepson. Perhaps Miller would help Ethan. Matthew turned and retraced his path toward the pavilion. Miller still stood behind the Canadian lieutenant colonel. He tried to catch Miller's eye but the stupid boy looked blindly ahead. Again he raised his arm in signal. This time he was sure another man, a regular, had intercepted his motion. Matthew turned as if to say something to Hull, who still sat in the pavilion conversing with the British officers. Then, as if suddenly changing his mind, he turned and walked back across the parade ground. He would have to tell the news to Ethan.

General Brock and Tecumseh rode into Detroit side by side. The Forty-first Fife and Drum played a march, and the British regulars and volunteers and hundreds of Tecumseh's men cheered. Tecumseh had achieved something his predecessor, Pontiac, had never done. He had taken Detroit. The defeat at Tippecanoe was avenged. For Brock it was a great and bloodless victory but one that could not be savored long. Another American army threatened Upper Canada across another river, the Niagara. He would take the cheers of his Redcoats, his beloved regulars, men he had led on this long journey from Port Dover. They deserved this moment. Even the York volunteers and the Amherstburg militia—they too deserved it. He could lay aside his suspicion of their soldiering qualities. The moment was theirs to savor as well. For the Indians, especially for the strange man who rode by his side, the moment was especially sweet. Tecumseh would let them loot and take those things in Detroit that they coveted—furs, blankets, trinkets, muskets, and powder. But there was to be no massacre. He had the chief's word on that, and strangely enough he felt this Indian's word meant more than the word of most men. But always in Isaac Brock's mind was the need to move on. He had word from young Miller that his ship *Sophia* was at Amherstburg. He would sail tomorrow. His troops would follow, leaving Proctor with only enough men to guard prisoners. *Nancy* and the other boat would ferry his army back to Fort Erie and to the one front in Upper Canada that still remained. He would sail with Miller to Fort Erie, then he would ride as fast as his horse would take him to Newark on Lake Ontario. He had to be back in his capital at York and on to Kingston to raise new troops and to meet the next threat.

Stephen saw his uncle signal the first time. He cursed the fool mentally for not understanding that. He wondered how often he would risk giving himself away. He followed Matthew's path back across the parade ground with his eyes. He noted where the American went. That must be where Ethan hid. Once he was free to roam the fort he would begin his search there.

Ethan had wanted to join Matthew and march out of the fort as a prisoner of war. But Nowell had argued with him. His only chance was to wait until his friends among the Canadians could whisk him out of Detroit and back to his farm on the Canadian side. Once the threat of military operation was over and he could avoid arrest, he could begin anew, either in the Canadian or in the U.S. frontier. Ethan had listened to his brother-in-law and now he sat alone in the vacated officers' quarters of the fort. All around him outside he heard Indian war whoops. He wondered if Tecumseh's men had gone on a rampage but he heard none of the screams of the women and children that would have accompanied a massacre. No one was being killed. At least not yet.

Matthew had told him to expect Stevie. It had been hours and no one had come for him. He sat, his loaded dueling pistol in his lap, listening to Matthew's clock tick away, counting the hours and the half hours.

Finally there was a soft rap on the door. Ethan rose and stepped to the side of the door. It swung open slowly. Ethan saw his stepson enter. He slammed the door behind him. Stephen was startled and turned to face his foe, knife drawn from his side.

"Stevie," said Ethan, lowering his pistol and hugging the other man.

"Come on, we've got to get out of here," said Stephen.

"I didn't think there was much chance of that until Matt told me you had entered the fort."

"Marc's outside making sure the way is clear."

"Is that the boy we almost did in?"

"Yes."

"Can he be trusted?"

"He saved my hide on a few occasions and he's kin to mother."

Ethan nodded. The two men stepped out of the officers' quarters into the dusk. The Indians were looting the commissary. Some of them were drunk, despite Tecumseh's prohibition of alcohol. But on the whole they were friendly, not hostile.

Stephen and Ethan found Marc at the end of the alley behind Matthew's quarters. The three men moved cautiously from building to building until dark took over and they stood beside the great log walls at the foot of the ramparts. The Indians were shooting off muskets within the fort but there was even more gunfire from the town below.

Stephen's eyes had adjusted to the darkness gradually but still he had trouble seeing in front of him. He could hear Ethan's heavy breathing behind him. His stepfather was not a young man any longer. And his breathing sounded raspy.

Marc's hand touched his arm, signaling that it was clear to the north gate at the rear of the fortress. The plan was to stroll through, three militiamen with a bit too much to drink looking for a place to sleep it off in the woods.

Stephen put his arm about Ethan's shoulders and started to sing drunkenly. It was a ballad he had learned at Mackinac. Marc began to ramble on in French. They walked out into the traffic that came into the gate as the British took over the American stronghold. They had made it among the wagons, avoiding the carts' wheels and dodging horses. The red-coated sentries at the gate paid little attention to the traffic. They were annoyed that everyone else was enjoying the celebration.

Suddenly a shout was raised. Stephen turned around and saw the face of Corporal Case of the Forty-first along with Private Dash. They aimed their muskets at the militiamen. Stephen yelled. They dropped behind a wagon as it came between the Redcoats and the fugitives. The three men then made a rush for the gate. Dash fired and missed. His ball smashed a window of a settler's cabin that stood next to the fort's wall. Stephen was running now as fast as he could. He trailed Marc, who was already through the gate. The corporal screamed out and brought the sentries to life. One stepped in Stephen's path, but Miller did not stop. He crashed directly into the smaller man, sending him flying through the air. He turned and looked for Ethan and saw him struggling to keep up.

"Hurry," he shouted. He grabbed his stepfather's arm to hurry him along. He could see the corporal aiming his musket carefully. He shoved Ethan aside as the ball slammed into a second sentry's chest. His musket went flying into the air and discharged. The soldier was dead before he hit the ground. Ethan stumbled from Stephen's shove. He rose to his feet. Stephen could see the panic on Ethan's face. He was just about out of wind. But they couldn't wait. Marc had already made it to the woods. Stephen started to run but Ethan tripped and fell on his face. Stephen knew that their escape had failed.

Stephen was sentenced to one hundred lashes for attempting to aid an enemy. Normally he would have been hanged, but the enemy was his own stepfather. Even fussy General Proctor could see why he might try. The lashes were never given. The night before sentence was to be carried out, the side of the tent where Stephen was held was neatly slit open and ropes cut and the captive became a fugitive. In the search that followed, no sign was found of militiaman Miller.

It was noted in the company roll that militiaman Stiegler had disappeared also.

But there was no rescuing Ethan Morin, the arch traitor of Upper Canada. He was locked in the Detroit jail under heavy guard. Brock had pardoned most of those who has joined Morin but Brock was gone, sailed for Fort Erie, and Proctor was a more vindictive man. The court martial sentenced Ethan to hang. The most damning testimony against him was evidence given by Corporal Cass of the Forty-first, who recalled for the court Morin's orders to kill the prisoners at Turkey Creek and recounted vividly the death of Private Robinson and Private Evans at the hands of this man's troops.

Ethan stood before the red-coated judges. His shoulders, which had began to stoop over the years, straightened as the sentence was read.

Amy sat in the courtroom. She too seemed to grow taller as she realized what her husband's fate was to be. She had no family with her. Charles had sailed with General Brock and Stephen was in hiding. Elizabeth sat by her side, however, and held her hand, and Eli Stoddard put aside politics to help a friend in need. He sat on Amy's other side.

"Have you any response to the sentence?" said a Major Philps, who was the president of the court.

Ethan hesitated a moment and then he said in a soft voice, "God bless the United States of America."

"Take him away," said the major.

Amy looked into her husband's face as he was led to the door. She knew he was afraid, but no one else would ever know it.

Eli put his head in his hands.

"The fellow is deranged," he moaned. "He doesn't know what he speaks of. There must be an appeal." He was on his feet now. "The lady, the prisoner's wife, appeals to General Proctor and requests a delay of sentence until General Brock can be reached."

"The sentence of the court is to be carried out within the hour," said Major Philps. "It can be carried out with only General Proctor's approval. You have no chance of an appeal to the governor."

Amy rose to stand by Stoddard. "I will not beg the court for my husband's life," she said. "I will not bring that shame on him. I do ask permission to speak to him."

Philps looked away. He was not an unkind man. The strength in this woman was remarkable.

"Guard," he called to the sentry by the door, "take Mrs. Morin to see the prisoner."

The guard led her down a long garbage-strewn alley to a small shack. It was guarded by a platoon of regulars. He spoke to the sergeant in command of the guard detail. The sergeant looked over at Amy. He shook his head in resignation and opened the shack door for her.

The shack smelled of rat droppings. Ethan stood with his back to the door. Amy called his name. He turned around. She rushed to him and he enfolded her in his arms. She cried softly for some moments.

"It would have been better for you, Ethan Morin," she said finally, "if you had never met me back in Isle d'Orleans—a lovesick but soon embittered child."

"But then the past thirty years would never have been," he responded.

"I should never have brought you to Canada to find a child I never really regained and whose love was denied me by a villain—my brother."

"Let's not rehash the past. It's over. What's done is done," he said. "I put myself where I am, not you."

"I don't want you to die," she sobbed.

"But I'm going to," he said, holding her tightly.

The room seemed to close in on her, to confine her. She was terrified for him.

He looked at her eyes and saw the fear in them.

"Be brave, Amy. Tell the boys that I loved them more than if they'd been my own and make them promise, since they can't promise it to my face, make them promise on my memory to take care of you."

She kissed him softly on the mouth and pushed the locks of gray hair from his forehead.

The door of the shack was opened and banged against the wall. The Redcoats entered and motioned Ethan to step outside. As he did, he was grabbed roughly, his hands were tied behind his back, and he was shoved forward.

Amy leaned against the shack wall to steady herself. A soldier went to help her, thinking she was going to faint. She pushed his hand away. She watched Ethan as he was led down the alleyway. They turned the corner and then he was gone.

12

Aaron felt like an old man. Sixty-seven years old was certainly too old to be sleeping out of doors and paddling canoes again. He had not done anything like this in twenty years. But Isaac Brock had an effect on him. The general told him of his need of allies. Tecumseh's men had made the difference in Detroit. He needed the Grand River Mohawks—still neutral after five months of war. He knew what Brock wanted of him. He had been a Mohawk sachem. He rode to Fort Erie and then set out on the lake in Miller's sloop. His nephew deposited him in his canoe on the Grand River sandbar. Here Miller would wait at anchor until he returned. Aaron paddled to shore and entered the river. He pulled to the riverbank and removed his European clothes. His buckskin leggings were stiff from lack of use. He put the loincloth in place.

"Jessica should see me now," he said aloud.

The buckskin shirt was tight, too tight to wear. He did not wish to go bare-chested. It was chilly and he did not need to develop a cough. In addition, his chest muscles had sagged, making him look more female than male. He cursed advancing age. He put his white dress shirt on. It was a strange garb but most Iroquois today dressed in a mixture of Indian and European clothes. It was late now. He thought he would camp here for the night. He rolled out his bedding and built a small fire. Miller had given him a basket filled with ship's bread and meat and a bottle of rum to keep him warm. He rested against a log, watching the flames and eating the meat between two pieces of ship's bread. It was harder by far than the unleavened bread Jessica insisted on making every year.

He was sleepy even though it was still early. Sleep seemed to come earlier and earlier. Eventually, he thought, it would come so early it would be late, too late. He chuckled.

Some things had not left him. He knew there were others present.

"My brothers come to share my fire with me," he said in Mohawk.

Four men stepped out of the bushes. They were old men, some of them as old as Aaron and some a bit younger. He recognized each of them. He had fought alongside them.

252

"Kenonranon has not visited the Mohawks in many years," one of them said. "He was replaced long ago as the sachem. What has made him leave the city of whites on Ontario and come to the home of his people?"

Aaron gestured to the other men to sit around the fire. They did. One took tobacco and filled a pipe. He puffed and passed it on to the man next to him. When all had smoked, Aaron addressed his old comrades.

"General Brock has sent me to you. He is sad that the children of He Who Does Great Things, my stepfather, and the people of the Brants have not joined in the war against the Americans."

"The last time you, Kenonranon, and Thayendanegga and the clan mother urged us to war on the Americans we lived on the eastern door of the longhouse—part of a proud confederation. Now you ask us to war again. Could we not lose even our present home?"

Aaron shook his head. "You speak like an old woman, Hiadenoni."

The old man clutched his crotch. "I may well be an old woman," he said, patting himself. "Not much going on anymore."

The others laughed at his joke. But Aaron knew these men did not come to joke, they came because they were worried. They had lost much in the late war and they feared more losses. But Aaron knew they would not be here if they felt they could control the young men. The Mohawks must be badly divided and the young men were itching for war. The older, more cautious, heads feared they would not be obeyed.

"My brothers," said Aaron, "the call has also gone out from Tecumseh and other people have answered. Shawnee, Winnebago, Ottawa, Ojibwa, Sioux, Saux, Foxes, Wyandot—the name the western tribes give our old enemy the Huron. Only the people of the longhouse hold back."

"We have not allowed the young men to put on paint and take up the tomahawk, nor will the women agree to a war in council. It angers the Chipmunk Who Wishes to Roar Like a Bear."

They all chuckled at the long name.

Aaron looked puzzled.

"Your cousin," said Houedto, "John Brant. His father wished him to be a sachem, although he was only a boy. When he lost his oldest son, Isaac, we sought to honor the boy and

253

made him a sachem. His heart was failing him and Joseph Brant was a great leader, greater than Hendricks and Old Brant his grandfather—as great a leader of our people as Degonawida or Hiawatha. So we humored him and the boy is a good boy."

"But you do not respect him," said Aaron.

"Should an old man respect a child?"

"When he is Joseph Brant's child—yes," responded Aaron.

"But the Chipmunk is not the one we fear. It is the other one—the one who is not of us yet, who calls himself a son of the longhouse. His name is Norton. We call on you who are one of us, but claim not to be, to neutralize him who claims us but is . . ."

All five men started to howl with laughter. Hiadenoni became so confused with his words that he could not get it straight. He started to say it again but Aaron interrupted.

"I know what you mean, friend, but I have come to urge the Mohawks to make war on the Americans again. I side with this imposter Norton and with my cousin, the son of my Turtle uncle, Joseph Brant."

"We know that war comes, Kenonranon, but we have no one who can force the young men to listen. We do not wish widows and orphans in our lodges on the Grand River. We want you to resume your duties and lead the Mohawks to war. If you do, our sons will return home to us."

Aaron was shocked but his face remained impassive. "I am too old. Older than some of you. Why can't some of you lead the men?"

"They will not listen to us," said Conneusut, who was an Onondaga, "nor will they follow us. Instead if we try to lead, young Brant and Norton will take over and charge into the mouths of cannons. But if the legendary Kenonranon, son of Molly Brant, were to return to lead his people, then they would be saved. Proper caution would be observed and our sons would return to us."

Aaron knew the older men were offering him exactly what Brock wanted—Indians on the Niagara front. He knew the general well enough to suspect that Brock did not value them as soldiers but he knew the effect their presence would have on the farmers who helped make up the New York militia: "The Mohawks were with the British"—those words would be worth regiments of regulars to him.

Aaron looked at his friends. He smiled and nodded. He knew it would be too much for him but the stakes were high. Despite the victory at Detroit, Canada was at risk.

Sergeant Devers, who was originally from Kingston but had moved his printing business to York when it became the capital of Upper Canada, walked along the fortifications at the docks, checking with each soldier.

"Keep your eyes peeled over at Lewiston. The Yanks may be up to something."

Michael Brant stood guard with Joseph Ashton, also of York. His father was a merchant with offices at Montreal and York and a trading post at St. Joseph's Island.

"Here comes old Lard Ass," whispered Joe, as Devers approached their post on the docks. Michael laughed.

"Hey, Sergeant," yelled Ashton, "just what are the Yanks up to over there?"

"Pulling their peckers for all I know. I just got word that they're restless. There are signs, boats at the riverfront, things like that."

"We've seen all that before," said Michael.

"No reason to get lazy," said the sergeant as he passed down the line toward the next post.

The two young men were quiet. The river rushed by them, still churning and noisy after its great drop onto the rocks below the falls. Somewhere downriver the waters began to settle down and prepare to enter Lake Ontario, still moving on its restless journey from the fresh inland lakes to the salt sea of the Atlantic.

"Do you ever get scared by all of this?" Michael asked.

Joe shook his head. "I did at the beginning. The first time a Yankee bugler let loose across the river I thought for sure a thousand Kentucky wild men would fly right across, string me up by my heels like a buck, and slit open my belly. Well, they didn't come and I'm beginning to think they might never come. What's more, Detroit taught me that those Kentucky and Tennessee boys are human after all. They get captured too and I guess they get scared just like you and me."

"I think they're going to move and they're going to move here. They have to do something after Detroit. Their morale must be low."

"The problem is that the Yanks came into the war divided.

New England isn't even fighting and the militia feel that they'll defend their homes and no more. If we attack them, they'll fight but I don't think General VanRensselaer can move them across the river."

"Devers thinks he can," suggested Michael.

"Ah, yes, 'General' Devers."

"But Brock thinks VanRensselaer can and he is a general."

Joe remained silent. No one in Upper Canada had the nerve to second-guess Isaac Brock.

"Well," he said finally, stretching his muscles and watching for a glimpse of old Lard Ass disappearing down the line, "they won't be coming in broad daylight. Wake me if you hear a bugle."

He pulled the collar of his uniform coat about his ears and sank down onto his bottom against a dock piling. He was asleep within a minute.

The night came and soon Michael was relieved from his post. All during the night he dreaded the call that he knew was inevitable. At three A.M. he would be shaken roughly by Sergeant Devers. He dreaded the moment but he had at least another hour to go. Suddenly he felt the hand on his shoulder. He awoke with his fist raised ready to strike out.

"Easy, fellow," said the sergeant. "It's time to get on your feet."

Michael had lost his sense of time. He could have sworn he had just looked at the pocket watch his father had given him and it was two o'clock. He removed it from his pocket.

"You're right," said Devers, "special orders. There is too much activity across the Niagara. The Yanks are on the move."

Michael was now very awake. The moment he had waited for with anticipation and fear could well be at hand. He had slept in his clothes. Well, thank God for his mother's foresight in packing warm clothes for him. Some of his York friends were shivering in garments worn to war in July. He rolled up his blanket and strapped it to his backpack. His musket was cleaned and it was loaded.

"Where do we go today?" called out Jervis, whose family lived not far from Michael's.

"It's up to the escarpment, to guard the big gun up there. The Yanks will be coming across at last."

Michael picked up his musket and started to march. It was an exhausting march from Queenston up the road to the escarpment. The night was black. Clouds, he thought, must be covering the moon and stars. The path was steep. He wished he was in the navy like his cousin Charles Miller. Charlie always had a warm bed and hot food. Soldiering was tough, although so far he had only heard cannons fired in anger across the border. Everyone else in the family had seen more of the war than he had. Charles had ferried Brock's troops to Detroit, Steve Miller had fought the Yanks at Mackinac and at Detroit—two overwhelming victories, two captured forts. His father, according to Jessica's letter, was again declared war leader and sachem of the Mohawks. Even Elizabeth and Uncle Eli had been to the front. Only he, the young warrior they had so proudly sent off to war, remained unbaptized by battle. Joe Ashton, who marched ahead of him, stopped and reached for Michael's arm. He pointed down across the river onto the American side. Lights—torches—could be seen along the river. Michael nodded. Brock was right. The Americans would attack. Now all that needed to be determined was where. Given the activity at Lewiston, Michael was sure they would come straight across the river. Queenston was their target. He would not remain unbaptized for long.

American regulars and militia attacked during the early morning hours. They crossed about a thousand strong but in a badly coordinated landing. Many of the regulars never made it across because of defective boats. The dock defenders, British regulars and provincial militia, fought desperately to keep them out of the town. Most of the Americans ended up pinned down along the river beneath the cliffs of the escarpment.

Stephen ducked behind the stones that dotted the shore as the firing from the dock became heavier and heavier. The damned American generals had made a mess of it again, he thought. This was a battle he was sure he should have missed. The British gun on top of the mountain was raining a devastating fire on the American troops that attempted to cross the river. So devastating, in fact, that no longer were the boats trying to make a crossing. It was a fine pickle. They couldn't move ahead and they couldn't retreat. Why, in God's name, he thought, had he decided to join up with the Americans? He was a Canadian. And here he was attacking his own people in the company of farmers from New York State and hard-bitten regular U.S. troops. But he knew why. It came to him in his nightmares. The soft drawl of the only father he had ever known—a gentle man, murdered for his beliefs. Stephen did not like Americans, but he hated the British because of Ethan.

He ducked when the gun on the escarpment went off. He knew it was silly. If it was aimed at him he would not hear of it.

Captain Wool, his commander, crawled past him toward Colonel VanRensselaer, the general's nephew, who had led the advance force. The colonel had been cut down by musket balls and lay helpless, bleeding, trapped on the Canadian shore of the Niagara with his entire force of a thousand men.

Wool spoke to VanRensalaer in agitation for some minutes and then finally the wounded man waved him away in disgust. Wool crawled back to his own company. He called his officers and sergeants together and conferred with them.

Lieutenant Gresham came to Stephen's troop to explain.

"The captain says he has learned of an old goat path up the front face of the mountain. He wants us to scale it. The colonel has agreed. You're all to take as much equipment, powder and ball as you can carry and you're to follow me."

Stephen moved quickly to follow the lieutenant. Anything was better than lying on the rocks waiting to be picked off. They crouched low and ran along the base of the cliffs going south upriver from Queenston. After running about a thousand yards Stephen felt winded. The escarpment above seemed to loom over him. How the hell were they to climb up?

Wool seemed to be searching for something in the underbrush that grew at the base of the cliffs. He ran back almost a hundred yards. He seemed confused. He had not found his path. Then suddenly he stepped through the bushes and disappeared. A few moments later he reappeared and signaled his men with his hand. One by one they followed him single file onto the path.

Stephen was near the front. The path led gradually up the face of the cliff. Stephen did not like high places and the path was climbing higher and higher. He forced himself to look away from the edge and to concentrate on what was going on in front of him. He stumbled and fell into a ditch that lay right in the middle of the path. It had been uncovered and logs had been placed over it, but Stephen had not been the first in the column to fall in and he would not be the last. He rubbed his shins, which had been bruised in the fall. He crawled out of the ditch and began to move ahead again. Now the way was steeper. Stephen had to search for handholds and to pull himself up higher. He was gripped with fear and was becoming weary. The climb was slow because he had to wait for the man in front of him. At times he felt his grip on the side of the hill was precarious, yet he could do nothing but hang on for dear life and wait for his colleague to move ahead. They were like seabirds clinging to the cliff, but nesting on rock ledges was natural to birds. Stephen felt anything but natural.

He had been climbing for almost an hour now. The muscles in his arms ached from grabbing rocks and branches of trees and hauling himself upward, ever upward. He could see the top up ahead. The path led into the woods on the right flank and to the rear of the British gun. It was just a bit further now. His fingernails were cracked and bleeding from grabbing the sharp gray rocks of the cliffside. A few more feet now. He was up. Wool, his face covered with scratches, signaled those who had arrived to fan out into the woods. Stephen crawled carefully among the bushes. Directly ahead of him he could see the Redcoats firing the gun. He stared at the tall figure in the scarlet coat. He could not forget that form—that coat with the gold braid. Isaac Brock himself commanded the great gun.

Michael watched the gun crew on the redan fire round after round into the river at army boats attempting to cross over to the American shore and at any force attempting to regroup. The British artillery was determined to stop any attempt to reinforce the trapped American forces.

There was a cheering from the town below and a few minutes later from the narrow road that Michael and the York men had followed up the cliffs to the summit during the night. Michael, who sat in some bushes guarding the road up, along with Joe Ashton and the rest of Devers's troop, strained to see what was causing the cheering. Then the reason came to view. Splendid atop his gray horse, Isaac Brock in scarlet-and-gold coat, now a revered sight among Canadian troops as well as the men of his old regiment, the Forty-ninth, had arrived at Queenston. Michael found himself shouting hoarsely. Before, he had been afraid. Now he was confident. The savior of Canada was on the field.

Brock rode to the redan and dismounted. His staff officers

MacDonell and Glegg were right behind him. He watched the regulars manning the gun. And he watched the fall of the shot. Then he made several suggestions for resighting. He exuded confidence. Michael watched him in awe. The general turned to Glegg.

"Most of this guard is unnecessary," he ordered. "Send them down to relieve Captain Dennis. He has his hands full defending the town."

Devers was soon on his feet, rousting the volunteers for a march back down to the town. Jervis cursed. His Methodist parents would have been shocked by some of the foul expressions he had learned in the army. "I wish these generals would make up their minds. First up the hill and then down the hill."

"No talking in the ranks," screamed Devers, "and watch how you criticize generals. You, Brant, Colonel MacDonell wants to see you."

Michael was surprised. He did not know MacDonell. He walked to the redan. He was deeply distressed that Devers had given the order to march without waiting for him. His friends were disappearing during the height of the battle. He felt naked and scared.

He saluted MacDonell.

"Are you Brant?"

"Yes, sir," Michael responded.

"General Brock, sir, this is Mr. Brant's son."

Brock, who was looking across the river, turned suddenly, his blue eyes fixing on Michael. He smiled at MacDonell.

"It would be hard not to guess, wouldn't it, John?"

"Mr. Brant, your father is in the area. I spoke with him some hours ago. I think you might have some difficulty recognizing our distinguished member of the bloody House of Assembly. He is wearing a loincloth and his very distinguished features are covered with paint."

"The Mohawks are here, sir?" said Michael excitedly.

"Indeed they are, at the front. They're six months late, mind you, and as undisciplined a group as any I have ever encountered. But your father tells me he can control them. I hope so. Now, young man, I promised him I'd keep you by my side during this engagement."

A look of anger appeared on Michael's face. His father did not trust him to face battle.

"Don't give me that wounded look, Private," said the general. "I think you'll find action enough where I am."

As if to accent his remarks, a war cry came from the woods to the rear of them. Brock looked beyond Michael. A look of surprise crossed his face. The surprise turned to incredulity. There were American troops in the woods to the rear of them.

"Good God," said MacDonell, "how did they . . ."

"They must have wings," said Michael.

"That's not the issue," said Brock, instantly swinging into action. "Somehow or other our clever enemy has flanked us and just after the 'Savior of Canada' has sent all his defenders away from the most vital spot in all of Upper Canada." His tone was filled with self-disgust. "Soldiers," he called out, "we must spike the gun."

He picked up the ramrod himself and drove it into the touchhole of the cannon. The rod broke in two. A soldier picked up a heavy mallet and pounded the piece of rod standing up from the gun deeper and deeper into the hole.

There was another cheer from the woods, followed by two hundred men charging from cover toward the redan.

"I think it is time for generals, colonels, majors, and even privates," Brock said, looking at Michael, "to beat a hasty retreat. But mark my words, gentlemen, it is a temporary withdrawal because whoever controls this spot when night falls will be the master of Upper Canada."

They began to scurry down the side of the cliff toward the road to Queenston. Michael scrambled over some rocks and through some bushes. He slipped at one point and fell on his face. Colonel MacDonell, who came stumbling behind him, stopped and grabbed Michael's hand, pulling him to his feet. He felt a musket ball pass by his shoulder. He looked behind him. The blue-coated American regulars were firing down at the fleeing general, his staff, and his gunners. But they were not following.

"Whoever commands the enemy," said a huffing General Brock, when he reached bottom, "knows what he is doing. He has the most vital piece of real estate at the front and he has turned this battle to his favor. Glegg, get word to Captain Dennis that I want as many regulars as he can get here and I want the town's defenses stripped except for a token guard of militia. We must retake the Heights."

Michael could see the Americans beginning to fortify their

261

position. Brock kept pacing back and forth waiting for reinforcements. His anger grew with each passing moment and his
face was flushed.

"I am sure Dennis and his men will be here shortly,"
offered MacDonell.

"Shortly is already too late. Damn it, John, I've lost this
battle through my own stupidity. How could the Americans
have taken the Heights? I was blind. All I could think of was
helping Dennis hold the town. I had no thought to the safety
of the Heights. How did they get up there?"

"I've been asking militiamen from around Queenston, General. There is an overgrown path winding up the front face of
the escarpment. Most of the locals don't believe a force could
have made it up, not carrying equipment anyway."

"In short," said Brock, "it's unscalable. And so we need not
defend it. Son of a bitch," he cursed, kicking the soil with his
black leather boot. "God save us from impregnable fortresses
and unscalable mountains. From the time of Julius Caesar
they have meant a general's downfall. I'll be damned if England
will lose the remnant of her empire because of my mistake.
MacDonell, where is Glegg and where is Dennis and where
is the Forty-ninth?"

The first sign that Brock's orders had been received at
Queenston's dock was the arrival of some of the York volunteers. Sergeant Devers and Michael's comrades came to the
stone wall at the edge of the town. Michael threw his arm
around his friend Joseph Ashton.

"What are you doing down here, Brant?" he asked. "I
thought I left you on top of the mountain. My God, can't you
and Brock do anything right without me?"

"We got chased off the top, Joe, and Brock is determined
to go back."

Ashton's face went white. "I was joking. I thought you had
been relieved. You mean the Yanks have the Heights?"

Slowly at first, but then in a rush, the red-coated regulars
of the Forty-ninth Regiment filed along the same stone wall.
Brock stood on the wall. He shouted to the men of his old
regiment.

"Follow me, boys," he called out, and leapt onto his gray
horse. He pointed his hand toward the Heights above. Officers called out commands. Bayonets were fixed. Slowly the
red line began to move forward up the hill. It was a steep
climb and soon the line became ragged. Men slipped on

brightly colored, wet fallen leaves and stumbled. Brock dismounted and began to lead his horse. The Americans opened a ragged fire and gaps appeared instantly in the British line. Still they came on. The two forces crashed into each other and the sound of metal striking metal as bayonet was fended off by bayonet resounded to the valley below. The red line inched forward, driving the blue one back.

Michael was terrified but he and Ashton, side by side, followed behind the regulars. Brock himself, splendid in his uniform of scarlet, his sword in his hand, was in the forefront. He had wrapped his handkerchief about his hand, which had been struck by a musket ball. It had become blood-soaked.

Then the Americans began to break and fall back along the front of their defensive line. Brock rushed forward.

"Christ," yelled Ashton to Michael, "we're going to go over the top. We're going to make it. Look at the Yanks pull out."

He began to scream a cheer but he never finished it. A ball struck him in the face and he fell forward, face down in the mud. Michael bent down and turned his friend over. He knew from the blankness in his eyes that he was already dead. He started to scream curses at the retreating Americans, shaking his fist. He rose from his knees, filled with anger and the blood lust of his Mohawk ancestors. He raced forward toward the American line. The fleeing Americans were in good order. But there were some stragglers. Michael was soon in the front line amid the red-coated regulars. The general was only a few feet to his right. An American soldier had fallen on one knee, wounded in the thigh. The red line came at him. He raised his musket to fire. Michael's bayonet caught him in the chest with such force that it pierced his back. He fell over backward and was impaled on the ground. Brant let loose with a scream that he would never have recognized as having come from his lungs.

The Americans, who numbered about a hundred, regrouped under their commander, Captain Wool. Some began to throw up their hands. They were trapped on the Heights with no reinforcements in the offing. But Wool rallied his force and gave the word to meet the oncoming British with a charge of their own. Again metal clashed against metal. Michael saw the blue line come from nowhere in front of them. He thrust with his bayonet and felt it strike flesh. The face in front of him was a blur of skin and yellow hair. The Redcoat next to him went down with a guttural scream. The Redcoat on the other side pulled back. Michael thought himself alone facing a determined-looking American. He heard Brock yell. The men of the Forty-ninth were pulling back. Michael stepped back reluctantly. Brock waved his sword. His hand was dripping blood, which sprayed with each passage of the blade over his head. Michael stepped next to him.

"They're retreating, sir. You have to go back."

"They can't retreat. This regiment doesn't retreat," he yelled.

In exasperation he lowered his sword and watched his men retreating. Then suddenly he grabbed his chest, a gaping hole gushing forth blood.

"The general's hit," Michael screamed out. He looked on in horror as blood gushed from the wound. A British soldier bent down to assist the general. A cannonball literally tore him in half. His blood mixed with Brock's, covering the general's whole body with gore.

Other men of the Forty-ninth now ringed the body of their leader. They picked him up and began to run back down the hill they had fought so hard to capture.

Michael ran the rest of the way. His will to fight had been destroyed by the anguish he felt. He knew that Brock would never survive such a wound. Tears of rage and misery came pouring down his powder-blackened face, leaving lighter lines.

When they again reached the stone wall at the base of the Heights, they heard a cheer go up from the Americans above them. Michael was openly crying now. John MacDonell bent his head over his leader's chest. He pulled his face away contorted with pain and rage.

"Oh, God," he called out toward the sky, "he's dead." He shook his fist toward the Heights. "Get me my horse," he screamed. He climbed onto its back. "Those of you who loved this man, come with me to avenge his death." He turned his mount and began to move up toward the Heights again. Michael reloaded his musket and ran forward to catch up with MacDonell and about seventy men who followed him. They were joined halfway up the hill by others of the Forty-ninth who came from their concealed spots in the clumps of underbrush that dotted the hillside. MacDonell kneed his horse and it surged ahead. The Redcoats began to yell. Michael felt his chest burning. He wanted to take a deep breath to get his wind back but he couldn't. He was yelling again a scream that would have been familiar to Old Brant, and to Nicus Brant

Now the Americans appeared on the rim of the Heights hundreds strong. They had been reinforced from the road in the village of Queenston, which was now in their possession. They opened a devastating fire on the British line as it charged up. MacDonell, astride his mount, was an obvious target. He threw up his hands when the first musket ball struck his arm. The horse turned and a second struck him in the back. He fell off the horse. Once again leaderless, the British charge ground slowly to a halt. Michael dropped to his knees. He took aim and fired up at the blue line on the rim of the Heights. He wanted to rise up and charge again but he could feel the men on either side of him begin to fall back. He was overwhelmed by a sense of defeat. Brock was dead. From the look of him when Michael saw him, MacDonell was about to join him. There were only a handful of regulars and militia left in Queenston and the Americans seemed to be pouring up to reinforce their comrades on the Heights overlooking the Niagara.

Aaron heard the firing off in the distance. He was tired. The journey with the hundred warriors from the Grand River had exhausted him. Yet he could not let young John and his friend Norton know this. The old men, his friends, had won in the council and Kenonranon was chosen to lead the Mohawks to war. But Aaron had learned much in his years in the House of Assembly. He had learned the value of compromise in politics. The old men who elected him would not be coming with him. The young men knew of him only by reputation. He was almost a legend. These men barely remembered Joseph Brant, his uncle, who had lived among them until recently. Aaron had left the Grand River twenty-eight years before.

The young men knew John Brant, his cousin, who was really only a boy, the child of Joseph Brant's old age. He selected John as co-leader of the war party.

The young men might not have known how to compromise but they could canoe and move through the woods in a way that would shame an old man of sixty-eight. Aaron had strained beyond what was good for him to keep up. Although the youngsters had deliberately set a pace to embarrass him, he was too stubborn to assert his authority and force them into a face-saving walk.

His chest hurt him. Eli had warned him to exercise. "Well, the old bastard should be happy now." He cursed under his breath. "I've had enough exercise to last me for the next dozen years."

John Norton, who aspired to be another William Johnson, adopting all aspects of Mohawk life, dropped to the rear of the Mohawk line of march through the woods.

"Kenonranon," he said in a heavily accented Mohawk.

"Speak English," said Aaron. "I'll understand you better." Norton looked deeply offended.

"No insult intended, Norton. It's just my Mohawk is rusty. It's been almost three decades since I've used it."

Norton's expression changed instantly.

"Brant," he said, "we've had word. The Americans occupy Queenston Heights directly in front of us. We're too late; the British have lost the battle."

Brant moved quickly up to the front of the line. His cousin stood waiting for him. The scout stood next to young Brant. Aaron began to question him in fluent Iroquois and Norton, coming up behind him, was filled with hate for this old man who had stolen his chance.

Aaron realized instantly from the scout's report that the situation was desperate. His hundred Mohawks, superb guerilla fighters, were not a sufficient force to turn the tide. The Americans had the Heights. The British were seemingly routed, although it was not yet clear that the main British force had entered the fray. Surely Brock would bring down his reinforcements from the Niagara line, from Fort George, and from Newark. But he remembered Brock's remark to him that the Mohawks of the Grand River were worth a regiment of regulars to him if he confronted New York militia. Terror—that's what Aaron had to strive for. He could do that and avoid casualties if his men stuck to hit-and-run tactics. He passed on the word, using mostly hand signals. The warriors were spread out through the woods. They were to strike at his command. A surprise charge on the Americans' rear. They could take scalps but if the Americans ran they were not to pursue if they heard his whistle.

Mohawk warriors slipped away, spreading out through the deep woods until they reached the edge of the pasture that dominated Queenston Heights. Aaron rose from his hiding

266

place. Most of the Americans, who must now have numbered close to a thousand, were fortifying the edge of the Heights above the village, the spot where Brock had struck at them.

The Mohawks would take them on their flank and on their rear. Aaron Brant, now dressed as a warrior, stepped out of the woods, raised his hand, and then dropped it. Suddenly the whole woods seemed to erupt with screaming painted warriors who fired their muskets at the totally surprised Americans. The small rear guard of the militia dropped their weapons in absolute terror and turned their backs and fled toward the safety of their more numerous colleagues on the edge of the escarpment. Some tripped and fell and the Mohawks were upon them like wolves. Scalps were ripped from their victims while they still lived. Screams of terror and pain filled the afternoon.

Aaron knew that John Brant would not heed his call if he were allowed to go any further. He placed his fingers in his mouth and his piercing whistle rang out over the war cries and screams of terror. Reluctantly the warriors withdrew, and none too soon. The American regulars, moving in precise military formation, wheeled away from their fortified position and moved toward their rear and the woods. The Mohawks faded quickly into the cover of the forest and out of the battle. They would scream their war cries and their battle song from the woods.

Matthew Nowell had joined Colonel Winfield Scott in climbing up the road with the troops that had huddled beneath the escarpment to escape the fire of the British eighteen-pounder. Now they had the gun, even if it was useless. Scott relieved the wounded Captain Wool and now commanded the strong position with a thousand men. More than half of them were militia. But the position was precarious. General VanRensselaer had promised reinforcements from across the river. Nowell could see regiments of American troops on the American side of the Niagara. The British, in the early hours after the capture of the gun on the escarpment, could bring no cannon to bear on the river. VanRensselaer should have been able to ferry his entire army across, but he had not. Matthew could guess the reason why. The New York militia would not cross the international border. It enraged him. They would now have to face the British army with a skeleton force of a thousand in full view of an enormous American army of much greater numbers. Yet this army would not come to their assistance. It was a disgrace. It was treason. His face was red with rage. He was on the verge of an anger fit of enormous proportions. And then the Mohawks had come. Their timing had been perfect. The front was quiet. On the American side of the Niagara the war screams of the Mohawks drifted in the air. No one would cross now, and his own men, especially militia, were terrified. The British were on their way. This time they would not come up the steep grade in front of him. They would take the long way around and strike him from the woods as the Mohawks had. Matthew went to Scott to advise him to move his troops and protect the rear of the escarpment. But Scott saw the problem as well and, waving his sword, ordered them to leave the fortifications they had dug. They must confront the real danger now from the rear. The men groaned as they left their positions and lined up for the brief march. The regulars fell into ranks and began to march out of the open pasture. The militia had lost their nerve. Men could be seen scrambling down the side of the escarpment as Brock's men had done earlier in the day. The American force was dwindling down to a few hundred regular troops. Nowell became terrified that once again he would become a prisoner of war. And this time he could not expect rapid exchange. He had already violated his parole by joining this campaign.

Major General Roger Sheaffe was sitting astride his horse when Aaron came up to him.

"Brant," the general greeted him, "it's a tragedy."

Aaron looked in surprise. "We can regain the day, Roger. I expect to drive every American who has crossed the Niagara back into it."

Sheaffe looked at Brant, his eyes filling with tears.

"You haven't heard yet. I am sorry to be the one to tell you. Brock is dead. He died leading a charge on the Heights earlier today."

Brant wanted to scream. He felt a choking feeling in his throat.

"Not Brock" was all he could say. And then he thought of Michael and fear gripped him. Michael had been with Brock.

Aaron walked away from Sheaffe toward the front. The British lined up across a plowed field. They would have to march through the woods and emerge out of the pasture. The

Mohawks lay waiting in the woods. They would allow the British to pass through their ranks. They would linger on the flanks and prevent any of the Americans from escaping.

John Brant joined Aaron as he came to the edge of the pasture clearing. In front of them was a meager American force.

"This time, my cousin," he said to the boy, "it will be more than screaming. The Redcoats will want to avenge their chief. Brock is dead."

Joseph's son nodded without looking at Aaron. He had the look of anticipation on his face. Aaron imagined that it was similar to the look on his own face at his first battle.

Commands rang out behind him and the Redcoats were on the move. The sound of marching feet filled the woods. The Mohawk scouts stepped aside as the British regulars and the York volunteers marched into the clearing. Two small American cannons opened fire and dirt sprayed into the air where the cannonball struck. A long line of Redcoats moved irresistibly forward. Aaron whistled again and the war cries of the Mohawks were heard in the woods. They came rushing out of the woods on the Americans' flanks. Aaron rushed out onto the field with John Brant. The young man raced ahead of him, his battle cry screaming from his mouth. Aaron tried to keep up with him. Musket balls filled the air as the Americans fired a volley, but that was their last resistance. All the militia in the American line broke and ran. The regulars fell back in order. But they had no place to retreat. They were trapped on the Heights high above the raging river of the Niagara.

Aaron saw John catch up with an American militiaman. He raised his tomahawk and it seemed to stay in the air for an endless time and it seemed to come down in slow motion. He could see the terror in the American's face as the steel edge crashed into his skull.

He must not allow his people to become involved in this massacre. The Americans were beaten. Their commander had raised the white flag. He raised his fingers to his mouth to whistle but instead pain gripped his chest with terrifying force. It paralyzed his left arm and shot up into his shoulder and jaw. He stood still in his tracks and began to collapse as if someone had slammed him between the eyes. Images began to flash before him. Shooting colors, red and orange, blurred his vision. He heard the war cries of the Sioux and the Saux and the Foxes as they slaughtered the English garrison at Michilimackinac; he saw the flames of Fort Vaughan climbing high into the night sky. These were the images of war—these were what he had left behind him. He could not see any longer. The chest pain had taken over his being. His eyes bulged and ached. His ears rang with a clamor that was louder than the sounds of the battle. Then suddenly the noise vanished and the pain decreased. The colors before his blind eyes changed to blue and soft purples. He felt the cool waters of the Connecticut engulf his body. He felt her cool hands on his fevered brow. He opened his cracked lips and called out her name.

"Jessica."

Stephen Miller scrambled down the side of the escarpment. It took him much less time than to climb up. He slipped and rolled halfway down the side of the hill, grabbing for any handhold in an attempt to stop himself. A rock stopped him instead, taking his wind away. Dozens of other men were trying the same tactic. Most of them were militiamen like himself, angry at themselves for having made the mistake of leaving their state to begin with and furious with their colleagues who had left them to their fate, which could very well have meant death at the hands of the Mohawks.

To Stephen's surprise, one of the retreating men was wearing a battered officer's coat. He rose to his knees, attempting to regain his breath. He recognized Matthew Nowell, despite his haggard face and bloodshot eyes. Nowell did not see him at first. Stephen had never been fond of the man and that lack of fondness had developed into a strong dislike that day before the fall of Detroit on the River Rouge—God, how that seemed years earlier to him and it was only a few short months ago.

"Uncle Matthew—Matthew Nowell," he called out.

Nowell looked about furtively. He wanted no one to think he had run from the battle. He was an officer. He should have remained behind. But he feared he would not be exchanged a second time and he could not stand the thought of being a prisoner of war for the rest of this conflict.

He recognized Stephen and looked deeply puzzled.

"Whose side are you on, boy?" he asked finally.

"I can't fight for anyone who hangs a man like Ethan Morin."

Pain crept into Matthew's expression. He had loved his

friend and he was primarily responsible for what had happened to Ethan.

"How do we avoid being taken?" Stephen asked. "I got a pretty wicked sentence hanging over my head if they catch me. I don't intend to be taken."

Matthew nodded. He felt much the same way.

"We head away from the direction the British would expect stragglers to follow. We go south, above the falls to Chippewa. We can steal a boat and get across the river and join our more fortunate noncombatant colleagues."

"Lead the way," said Stephen, brushing the dirt and twigs from his clothes. "Get me across that river and to safety, and I'll follow you to hell and back."

Margaret had never thought about his return to Boston. She had moved out of the old Charlestown house years before and she had established herself in a town house in Louisbourg Square on Beacon Hill.

The message from the castle in the harbor that Colonel Nowell would be in Boston within a few days was ignored. On this night she was giving a party in her drawing room in honor of Captain James Lawrence of the frigate *Chesapeake* and nothing was going to ruin it. She would worry about Matthew at a later time.

Most of her merchant friends were federalists who disapproved totally of this war with England. Some, in fact, had refused to attend the party, but Lawrence was dashing, she thought, and he was very attractive.

Margaret did not disapprove of the war. It provided her with a handsome income. She had four heavily armed swift brigs under letters of marque and the prizes that they sent back to port had made her rich many times over again. Her earnings from trade had dropped to nothing because of the blockade of American ports and the actions of the Royal Navy, but her privateers more than made up for it.

She sat down at her dressing table and checked her face in the mirror. Her complexion was perfect. Pale white skin, unblemished by any freckles, was unusual, she realized, for someone of her coloring. She highlighted her high cheekbones lightly with her rouge, just a hint of color. She swept her hair up on the top of her head and then pinned it in the back in the style of the Greek classical period. Her hair was shining in the reflected light of the mirror. As a child she had hated its color. It had marked her out as different and the result of being different had been traumatic for a small child among strangers. But now she reveled in the beauty of it. Sometimes she let it fall down about her shoulders as she sat before the mirror just to enjoy the sight of it.

Her dress was of the latest cut from Paris—high-waisted, outlining the fullness of her breasts. It was cut as low as decency would allow—even lower. It was a fine, sheer white linen, so sheer as to be almost transparent. It fell straight from her waist to her ankles. In Paris, she had been told, women had worn transparent dresses, but Boston was not Paris. She would scandalize the town as it was by what she did with her feet. She would go barefoot, with her toenails painted a startling red—the same color as her hair. And she wore a pearl-and-gold toe ring on the second toe of her left foot. No lady in Boston had ever appeared in Boston with naked feet—until tonight.

Walker, her butler, whom she dressed in the style of the eighteenth-century French court, powdered wig and all, knocked to tell her that most of her guests had arrived.

She rose, took another long look at herself in the mirror, and deliberately loosened a tiny curl at her temple so that it looked slightly out of place. She was satisfied.

As Maggie Nowell descended her own circular staircase to the foyer off the drawing room, every guest, man or woman, focused on her, the women in horror and the men in lust.

She smiled when she caught sight of Lawrence in naval uniform.

"Captain Lawrence," she called out as she descended. "I am so sorry I did not greet you as you arrived but I've become so disorganized. It takes me so frightfully long to get myself ready and my maids are hopeless."

Lawrence bowed slightly when she greeted him. He could not take his eyes off her. She swept up to him and grabbed his arm and led him into the drawing room.

The rug had been removed from the floor to allow dancing on the intricately designed light oak parqueted wood. The furniture, including the cream-white silk-upholstered couches, was pushed against the wall. Yet even with this disruption the room was exquisite. The tables were of a black wood with straight legs carved with the face and body of the Sphinx. Bonaparte's campaigns in Egypt had influenced even styles of furniture. The Empire style was the rage in Europe and

Margaret was the first to bring it to Boston. The room was dominated by a large fireplace over which she had hung a giant mirror whose frame was decorated with the gold eagles of Imperial France. A small string orchestra played marches and polkas. Margaret thought they suited the spirit of her guest of honor.

The male guests crowded around Lawrence and his hostess while the women moved off to the end of the room where servants passed out tiny chocolate sweets, raisins, and nuts.

"Captain Lawrence," said a state senator from Lynn, Massachusetts, north of Charlestown, "do you think you'll break the British blockades and sail with *Chesapeake*?"

"I don't see why not," said the captain.

"Well, the British have a massive fleet. I was hoping, as I believe many of my constituents hope, now that this western Jeffersonian madness about conquering Canada is over, we might come to our senses and accept the mediation of the czar and begin to talk peace. This war is ruinous to trade."

"Not to mine," laughed Margaret. "Senator, the captain is not here to discuss politics. He's a sailor."

But the senator was not so easily put off.

"But, Lawrence, don't you people in the military realize that Bonaparte is beaten in Russia? It is the end for him. Hundreds of warships of the line will be released from European blockade duty and sail here to destroy our seaport towns."

"I'd hoped you valued our fighting ability more highly, sir."

"Captain, there's not a battleship of the line in the entire American fleet. What will you resist them with?"

Lawrence didn't answer. Margaret had pulled him away from the senator's corner.

"James," she said loudly, "I will become furious with you if you keep this up. You promised me a chocolate."

There was a sudden commotion in the foyer. Loud angry voices pierced the serenity of the environment that Margaret had carefully created. Her eyes flashed toward the noise in anger. But her look turned to surprise when she saw a dirty, unshaven Matthew Nowell appear in the entrance to the drawing room. His blue military coat was muddy and torn, his once-white breeches were stained brown and black, and his boots were muddy and shabby. Behind him stood a man equally unkempt but of far greater interest to Margaret. He was tall with stocky broad shoulders. His face was covered with a golden blond fleece. He was a handsome, rough-looking, attractive man. And Margaret could not resist imagining the way the rest of him looked.

"Uncle Matthew, I didn't expect to see you here."

"Nor I to see you here," he said, gaping around him. "What was wrong with the house at Breed's Hill?"

"Excuse me, everyone," she said, "I must introduce you. Ladies and gentlemen, most of you do not know, but this is my uncle and guardian, Matthew Nowell, who has served gallantly with General William Hull at Detroit and with my dear kinsman Stephen VanRensselaer at Niagara."

A murmur ran through the room. VanRensselaer was being denounced throughout the country for his failure at Queenston Heights and William Hull was branded a traitor and many expected he would be shot for cowardice in surrendering Detroit. The niece would have to be excused for not knowing these things but she had associated her uncle with military failure and personal cowardice.

"Margaret, I must speak with you . . . in private."

"But, uncle, my guests. I just can't leave them."

"Go ahead, Margaret," said Lawrence. "After all, we must honor the conquering hero. I'll entertain your guests for you."

Margaret led Matthew into the foyer and across it to a small coatroom.

"Who is this?" she said, looking at Stephen as she entered the coatroom.

"Stephen Miller, your half brother."

Stephen made an exaggerated bow and winked at her.

"Hi, sis," he said.

She turned her head away from Matthew and winked back and closed the door on him.

"Well, we'll be out shortly," she said, fascinated to see how much her brother had changed since she last saw him. Then she turned back to Matthew. She placed her hand on his shoulder and reached up to kiss his cheek. He grabbed hold of her and kissed her passionately on the lips. She pulled back and wrenched herself from his grasp.

"Not again, Uncle Matthew. Never again."

The longing look in his eyes was pitiful, she thought. The man would never change.

"We can't be in the same house together, uncle." She began to cry. "Why else do you think I bought this house? I knew you would return to Breed's Hill and you'd find me there and I would not be strong enough to resist you. I can't go back to the way I was. I am a proper lady now who can live with her own conscience."

Matthew began to cry, to beg.

"Please, Margaret, come back to Charlestown with me. I am alone. I am beaten. You're all I have."

She looked away and remained silent. Matthew's face seemed to sag. He looked suddenly older than his fifty years. He stepped past her and opened the door.

"Where are you going?" she asked, staring directly at Stephen, who leaned against the far wall of the foyer.

"To Breed's Hill," Matthew responded.

"The house is closed up," she said, still staring at Stephen. "You'll have to spend the night here. I'll provide you both with your own bedrooms."

Matthew looked at her, hoping that she might be weakening in her resolve. But she seemed not to pay any attention to him at all.

Stephen stood naked by the washbasin. He poured half the water pitcher into the basin. He cupped it in his hands and splashed it on his face. It was cold water and it felt good. He splashed some under his arms and on his crotch. There was soap beside the basin and he worked up a lather on his face and armpits. He picked up the linen towel and dried himself. It smelled of her perfume.

So this was the sister his mother had pined for all of these years. She was beautiful but there was no doubt in his mind what she was. He had slept with enough women to know the type. She enjoyed rutting just as he did. Her grand manner couldn't disguise it from him.

He pulled back the covers on the bed. The bed linen was soft. It had been ages since he had slept in a bed, not since Amherstburg.

He eased himself down onto the soft mattress and groaned with the pleasure of it. He would fall off to sleep quickly tonight, he thought.

There was no sound in the house now except for a ticking of the hall clock. The party had ended an hour ago. He closed his eyes and was at ease, but then his body tensed. He heard her call out in fear.

He pulled on his breeches and ran down the hall toward

where he heard her cries. It was the room at the end of the hall. He threw open the door. Matthew Nowell had thrown himself on top of Maggie as she lay in the bed.

"What the hell is going on here?" Stephen called out.

Matthew looked about him in confusion. "Didn't you ever hear of knocking?" he asked, trying in vain to salvage some little portion of his dignity.

"Stephen, brother, help me. He is trying to force me."

"Jesus" was all that Stephen could force from his lips.

Matthew's face was ashen. "Don't say any more, Maggie." He was afraid now that she would say too much. "Stevie, don't listen to her," said Matthew, now in a panic.

"Yes, Stevie, listen to me. Your uncle, my guardian, has been screwing me for years, from the time I was a girl. He found me with the Indian—Geyasada. My first guardian took me when I was barely old enough to talk, and Uncle Matthew, he took me too. They taught me all I know."

"Stop this. Stop it," Matthew yelled, and struck her in the face. Then, terrified by what he had done, he tried to stroke the spot he had hit. She blocked his hands with her own arm.

"Get out of my life, you evil little man, you underdeveloped misfit, you perverter of children. Don't lay a hand on me again. Don't ever come into my life again."

"But, Maggie, I love you!"

"You've always claimed that, but everything is done to satisfy your perverted needs. Get out of my house. Go to your gloomy tomb on top of Breed's Hill."

Matthew seemed to back away from the fury of her attack. His eyes darted from her to Stephen. Finally he cried out in anguish. It was a scream of pain. He raced from the room and down the stairs. He flung open the front door of the house and ran into the street. It was raining and the cobblestones of Louisbourg Square reflected lights from some of the houses fronting it. Matthew didn't know where he was going. All he knew was that he had to flee her anger. She was right. He was just like Geyasada. He knew that. But she hated him as much as she had hated the Indian. He could never face her again. She had called him a pervert. He had called himself that for years. But he never thought she felt that way about him also.

He walked blindly to the bottom of Beacon Hill. The Common stretched out before him. The rain had soaked through his shirt and the winter air was chilling. Geyasada, she thought of him as another Geyasada. She had crushed the Indian with rocks. He stumbled across the pastureland of this park within the town. He stepped out from behind the bushes into State Street. He had no idea where he was. Even if he had heard the noise of the fast-moving wagon he could not have avoided it in time.

"Watch out," screamed the driver. The horses swerved away from him in fright but the rump of one crashed into Matthew, knocking him off his feet. The heavy wood-and-iron wheel smashed into his face, crushing his head with the full weight of its freight.

The ice had formed a solid cover on top of Lake Ontario. The village of York had greeted the new year quietly, which was proper for a nation at war. The house on Bay Street was filled on New Year's Day with friends and family.

Amy, her sorrows almost overwhelming her, had left the Brant household. Marc Stiegler, her nephew, suddenly appeared in the town after spending the fall in Quebec. There were no charges against him. No one knew what role he had played in the attempt to rescue the traitor Ethan Morin. Marc took Amy Nowell back to Isle d'Orleans to visit her ancient mother, Katherine Schuyler, now eighty-three. Katherine had left Saint John and was now living with her son, Marc's father. Amy wanted to see her once more before anything happened. She smiled wanly when she thought about it all. Her mother would probably outlive her. The Schuylers were long-lived—Aunt Margaret Schuyler had not died until she was ninety-four.

Amy left York for Quebec before the first winter snows came.

But the rest of the clan had congregated in York. Jessica had ordered a lamb from the local butcher shop and told the cook to roast it for New Year's Day. It came to the table surrounded by boiled potatoes along with a great brown baking pot filled with baked beans cooked in molasses and brown sugar. The cook had slipped a piece of salt pork in as well. Mrs. Brant need not know. She would fish it out before she served the beans. But no self-respecting cook could cook beans without a bit of pork for flavor.

Charles Miller came into the sitting room where they were to congregate for a toast before dinner. He escorted Elizabeth and seemed to have eyes for no one else. She had agreed to marry him. She wanted to have the preacher in as soon as he had asked her, but he had begged off, claiming the only proper, cautious path was to wait until the war's end. He could not live with the fear that she might be widowed with children if he married her while the Americans still posed a threat to Canada. But Elizabeth had changed. Charles was now the main force in her life and his gentle, persuasive caution was winning her over. Eli disapproved. Not of Charles as a man. But he liked the old impulsive Liz. She had been more fun, more unpredictable, more easily spoiled, more like him.

Eli had trimmed his hair right after the last time Jessica had referred to him as Dr. Franklin. He was almost entirely bald now, with just a fringe of snow-white hair on the sides of his head.

"Where's Michael?" Eli yelled. "I want the lad to recite the details of our glorious and tragic moments at the Heights of Queenston. Where is the boy?"

"Up here," said Michael, who could hear the old man from the landing of the second story. He came down the richly carpeted stairs. And he carried his once-mighty father in his arms.

Eli rose from his chair. "Set up Thomas's chair," he called out. "The head of the household arrives."

Aaron's face broke into a great, toothy smile as he was carried by his son into the sitting room. Charles, Elizabeth, and Jessica broke into applause. Michael placed his father in a chair while Eli fussed with the blanket, which he placed on Aaron's lap and wrapped around his legs. It was Aaron's first trip downstairs since the day he had arrived home in York near death. The heart attack should have been fatal, would have been fatal, according to Eli, had he not been brought under Stoddard's care so soon. As it was, Eli knew that the damage had been severe enough that Aaron had little chance to live to see the same age that he, Eli Stoddard, had already attained. But he was lovingly cared for in this Bay Street mansion house.

Jessica stepped to Aaron's side and kissed his haggard cheek.

"Woman," called out Stoddard. "None of that. The man's in no condition for that kind of excitement."

Jessica blushed. But Aaron reached up and held her hand.

"Speak for yourself, you old reprobate," he said in a low

and weak voice. "Don't tell me what I'm up to. I know better than you."

He looked about at his family and was filled with an enormous sense of contentment. The country was saved. Its savior lay in his grave at Niagara but his death had not been in vain. Brock's efforts had thwarted the initial American invasions. The enemy had been defeated on every front. The danger was not over and Canadians, if they wished to preserve their nation born at Detroit and Queenston, would need to be vigilant. When the ice melted, even this capital of Upper Canada at the Toronto carrying place, this York, could be vulnerable, as was Montreal. Everywhere in Canada was but a few miles from the Yankee republic. Next year would see more fighting. But the word was that Bonaparte was beaten. Soon, very soon, England would come to their rescue with the veterans of armies that had brought the emperor to his knees, and then all would be placed under the protective loving wing of Mother England. No longer would they need to fear the radical Americans. These Americans did not seem to understand that society must be structured. That some must lead and some must be led.

He looked at the youngsters. Charles, his career was clearly in trade, plying his ships on the lakes. He was such a serious young man but he was a superb influence on Elizabeth. He watched his daughter smiling up at this man, whom she clearly loved so much. At last, thank God, someone she'd listen to. But deep down inside himself he knew he deluded himself. No one, not Aaron Brant, not Eli Stoddard, and not even Charles Miller, ever really controlled Elizabeth.

And then there was Michael. Still really a boy, blooded at Queenston, but so bright, with his career already clearly delineated. Strachan and Allan had already been by and suggested that as soon as the boy was admitted to the bar he should be groomed to fill Aaron's seat in the Assembly. The father was extraordinarily proud of him.

He had been frightened that he would never see any of this again. That he would die away from Jessica. He did not know how much more time was allotted to him but he knew he must cherish these moments.

"It's time for the toast," he said.

Eli hushed everyone, although all were already silent.

Charles passed around glasses filled with a fine madeira wine. Aaron raised his glass. His hand shook and he spilled a

279

bit of it. The fine brown wine trickled down the back of his hand to his wrist. He ignored it.

"First, I toast my patriot sons, Charles and Michael, who have braved death on our behalf. And I toast all of us patriots, all of us who have saved this land and laid the cornerstone of a great nation. We must persevere in the months ahead to preserve what we have achieved. Isaac Brock and our brave brothers in arms must not be allowed to have died in vain. To Canada."

They all sipped the wine.

ABOUT THE AUTHOR

A Canadian citizen since 1976, ROBERT E. WALL draws on his love for Canada and his native United States in creating the saga of *THE CANADIANS*. He perceives the histories of the two nations as deeply entwined and, influenced by the writings of Kenneth Roberts, seeks to teach those histories through the historical novel. *Blackrobe*, the first in the series, is Wall's first novel, followed by *Bloodbrothers* and *Birthright*.

Robert Wall is married, has five children (one is an adopted Cree Indian, the most authentic Canadian in the family), and divides his time between New Jersey, where he is provost at Fairleigh Dickinson University, and Montreal, where his family lives.

BLACKROBE
BLOODBROTHERS
BIRTHRIGHT
PATRIOTS
and now . . .

THE INHERITORS

Book Five of *The Canadians*

by
Robert E. Wall

Read the thrilling opening pages to the magnificent
fifth volume in this sweeping historical saga.

PROLOGUE
September 1813

The sun burst through the early morning grayness, touching the sails of the ship with gold. The wind was light and *Detroit,* a three-masted ship built at the Amherstburg yards and just launched and rigged, glided across the rolling waves of the broad expanse of Lake Erie. In her wake sailed her sister ships—the smaller *Queen Charlotte* and the brigs and schooners *Lady Prevost, Hunter, Little Belt,* and *Chippewa.*

Charles Miller, lieutenant of the Provincial Marine had sailed the lake for most of his life. But this entrance into its waters was different. Never before had he sailed to war. The British had only one purpose now, to find the American fleet that had left Presque Isle in Pennsylvania and to destroy it. Upper Canada, west of Niagara, was untenable without control of Lake Erie, and the glories of Fort Detroit last year would be squandered if the Americans were not found and destroyed immediately.

Captain Robert Barclay paced the quarterdeck. His one empty sleeve—trophy of his long Royal Navy career—was pinned to his coat. Lieutenant Morse, Charles's colleague in the Provincial Marine who had sailed with him in the old *Nancy* ferrying Brock's men to Detroit, shared the watch with him.

"The bloody wind is fickle, this morning," Barclay said half aloud.

"Aye, sir," responded the helmsman instinctively, although it was clear that Barclay had not been addressing anyone in particular.

Both Charles and his companion kept to their side of

the quarterdeck, trying to give to the captain privacy, as was traditional in quarterdeck behavior, but Barclay wanted to talk. He walked over to his subordinates.

"This will be the decision day, gentlemen," he addressed them.

"Aye, aye, sir," they both responded together.

"All these months of worry and work and of scarcities—they all stop today. The enemy fleet is out and we will find and destroy them."

"It has been difficult, sir," offered Morse.

Barclay chuckled bitterly. "Difficult is considerably understated. Building a fleet in the godforsaken wilderness with no iron foundries, no seamen, importing everything from Montreal to Kingston by almost nonexistent roads. It was a nightmare, and even though we've put out to sea I've only a handful of experienced seamen. We're not used to it. We command the world's oceans, our ships have won every major engagement since the first American war, and here we find ourselves contested for control of this little lake. But we'll win again. We outgun them, gentlemen. Our cannon don't have their weight, but we've got the range. We'll fight them at a distance. So long as we have the weather gauge."

He looked up at the sails. "The damned wind."

He looked across the lake toward the vague outline of the American shore. The sky was now a pale blue and the sun on the port side gave a welcome warmth, driving away the chilly dawn air.

From the mast above there came a shout. Charles looked up and then realized that the inexperienced seaman was pointing ahead. Charles raised his glass in the direction the sailor pointed. There were islands off to the east. Yes, and clearly now sails were emerging, distinguishable from the gray outline of the land itself.

"Put in Bay," he said aloud. He himself had anchored his schooner there during storms.

Barclay reached for Charles's glass. Morse held it up for him as he put it to his eye and then steadied it with his arm.

"The islands, sir, there's a good anchorage there," said Morse.

"The American fleet is coming out," said the captain. "My esteemed opponent, Commodore Perry, has erred. He's coming out of the anchorage directly to face me. He's giving me the wind. We shall beat him."

Morse had his glass trained on the American fleet.

"There are nine of them, sir, and only six of us. Even odds, I'd say, for the Royal Navy."

Barclay pulled his eye away from the glass.

"This battle will be won or lost, gentlemen, by our two ships and their two brigs."

The fleets continued to approach each other. The breeze was slight and their progress was slow. Barclay remained on deck. The guns of *Detroit* and the other ships were run out; sand was scattered on the decks and a hot breakfast was ordered for all hands.

Charles's body felt clammy and he could feel the sweat trickle down his sides under his coat. He was unsure if it was the effect of the hot September sun or just plain fear. He had never been more frightened in his life. He tried to steady himself. He thought of his family, attempting to calm his nerves. He thought of Elizabeth, who loved him, of her brother Michael, seven years younger than himself but already a veteran of Queenstown Heights. He thought of Michael's father, Aaron Brant, a legendary warrior even if now a broken invalid. None of them had been found wanting in the face of battle. His own twin brother, Stephen, was fighting on the other side—and damned by all, but no one said anything against his courage. Every male in the family had been tested by war. Even his mother had faced the loss of her husband with extraordinary courage. Now it was his turn. His mouth was dry and he couldn't swallow.

"Damn it," shouted Barclay, "the wind—it's changing."

Charles broke out of his daydreaming and glanced in the direction of his captain and then at the ensign that had been nailed to the mast. The wind had shifted and came from the southwest. Now the Americans sailed with the wind and the British–Canadian fleet would have to await their assault.

Captain Barclay slammed his hand down on the green wood of the railing of the quarterdeck, cracking it with the snapping sound of a sharpshooter's rifle. Several veterans on the gun deck actually ducked at the noise.

Barclay looked at the damage with an amused grin. "If a one-armed man can do that with his hand, imagine what Perry's carronades will do." He turned to face the two Provincial officers and saw their mutual look of concern. He clapped Morse on the shoulder.

"No matter," he continued. "The Yankee ships will be no stouter. But we have a new factor with the wind change, gentlemen. Our guns will still outrange theirs but we can't stand off and pick them off one by one from afar. They'll be able to close. We must damage them so badly that by the time they're within range with their carronades they'll be too devastated to fire them. Lieutenant Garland . . ." Barclay called out for his first lieutenant. "Join me please on the quarterdeck. Morse, Miller, thank you, gentlemen. Your knowledge of the lake has given confidence to all of us. You may now go to your gun crews."

Charles and his friend descended the stairs to the gun deck. Morse was commander of the portside guns; Lieutenant Inglis of the Royal Navy had charge of the starboard side. Charles's task was to assist the commander whose side was most heavily engaged. With the Yankees sailing directly toward them from the southeast and Barclay turning his fleet to the southwest to pick up wind, it was clear that Charles would be joining Morse on the port side.

The lake was calm, with almost no noticeable roll. The sun was hot. Most of the gun crews had stripped to the waist and tied pieces of cloth about their heads to keep their hair and sweat out of their eyes. Charles envied them. His officer's coat felt heavy and dreadfully conspicuous.

He could see the American ships clearly now. One of their brigs was surging forward toward *Detroit* while her twin lagged behind.

"That will be *Lawrence*—Perry's flagship." Barclay's voice broke the deathly silence aboard *Detroit*. "It is a vessel, my lads, named after an American captain who was defeated and killed off Boston by our own *Shannon*. Let that be an omen."

The crew of *Detroit* cheered. Barclay waved his hand. Charles tried to cheer but his throat felt so constricted that only a hoarse rasp emerged. This was all madness, standing exposed on an open deck while across the water of his lake, his beloved Erie, other men approached, determined to blast his ship out of the water and to send him, Charles Miller, to the bottom to feed the fish.

The fleets continued to converge. On the quarterdeck, Barclay signaled his cabin boy, who raised a bugle to his lips. The lonesome cry reached out over the calm water toward *Lawrence*, which inched along through the blue-green water. It was Morse's signal. He dropped his raised sword and his first gun belched flame and lurched backward against the restraining ropes. Charles moved forward to the railing to watch the shot fall.

"Short," he yelled, his voice high-pitched, excited, and unrecognizable even to himself.

Wedges were placed under the gun to raise its elevation.

"Fire," Morse screamed.

This time the shot struck the railing of the Yankee flagship, sending deadly foot-long splinters flying in all directions.

"Continue to fire all portside guns," Barclay called out.

Charles lowered his sword and the five guns under his command thundered as one. Smoke and the acrid smell of gunpowder filled the air about him. He could see spars on *Lawrence* crash onto the deck.

"Too high, Mr. Miller," yelled Lieutenant Garland, who stood on the quarterdeck next to Barclay.

"Dislodge those carronades she carries before she can get into our range."

Charles bent down and sighted each of his guns. *Lawrence* continued to approach. Her guns were still silent, still out of range, but her very approach, silent and unalterable, sent shivers through Miller.

He screamed out, "Fire," once again, and for a second time the roar of the cannon crashed into his ears and the smoke and stench filled his lungs. He coughed and tried to swallow; his lips were dry and cracked when he shouted. Now his guns no longer fired in volleys. The gun crews swabbed out the muzzles, rammed home the cartridges of gunpowder, and placed the heavy shot into the tilted muzzles and touched the powder holes with a slow match. Each cannon roared as it was fired, and the crews began all over again. White splinter marks appeared along the bow and starboard hull of *Lawrence* but still she came on, while the rest of the Yankee fleet seemed to hang back.

On *Detroit's* stern the eight guns on the port side of *Queen Charlotte* opened up on *Lawrence* as well. The American ship was taking heavy damage now but still she came on.

Then *Lawrence* veered. At first Charles thought she had had enough and she was breaking off, but suddenly the world about him came apart. Hot metal seared the air, splinters of wood smashed into metal with a clang, into human flesh with a sickening dull thud. Men screamed and blood sprayed in all directions.

Charles felt the breath knocked out of him and he fell to his knees. He looked about him dazed. One of his guns lay on its side, dislodged from its carriage. The gun captain lay beneath it; his mouth was open. Charles knew he was screaming but the roar of guns drowned it out. He looked himself over, fully expecting to see blood seeping from some open wound. But he was untouched. The gun crew had lifted the cannon with a lever and dragged the broken body of their comrade from under it. He had ceased his screaming and soon disappeared, dragged below deck at the mercy now of the surgeon's pitiless knives and saws.

Detroit's port guns continued to fire. Charles rose to his feet. His sword had been knocked from his hand and his hat was missing. He knew he should be giving orders but his crews were firing, paying no attention to him. He knew that *Lawrence* would fire a second volley any minute now and the thought paralyzed him. He heard his name called. It was Garland.

"Get your guns under control, Miller. The enemy is still too far off for blind shooting. You must sight your guns. You . . ." The rest was drowned out again as the decks of *Detroit* were ravaged by grapeshot. Men screamed and cursed. Charles looked for some place to duck, to flee, to leave this horror behind him. But he could not move, no matter how much he wanted to. The sand on the deck had been dyed red with blood. Men oozing gore staggered aimlessly on the deck.

George Inglis grabbed hold of Charles's arm and shouted into his face. The roar of the guns had deafened Charles and he could not understand what the English lieutenant was saying. His eyes followed his comrade's pointing arm toward the quarterdeck. It was a shambles. The helmsman was crawling down the stairs. His leg was dragging behind him. His breeches had been torn off of him and his wounded leg was attached only by sinew.

Inglis moved toward the helmsman, yelling at an uncomprehending Charles to take command of the starboard gun crews. Charles followed his fellow officer toward the quarterdeck. The helmsman tumbled the last few stairs to the gun deck and fainted, lying in his own blood. Garland, the first lieutenant, lay in a heap against the railing. He was dead. Barclay lay at the base of the wheel, propped against it. He was awake, but from his thigh blood trickled down his leg and into his boot.

"Inglis, take command," Barclay croaked, "while Miller here takes me below to the butcher. If he can stop the bleeding in time, I'll return to the deck to finish off the Yankees. They've hurt us but we've hurt them worse. Signal *Queen Charlotte* to work her way in close and keep firing."

Charles lifted Barclay in his arms. The captain held on with his one arm about Charles's neck and was half carried, half dragged down the stairs to the main deck.

"It's just a scratch, lads," Barclay called out to his men, who stared at him with anguish and with fear. They could not have heard him. The roar of cannon drowned out his voice, but the fact that he addressed them inspired some with confidence that he would soon resume his command.

"Just as soon as the surgeon digs the ball out, I'll be back up to give the Yanks the drubbing they deserve. Keep the guns firing."

He called into Charles's ear. "Get me below fast, Miller. I can't have the men disheartened looking at me."

Below decks was even more terrifying to Charles. Men lay about in dark corners, rags tied over their wounds to stop the bleeding. At a low table, lit by his assistant holding a lantern high above his head, the ship's surgeon grimly sawed through the bone of a screaming sailor pinned to the table by four of his comrades.

"It's the captain," called out one of the wounded.

The surgeon glanced up from his grisly work with his quick eye discerned that Barclay's was not a mortal wound, and he continued to cut through the bone.

Charles laid Barclay down on the floor and covered his ears with his hands, not only to drown out the screams of the poor sailor and the groans of the other wounded but also to hide from the hideous thunder from the decks above.

"Go back to your command now, Lieutenant," Barclay said to him. "You're needed on deck."

"But someone must stay with you," protested Charles.

"I have an appointment with yonder surgeon, Miller. I'll need no one to help me keep it. He'll see to that."

Charles hesitated.

"That's an order, Lieutenant," Barclay said through gritted teeth. "Your concern for me is misplaced. Do your duty."

Charles stepped back out of Barclay's line of vision. It was not concern for his commanding officer that had made him hesitate. For all the horror found here below the water line, at least here no grapeshot clanged against metal. He was afraid to go back up into that hell.

He saw the surgeon carelessly fling the leg he had been working on onto the gory floor. His victim had fainted at last and would not feel the searing flame that cauterized the stump of what had once been a powerful, muscled limb.

The surgeon looked over at him quizzically.

"Are you hurt, Lieutenant?" he called up to Charles.

Charles shook his head and pointed toward Barclay. The captain had been dozing and the surgeon's question had awakened him.

"Is Miller still here?" he called out. "I must protest to you, sir. I can't see you, but if you remain below I'll press charges of cowardice in the face of the enemy against you."

Charles had no choice now. He climbed the stairway leading back to the gun deck. George Inglis, with a new helmsman, stood fearlessly on the quarterdeck. Lieutenant Garland's body had been removed. Lieutenant Morse, his hat and coat removed and his white shirt sticking to his soaking torso, was personally shifting one of the great guns back into firing position. He waved at Charles. He shouted but his voice was drowned out by the roar of the guns. Charles went to Inglis's position on the starboard side. So far no guns on the starboard had been fired and its crews were being denuded to replace casualties on the portside guns.

Miller caught sight of *Lawrence* for the first time since returning on deck. He was astounded. It was a mere hulk lying still in the water, but her guns flashed and her metal tore holes into *Detroit*'s sides, although she fired less often now. Suddenly the crew of *Detroit* cheered loudly. The commodore's flag on *Lawrence* was coming down. The Yanks were surrendering. Then a small boat pulled away from *Lawrence*'s side, making straight for the second American brig, so far untouched by any British fire but coming up rapidly from the rear of the American line.

Inglis yelled to the marksmen to get into the rigging and to fire at the retreating boat.

"That's Perry and he's escaping," Inglis shouted.

"The coward," screamed Morse. "His ship has surrendered. He can't leave it."

Charles stared incredulously at his friend. It was as if they were playing some sort of game and someone had broken the rules. What kind of game was this, a game that tore limbs from bodies and scattered brains and blood about the deck?

"Not true," Inglis shouted. "He's changing flagships in the middle of the battle." He pointed at the Stars and Stripes, which still flew from the stumps of what had once been *Lawrence*'s masts.

"The Yanks haven't given up yet, lads. Pout it into them."

The cheering grew louder when the form of Robert Barclay, supported by two surgeon's assistants, reappeared on deck. The captain, his face pale from loss of blood and in pain, again waved to his crew. He was carried back up to the quarterback and, holding on to the rail, reassumed command of his ship and his fleet.

As soon as the second American brig took aboard the American commodore, it began to inch forward toward *Detroit* and *Queen Charlotte*. *Detroit*'s sister ship had taken an equal beating and had signaled that all her senior officers were dead and the ship had fallen to the command of the lieutenant of the Canadian Provincial Marine, as inexperienced in war command as was Morse or Miller.

As Charles stared out at the American fleet, he saw the

calm surface of the lake ripple and the American brig and its escorting gunboat seemed to leap forward.

"The wind's picking up," shouted Morse, who had noted it almost simultaneously with Charles.

Barclay gripped the rail with his arm.

"Inglis," he shouted. "He's going to try to split our line and cross the *t* and rake us. We can't have it. Damn it, I'll not have the enemy pull a Nelson on me. Wear ship and bring the starboard guns to bear on the American. What is she called?"

"It's *Niagara,* sir," said Inglis.

"It's a good name. We'll keep it after we take her. After all, Niagara is British soil and a British river, or at least it will be when this war is over."

The American gunboats, up to that moment, were lagging far to the rear but now came into range with their single heavy gun, and they opened fire on *Detroit.* Barclay looked around for his small vessels and signaled them to drive the Americans off. But *Chippewa, Little Belt,* and *Lady Prevost* had been driven off by their American counterparts and had run to the head of the line to escape the American fire. *Hunter* lay dead in the water, her crew all but decimated by *Lawrence*'s brutal pounding earlier in the engagement.

"Keep those guns firing," Barclay screamed above the shouts of his men. "Helmsman, bring us about."

But suddenly out of the smoke *Queen Charlotte* loomed. An experienced officer could have avoided collision but none remained on *Queen Charlotte.* The two ships crashed into each other with a sickening wrenching of timbers and a whine of taut rigging and a ripping of canvas.

"Try to disengage," called Barclay, who had been knocked to the deck by the collision. He knew now that they were in mortal danger. Unless he could untangle *Queen Charlotte* from his flagship, only *Detroit*'s battered port side would be able to fire on *Niagara* as she crossed his line and raked both of the ships from stem to stern.

Charles watched *Niagara*'s approach with an almost fatalistic fascination. She seemed almost to fly across the tiny waves. Barclay was back on his feet. Charles felt Morse grab hold of his arm. He stared blankly into the wide-eyed face of his friend.

"Charles, all your crew's to the port side. The starboard guns are useless now. Help me."

Morse's last plea was punctuated by a shove that sent Charles toward the stern and rear portside guns. At that moment, grapeshot loosed by the American schooner *Caledonia* raked the quarterdeck of *Detroit*. Barclay screamed as a ball struck his shoulder. Then he stared at the wound. His good arm, his only arm, was he to lose it also? Blood rushed down his side. Inglis grabbed the wheel from the helmsman.

"Take the captain below," he ordered.

Barclay was slipping into shock, and in the far recesses of his mind the fear of losing this battle was suddenly coming to light.

"Fight her," was all he said as the helmsman helped him below to face the surgeon again.

And now as *Niagara* sailed through the British line, her guns, both port and starboard, fired at once. She seemed almost to be lifted out of the water by the power of her broadside. Her metal tore into the crippled *Detroit* and *Queen Charlotte*. Shot passed over Charles's head. He was about to order his crew to fire when suddenly the gun was dislodged and tumbled onto the crew servicing it. The hiss of hot metal burning into flesh seemed to chase all other sounds from Charles's mind. Again *Niagara* flashed. Charles opened his mouth and screamed as he saw Lieutenant Morse's lower body torn from his torso, his legs quivering uncontrollably on the deck. It was more than his mind could stand. He reeled from the chaos on the gun deck and tore down the stairway. Below decks, he found men lying all over the blood-drenched floors. He dropped down among them, sobbing, his chest heaving. He could feel vomit rising in his throat. He retched and gave up the hot breakfast so thoughtfully provided for them all before the slaughter began. He lay there, not moving, lying in his own puke. He did not even notice the quiet when Lieutenant Inglis waved the white handkerchief. Barclay's ensign had been nailed to the mast and could not be lowered.

Read THE INHERITORS, *on sale in mid-1983 wherever Bantam paperbacks are sold.*

Don't miss any of the novels in this stirring
historical series

THE CANADIANS

by

Robert E. Wall

Book One: BLACKROBE
This is the story of Stephen Nowell—a man caught in the
whirlwind of history. Torn from the arms of his family as
a child, he is captured by Indians and raised by Jesuits. In
his search for his roots, Stephen finds that his fiercely
guarded past has become a burning issue of the present
and of the future. And he finds the love he seeks in the
arms of a passionate and powerful Indian princess.

Book Two: BLOODBROTHERS
From massacres on the Hudson to the battlements of
Quebec, from the Seven Years' War to the fall of the New
France, Stephen Nowell and Karl Stiegler were bound to-
gether by the brotherhood of shared experience. In one
act, they swore that nothing would come between them.
But could their vow withstand the strength of their
desires?

Book Three: BIRTHRIGHT
The magnificent saga continues into a new generation as
sparks of revolution blaze into a mighty conflagration.
These are a people divided—father against son, brother
against brother—as from the seeds of passion and the
fires of war, mighty nations struggle to be born.

*Read THE CANADIANS, available wherever Bantam
paperbacks are sold.*